CAROLINE AND THE RAIDER

Books by Linda Lael Miller

Angelfire
Banner O'Brien
Caroline and the Raider
Corbin's Fancy
Desire and Destiny
Emma and the Outlaw
Fletcher's Woman
Lauralee
Lily and the Major
Memory's Embrace
Moonfire
My Darling Melissa
Wanton Angel
Willow

Published by POCKET BOOKS

CAROLINE AND THE RAIDER

LINDA LAEL MILLER

POCKET **STAR** BOOKS

New York   London   Toronto   Sydney   Tokyo   Singapore

An *Original* Publication of POCKET BOOKS

A Pocket Star Book published by
POCKET BOOKS, a division of Simon & Schuster Inc.
1230 Avenue of the Americas, New York, NY 10020

POCKET STAR BOOKS and colophon are registered
trademarks of Simon & Schuster Inc.

Cover art by Gregg Gulbronson

Printed in the U.S.A.

For Janet Carroll,
a friend for centuries

CAROLINE AND THE RAIDER

Prologue

Lincoln, Nebraska
December 9, 1865

*T*he train whistle gave a piercing shriek. Feeling her six-year-old sister, Lily, tremble beside her in the stiff, sooty seat, Caroline slid an arm around the little girl's shoulders.

Lily's brown eyes peered at Caroline from beneath straggly, white-blond bangs. Emma, who was seven, sat next to the window, watching the snow-laden frame buildings of the prairie town slip past. Her coppery hair glinted in the thin light of a winter day. Like Lily's, it needed brushing.

Caroline despaired of making her sisters and herself presentable. There were no hairbrushes, no changes of clothes—all they had were their worn coats, shoes, and plain dresses, given them by the nuns at St. Mary's in Chicago.

The conductor lumbered along the narrow aisle, a big, beefy-looking man without a whit of charity in the whole of his being. "This here's Lincoln, Nebraska," he boomed out. "Got your farmers and storekeepers and blacksmiths." He paused and let his beady gaze sweep over Caroline, Lily, and Emma. "I reckon folks like that will be looking for boys," he finished.

Caroline held Lily just a little closer and glared fearlessly up into the conductor's face. His nose was big as a potato,

1

with tiny purple and red veins all over it. "Girls are every bit as good as boys," she said staunchly, calling upon all the aplomb she'd managed to gather in eight years of living. "And they're a whole lot less trouble, too."

"Just get out there and stand on that platform with the others," the big man commanded, as a dozen boys scrambled toward the back of the car. They were all unwanted children, or outright orphans, with little papers bearing numbers pinned to their clothes, hoping to be adopted by one of the families waiting along the line.

The train rattled, and the metal wheels screeched against the tracks. Puffs of steam billowed past the windows.

"Everything will be all right," Caroline said softly, looking from Lily's dark, troubled eyes to Emma's fearful blue ones. She knew the words were probably a lie even as she uttered them, but she had no choice. She was the eldest sister; it was her place to look after Lily and Emma.

Fat snowflakes wafted down, nestling in Lily's and Emma's tousled hair, as the three girls trooped out onto the platform.

Standing just behind Lily, Caroline gripped the little girl's narrow shoulders tightly, trying to give her courage. She'd been pleading with God to let the three of them stay together ever since Mama had tearfully ushered them onto the orphan train in Chicago, but in her heart, Caroline knew He wasn't going to answer her prayer.

Come to that, Caroline couldn't remember the last time God *had* answered a prayer. Sometimes she wondered why she even bothered talking to Him.

A huge man with a black beard and a dirty woolen coat stepped onto the platform; his dark eyes narrowed as he surveyed the small crop of orphans lined up for his inspection.

Caroline breathed a sigh of relief when he chose two boys and left. Maybe, just maybe, she and Lily and Emma would have a little more time together before they were parted. She crossed chilly fingers where they rested on Lily's shoulders.

A fat woman in a faded calico dress and an old woolen cloak huffed up the platform steps, stomping snow off her feet as she went. Her cheeks were round and red, but there was no merriment in her gaze.

"I'll take you," she said, pointing at Caroline.

Caroline swallowed. *No,* she pleaded silently. *I can't leave Lily and Emma.* She tried, one last time. *Please, God— they're little, and they need me so much.*

Remembering the manners her grandmother had taught her, before her death a year before, Caroline curtsied. "Ma'am, if you please," she blurted out, "these are my sisters, Emma and Lily, and they're both good, strong girls, big enough to clean and cook . . ."

The dour woman shook her head. "Just you, miss," she said sternly.

Caroline couldn't hold back the tears any longer; they brimmed in her eyes and trickled down her cold, wind-burned cheeks. She'd hoped to be chosen last, if she was to be separated from her sisters, because she was the oldest and the most likely to remember where the others had left the train.

But God wasn't willing to grant her even that much.

"Remember all that I told you," she said softly, after frantic hugs had been exchanged. She crouched down and took Lily's small, chapped hands in her own. "And when you get lonesome, just sing the songs we learned from Grandma, and that'll bring us close." She paused to kiss Lily's cheek. "I'll find you both again somehow," she added. "I promise."

She rose and turned to Emma. "Be strong," she managed to say. "And remember—*please* remember."

Emma nodded, and tears moved down over her reddened cheeks. She mouthed the word "good-bye," unable to say it out loud, and Caroline understood.

The conductor herded the remaining children back into the railroad car then, since it was plain that no more orphans would be chosen. Caroline followed her adoptive mother down the slippery platform steps, not daring to look back.

"If you ask me," muttered the strange woman, broad hips swishing from side to side as she led the way through the ever-deepening snow, "Miss Phoebe and Miss Ethel are tempting fate, taking an outsider in like this, just because they need a companion—"

Caroline was paying little attention; her grief was too raw and too keen. Only as the train lumbered loudly out of the station did she turn to watch; the noisy beast was carrying away the two people she loved most in the world.

The woman grabbed her roughly by one shoulder and pulled her along. "I don't have the day to waste on this fool's errand, you know," she fussed, intent on her progress again. "I dare say, Miss Phoebe should have done this herself, instead of sending me."

The snow was deep and muddy and dappled with manure, and Caroline had a difficult time keeping up. She hardly heard the woman's prattle, for her heart was on board the train, chugging steadily west, and she longed to chase after it.

"What's your name, anyway?" the woman demanded, as they passed a general mercantile and made their way toward a brick hotel.

"Caroline Chalmers," Caroline answered regally, straightening her charity coat and tossing back her long, dark hair. She could feel the snow seeping through to wet her scalp. "What's yours?"

"Mrs. Artemus T. Phillips," the woman replied, at last troubling to look at Caroline as she dragged her along the slippery sidewalk, past a store and a hotel. "Merciful heavens, now that I truly look at you, I see you're a scrawny little thing. You probably won't last the week."

Caroline was determined to hold on as long as it took to find Lily and Emma. She raised her chin. "I'll last, all right," she said.

"Don't you be pert with me!" warned Mrs. Artemus T. Phillips, gripping Caroline by a frozen ear and propelling her around a corner. "I declare, the poor haven't the sense to know when they should be grateful . . ."

Caroline flailed one arm to free herself, but Mrs. Phillips was strong, and there was no escaping her.

They turned another corner onto a street lined with

4

houses and Mrs. Phillips stopped in front of a snow-frosted picket fence and pushed open the gate. "Here we are," she said, with no small measure of relief in her voice.

Caroline lifted her eyes to take in the house. It was a sturdy two-story place with green shutters on the windows and smoke curling from a brick chimney, the kind of home she'd always dreamed of having.

There was an oval of frosted glass in the front door, and Caroline thought she saw the suggestion of a face behind it. A moment later, a brown-haired woman in a pink crepe dress stepped out onto the porch. She wore a shawl around her shoulders, and there was a cameo brooch at her throat.

She smiled at Caroline, and despite everything, Caroline smiled back.

"So this is our girl," she said. She was neither beautiful nor plain, young nor old. "Come in, come in."

Caroline was ushered into a house that smelled pleasantly of lavender and cinnamon.

Another woman, looking exactly like the first except that her dress was blue, came down the steep stairway, one hand sliding graciously along the banister. "Is this the child?" she asked, coughing delicately into a handkerchief. Her eyes moved to Mrs. Phillips. "Oh, Ophelia, you chose wisely. She's lovely."

Caroline gulped and stepped back, assessing the two women with wide brown eyes.

"I dare say she has a mind of her own," complained Ophelia Phillips, dusting snow from the shoulders of her plain brown cloak. For all her talk about the poor, she didn't look too prosperous herself.

"That's as it should be," said the woman who had opened the door to admit them. She bent to smile into Caroline's face. "I'm Phoebe Maitland," she said. Then she gestured toward the woman in the blue dress. "And this is my sister, Ethel."

Caroline liked the middle-aged sisters, and despite the heartache of that day, she was grateful to know she'd be staying with them, instead of the fearsome Mrs. Phillips. She curtsied. "How do you do?"

The sisters twittered, obviously charmed.

Mrs. Phillips cleared her throat loudly. "Now that I've done my Christian duty," she said, "I'll just go and see to my own affairs."

Miss Phoebe thanked Mrs. Phillips warmly and ushered her right out the door.

"For a while, I was afraid *she* was going to adopt me," Caroline confessed to Miss Ethel in an earnest whisper.

Miss Ethel laughed prettily, then coughed again. "Bless your buttons, child. Ophelia's our neighbor, and Sister only sent her to meet the train because I was feeling poorly and she didn't wish to leave me."

Caroline looked around at the tall clock and the umbrella stand and the oak wainscoting. To think this was only the entryway. "I've never been in a house this big," she confided, stepping closer to Miss Ethel. "Am I supposed to clean it?"

Just then Miss Phoebe reappeared, shivering as she was borne in on a cold winter wind. "How Ophelia does run on," she said, pushing the door closed with visible effort.

"Caroline thinks she's supposed to clean our house," Miss Ethel imparted to her sister, looking chagrined.

Miss Phoebe came and laid a gentle hand on Caroline's shoulder. "Oh, dear, no," she said. "You're to be a companion to Sister and me as we undertake grand adventures in the West."

Caroline felt her eyes go wide. Maybe there was still hope that she and Lily and Emma would be reunited. "The West?" she echoed.

"We're off to Wyoming," said Miss Ethel, with a pleased nod. "We'll all make a fresh start."

Caroline had never heard of Wyoming, but she'd discerned that the place was in the west, that great, mysterious land that had swallowed up Lily and Emma. She was eager to set out.

Miss Phoebe started off through the house in a determined rustle of taffeta petticoats. "Come, child—you must be hungry, and you do look a fright. Sister and I will see that you're fed, and then we'll decide what to do about those dreadful clothes."

Despite her reduced circumstances, Caroline still had a measure of pride, and she bristled. Maybe her dress and stockings had come from the parish ragbag, but they were hers and they weren't dreadful, only shabby. "I don't need anything," she said firmly, though she followed close on Miss Phoebe's heels.

They ended up in a kitchen grander than anything Caroline could have imagined. Miss Ethel offered her a seat at the giant oak table, and Caroline took it.

"Of course you need things," said Miss Ethel, laying a gentle hand on Caroline's shoulder before sitting down. "What a treat it will be to sew for you."

"You're our child now," said Miss Phoebe resolutely, taking a plate from the warming oven above the stove, with its glistening nickel trim. "Sister and I will take care of you."

Even though Caroline had made up her mind not to eat, when Miss Phoebe set the food before her, she gobbled it down, desperate to ease the gnawing ache in her belly.

"Poor darling," said Miss Phoebe, much later, clucking her tongue as she poured fragrant tea from a squat brown china pot. "Do tell us—how did you come to be traveling all alone on an orphan train?"

Caroline eyed the remains of her reheated meat loaf, mashed potatoes, and creamed corn glumly. Lily and Emma were hungry, too, but all they would get today would be a piece of bread and some spotty fruit. It shamed her that she'd eaten while her sisters had to do without.

"Caroline?" Miss Ethel prompted.

Caroline drew a deep breath and sat up very straight in her chair. "I wasn't alone," she said, near tears again. "I was with my sisters, Emma and Lily."

The Maitland sisters exchanged sad looks.

"Oh, dear," whispered Miss Ethel. "We've parted her from her loved ones, Phoebe. She's like a little bird, plucked from the nest!"

Miss Phoebe patted Caroline's hand. "From now on, we'll

be Caroline's family," she said. "We'll travel west, the three of us, and make a fine home for ourselves."

Miss Ethel sighed philosophically, lifting her teacup to her mouth. "Papa did make us promise to look out for his mining interests out there," she reflected. She paused to smile fondly at Caroline. "With Phoebe marrying Mr. Gunderson almost the moment we step off the train, I would have been very lonely."

After tea, Caroline stood on a stool in the parlor and was measured for new clothes. Although she couldn't help grieving for Lily and Emma, she did take a little joy in her own good fortune.

Caroline was warm and full for the first time in days, and she was going to have new clothes that had been made just for her, rather than bought from rummage or scrounged by the nuns. Miss Ethel sat at the spinet playing "What A Friend We Have In Jesus," and snow drifted lazily past the parlor windows.

It was easy to be optimistic. Surely it followed that if she and Lily and Emma were all headed west, the three of them would be together again soon.

Chapter

❧ 1 ❧

Bolton, Wyoming Territory
April 15, 1878

*H*e was the most disreputable-looking man Caroline had ever seen, and everything depended upon him.

Squinting, she took a neatly pressed handkerchief from the pocket of her coat and wiped away some of the grime from the saloon window to take a closer look. If anything, Mr. Guthrie Hayes seemed even less appealing after that effort. He certainly didn't look like the war hero her student had told her about with such excitement.

A muscular man, probably only a few inches taller than Caroline herself, he sat at a corner table, engrossed in a game of cards. A mangy yellow dog lay at his side on the sawdust floor, its muzzle resting on its paws. Mr. Hayes wore rough-spun trousers, a plain shirt of undyed cotton, suspenders, and a leather hat that looked as if it had been chewed up and spit out by a large, irritable animal. His face was beard-stubbled, and he sported a rakish black patch over one eye.

Caroline couldn't see his hair, because of the hat, but she figured it was probably too long. She sighed, dampened a clean corner of the hanky with her tongue, and cleared a bigger area on the glass.

Just then one of the men at Mr. Hayes's table must have

9

pointed Caroline out, for he raised his head and looked her directly in the eyes. An unaccountable shock jolted her system; she sensed something hidden deep in this man's mind and spirit, something beautiful and deadly.

He had the audacity to smile around the stub of a thin cigar clamped between his strong white teeth. As far as Caroline was willing to admit, those teeth were his only redeeming feature.

Mr. Hayes spoke cordially to the other men, threw in his cards, and pushed back his chair. The dog got up to follow him as he came toward the swinging doors.

Caroline stepped back, alarm and excitement colliding inside her and driving out her breath. Her fingers trembled a little as she stuffed the soiled hanky into her handbag. She squared her shoulders and lifted her chin, even though she was patently terrified.

Mr. Hayes approached her idly, the cigar stub still caught between his teeth. In the bright sunshine of an April afternoon, Caroline saw that his one visible eye was green, and she just assumed the other was, too—provided there *was* another one, of course. There was a quirky slant to his mouth, and his beard, like what she could see of his hair, was light brown.

His very presence had an impact, despite his appearance.

"Ma'am," he said, touching the brim of his seedy hat, and Caroline heard just the whisper of a southern drawl in the way he uttered the word.

She drew a deep breath and let it out slowly. Lord knew, she wanted nothing to do with the likes of Guthrie Hayes, but he might well be Seaton's only chance. She was prepared to do almost anything to help the man she hoped to marry.

She put out a hand. "My name is Miss Caroline Chalmers," she said.

An impudent green eye moved over her slender figure slowly then came back to her face. The amusement Caroline saw in its depths nettled her, and she felt a peculiar sort of sweet venom spread through her.

"What can I do for you, Miss Caroline Chalmers?" Just

behind him, the yellow dog whimpered forlornly and ker-plopped to its belly on the dirty wooden sidewalk.

Caroline ran her tongue over dry lips, and even though her errand was urgent, she was compelled to hedge. "Is that animal ill?" she asked.

"Tob?" Hayes chuckled, and the sound was warm and rich. It hid itself in Caroline's middle and melted there, like beeswax left in the sun. "Not really. He's just hung over—bad habit he picked up before he and I became partners."

Caroline took a step backwards and felt her cheeks redden. Inside the saloon, a tinny piano made a *chinky-tinky* sound, and wagons and buggies rattled through the mud-and-manure-filled street. "Tob is a very strange name," she managed to say. "Why do you call him that?"

Mr. Hayes sighed in a long-suffering fashion, probably yearning to get back to his debauched pursuits inside the Hellfire and Spit Saloon, took off his hat, and put it back on again. In the interim, Caroline caught a glimpse of tousled brown hair with a golden glint to it.

"Miss Chalmers," he said, with irritating patience, "I didn't come out here to discuss my dog. What do you want?"

Caroline's cheeks went even redder, and out of the corner of her eye, she thought she saw Hypatia Furvis peering at her through the window of the dress shop. Before sunset, every warm body in Bolton would have been told that the school-teacher had been seen talking to a man who was hardly more than a criminal.

"Miss Chalmers?" Mr. Hayes prompted.

"Is it true that you used to—to rescue people from Federal prisons, during the war?"

He took a match from the pocket of his shirt, struck it against the sole of one scuffed boot, and lit the cigar stub. Clouds of blue smoke billowed into Caroline's face, fouling the fresh spring air. "Who told you that?"

Caroline coughed. "One of my students," she admitted.

A mischievous grin lifted one corner of his mouth. "I thought you looked like a schoolteacher," he said, and once more, his brazen gaze took in her figure. "You're surely a scrawny little thing. Don't they pay you enough to buy food?"

Caroline was patently insulted. Maybe she wasn't fashionably plump, but she wasn't exactly thin, either. She took another deep breath to show that she had a bosom, however modest. "My wages are adequate, thank you. In fact, they allow me to offer you a sizable sum in return for your help."

Hayes took a puff of the cigar. "How sizable?"

"Two hundred and thirty-six dollars and forty-seven cents," Caroline replied, with dignity. She'd saved literally from childhood to amass what she considered a small fortune. And she loved Seaton Flynn enough to hand over every penny in return for his freedom.

He gave a slow whistle and shook his head. "That's a lot of money, Miss Chalmers. Exactly what would I have to do to earn it?"

Caroline looked carefully in every direction, then dropped her voice to a whisper to reply, "I want you to free my—friend from jail."

The eye narrowed, and Mr. Hayes tossed the cigar into the street. "What did you say?"

Caroline bit her lower lip for a moment, then repeated her request, slowly and clearly, the way she would have done for a slow student.

"I'll be damned," swore Mr. Hayes, resting his hands on his hips. "You're asking me to break the law!"

"Shhh!" Caroline hissed. Then she took his arm and fairly dragged him into the little space between the Hellfire and Spit Saloon and the Wells Fargo office. There was no telling what Hypatia would make of that, but Caroline felt she had no alternative. "You wouldn't be breaking the law," she insisted furiously, still gripping Mr. Hayes's arm. "You'd be striking a blow for justice. Seaton—Mr. Flynn is innocent. He was wrongly accused." Tears welled, unbidden, along her lashes. "They're going to hang him!"

There was a certain cautious softening in Mr. Hayes's manner. His dog was at his side again, nuzzling the back of his knee. "I read about that in the newspaper," Hayes said with a frown, rubbing his bristly chin with a thumb and forefinger.

Desperation kept Caroline from remarking on the surprising fact that Mr. Hayes could read. "He didn't rob that stagecoach," she whispered frantically. "And I *know* he didn't gun down the driver. Mr. Flynn would never do a reprehensible thing like that."

Mr. Hayes looked both pitying and skeptical, and Caroline wanted to slap his face for it, but she restrained herself.

"What makes you so sure?" he asked.

Caroline huffed out a ragged, beleaguered sigh. "Because he *told* me he didn't!"

Hayes spread his hands wide. "Well, why didn't you say so?" he retorted sarcastically. "That changes everything!"

Caroline sniffled. The tip of her nose was probably turning red, but she didn't care. Practically everything that mattered to her was at stake. "If Mr. Flynn can just get out of jail, he can prove his innocence."

"Or hightail it for the ass-end of nowhere," Hayes agreed. "Flynn was convicted of robbery and murder, Miss Chalmers. He was sentenced to hang. And there isn't a damn thing I can do about it." He turned to walk away, and Caroline gripped the back of his sleeve.

"Wait," she pleaded. "Please."

He faced her again. "Breaking into Yankee jails during wartime was one thing, Miss Chalmers. But now the fighting is over, and I've got no intention of getting in the way of justice."

"Justice?" Caroline cried. "The territory's about to execute the wrong man! Do you call that justice?"

Hayes hooked one thumb under a suspender and regarded Caroline thoughtfully. "You really love this jaybird, don't you?"

"Yes," Caroline admitted, in a whispered wail. The dog at Mr. Hayes's feet seemed to echo the sound.

"Hell," cursed Mr. Hayes. "I do powerfully hate it when a lady cries."

Since her handkerchief was filthy, Caroline had to dry her eyes with the back of one hand. "Will you help me?"

"No," Mr. Hayes answered flatly. And then he walked away, the pitiful dog scrambling along at his heels.

Caroline took a few moments to recover her dignity, then followed him. That snoopy Hypatia was standing out on the sidewalk in front of her Aunt Gertrude's shop now, her arms folded, watching with a smirk on her face.

"Hello, Caroline!" she called out in a sunny voice.

Caroline only glared at her and went back to the saloon window.

Guthrie Hayes was once again embroiled in his card game. As Caroline watched, a dance hall girl in a skimpy pink and black striped dress minced her way over the sawdust toward him, carrying an enameled bowl in one hand.

Reaching the table, she picked up a whiskey bottle and poured the amber-colored liquor into the bowl. She set the dish on the floor, showing her garters when she bent over. The dog drank the whiskey in shameless laps, then lay down at Mr. Hayes's feet again.

Caroline wasn't concerned with the dog's apparent lack of moral fortitude. It was the dance hall girl who irked her. While she watched, the shameless hussy sat down in Mr. Hayes's lap with a distinct wiggle and wrapped one arm around his neck.

For the moment, Seaton Flynn and his predicament were forgotten.

The harlot took Mr. Hayes's hat from his head and put it on her own, then bent to whisper something in his ear while he dealt the cards.

Caroline tapped insistently at the window, but Mr. Hayes's attention was all for the strumpet squirming and simpering in his lap.

A slow grin spread across his face as he listened to whatever the soiled dove was saying and then he nodded in response. In that moment, Caroline lost all concern for appearances and marched along the sidewalk to the swinging doors.

Without stopping to think—if she had paused to consider

14

the implications of her actions, she wouldn't have had the courage—Caroline strode into the saloon, her prim black shoes kicking up little clouds of sawdust as she moved.

The bawdy tinkle of the piano ceased, as did the clinking of bottles against glass and the low hum of conversation.

Everyone turned to stare blearily at Caroline through a blue haze of smoke as she came to a halt beside Mr. Hayes's chair and folded her arms.

Tob whined and put one paw over his muzzle. Mr. Hayes looked up at her and grinned, and the dance hall girl, still wearing the hat, gazed at Caroline with a combination of challenge and contempt in her saucy, kohl-lined eyes.

The impetus that had swept Caroline into the saloon promptly deserted her, and she was at a total loss. After all, she couldn't very well argue her case in front of all these witnesses; the whole plan depended upon the utmost discretion.

"Mr. Hayes," she said awkwardly, operating on sheer bravado, "I demand that you speak with me. Privately."

He arched one eyebrow, his arm resting nonchalantly around the saloon girl's middle. Playfully, she put the hat back on his head. "Oh, you do, do you? What about?"

Caroline's face was flooded with color. "You know very well *what about,* Mr. Hayes. You are simply being difficult."

Much too gently for Caroline's tastes, he displaced the young woman on his lap and stood. "I believe I made myself clear when we talked before, Miss Chalmers," he said evenly, hooking his thumbs in his suspenders.

Caroline was terrified. If he repeated the request she'd made of him in front of these people, all would be lost. She might even end up in jail herself.

Almost suavely, he gestured toward the swinging doors, inviting her to leave.

Chin trembling, Caroline turned on her heel, picked up her skirts with one hand, and stormed out of the saloon and down the sidewalk.

She didn't stop to think about what she'd done until she reached the picket fence surrounding the brick schoolhouse, three streets away. Pushing open the gate, Caroline stumbled blindly up the walk, one hand to her mouth, and let herself into the building.

All her students were gone for the day, since she'd dismissed classes before venturing to the saloon in search of Mr. Hayes, so she had the privacy to cry.

She sat down on one of the small desks, attached to each other by long runners of black iron, covered her face with both hands, and wept in earnest. She hadn't felt this bleak or hopeless since that long-ago day in Nebraska, when she'd been forced to leave Emma and Lily behind on the orphan train.

With Seaton Flynn, a handsome young lawyer who had appeared in town on the afternoon stagecoach one day two years before, she'd found the hope of a home and children of her own, a real family. He'd charmed her easily, with his dancing brown eyes and ready smile—he had a grand sense of fashion and propriety, too, unlike Mr. Guthrie Hayes— and he'd soon built a respectable practice. Although Caroline had caught glimpses of a cold, quicksilver temper in Seaton, she'd felt that his good qualities outweighed such a transitory flaw.

Then he'd been accused of robbing a stagecoach and actually shooting another person to death! Seaton had been whisked away to Laramie, tried, and convicted, but Caroline was convinced it was all a colossal mistake. She loved Seaton Flynn, and that wouldn't have been the case if he were a murderer and a thief. She would have known.

When the door creaked open behind her, interrupting her reflections, Caroline thought one of her students had returned for a forgotten book or slate. She sniffled once, lifted her chin, and scraped up a smile to put on. But when she turned to look, she saw Guthrie Hayes standing at the back of the schoolroom.

Instantly, the room was too warm. Caroline bolted off the desk top and went to take a long pole from its hook on the wall. Her heart pounding at a rate all out of proportion to the activity, she went from one high window to another, opening them from the top.

Soon, there was nothing to do but face Mr. Hayes again. "What do you want?" she asked.

He was still standing in the framework of the inner door, next to the entrance to the cloakroom, one powerful shoulder resting against the jamb. "You've been crying over Flynn," he said seriously. "Has it ever occurred to you that he might not be worth your tears?"

Caroline thought of picnics and long Sunday afternoon walks with Seaton Flynn, of shared kisses in the moonlight and her many bright dreams. Caroline's heart had gone tumbling into infinity the first moment she saw him, when they'd collided at the base of the outside stairway leading up to his office over the feed and grain.

"You don't know Mr. Flynn," she said, as reasonably as she could, putting the window pole back in its place. "And may I say I think it's abominably cruel of you to come here and torment me further."

The barb didn't appear to catch Mr. Hayes in a tender place. He shrugged. "Evidently, the judge and jury didn't know him either. They convicted him of murder, among other things."

Caroline was tired, discouraged, and exasperated. "Why did you come here?" she demanded.

He pushed off his hat and thoughtfully scratched his head. "I'm not sure," he replied, "considering that I had better things to do."

Recalling the trollop who'd practically draped herself across Mr. Hayes's muscular thighs, Caroline was stung. She gathered the first-grade arithmetic primers into a stack and slammed them down onto her desk top. "That isn't a satisfactory answer, Mr. Hayes."

Again he indulged in that obnoxious, off center grin. "I seem to be flunking this conversation, Teacher."

For some reason Caroline couldn't begin to divine, he was toying with her. She swept him up in one contemptuous glance. "You seem to be flunking this *lifetime*," she replied.

He laughed and slapped one hand to his chest as though she'd sunk a knife into him. Then he hoisted himself away from the door jamb and ambled toward her, until he was standing very close.

"Maybe you shouldn't insult me quite so freely," he said, in a low voice that caused a warm, quaking sensation somewhere deep down in Caroline's person. "From what you've told me, I'm the only hope you've got of springing your gentleman friend from the hoosegow."

She took a step backwards and raised one hand to fidget with the loose tendrils of dark hair at the back of her neck.

Mr. Hayes's single eye slipped to her breasts at the motion, then came moseying back to her face. Again, one corner of his mouth tilted in a quirky grin. Caroline felt dizzy and took refuge in her official chair.

"Are you going to help me or not?" she asked breathlessly, looking up at Guthrie Hayes as he bent over her, his hands braced on the gouged oak surface of the desk.

"I haven't decided yet," he answered. "This isn't the kind of thing a man enters into lightly, Miss Chalmers. There are a lot of variables to consider."

It struck Caroline then that Mr. Hayes was better educated than his clothes and general personal appearance would indicate. "But you're not saying no?"

He shook his head, and the expression in the eye Caroline could see revealed bafflement. "No. Why the hell I'm not is anybody's guess, because this whole idea of yours is just plain crazy. One or both of us could end up in jail, right alongside your beau."

To her own surprise as much as his, Caroline smiled, and he drew back slightly, looking mildly alarmed and more confused than ever.

"Thank you," she said.

Mr. Hayes muttered a curse word, wrenched his hat off, then put it on again. After that, he waggled an index finger at Caroline. "I haven't made my final decision yet, Teacher, and don't you forget that."

"I won't," Caroline replied, unable to keep the little trill of joyous triumph out of her voice.

Mr. Hayes swore again, turned on one heel, and strode

back along the aisle between the desks to the inner door. He was muttering to himself as he went out.

For the first time since Seaton's arrest, Caroline's heart was light. She closed all the windows, washed down the blackboard, swept the floor, and left, her lesson book clutched to her chest.

Miss Ethel, gray-haired now but as delicately spry as ever, was in the front yard when she arrived home, examining her cherished rose bushes for buds. She beamed when Caroline swept through the gate, humming happily.

"You've finally gotten over that wretched Mr. Flynn!" the older woman said, looking delighted.

"On the contrary," Caroline replied, in a conspiratorial whisper, "I'll soon prove to the entire world that Seaton isn't guilty."

Miss Ethel's wrinkled face fell. "But he is, dear," she said. "Don't you remember? One of the stagecoach passengers identified him."

Caroline continued up the walk toward the front steps, though her gait wasn't so springy now and her spirits were drooping just a little. "It was a mistake," she insisted. "The real robber is someone who resembles Seaton, that's all." She didn't look back, because she knew if she did, she'd see Miss Ethel shaking her head.

In the front parlor, Miss Phoebe was perched on the settee, sipping tea and gossiping with a neighbor. She inclined her head and waggled her fingers slightly as Caroline passed by in the hallway.

Miss Phoebe had planned to marry a Mr. Gunderson immediately after she and Caroline and Miss Ethel arrived in Bolton thirteen years ago, but a Shoshone brave had shot the prospective bridegroom dead before she'd even finished unpacking. Despite hordes of eager suitors—like all the western territories, Wyoming suffered a drastic shortage of marriageable women—neither Miss Phoebe nor Miss Ethel had ever expressed interest in matrimony again.

Reaching the spacious kitchen, Caroline hung her sensible navy blue cloak from a peg beside the back door and snatched a piece of fresh bread from the box on the counter. The scent of a mutton roast simmering in the oven made her stomach grumble.

She buttered the bread and went to the stove for the teakettle. Soon, she was seated in one of the sturdy oak chairs, her lesson book open on the red-and-white checked oilcloth covering the table, her feet up on another chair. While she ate and drank her tea, she was planning assignments for the next day's classes.

Presently, Miss Phoebe came in to open the door of the oven and peek at the aromatic mutton. There were carrots, potatoes, and onions stewing in the pot along with the meat.

"Is Mrs. Cribben gone?" Caroline asked. That lady was the head of the Bolton Community Literary Club and the author of reams of truly wretched poetry, and in Caroline's opinion she was a terrible bore.

"Yes," Miss Phoebe replied, with exasperated goodwill. Her hair had turned gray, like her sister's, but she was still an attractive woman. "It wouldn't have hurt you to stop and greet her, you know. She was instrumental in persuading the mayor to levy a special saloon tax so that we could buy new textbooks last spring."

Caroline sighed and nodded. She was a dedicated teacher, and the concerns of the school were her concerns, but her mind had fastened onto Mr. Guthrie Hayes and she couldn't seem to pry it loose. What had that saloon woman whispered in his ear, to make him grin like that? Had the two of them gone upstairs together to do scandalous things?

Caroline clenched her fist.

What was Guthrie Hayes doing in Bolton, anyway?

"Caroline," Miss Phoebe scolded.

Caroline jumped. "I'm sorry," she said, flushing. "You were saying—?"

"I was saying that Mrs. Cribben told me that Hypatia Furvis told *her* that you walked right into the He—that awful saloon—" She paused to shudder. "In the broad light of day!"

Caroline swallowed and stared at her kindly guardian, heat climbing her neck to pulse in her cheeks. She saw no anger in the fragile, well-bred face, but Miss Phoebe did look disconcerted. "There was a gentleman there I needed to see," she explained lamely.

"Why?" Miss Phoebe wanted to know.

Only with the severest difficulty did Caroline lie to the woman who had been a mother to her. "H-he's the father of one of my students," she said, looking down at her lap and smoothing her crumpled sateen skirt with nervous fingers. "Calvin has been missing school, and I wanted to know why."

"Couldn't you have gone to the family home and inquired?" Miss Phoebe pressed.

Caroline forced herself to meet the other woman's gaze. A lie was a lie, but this was an extenuating circumstance. After all, Seaton's life hung in the balance. "Calvin told me his mother was very ill," she prevaricated, her eyes wanting to dodge away from Miss Phoebe's. "I didn't wish to disturb the poor woman."

Miss Phoebe sighed. "I don't think I need to remind you, Caroline, that a teacher cannot afford so much as a speck on her reputation. If word of what you did gets back to the school board—and it most certainly will—you could lose your job."

Caroline imagined herself as Seaton's wife, returning to Bolton in triumph. Cleared of all charges by his own efforts, Mr. Flynn would reopen his law office and Caroline would be busy sewing curtains and having babies. Her job wouldn't be a concern anymore.

"I'll be more careful," she promised, not daring to tell Miss Phoebe that Guthrie Hayes had virtually agreed to break Seaton out of jail.

Miss Phoebe reached out and patted her hand. "See that you are, dear." She sighed as she rose from her chair and went to the sideboard for supper china. "I do hope you've put that lawyer fellow out of your mind," she said. "Heaven knows, there are plenty of other young men in Bolton who would be thrilled to marry you."

Caroline hid a smile as she got up from the table. After closing her lesson book and setting it aside, she tossed away her bread crusts and began taking silverware from one of the wavy wooden drawers in the sideboard. In its round mirror, she saw that her color was high and her brown eyes were twinkling. "Don't worry, Miss Phoebe," she said cheerfully. "I'll be married before you know it."

Just then, Miss Ethel came through the dining room doorway, carrying her straw gardening hat in one hand. "Who's getting married?" she inquired eagerly.

Caroline laughed as she set silverware alongside the plates Miss Phoebe had already laid out. "I am," she said.

"Caroline is teasing, Ethel," Phoebe put in gently.

Miss Ethel looked downright disappointed, but she brightened after only a moment. "There was a letter for you today, Caroline," she announced, patting first one skirt pocket and then the other. "Here it is."

Caroline rarely received letters and, when she did, her heart always did a cartwheel. She'd never given up the hope, even after all these years, that she'd hear from Lily or Emma.

But the envelope bore a return address in Laramie, and Caroline instantly recognized Seaton's elaborate handwriting. Of course it followed, because Mr. Flynn was being held in that town, and had been since his trial.

Her fingers shook a little as she opened the letter, and there was a feeling of dread in the pit of her stomach.

It wasn't at all the reaction she would have expected.

Dear Caroline, he had written, *It's lonely in this place, and I miss you with all my heart . . . somehow, we must find a way to secure my release . . . I swear to you, by all that's holy, I didn't kill that man . . . we'll go away together, start a new life . . .*

Caroline refolded the letter carefully and tucked it back into its envelope. In her mind, she stood before Seaton, looking up into his sincere dark eyes, touching his rich ebony-colored hair, being held against his tall, lithe frame.

And for the very first time since the whole nightmare had begun, she felt a whisper of doubt brush against her spirit. Could Seaton be lying?

"Excuse me," she said to Miss Phoebe and Miss Ethel,

who were watching her with worried puzzlement. And then she hurried up the rear stairs and along the narrow hallway to her room.

Safely behind her own door, she laid one hand to her heart and breathed deeply until the dreadful suspicion began to pass. Seaton Flynn was innocent of any crime, no matter what the judge, the jury, and Guthrie Hayes happened to think. He was just as much a victim as that poor stagecoach driver.

Wasn't he?

Resolutely, Caroline went to her bureau and picked up the framed sketch she'd done herself, from memory, of Lily and Emma. One by one, she touched their faces, aching to know where they were and whether they were safe and happy.

"He didn't do it," she told her lost sisters, and their large eyes regarded her solemnly from behind the glass

Chapter

❧ *2* ❧

*G*uthrie drew the buckboard to a halt when he reached his camp in the foothills, pushed the brake lever into place with one heel, and dropped the reins. Tob jumped down from the back of the wagon with a little whine and came around to get underfoot while Guthrie unhitched the liver-colored gelding, and chickens scattered everywhere, squawking.

Thinking of Caroline Chalmers's visit to the Hellfire and Spit Saloon, Guthrie grinned and pushed the eye patch up onto his forehead—he wore it in case there turned out to be somebody in Bolton he didn't want to recognize him—then led the horse into a stand of cottonwoods nearby. Beyond them was a stream flowing from a mountain spring somewhere higher up, and there was plenty of green grass along its banks.

Using a long leadline, Guthrie tethered the animal to a stake in the ground and left the horse to graze.

His mind was still on Caroline when he returned to camp, where Tob greeted him with a series of yips. Frowning, he reached down and patted the dog's grizzled head. If one scrawny schoolteacher had figured out who he was, it wouldn't be long until word of it was all over the territory.

He took an armload of wood from the pile he kept just inside the opening of his mine shaft and carried it back to the ring of stones in the center of camp. If the Yankees were going to throw him into prison for the things he'd done during the war, he reasoned, they would have done it by then. There was no need to run.

Guthrie's hands worked independently of his mind, due to long habit, as he laid the fire and picked up his blue enameled coffeepot. He started back through the shimmering cottonwood trees, toward the creek.

There was a small deposit of copper not twenty yards from where his tent stood, and Guthrie meant to stay and work the mine. He grinned as he squatted to fill the coffeepot from the stream. He was through rambling from place to place.

As soon as the mine started producing, he was going to build himself a house at the edge of Bolton—the best one in town. Then he'd go back to Cheyenne and fetch Adabelle Rogers, a woman with particular promise as a wife. If she was still available, of course.

He smiled as he carried the fresh water back toward his camp. Adabelle had blue eyes and blond hair and a body like a featherbed, and Guthrie looked forward to sinking into her warm softness every night. With luck, there would be four or five kids running around before too much time had passed.

Squatting by the campfire, he set the pot in the embers and spooned coffee grounds into it. His anticipatory grin faded away as Caroline Chalmers elbowed her way into his mind, pushing Adabelle aside, looking at him with those wide brown eyes.

Guthrie stood up, tore off his hat, and flung it toward the dusty tent standing a few yards away. He wasn't going to risk the mine and Adabelle and all the attendant dreams just because some skinny schoolmarm needed his help.

Was he?

He shoved splayed fingers through his hair, then jammed his thumbs behind his suspenders. Caroline was nothing like Adabelle, and yet her face and shape and voice filled his

25

brain. When she'd smiled at him unexpected-like, back there at the schoolhouse, he'd actually thought for a moment that the ground was moving under his feet.

With a ragged sigh, Guthrie threw back his head and gazed up at the spring sky. Although the days were definitely getting longer, there wasn't much light left. If he was going to hunt down some supper, he'd better get busy.

He pulled his .45 from its holster on his hip and checked the chamber. Then, with Tob at his heels, he started off into the woods.

Twenty minutes later, he returned with a couple of grouse. He cleaned and plucked them alongside the stream, then brought them back to camp and put them onto a spit over the campfire. Once the meat had cooked a while, it began to give off an aroma that made his stomach grumble with anticipation.

He lifted the coffeepot from the coals, using an old piece of rawhide to protect his hand from the hot metal handle, and poured the foamy brew into a mug. While he sipped his coffee, pausing every now and then to spit out a few grounds, he watched the sun set and wondered if Caroline was right.

She was pesky as a horsefly, that woman, but it seemed to Guthrie that her head was on straight, and the fact that she believed in the lawyer carried weight with him. Maybe Flynn *was* innocent. Maybe a man was about to die for a crime he hadn't committed.

Guthrie set his mug down on a tree stump that served nicely as a table. Then he brought a kerosene lantern from the tent, lit the wick, and hung it from one of the crude poles he'd erected to support the clothesline.

The lantern light, coupled with the blazing campfire, pushed back a little of the darkness, but Guthrie still yearned to have walls around him again, and a real floor under his feet. When he sat down on an upended apple crate to wait for the grouse to finish roasting, Tob came to him and rested his muzzle on Guthrie's knee.

Guthrie stroked the dog with one hand and held his coffee mug in the other, staring into the snapping flames of the fire.

Tonight, the loneliness that had been plaguing him for the last few years was keener than ever.

He called Adabelle to his mind, but once again it was Caroline who answered the summons. Her beautiful eyes pleaded with him and her lower lip trembled slightly.

Guthrie groaned. "Get out of here and leave me alone," he muttered. But she stayed. She stayed through supper and hung around while Guthrie was washing up at the stream bank. And she was there when he crawled into the tent and stripped down to his long underwear to sleep.

Mr. Flynn is innocent, he heard her say. *He was wrongly accused.* He saw the tears rise in her eyes. *They're going to hang him!*

"He probably deserves it," Guthrie grumbled, shifting uncomfortably and punching his pillow, remembering the newspaper accounts of the trial, which had taken place miles away in Laramie. Flynn was still in jail there, awaiting his execution.

Guthrie closed his eyes determinedly, expecting to lie awake for hours, but the moment his lids dropped, he was back in northern Pennsylvania, within the high barbed wire fences of Slaterville, a makeshift Yankee prison camp . .

The bayonet wound in his side alternately burned and ached. In the fetid darkness that surrounded him, he could hear other men, some moaning, some weeping, some screaming in the throes of a nightmare or in the clutch of hot steel fingers of pain.

"Guthrie." The ragged whisper came from right beside him and he tensed, tried to raise his head from the straw pallet on which he lay. The effort was too much.

A hand found his shoulder in the gloom and shook him gently. "Guthrie, that is you, isn't it?"

Despite everything, the pain and the helplessness and the fever he felt brewing under his flesh, Guthrie grinned. The voice belonged to Jacob McTavish, the closest thing he had to a brother. He and Jacob had grown up together on the McTavish plantation in Virginia, where Guthrie's father had worked as a sharecropper.

Because of Jacob's mother's Christian bent, Guthrie had been educated, right along with her own two sons, in the study of the main house.

"So this is where you've been hidin' out, you yellow-livered Yankee lover," Guthrie managed, with a raspy laugh. "According to the last letter I had from home, your mama and daddy think you're dead." Now, when his eyes had had a chance to adjust, he could see the outline of Jacob's tall, gawky frame kneeling there beside him.

"I'm as good as dead if we don't get out of here," Jacob whispered. "There's this guard, Sergeant Pedlow, and he looks for any chance he can get to devil me. He put a brand on a man from Tennessee just last week."

Guthrie closed his eyes against the image and murmured a profanity. "Try to stay out of the bastard's way," he said, as a beam of moonlight came in through a crack in the wall and gilded his friend's profile in silver. "Maybe you didn't notice, Jake, but I'm in no condition to climb over barbed wire with fifty Yankees aiming rifles at my ass."

Jacob shoved a hand through his auburn hair. "I saw you were hurt when they brought you in on that meat wagon. I watched to see what barracks they put you in. You're just lucky you didn't end up in one of those field hospitals."

A strangled sound erupted from Guthrie's throat; meant to be an ironic chuckle, it came out as a sob. He could still smell the blood and hear the shrieks. "I did," he answered, after a long moment. "They poured carbolic acid into my wound and sent me here."

"You fell at Gettysburg?"

Grimly, Guthrie nodded. "Do you think it's true what the Yankees say—that they routed General Lee and the war's almost over?"

Even in the dim light, he saw Jacob's thin shoulders move in a shrug. "The war's over for you and me," he said, "unless we get out of this place. And I'm not going to see home again, if Pedlow has his way."

Guthrie wanted to rage against the helplessness he felt, but he didn't have the strength. "Why does he hate you so much?"

"Why do you think he hates me, Hayes? Because I'm a Rebel."

Guthrie sighed. "Lay low, Jacob—try not to attract the sergeant's attention. I'll think of something."

"I'd better get back," Jacob said, sounding as dejected as Guthrie felt. After laying a hesitant hand on his friend's shoulder, he disappeared into the darkness.

Guthrie lay still in the straw, listening as a man retched somewhere close by. A putrid smell was added to the general stench of sweat and misery and rotting skin.

He knew now that Mrs. McTavish, Jacob's religious mother, had been right. There truly was such a place as hell; he was in it.

By the next morning, the wound in his side was infected and he lapsed into a fever. Everything around him was a heat mirage, shimmering just out of reach, but he heard the scream from outside and, somehow, he knew the cry was Jacob's.

Probably because he was so cussed, as his daddy would have said, Guthrie survived and, after a fashion, recovered. As soon as he could walk, he went looking for his friend.

He found Jacob, cowed and hollow-eyed, shoveling lye into a stinking sewage pit. Flies buzzed around in black clouds. Jacob's lips didn't move, but his eyes said, *You're too late.* He pushed aside his filthy shirt and revealed an ugly scab on his left shoulder—a brand in the shape of a diamond.

Until that moment, Guthrie had not really hated Yankees. He'd figured most of them were just green kids, like himself, who'd expected the fighting to be a game and found out it was in deadly earnest. "Which is Pedlow?" he asked, taking up a shovel so he wouldn't draw undue attention.

Jacob worked on. "The one standing over by the gate," he mumbled, "cleaning his fingernails with a bowie knife."

Guthrie found the man and measured him in a surreptitious glance. The guard was about his own size, though he was older and beefier, and his skin was so badly pockmarked that his features seemed distorted.

After a while, Pedlow raised his eyes just in time to catch

Guthrie looking at him. The two men regarded each other in silence for a time, then Pedlow turned his head, spat into the muddy dirt, and walked away.

For three days, Guthrie watched the sergeant, memorizing his habits and mannerisms, learning his routine. He was weak and sick but, by some twisted irony, Pedlow became his reason for surviving. All he had to do when he felt himself slipping was to imagine the brand making contact with Jacob's flesh.

At last, Pedlow was put on night duty at the south gate, and that seemed fitting to Guthrie, because he fully meant to travel in a southerly direction.

An hour after nightfall, he slipped up behind the sergeant and struck him in the back of the head with a rock he'd been saving for that express purpose. He dragged Pedlow behind a line of rain barrels and took his knife and uniform.

In moments Guthrie had exchanged his own worn, bloody clothes for Pedlow's Union blue, and his palms sweated where he held the rifle. He kept to the shadows when half a dozen Yankees passed by, a few minutes later, greeting him without particular enthusiasm, and he answered with a grunt.

When Pedlow started to come to, Guthrie put the heel of one boot on the man's throat and told him, "It wouldn't trouble me at all to smash your windpipe like a summer squash, blue-belly, so don't give me any more cause than you already have."

The Yankee made a sickly whining sound, and Guthrie bent to gag him with his own bright yellow bandanna and cuff his hands together.

After that, Guthrie walked boldly into the barracks and roused Jacob, as well as half a dozen others who looked strong enough to travel. When he marched the men out of the south gate, in the thin gray light of that cold morning, anyone who observed him would have thought he was a Union sergeant, taking a detachment of prisoners out on a work detail.

Even though, in reality, he and the others had escaped, at that point in the dream Guthrie was almost invariably wrenched back into that stinking prison camp and branded just the way Jacob had been. The experience was so real that Guthrie awakened with a violent start, rising up on his elbows and looking around. Tob, curled up at his feet, gave a soft whimper of commiseration.

Guthrie's body was drenched with perspiration. He found his pistol in the darkness of the tent and gripped the handle against a slippery palm. It took him nearly five minutes to untangle *then* from *now* and slip into an uneasy, guarded rest.

A deafening blast sounded, rattling the schoolhouse windows in their frames, and Molly Haggart, a six-year-old with jet black braids and cornflower blue eyes, leaped out of her seat. Waving one little hand in the air, she cried, "Teacher, are we having an earthshake?"

Caroline's heart was just slowing down to its regular beat. "No, Molly," she said, raising her voice to be heard over the nervous laughter of the other children. "That was dynamite. And the word is earth*quake.*"

"Maybe somebody's robbing the bank!" said Johnny Wilbin, his many freckles standing out against his pale skin.

"Or the old Maitland mine might have caved in," speculated Pervis Thatcher.

Miss Phoebe and Miss Ethel's inherited coal mine had been shut down for five years, but it had made enough money in its time to support the old ladies for the rest of their natural lives.

"Hush, children," Caroline said firmly. "If it's anything we need to know about, someone will come and tell us."

"It's just Mr. Hayes, blasting for copper," said Martin Bates, the same young man who had told Caroline about Guthrie Hayes's escapades during the war after proudly pointing him out as a friend of his father's. "You can't work a mine without using dynamite. He's got a place out by Ribbon Creek."

Caroline made a mental note of that information and determinedly turned the children's attention back to their work. Once school had been dismissed, however, and she'd washed the blackboards, swept the floor, and brought in the flag from its holder beside the front door, she rushed to the livery stable and asked for a horse and buggy.

After paying the ten-cent rental, she set out for Ribbon Creek.

It was four-thirty in the afternoon when she found Mr. Hayes's camp by the smoke of his campfire and drove in.

Furious chickens scattered before the swaybacked horse, flapping their wings, and Tob came loping toward her, barking uncertainly.

Guthrie Hayes was not inside his mine, as Caroline might have expected, but standing over a washtub, the sleeves of his underwear shirt pushed up, his arms up to the elbows in soapy water. She saw him fidget with his eye patch, then come toward her at a leisurely pace, passing a clothesline where several pairs of trousers were hung out to dry.

"Hello, Miss Chalmers," he said, in that impudently cordial way of his. His hands were resting on his hips now, and he wasn't wearing a hat, so his rich brown hair glistened in the sun.

Caroline leaned slightly forward in the buggy seat, still holding the reins, and squinted. "I could have sworn you were wearing that patch over your right eye yesterday."

Mr. Hayes touched the patch briefly, then dropped his hand again. "You were mistaken, Miss Chalmers," he said politely.

She sat up straight and wrapped the reins carefully around the brake lever. "I don't think so," she replied. "I'm usually right about things like that. I notice details. Will you help me down, please?"

He hesitated a moment, then walked toward her. When Caroline stood and his hands closed around her waist, she regretted forcing him into this particular courtesy. Jets of sweet fire shot down her legs from the points of contact, curled her toes, and raced upwards again to collide hard at the crux of her thighs.

Caroline drew in her breath and her face went pink when she saw that Mr. Hayes was aware of her scandalous reaction. He was smiling his tilted smile, and his gaze was fixed on Caroline's mouth.

For one moment, she thought he was going to have the audacity to kiss her.

Instead, to her profound relief and boundless disappointment, he let her slide down the length of his frame to stand, trembling, on the ground. He was still so close that she could smell sunshine and sweat on his clothes and feel the hard heat of his body.

"You know," he said easily, "it isn't entirely proper, your coming out here alone."

Caroline's heart pirouetted over a beat, and she felt perspiration dampen the space between her breasts. "Surely you're a gentleman," she said, although she was sure of no such thing.

His green eye twinkled. "If you say so, Miss Chalmers."

"Perhaps you wouldn't mind—stepping back? Just a little?" Caroline inquired breathlessly. Even though it was a mild April day, with a fresh breeze coming down from the mountains, she was feeling the heat of August.

"Of course," Mr. Hayes replied. But he didn't move.

Except, that is, to lower his mouth to Caroline's.

She stiffened when his lips touched hers, as though she'd stepped into a puddle of lightning, and gave a little whimper of both protest and acquiescence before he kissed her in earnest.

It was in every way unlike the discreet pecks Seaton had stolen during their walks together, or in the parlor, when Miss Phoebe and Miss Ethel weren't around. Guthrie's lips were warm and supple, and yet they tamed Caroline's, with the skillful aid of his tongue.

Caroline's eyes had drifted closed after the initial shock, but they went wide again when she felt this first brazen intrusion. To her utter mortification, she could not pull away; her tongue moved against Guthrie's like an eager lover.

Finally, he drew back, his lips curved into a sleepy smile, his hands still resting on Caroline's waist. "Did your

33

gentleman friend ever kiss you like that? This man you claim to love?"

Caroline's cheeks flamed, and she twisted away from Guthrie's grip to smooth sweaty palms over the skirts of her checkered gingham dress. "Of course he did," she lied. "All the time."

Guthrie's expression bordered on a smirk. "Did he, now?" he teased. And then, as easily as that, he turned and walked back to his washtub. "That was a test, Teacher, though whether you failed or passed is a difficult question to settle. You may think you love Seaton Flynn, but you don't."

Caroline watched in amazement as he took a blue cotton shirt from the suds and tossed it into a bucket of somewhat clearer water. Once he'd rinsed the garment, he wrung it out, gave it a hard shake, and hung it expertly on his clothesline, along with several pairs of trousers.

She was so overwhelmed, first by his kiss and now by his pure nerve, that she couldn't speak.

"What are you doing out here, Caroline?" he finally asked, watching her as he returned to the washtub to scrub another shirt.

Her mouth moved, but nothing came out, so she tried again. That time, she managed to speak. She would simply let his outrageous claims pass, for now. "I'm here to find out what your decision is. A-about Mr. Flynn, I mean."

He shrugged. "I haven't made a decision," he said, industriously rubbing another garment along the tin ridges of his washboard.

Caroline began to pace. She'd never seen a man do wash before, and the sight was all the more disconcerting for all the other shocks she'd suffered already. She knew she should get back in her rented buggy and leave, but she couldn't bring herself to do it. "I'm surprised you don't have a wife, Mr. Hayes," she said.

"After that kiss," he responded, giving her a cocky wink, "I think you'd better call me Guthrie."

Caroline turned away for a moment, her arms folded, because she was sure every bit of skin she had showing was

34

crimson. When she looked again, he was rinsing the second shirt.

The muscles in his tanned forearms corded powerfully as he wrung out the garment. "Well?" he prompted.

"Is that a condition you're setting? That I have to call you by your first name, I mean?"

He considered. "Yes."

"And if I do, you'll promise to rescue Mr. Flynn?"

"No," he replied, snapping the wet shirt and pegging it to the clothesline.

Caroline's frustration was rising. "This is not a game, Mr. Hayes. Someone's life is at stake!"

"Guthrie," he corrected intractably. "And someone else's life ended during a stagecoach robbery."

"All right!" Caroline yelled. *"Guthrie!"*

He grinned. "You don't love him," he reminded her. Apparently he'd finished his laundry, because he was tugging down the sleeves of his underwear shirt.

Caroline entertained a fantasy wherein she drenched Guthrie Hayes with the entire contents of his washtub. Of course, she didn't dare follow through, but she did derive some pleasure from imagining it. "I *do* love him," she insisted.

"No, you don't," Guthrie replied calmly. Then he gestured grandly toward a smooth-topped tree stump beside the embers of a campfire. "Have a seat, Caroline, and I'll explain it all to you."

Mr. Hayes's arrogance was exceeded only by his bad breeding. "It's Miss Chalmers to you!" she said, folding her arms and stubbornly standing her ground.

"Not if you want me to get your beau out of jail," Guthrie reasoned cordially. "Now, *Caroline,* sit down before I forget that I was raised to treat even bad-tempered hoydens like ladies."

Caroline edged reluctantly over to the stump and sat. "What happened to your eye?" she asked, to distract him from the fact that she'd had to concede that particular battle

He bent and poured himself a mugful of coffee that looked thick enough to grease a wagon axle and regarded her over the rim for a few moments before answering. "Maybe I lost it in the war," he said cryptically. "Would you like some coffee?"

She smoothed her skirts. "I would prefer tea."

Guthrie executed a mocking half bow. "I'm sure you would, Teacher, but all I've got is coffee."

Caroline remembered the consistency of the stuff and unconsciously curled her lip. "No, thank you," she said, with cool politeness. "Now, if we could get down to business—"

He dragged up a wooden crate and sat next to her. "What business is that?"

She drew a deep breath and let it out slowly, struggling to control her temper. "Mr. Flynn's rescue, of course."

Guthrie swirled his coffee cup, watching the dark waves and ripples. "Are you always this persistent?"

"Yes," Caroline replied, quite truthfully. She'd never failed at any task she'd really set her mind to, except for finding her lost sisters, and she hadn't given up on that, of course. It was just that she'd had to give Mr. Flynn's predicament priority, since it was a matter of life and death.

Mr. Hayes took another sip of his coffee, then tossed what remained into the dying fire. "Well, Teacher," he said, leaning forward slightly and resting his arms on his knees, "sometimes, you just have to wave a white flag."

For a moment, his face took on a haunted, distant expression. "Yes," he answered, and his voice was rough as rust.

"What was it?" Caroline asked, genuinely interested.

"The Confederacy, for one thing," he said. The look in his eyes hinted at a host of other dreams, all cherished, all lost.

She sighed, feeling a deep sadness. "There must be something else," she finally said, her voice soft.

His grin was sudden and bright, like unexpected sunshine, as he viewed some picture passing through his mind. "If there is," he replied presently, "it would be none of your business."

Caroline was nettled. "I don't care anyway," she lied.

There was a long, difficult silence.

"Well," Caroline burst out finally, "you must want *something!* Everyone does."

Guthrie was in no hurry to reply. His gaze slid down over her slender figure and then came back to her face. He shrugged. "I want a wife, Caroline," he said. "A soft, warm, cushiony wife."

Even though she had no aspirations to marry this man, Caroline was stung by his remark. She was as soft and warm as anyone, but when it came to the cushiony part, she fell short. "You mean, you want somebody *fat,*" she said, for the sake of her pride.

Guthrie laughed. "I'm sorry, Caroline. I didn't mean to hurt your feelings."

"You didn't," she lied huffily, straightening her skirts. Then she looked at him directly again. "Have you chosen this—wife?"

"In a manner of speaking," he said, with a lusty, contented sigh that heated Caroline's blood, "Her name is Miss Adabelle Rogers and she lives in Cheyenne."

Caroline looked away, hoping to hide the unexpected stab of pain his announcement had caused. She couldn't think why she cared whether or not Mr. Hayes meant to take a bride, when she was about to marry Seaton. But she did.

"I wonder what she'd say if she knew you kissed me," she said, to repay him.

"She'd claw out my other eye," Guthrie replied, with amusement in his voice.

Caroline shuddered and then bolted to her feet. "That was a disgusting thing to say!" she blurted.

Guthrie regarded her with a patient sort of sympathy that dealt still another injury to her dignity. She was sure he was thinking that she wanted to get Seaton out of jail because nobody else but a criminal would ever want a skinny schoolmarm like her.

Suddenly, she could no longer bear Mr. Hayes's presence, even if it meant saving Seaton from the hangman's noose. She was near tears, and self-respect decreed that she couldn't allow herself to let this man see her cry again. "I'm sure the two of you will suit each other very well," she said, and then she marched off toward the buggy and stepped up onto the runner.

She wasn't aware that Guthrie was behind her until he caught her by the waist and gently lifted her back down.

Startled, she twisted in his arms. She gave a small whimper of protest, then her hands moved automatically to his shoulders, while his mouth found and conquered hers.

"I'm leaving now," Caroline told him, in a dazed whisper, when the kiss finally ended.

"You're staying for supper," Guthrie countered, his voice a low rumble, and then he took her hand and led her back to his campfire.

Chapter

❧ 3 ❧

*T*ell me about yourself," Guthrie said, squatting down to take the lid off the pot sitting in the embers of the fire and stir the contents. The savory scent of stew rose in the spring air, intensifying his hunger.

Caroline was seated on the same stump where she'd sat before, looking defiant and like she wanted to bolt into the woods, both at once. She smoothed her skirts over her knees and lifted her chin a notch. "I'm a teacher," she replied, in a prim effort to cooperate. "And, as you know, I'm a close friend of Mr. Seaton Flynn—"

"Don't you have a daddy?" Guthrie interrupted, slamming the lid back down onto the pot of simmering stew. These Yankees never ceased to amaze him. Where he came from, men looked after their womenfolk instead of letting them wander all over the countryside getting themselves into dutch. "Or a brother?"

Caroline stared at him. "I beg your pardon?"

"You must not have any male relations," he said quietly, sitting on the wooden crate now. "If you did, you wouldn't be running around the territory like a scalded chicken, pestering men you shouldn't even speak to."

She did not flinch or look away. "Men like you, Mr. Hayes?"

"Yes. Men like me. If I had a daughter, and she walked right into a saloon the way you did yesterday, I'd turn her over my knee. As for coming to a man's camp, all alone—" He paused and shook his head, marveling.

Color rushed up Caroline's graceful neck to glow in her cheeks. She started to stand, but he immediately caught hold of her arm and prevented her escape.

"Are you alone in the world, Caroline? Except for Flynn, I mean?"

Tears glistened in Caroline's eyes, but Guthrie had to give her credit. She blinked them back. "No. I have two guardians, Miss Phoebe and Miss Ethel Maitland. They adopted me when I was eight and I love them very much."

Guthrie let his elbows rest on his knees and propped his chin on intertwined fingers. "Why did you need adopting when you were eight?" he asked. His interest was genuine.

Caroline sighed. "I lived in Chicago, with my mother and my two sisters, in my grandmother's house. Grandma died when I was seven, and we had to move to a flat because there wasn't any money. Mama—drank a little. She tried working in a shoe factory, but mostly she couldn't concentrate." Caroline hesitated while she searched his face for a moment, as if to determine whether or not it was safe to go on. "After a bit, Mama started bringing home different men." Her eyes skirted Guthrie's steady gaze for a moment, then returned. "They'd g-give her money, and things would be all right for a time. But then the soldier came along—Mr. Harrington."

Guthrie nodded to encourage her to go on.

"Mr. Harrington was a sergeant, I think, and he wasn't fond of children. It didn't take him long to persuade Mama that Lily and Emma and I would be better off taking our chances on an orphan train than growing up in Chicago." She looked down at her fingers, which were locked together and white at the knuckles. "Maybe he was right. We probably would have ended up in the factories. Or worse."

Guthrie reached out and closed one hand over both of

hers, wishing he could have protected her somehow. "Your guardians didn't adopt Lily and Emma, too?"

Caroline bit her lower lip for a moment, clearly battling some old and well-worn grief, and shook her head. "They sent a neighbor to fetch them a girl from the train, because they wanted a companion to travel west with them. The pity of it is, Miss Phoebe and Miss Ethel are the kindest, most generous women in the world. I think they probably would have taken in my sisters, too, if they'd been at the station to see them."

He moved his thumb over the back of her hand, wanting to take her into his arms and hold her. The more Guthrie heard, the better he understood her desperate need to believe in Seaton Flynn. It probably seemed to her that the lawyer could offer her a home along with all the things she'd missed as a little girl.

"Did you manage to stay in touch with Lily and Emma?" he asked.

Caroline shook her head. Moisture glimmered on her lower lashes again. "I don't have any idea where they are. I don't even know if they're alive."

"What have you done to find them?"

She averted her eyes for a moment. "I wrote a letter to the agency in Chicago that sent us west, but they couldn't tell me anything. So then I wrote a book."

"A book?" Guthrie didn't release his hold on Caroline's hand, and she didn't try to pull it away, though he figured that was only because she'd forgotten they were touching.

She nodded. "It's just a thin volume, telling what happened to Lily and Emma and me—how we had to leave home on the orphan train and everything. I'm hoping, when it's printed, that my sisters will see the book, or hear about it, and get in touch with me."

"You've already made arrangements to have it published?"

Caroline glowed with pride, clearly pleased with her literary effort, and Guthrie found himself wanting to read it. At the same time, he wasn't sure he could stand to dwell on the idea of three little girls on a train with nobody to look out for them.

"I was paid one hundred dollars for it," she said.

Guthrie grinned. "That's a handsome sum of money," he replied, letting go of her hand, finally, in order to stir the stew again.

"What about you, Guthrie?" she asked, catching him off-guard. "Do you have a family?"

He felt his grin fade. "You might say that," he conceded, "if you were being real generous. My daddy was a drunken sharecropper, working on a place just outside of Richmond, Virginia, and my mama ran away when I was four. I was raised by my sister, Iris."

"You seem well-educated," Caroline commented. "I didn't get to school until after the Maitland sisters adopted me, although my grandmother taught me the alphabet and showed me how to write my name."

Guthrie was touched by this new confidence, and he didn't want Caroline to see that he felt sorry about her childhood, so he went into the tent and returned with two enamel bowls and two spoons before answering. "I was taught up at the big house with the planter's sons."

Caroline watched as he dished stew into the bowls with a ladle. "What about your sister?"

"She was gone by that time."

"Gone?" Caroline swallowed. Guthrie could see the fear plain in her eyes; she was afraid of finally tracking her sisters down, only to find that their trails ended at a pair of tombstones.

"Not dead," Guthrie corrected, handing her one of the bowls, along with a spoon. "Iris ran off with a medicine peddler. I'm only guessing, but I figure she probably had to get away from the old man."

Caroline nodded sympathetically. "Did she ever write?"

"Once," Guthrie answered, concentrating on his stew. "From down around Atlanta somewhere. The peddler was conscripted and she was working for a dressmaker."

The sun was gradually sinking behind the mountains, and Caroline's gaze started wandering toward town. Clearly, she wanted to get back to Bolton before darkness fell. Already she had behaved daringly, for a lady, visiting his camp alone. To stay past sunset would probably create the kind of scandal people talked about for years.

"The stew is good," she said, lifting a piece of meat on her spoon. "Is this beef?"

"Bear," Guthrie replied.

Caroline lowered the spoon again. "I saw a trained bear once. He came through town with a shoddy little carnival, and he had mangy hide and sad eyes. They kept him in a cage, and he made sorrowful sounds 'til I thought my heart would break."

Guthrie decided that if it weren't for sorry luck, he wouldn't have any at all. It seemed every subject that came up was bound to stir some unhappy memory for Caroline.

He watched, fascinated, as she shook off the melancholy recollections, straightened her shoulders, and set the bowl aside. Tob immediately appeared to lap up the leftovers.

"I can't tolerate the suspense for another moment," she said. "I must know whether or not you've changed your mind. About helping Mr. Flynn, I mean."

Guthrie put his bowl down, sighed, and ran his fingers through his hair. "I don't think so," he said reluctantly. "I want to work this mine and build myself a house, and, frankly, I don't need the kind of trouble your plan would stir up."

He could see that his words not only disappointed Caroline bitterly but wounded her as well. He hadn't intended that.

She covered her face with both hands, in an obvious effort to keep from losing her composure, but her shoulders shook and she couldn't seem to stop that snuffling sound she was making.

Guthrie felt as though a Yankee bayonet had just been driven through his middle. "Caroline, please don't cry. You're going to find another man one of these days—"

Caroline emitted a stricken wail. "I don't want another man!" she sobbed. "I want Seaton Flynn!"

Guthrie muttered a swear word and hoisted himself to his

feet to pace on the other side of the campfire, while the dog sat watching with his homely head cocked to one side.

"In all likelihood, the man is a robber and a murderer!" Guthrie spat. "Hell, Caroline—even you could do better than that!"

Caroline shot to her feet, causing the dog to hunker down in fear. " '*Even you*?" she shouted, her hands resting on her hips. "Just what do you mean by that, Guthrie Hayes?"

He stopped and flung his arms out wide of his body, then let his hands slap against his thighs. "You're pretty enough," he conceded miserably. "It's just that you're kind of skinny."

Livid, Caroline folded her arms across her compact but well-shaped bosom. "If I eat cakes and pies until I'm fat as an old cow put out to pasture, *then* will you help me?"

In spite of himself, Guthrie laughed, but that didn't mean he wasn't discouraged and annoyed. He was, and mightily so. "Caroline, we're not discussing your figure here. We're talking about freeing a convicted killer from jail. Do you have any idea how serious that is?"

"If the charges against Seaton were true," Caroline persisted, "it would be serious. Since he's been wrongfully arrested, saving him from the hangman is plainly the right thing to do. You'd be a sort of Robin Hood."

"Please," Guthrie breathed the word, rubbing his eyes with a thumb and forefinger without displacing the patch. His head was throbbing.

"Well, if you can live with an innocent man's death on your conscience, so be it," Caroline said. She started toward the buggy again and, as before, Guthrie stopped her.

"What are you planning to do?" he demanded, narrowing his eye.

Caroline wrenched her arm free. "If you won't help me, I'll simply have to handle the job myself."

Guthrie groaned. "You'd do it, too, wouldn't you?" he burst out angrily, a moment later. "You'd risk your fool neck to get that spitwad out of jail!"

"He's not a spitwad," Caroline maintained indignantly,

slapping dust from the sleeves of her dress. "And I'll thank you not to use crude language in my presence."

"Oh, you will, will you?" Guthrie drawled, his eye glinting. "Aren't you forgetting, Teacher, that you need my help?"

"I've never forgotten it for a moment," Caroline said, in a defeated tone. "Now, if you'll just let me be on my way. I have arrangements to make."

He gripped her shoulders and gave her a little shake. "Look," he said, "I don't want you going anywhere near Laramie, do you hear me? And I especially don't want you sashaying into the jailhouse!"

"What you want," Caroline replied primly, "has nothing to do with me. Good evening, Mr. Hayes, and thank you very much for the stew."

She got all the way to the buggy and up into the seat, and Guthrie knew if he didn't take a strong hand in the situation, she was going to do some damn fool thing to help Flynn and end up getting herself either shot or arrested. Or both.

"All right," he sighed, looking up at her. "I'll talk to the witnesses, and to Flynn and the marshal who brought him in. If I still think he's guilty when I've done those things, I won't lift a finger to set him free. Do we understand each other, Caroline?"

A jubilant smile burst over her face, glorious as an Easter sunrise, and even though it was the prettiest sight Guthrie had ever seen, he found himself injured by it. "We'll expect you to supper tomorrow night at six o'clock," she announced, taking up the reins. "You and I will discuss the details of Seaton's rescue afterward. They've got the wrong man, Guthrie. You'll see!"

He stepped back. "You'd better get out of here. People are probably talking as it is."

The set of Caroline's jaw said she didn't care about petty gossip. Clearly, all she wanted was a chance to build a happy life with the man she thought she loved, and Guthrie had all but volunteered to make sure her wish was granted.

He sighed and shoved a hand through his hair. Funny how a man could go right on growing older without necessarily getting any smarter.

The next morning, Guthrie went to work in the mine as usual. He alternately dug and swung a pickax until sweat soaked his hair and ran down his forehead. His shirt stuck to him, both in back and in front, and he figured he probably smelled worse than the Hellfire and Spit Saloon on a Saturday night in August.

If he was going to keep Adabelle happy, once she came to live with him in Bolton, he would have to pay more attention to life's delicacies.

He worked until the sun was getting ready to set, then stumbled out of the mine shaft. He found a bar of soap in one of his saddlebags, then wrenched a clean shirt and a pair of trousers from the clothesline, where he'd hung them the day before

By rights, he reflected, as he made his way between the cottonwoods to the stream, he shouldn't be taking supper with Caroline. It would only get her hopes up that he was going to spring that no-good beau of hers from the hoosegow and, besides, her invitation had been a little on the offhand side.

It was just possible that she wasn't expecting him at all.

Reaching the creek, Guthrie eyed it, shivered once, and sat down on the grassy bank to pull off his boots. The food probably wouldn't be very good, either, he thought, judging by Caroline's trim figure.

He lowered his suspenders and took off his filthy, sweat-soaked shirt. Tob joined him, yipping as he ran back and forth between his master and the icy stream.

"I'm going to regret this," Guthrie told the dog, unbuttoning his pants and shoving them down.

The dog yowled pitifully as Guthrie scrambled down to the water, his soap clutched in one hand.

Stepping into the creek, Guthrie shouted a curse word. The stuff was nothing more than melted snow. If he'd waited until Saturday, he could have had a warm bath upstairs at the Hellfire and Spit.

Cussing the whole time, Guthrie scoured himself from head to toe, and his teeth were still chattering when he got out and began dabbing at his goose-pimpled flesh with his clean shirt. One of these days, he was going to have to buy himself a towel.

Dressed again, he picked up his dirty clothes and went back to camp. There he propped a small mirror in the rocks next to the opening of his mine shaft and inspected himself.

His brown hair stood out all over his head, and his beard was getting winter-thick. Grumbling, he fetched his razor and filled a washbasin with warm water from the kettle sitting in the fire. He used the yellow soap to make lather and began to shave.

Maybe he should tell Caroline that he'd misled her in making her think he'd lost his eye. After all, he'd already spilled more about his old life to her than he'd ever told Adabelle.

Then again, she might not understand that he liked wearing the eye patch because it gave him a menacing look and kept most people at their distance, where it was hard to ask too many questions.

After splashing away the last of the soap lather, Guthrie brushed his hair and put the eye patch back in place.

At five forty-five, by the watch his daddy had given him after the war ended, Guthrie fed Tob what remained of the stew and saddled the nimble bay horse that usually pulled his buckboard. He made sure he didn't arrive at the tall white house, with its picket fence and budding rosebushes, until the stroke of six.

Caroline answered his knock, and her eyes widened in surprise when she saw him. He didn't know whether it was his grooming that took her aback, or the fact that he'd come at all.

"Come in," she said. She was wearing a trim black skirt and a pink ruffled shirtwaist that definitely became her.

Guthrie stepped over the threshold and was immediately assailed by the scent of fried chicken. His mouth watered.

Caroline closed the door, then touched the eye patch with an exploratory finger. "If you're going to wear that awful

47

thing," she whispered, "at least put it over the same eye every day."

Before he could respond to that, she whirled away in a rustle of crisp skirts and led the way into a nearby parlor.

The old yearning possessed Guthrie as he looked around at the fireplace, with its carved mantel, the spinet, draped in lace and supporting a forest of framed photographs, the horsehair chairs and settee. If he never had another thing, besides a house like this and a woman to share it with, he'd be satisfied.

Two elderly ladies entered from another room, looking at him with pleased, maidenly eyes. After Seaton Flynn, Guthrie reasoned, anybody their charge brought home would probably be an improvement.

"Miss Phoebe and Miss Ethel Maitland," Caroline said formally, "may I present Mr. Guthrie Hayes of Virginia."

Guthrie permitted himself a half smile at that. She made him sound like a gentleman, instead of a sharecropper's son with a reputation for raiding Yankee prison camps. Of course, she probably hadn't told them about that last part. "How do you do?" he said, as the words echoed back at him in two other voices.

"Caroline cooked tonight's dinner herself," one of the Miss Maitlands twittered, beaming proudly at her ward.

Guthrie supposed that news was supposed to encourage him, and he smiled, wondering if it was possible for chicken to smell that good and still taste bad.

"She can sew, too," said the other spinster.

Caroline flushed at that and averted her eyes for a moment. "Would you like to sit down?" she asked, taking Guthrie's arm and gently steering him toward a chair.

It felt good, that soft, cushiony chair, after a wooden crate next to a stump. The old women were hovering in a cloud of lavender, smiling at him. Clearly, they saw him as a potential husband for their darling, and he shifted uncomfortably.

Caroline probably hadn't told them about Adabelle, and the house Guthrie meant to build now that his mine was about to produce ore.

"Mr. Hayes is a miner," Caroline said, standing close by

his chair. If she'd rested a hand on his shoulder, they could have posed for a photograph.

"Our father was a mining man," said one sister.

"Do you mean to settle here in Bolton, Mr. Hayes?" inquired the other.

Guthrie smiled broadly. Things would be easier for Adabelle if a few of the town ladies were expecting her when she came. "Well, as a matter of fact, I—"

Before he could tell them about the woman he intended to marry, and the house he planned to put up for her, something struck the bottom of his chair. After a moment of confusion, he realized it had been Caroline's foot.

Obviously, his hostess didn't want him to mention his plans to bring a bride to Bolton. "Mr. Hayes is single," she told the old women resolutely. "Shall we eat?"

Caroline watched Guthrie out of the corner of her eye as he accepted a china bowl brimming with creamy mashed potatoes. He seemed as surprised by the abundance and quality of the food as she was by his striking good looks.

Under that layer of mine dust and all those whiskers was a very handsome man, despite the eye patch. Not that his appearance made any difference in her plans, of course. And just because his kiss had made her feel as though the world had picked up speed and flung her right off into the stars . . .

"Teachers make very good mothers, of course," Miss Ethel remarked, as she buttered a biscuit with a delicate motion of one wrist.

One side of Guthrie's mouth quirked in that way it had. "Yes, ma'am," he said politely, ladling gravy onto his potatoes. "I imagine they do."

Caroline lowered her eyes for a moment, embarrassed by the way her guardians were shoving her at Guthrie like a slice of choice roast beef. She knew she would have to go along with the charade if she was to explain keeping company with Mr. Hayes. It would take time to plan Seaton's rescue properly.

"Have you ever been married, Mr. Hayes?" Miss Phoebe wanted to know.

"Yes, ma'am," Guthrie said again.

Caroline choked on the delicate bite of chicken she'd just swallowed, and Miss Ethel immediately reached out to slap her on the back.

Their dinner guest smiled as Caroline recovered her composure, gazing at him over the linen napkin she'd pressed to her mouth.

"Did I neglect to mention that, Miss Caroline?" he asked indulgently.

Caroline glared at him and lowered the napkin slowly to her lap. "Yes, Mr. Hayes, I believe you did," she replied, as mildly as she could manage. Perhaps this was another lie, like the eye patch.

"Is your wife alive?" Miss Phoebe asked, looking concerned. She made no pretense of eating.

Looking into Guthrie's face, Caroline saw a deep sadness pass over him, like the shadow of a cloud. "No," he replied. "She died a few years after the war ended."

Caroline was stricken by his words; for a moment, his grief was her own. She mourned the unknown girl just as she would have Lily or Emma, or either of her guardians. "I'm sorry," she said.

"You must have been very young when you enlisted," Miss Phoebe observed practically.

Caroline could see that Guthrie was grateful for the change of subject.

"I was sixteen, ma'am," he replied, helping himself to another piece of chicken.

Miss Ethel made a *tsk-tsk* sound. "Too young to go a-soldiering, I'm sure," she said.

"There were a great many such tragedies on both sides," replied Miss Phoebe.

After supper, Caroline cleared away the dishes and brought out a fresh-baked apple pie. She set it down directly in front of Guthrie and sliced the first piece for him.

Miss Phoebe cleared her throat discreetly. "Perhaps you could serve dessert to Mr. Hayes on the front porch, dear," she said, consulting the little watch pinned to the bodice of her white shirtwaist. "Sister and I are due at choir practice, and it wouldn't be proper for you and Mr. Hayes to be alone in the house, of course."

Guthrie winked at Caroline, unbeknownst to the Maitland sisters, and pushed his chair back. "I'm sure Miss Caroline wouldn't want to do anything that would stir up talk," he said pointedly. He was making private allusions, of course, to her scandalous visits to the saloon and to his mining camp.

Caroline would have liked to kick him; instead, she smiled, baring her teeth. "One must guard one's reputation," she said.

While Miss Phoebe and Miss Ethel were crossing the street to the First Presbyterian Church, Caroline carried hot coffee and slices of pie out to the front porch on a tray Guthrie was sitting in the bench swing, his feet outstretched, a look of utter contentment on his face.

Caroline set the tray down on the little wicker table in front of the swing. For some reason, she was feeling all shivery with excitement, and her voice shook a little when she spoke. "Miss Phoebe and Miss Ethel seem to like you."

Guthrie watched her with a glint in his eye and a wry twist to his mouth as she sat down beside him in the swing, taking care to leave a generous wedge of space between them. The sun was going down, and the first stars were popping out in the sky, surrounding a thin wafer of a moon.

"They're pretty anxious to marry you off," he said.

Caroline fairly shoved Guthrie's pie into his hands. "They think my heart is broken," she told him. "They want me to go on with my life. And to them, that means finding a husband."

Guthrie accepted the pie and took a bite. His face registered unreserved approval. "Is it?" he asked, chewing.

Caroline had lost her train of thought, being so close to him and everything. "Is what?"

"Is your heart broken?"

The question took her by surprise. "Of course it is," she said, affronted.

Guthrie enjoyed another bite of pie, and there was something almost unbearably sensual in the way he took his

51

time, savoring the morsel. "You don't feel much passion for this beau of yours, do you?"

A delicate film of perspiration moistened the place between Caroline's breasts, and it was an effort to keep from fanning herself. She was careful to look away from Guthrie. "You're wrong, Mr. Hayes."

"Umm-hmm," Guthrie agreed, with skeptical good humor. He set the pie plate on the little table and spoke in a low drawl that was something of a caress in and of itself. His hand rested lightly on Caroline's nape, setting all the rest of her flesh a-tingle. "The way you responded when I kissed you last night tells me different, Teacher."

Caroline stiffened and turned her head to glare at him. "You are insufferably arrogant, Mr. Hayes!" she hissed. Organ music swelled into the twilight from the church across the street, and a dozen discordant voices tumbled out after it.

His thumb made a slow circle on the delicate skin at the back of her neck. "If a man can't make a woman breathe hard and whimper and then explode like ten tons of dynamite dropped straight into hellfire," he said, without the slightest compunction, "she shouldn't marry him, because she's not going to be happy."

Heat climbed Caroline's face, but she couldn't pull away. In fact, her breasts felt heavy, their tips jutting against the muslin of her camisole, and her womanly place ached.

Guthrie was still caressing her nape. He must have felt the tremor that went through her; Caroline couldn't bear to look at his face and see. She let her eyes drift closed.

"You didn't tell me you'd been married," she said evenly, after a scandalously long time. She needed to put some distance between herself and Guthrie Hayes before she melted.

The porch swing creaked slightly as Guthrie lowered his hand from the back of her neck, and the music from the church was a reassuring hum. "I had no reason to," he answered evenly.

"What was her name?" Out of the corner of her eye, Caroline saw Guthrie shove his fingers through his hair.

"That isn't important."

"I imagine it was to her. And to you."

Guthrie gave a sad sigh. "Anne. Her name was Anne."

Caroline folded her hands in her lap and propelled the swing into motion by bracing one heel against the floor of the porch and pushing. "Did you love her?"

"Isn't that kind of a personal question?" He wasn't prickly, exactly, but he sure sounded reluctant.

Caroline had not spent the last several years dealing with stubborn children without learning a thing or two about persistence. "Probably," she agreed. "But I still want to know."

Guthrie's jaw tightened slightly, and he turned his head, taking an exaggerated interest in the forsythia bush growing in a far corner of the yard. "I loved her."

Instinct warned Caroline to lighten the moment. "Was she fat?"

He gave a burst of laughter that was only partly amusement; in large measure, Caroline knew, it was relief. "No. Why the devil would you ask me that?"

Caroline's shoulders lifted in a coquettish little shrug. "You've made it very clear that you prefer fleshy women."

Guthrie grinned. "I was nineteen, going on twenty, when I married Anne. At the time, I didn't know I *had* preferences—I liked all women."

Emboldened by the fact that there was little illumination, except for the transparent moon and a block of light strained by the parlor curtains, Caroline reached out and gently pushed the black eye patch up onto Guthrie's forehead.

She wasn't surprised to see a perfectly healthy green eye gazing back at her. Her cheeks heated when Guthrie winked, and she retreated slightly.

He chuckled at her reaction. "I'm sorry," he said, in a husky voice. "I was planning to tell you."

"Why on earth would you want to wear that thing when you didn't have to?"

Guthrie stuffed the patch into the pocket of his clean but crumpled shirt. "I've been on the move for a long time," he said, leaving the swing to stand with his back to her and grip the porch railing. "Because of the things that happened during the war, I had to be careful about running into people who might remember me."

Caroline's heart stopped for a moment, then started up again. "Are you wanted for some crime?" she asked, her voice soft with dread.

He turned to look down at her, his arms folded across his rock-hard chest. "Not exactly. But I didn't make a lot of friends among the Yankees."

"You did something," Caroline insisted. She knew that as well as she knew her schoolroom, though she couldn't have said how.

Guthrie sighed. "I killed a man."

"There was a war—"

"This was afterward, Caroline."

She looked away, her fingers woven together in her lap. "Surely you had cause."

"That depends on your viewpoint," Guthrie answered. "And, frankly, I've never been particularly inclined to discuss the incident with a Union judge. Until I met Adabelle and then struck copper up there in the hills, I intended to keep moving for the rest of my days."

Caroline was stung by the reminder that the woman waiting in Cheyenne had been the one to turn Guthrie's life in a new direction, though she knew she shouldn't have cared. "I need to know the circumstances of the killing," she said, standing to face him. "Tell me what happened. Please."

He was still leaning against the railing, and his arms remained folded. Although that would have been the perfect opportunity to take Caroline into his arms and kiss her, as he had in his camp, he didn't move. "Why?"

"Because I can't keep company with a murderer," she answered, with quiet reason.

In the wispy light from the windows, Caroline saw a muscle tighten in his jawline. "Why not? You don't seem to have any misgivings about marrying one."

Caroline held her temper. However much she might

dislike Mr. Hayes on a personal level, she needed his help, and she couldn't afford to offend him too deeply. "That's because I firmly believe Seaton is innocent," she said, with dignity. "But you admitted, straight out—"

Guthrie put up both hands in a bid for silence. "The man I killed was someone I knew during the war," he said. His voice was low, even, and adamant. "And he needed killing."

"I could go to the sheriff," Caroline pointed out, though she knew even then that she'd never follow through. It was only after the words were out that she realized Guthrie had inadvertently handed her a weapon to use against him.

"You don't have any proof," Guthrie said. His eyes were watchful, though she couldn't read their expression.

She shrugged, operating on pure bravado. "Somebody, somewhere, probably does."

Guthrie stepped forward suddenly and gripped her upper arms in his strong, calloused hands. Then, as quickly as he'd taken her, he let her go again. "What I said before stands, Caroline," he said, after a long, uncomfortable silence. "If I decide Flynn's guilty, he'll hang if I have to put the noose around his neck myself. Thanks for supper."

With that, he turned and strode down the steps onto the walk. His horse was tethered to a hitching post just beyond the picket fence.

Caroline hurried after him. "I want to go with you," she blurted out. "When you go to Laramie, I mean."

Guthrie's shoulders tensed, and he turned slowly to face Caroline, the process of mounting his horse forgotten. "No," he said.

"Yes," Caroline replied, setting her jaw.

Chapter

❧ 4 ❧

*T*he next morning, Guthrie hitched up the buckboard and drove to town to buy supplies, Tob riding like visiting royalty in the back. Perhaps as a concession to Caroline, or maybe just because he was tired of running from the long tentacles of the war that constantly reached out to entwine him, Guthrie tossed the eye patch into some scrub brush as he passed.

There was a letter waiting for him at the general store, scented with lavender water, and he smiled as he tucked it into his shirt pocket. No matter what Caroline said, he assured himself, Adabelle definitely wasn't fat. She was plump, in the same pleasant way as a Christmas turkey.

While the storekeeper, a skinny little man with wisps of red hair surrounding his bald, freckled pate, took the items on Guthrie's list from the shelves and put them into boxes, he browsed. A selection of books lined a shelf, over in one corner, and he examined the titles with narrowed eyes, running one finger over their sturdy spines.

More than anything else, shelves full of books meant wealth to Guthrie. They made him miss Willow Grove, the McTavish plantation in Virginia, and mourn certain gracious aspects of the South that were probably gone forever.

56

His throat was constricted as he took a volume of Swinburne into his hands, but a grin lifted a corner of his mouth as he wondered how many of the ranchers, miners, and sheepherders around Bolton enjoyed reading poetry. The answer was in the layer of dust that wafted up from the book when he opened it.

He blew away the worst of it and flipped to the first page. When he built his house at the edge of town, there'd be a whole room reserved for reading and the like, just as there had been at Willow Grove.

"I'd be willing to give you a bargain on that there book," the storekeeper said earnestly, startling him out of his reflections.

Guthrie figured he must be slipping, since he hadn't heard the man approach. It was probably his just due for getting involved with a woman like Caroline in the first place. "How much?"

"Five cents," was the firm answer.

"Sold," Guthrie replied, handing the little man the book and moving to the nearest window. There he caught his thumbs under his suspenders and gazed out.

Tob was waiting patiently in the back of the wagon, though he was eyeing the Hellfire and Spit Saloon, just down the street. He probably had a bowl of good Irish whiskey on his mind, Guthrie thought with a grin.

He was just about to turn away when he saw Caroline walking purposefully down the sidewalk on the other side of the road. He didn't know whether to call out to her or duck out of sight, and before he could make the decision, she spotted Tob sitting in the wagon.

A moment later, she was cautiously wending her way across the road, looking primly pretty in a plaid dress with white lacy trim of some kind.

Guthrie stepped out onto the sidewalk, telling himself there was no way to avoid her. In truth, he didn't want to. "Why aren't you teaching school?" he asked, briefly touching the brim of his hat and speaking as cordially as if they hadn't had words the night before, in front of Caroline's house.

57

Her chin came up a notch, and he had a momentary sensation of tumbling head over heels into the saucy brown depths of her eyes. He set his feet a little farther apart on the splintery boards of the sidewalk to brace himself.

"It's Saturday, Mr. Hayes," she explained. Although her manner wasn't exactly cold, her lips didn't curve into a smile. "I'm happy to see you've gotten rid of that silly eye patch."

Guthrie had a sudden vision of himself laying Caroline gently on the lush green grass beside a stream and teaching her lithe little body every note in the scale of pleasure. There was a grinding sensation deep inside him, and he felt himself harden.

Then he remembered Adabelle and slapped his hand over the letter in an effort to make some kind of contact with her.

Caroline's gaze dropped to the scented envelope only partially hidden by his fingers and then rose to his face again. He saw a spark of fury in her eyes and, to his own confusion, he reveled in the sudden insight that she was jealous.

"From Adabelle?" she inquired sweetly.

Guthrie smiled a fond smile and then nodded.

Caroline rolled her eyes, but her words and tone of voice were concessionary. "I hope you're still planning to help me," she said.

Actually, Guthrie had been hoping their argument the night before had made her forget her crazy ideas about getting her beau out of jail, but now, in the bright light of day, he realized he should have known better.

Although he knew it was cowardly, he fell back on Adabelle as an excuse. "I'm not sure my future wife would approve."

Caroline's eyes narrowed, and she took a step closer to him. She smelled of sunshine and vanilla, and Guthrie's groin tightened further. "I *know* your future wife wouldn't approve of that kiss you gave me the other day," she intoned.

Guthrie jerked his hat off, then put it back on again.

Tarnation, if this woman wasn't irritating. "If you don't quit threatening me, Miss Chalmers," he breathed, "you and I are going to have a little set-to. And I promise you, I'll win!"

"Now who's making threats?" Caroline retorted, raising one dark eyebrow.

Not since his early teens, when one of Jacob's girl cousins had taken his favorite slingshot and thrown it down the well, had Guthrie yearned so fiercely to turn a female over his knee and blister her bustle. He smiled, baring his teeth. "May I remind you, once again, that you're the one who wants a favor here?"

Her bravado visibly deserted her—she paled and retreated a step—but her pride was still very much in evidence. "Like I told you last night," she said, in a voice low enough so passersby wouldn't hear, "if I can't get you to help me, I'll go alone."

Guthrie knew he ought to tell her to go ahead and do that, but he couldn't stand the thought of her taking such a crazy chance. "Why don't you just find yourself a nice man to bedevil," he whispered, painfully conscious that folks were looking at them, "and forget that polecat down in Laramie?"

Her eyes flashed with fury as potent as a summer thunderstorm, but she didn't rise to the bait. "The school term ended yesterday," she told him, "so that the boys could help their fathers with spring roundup and branding. There's no reason I can't go to Laramie."

With that, she turned and walked on down the street toward the post office, and Guthrie was afraid to touch her, even to grasp her arm. He spat an expletive, causing Tob to give a startled yelp from the back of the buckboard, then whirled on the heel of one boot and stormed back into the store.

After Caroline had seen Guthrie leave the mercantile and stride down the street to the Hellfire and Spit Saloon with that ugly dog at his heels, she left the post office and crossed the street to the dress and millinery shop.

Hypatia Furvis greeted her with a sly smile. "Well, *Caroline,"* she trilled. "What brings you in? Are you needing a dress for the spring dance?"

No one had asked Caroline to the dance, and Hypatia darn well knew it. She liked nettling her old schoolmate because she'd never forgiven her for winning the eighth-grade spelling bee and getting her name in the newspapers clear down in Laramie and Cheyenne. Besides that, Hypatia had had her own hopes when Seaton Flynn came to town and set up his law practice.

"Yes," Caroline said, with sudden resolution, even though she usually stitched her clothes instead of buying them ready-made or having someone else sew them up for her. "I want a dress."

Hypatia, who was small and plain, with big teeth and frizzy hair just the color of a field mouse's hide, looked quite taken aback. "I suppose that seedy miner's asked you," she said with a sigh, as she sorted through a rack in search of something in the proper size. "People are talking. They're saying you're entirely too friendly with that man."

Caroline widened her eyes at Hypatia. "Are they? I had no idea 'people' were so concerned with my private business."

Hypatia had the good grace to blush. "He spends a great deal of his time in the saloon," she said in a rush of daring. "And he wears that dreadful patch over his eye, like a pirate in a dime novel. I can't think what you'd want with him."

A frothy concoction of pink lace presented itself, and Caroline took the gown from the rack to look at it. Normally, she wouldn't have looked twice at something so fussy, but she felt a little leap in a corner of her heart when she held the dress in front of her and peered into the stand-up mirror nearby.

The color brought out a rose tint in her cheeks and made her dark eyes dance. If she wasn't mistaken, the ruffles on the low-cut bodice just might make her appear buxom. "How much is this?" she asked thoughtfully, forgetting Hypatia's comments.

"More than a schoolteacher could possibly afford," Hypatia said smugly.

After that, nothing could have kept Caroline from buying the dress, even though it required most of her last month's wages. "I'll take it," she said.

Hypatia's mouth dropped open, then she narrowed her eyes and snatched the dress out of Caroline's hands. "Very well, then," she fussed, "but don't go trying to bring it back tomorrow, after you've worn it."

Caroline might have smiled as she followed Hypatia to the counter if it hadn't been for the fact that she didn't actually have an escort for that night's dance. She couldn't very well show up alone.

In a state of distraction, she paid for her dress out of her hard-earned salary and left the shop carrying it under one arm in a large white box.

Guthrie was coming out of the saloon when she stepped onto the sidewalk. The dog, Tob, trotted along at his side, licking his muzzle.

Caroline drew a deep breath for courage, looked both ways, and walked across the street.

"I have a favor to ask," she said forthrightly, coming to a stop right in front of Mr. Hayes. "But I'd be willing to pay you if necessary."

Guthrie sighed and raised his hands to his hips. His manner conveyed distinct suspicion. "What now?" he asked.

"There's a dance tonight at the schoolhouse," Caroline said bravely, her voice trembling slightly, "and I'd like you to be my escort."

His green eyes twinkled, and she thought she saw his mouth twitch before he spoke. "You'd pay me to take you to a dance?" he asked. "You like me more than you're willing to let on, Miss Chalmers."

"I don't like you at all," Caroline maintained staunchly. "It's just that—well—I have my reasons for wanting to go."

"I imagine you do," he replied dryly. "You probably haven't done anything spontaneous since the day you were born."

Caroline struggled to hold her temper in check, and the task was made all the more difficult by the fact that Guthrie was clearly enjoying her dilemma to the utmost. "Well, will you go or not?"

Guthrie sighed and removed his hat respectfully. "I'd be honored, Miss Caroline," he said, and his lips were quivering again, almost imperceptibly, while his eyes danced. "And I've never allowed a lady to pay me for my attentions in my life. I'm not about to start with you."

Caroline's face burned at the implications of that last remark. "Thank you," she said uncertainly.

He put his hat back on, still grinning at her discomfiture, and there was something very cocky about his manner. "I'll be by the house to pick you up around seven," he said. "Be ready."

Caroline couldn't meet his eyes because she knew she'd see laughter there and she was capable of only so much self-control. She nodded briskly, turned, and walked purposefully away. All the way home, her cheeks pounded with color.

Miss Ethel was digging happily in a flower bed, but she rose awkwardly to her feet when she saw Caroline come through the gate. Her gaze touched the dress box, then swept to her charge's face. "You're going to the spring dance after all. Sister and I had about given up hope, since you didn't mention it—"

"I was trying to forget the dance," Caroline confessed, with a rueful sigh. "But Hypatia Furvis made that impossible."

Miss Ethel beamed. "Wonderful," she said, missing the reference to Caroline's arch enemy entirely. "Who is escorting you? I hope it's that marvelous young man who came to supper last night."

Caroline couldn't help smiling, since Miss Ethel's pleasure was so obvious. "Yes," she said, embracing the fragile woman with her free arm and kissing her forehead. "I'm going with Guthrie."

The spinster gave a twittering laugh. "He's got that smooth Virginia way of speaking." Her earnest little face turned solemn. "Say what you will about their politics, those southerners do seem to know how to turn out a gentleman."

In order to keep from laughing aloud at the concept of Guthrie Hayes as a gentleman, Caroline bit her lower lip and nodded. Then she excused herself to hurry inside.

Upstairs, in her bedroom, she took the luscious dress from its box and shook it out. It made a delectable whispering sound as it settled against her body.

Caroline admired the creation for a few minutes, then hung it carefully in her wardrobe and sat down at her vanity table. The face that looked back at her from the mirror was flushed with eagerness, eyes shining.

Reaching back with both hands, Caroline undid the heavy chignon at her nape and shook her head, letting her dark hair tumble around her breasts and shoulders. She ducked her chin and practiced the sultry stare she'd seen other women use with men.

As far as Caroline was concerned, it made her look dyspeptic. She lifted her head back to its usual proud angle and began brushing her mahogany-colored hair. The framed drawing of Lily and Emma distracted her, and she went to the bureau and picked it up. In her mind, she heard three childlike voices singing.

> *Three flowers bloomed in the meadow,*
> *Heads bent in sweet repose,*
> *The daisy, the lily, and the rose . . .*

Close to tears again, she gently touched each little face in turn, then set the picture down again. Lily would be nineteen now, and Emma twenty. She tried to imagine how they would look, all grown up, and silently prayed that they'd found strong, decent men to love them.

Maybe they hadn't survived to adulthood, though, Caroline thought glumly. After all, a lot of children didn't, especially when they'd never had proper care or enough to eat.

The sun was shining and that night she was going to

dance, even if it was Mr. Hayes's arms she'd be in, instead of Seaton's. Caroline refused to believe that either Lily or Emma had perished.

After winding her hair into a single braid, she took pen and paper to the porch swing and began a letter to Seaton. She wanted to reassure him, without giving away her plans to anyone who might censor his mail, but beyond Dearest Mr. Flynn, she couldn't think of a single thing to say.

Although his funds were getting low, Guthrie took himself to the saloon for a regular bath, and then he went to the barber for a shave and a haircut and a splash of bay rum that made his cheeks sting. He even bought a ready-made suit and a shirt over at the mercantile, though he didn't imagine he'd wear the get-up again until he and Adabelle stood before a preacher.

Adabelle.

It was on the way home, with Tob hunkered on the seat beside him because the wagon bed was loaded with supplies, that he remembered the letter.

Guilt swept over him as he took it from his pocket and opened one end of the envelope with his teeth. A thin blue sheet of writing paper slid out, and he snapped it open, annoyed now. It wasn't like he was betraying Adabelle by taking Caroline to the dance.

Frowning, he read the neatly written words on the page. She loved him. She missed him. She could hardly wait until they could get together and start a family.

Normally, such a direct mention of the natural ramifications of marriage would have drawn the fabric of Guthrie's trousers tight across his crotch. Now all it did was make his conscience smart.

Caroline Chalmers, for all her contentious nature and skinny framework, stirred something inside him. Something profound.

Guthrie bunched the letter back into its envelope and stuffed it into his shirt pocket again. He'd known that schoolmarm was trouble when she called him out of the Hellfire and Spit in the broad light of day.

Beside him, Tob whimpered sympathetically, as though following the train of his thoughts. He reached out and patted the dog idly on the head. He'd take Caroline to the dance, since he'd gone to all the trouble to bathe and buy a suit and get himself barbered, and he'd ride down to Laramie to talk with that Flynn character face-to-face. He'd practically given his word. But after that, he was going to head straight to Cheyenne, fetch Adabelle, and bring her back to Bolton.

A slow smile spread across his face. Once Adabelle was with him, wearing his wedding band on her finger, thoughts of that troublesome little schoolmarm would finally leave him alone.

Reaching his camp, Guthrie unloaded his supplies, storing most of them inside the opening to his mine shaft. He hung his new suit carefully on the clothesline and admired it. His grin faded when he imagined his wedding and the woman standing beside him was Caroline and not Adabelle.

He couldn't distract himself with work, not without spoiling the whole effect of the hot bath he'd taken in town, anyway, so he got out the volume of Swinburne and went down by the creek to read. Since he hadn't gotten any sleep the night before, after that verbal battle with Caroline, he ended up sprawled on his belly in the soft grass, snoring.

When he awakened, Tob was licking his face and most of the afternoon had passed. Swearing, Guthrie hoisted himself to his feet and made his way back to camp.

The fire was going out, so he built it back up again. Then he cut off a piece of the salt pork he'd bought in town that day and threw it into a skillet to fry. It was going to seem like sorry fare, he thought grumpily, after the chicken dinner Caroline had served him the night before.

Damn that woman, anyway. He was beginning to wish he'd never seen her face or heard her name.

He ate some of the salt pork without tasting it and gave a generous portion of the leftovers to Tob. Then he went down to the creek and brushed his teeth with baking soda.

He arrived at Caroline's right on time, having chastised himself every mile of the way for squiring one woman to a dance when he meant to marry another. When Adabelle came to Bolton, she was bound to hear rumors about him and the schoolteacher . . .

Then Caroline answered his knock, wearing a lacy pink dress that raised her breasts and thrust them toward him like a sweet offering. Her hair was a gleaming puff of ebony around her face, and her skin glowed like moonlight trapped in milk glass. Guthrie knew he was supposed to be in love with another woman, but he couldn't remember her name for the life of him.

Chapter

❧ 5 ❧

*I*t was disturbing, Caroline thought, the way Mr. Hayes seemed to get handsomer every time she saw him. On their first encounter, outside the saloon, she'd thought he was nothing more than a saddle bum. Now, standing on her porch, all dressed up in a suit and about to take her to the spring dance, he had an aristocratic air.

She was probably imagining that last part, she decided, smiling. "Come in, Mr. Hayes," she said, stepping back so he could pass.

Miss Phoebe and Miss Ethel were huddled close together in the parlor doorway, beaming with delight. Caroline guessed she'd probably been something of a disappointment to the sisters, turning away suitors—until Seaton, of course —to concentrate on teaching and writing her book about the orphan train.

"Don't you look handsome," Miss Ethel said to Guthrie, clasping her small, bejeweled hands together.

Guthrie smiled and bowed slightly. He'd guessed, of course, that the ladies admired courtly southern ways. "You will be at the dance, won't you, Miss Ethel?" he inquired, with just the right mixture of eagerness and mischief in his voice.

Miss Ethel blushed, and her eyes shone. "Oh my, no," she said, laying a fluttery hand to her breast.

Guthrie looked downcast. "I see," he said gravely.

Miss Phoebe took charge. "Do get started," she said to Caroline and Guthrie. "The dance is about to begin."

Caroline handed Guthrie her best shawl, one Miss Ethel had crocheted for her the Christmas before, out of gossamer silken yarn, and he draped it over her shoulders. She was feeling shy and somewhat off-balance, and the fact that she'd invited Guthrie to the dance was like a bruise on her spirit. But then, if he'd asked her, as custom dictated, she probably would have refused.

Mr. Hayes's horse was tethered to the hitching post beyond the gate. He'd known the schoolhouse was close by, having visited there once, and had probably seen no reason to bring his wagon.

They walked along the path at the side of the road, since the sidewalks didn't extend that far from the center of town, Caroline's arm linked comfortably with Guthrie's. The faint strains of fiddle music came from the direction of the schoolhouse, and the stars were like big splashes of silver paint against the dark sky.

For this one night, Caroline decided, she would forget her troubles and concentrate purely on the moment. She looked up at Guthrie's moon-shadowed face and smiled unsteadily. She'd probably been to a hundred dances in her life, and yet somehow this experience was very different.

Guthrie stopped, in the shadow of Doc Lendrum's big maple tree, and gently turned Caroline to face him. "I take it back," he said hoarsely. "What I said about your being skinny, I mean. Fact is, you look so womanly that I'm hard put to behave like a gentleman."

Sensing how difficult that confession had been for him, Caroline smiled softly, while her heart soared high above, playing tag with the bright stars. "Thank you," she said, and though she knew it wasn't right, with both of them virtually pledged to other people, she devoutly hoped he meant to kiss her.

As the fiddlers struck up a rousing reel inside the schoolhouse, Guthrie dipped his head and brushed Caroline's mouth with his. She felt a tremor begin inside her and then spread down into the very earth, like the roots of some intangible tree. Her hands fidgeted with Guthrie's lapels, then met and entwined at the back of his neck, and she stood on the balls of her feet to get closer.

With a low groan, Guthrie crushed her close to him and deepened the kiss. One of his hands rested just below her breast, and she felt the nipple tingle and then go tight, awaiting his touch.

But instead of caressing her, Guthrie swore and broke away. "I apologize for that," he said gruffly, turning his back to Caroline.

Because she didn't trust herself to speak—if he'd taken her somewhere private and made love to her, she wouldn't have been able to protest—Caroline lifted both hands to make sure her hair wasn't coming down from its pins, then hooked her arm through Guthrie's. They would just have to make the best of things.

Light, laughter, and music spilled into the schoolyard through the front doors, which were flung open wide, and Guthrie fairly propelled Caroline up the steps and inside.

The desks had been pushed up against the walls, and the schoolhouse brimmed with people. It seemed that with Caroline and Guthrie's entrance, all eyes turned to them. Caroline lifted her chin defiantly, even though her first urge was to turn and flee.

Guthrie sensed her quandary, it seemed, for he smiled down at her and immediately whisked her into the lively swirl of dancers. Tonight, Caroline thought, looking up at him in amazement, she could almost believe it was a contrary ex-Confederate she loved, and not Seaton Flynn. She wondered if Guthrie had learned to dance in the planter's big house, the way he'd learned his reading, writing, and arithmetic. Or had a woman taught him—the mysterious Annie for instance?

They danced until Caroline was breathless, and then they danced some more. Guthrie seemed unaware of the other women stuffed into the schoolhouse, hoping to catch his eye, and he left Caroline's side only to fetch a glass of punch for her when the amateur musicians went outside for a smoke and a few nips from their flasks.

"Is *that* the drifter who struck copper up in the hills?" Hypatia demanded, appearing the instant Caroline was alone. Her eyes were wide with disbelief, and she kept patting her field mouse hair with a hand that trembled slightly.

"His name is Guthrie Hayes," Caroline said, feeling flushed and, for the first time since before Seaton's arrest, happy. "And he's not a drifter." She told herself she was standing up for Guthrie because she wanted people to believe she cared for him, so they wouldn't guess who was behind the upcoming jailbreak.

Hypatia was fanning herself with her dance book. "We all know," she simpered, "what a sterling recommendation *means,* coming from you."

Caroline's blood heated. Hypatia was referring to her staunch support for Mr. Flynn, of course. Like the rest of the town, Hypatia believed Caroline's loyalty was misplaced. But before she could think of a suitably scathing response, Guthrie returned with a cup of punch.

His green eyes seemed to devour Caroline, while dancing with mischief at the same time, and his lips curved in that sideways grin that always made her feel a little dizzy.

"Thank you, Mr. Hayes," she said, as grateful for the interruption as she was for the punch.

Hypatia hovered, waiting for an introduction, and Caroline took a leisurely sip of the fruity drink before saying, "Miss Furvis, may I present my friend, Mr. Guthrie Hayes? Mr. Hayes, Miss Hypatia Furvis."

While Guthrie inclined his head to Hypatia, he hardly seemed aware of her presence. She finally skulked away.

"She wanted you to ask her to dance," Caroline said.

Guthrie took her arm and squired her toward the door. On the steps, men were tipping back flasks and laughing, but they stepped aside to make way, falling silent as the couple passed.

He led her to the playground, and Caroline settled into a

swing, still sipping from her punch. Guthrie took a cheroot from his pocket, lit it, and leaned against the framework that supported the swings, watching her.

She knew the moonlight glowed on the rounded tops of her breasts, but Caroline made no effort to hide herself as she normally would have. She decided she was under some kind of spell.

"Do they throw these shindigs often?" Guthrie asked. His voice sounded a little gruff, but Caroline attributed that to the nasty habit of smoking cheroots.

Inside, the fiddlers began to play again, and most of the people who were outside wandered in. "Once a month or so," Caroline answered with a shrug. She was remembering the kiss she and Guthrie had shared in the shadow of the maple tree, and the way it had felt to brush against him when they danced.

He drew on the cheroot and looked very deliberate as he exhaled the smoke. "I'll be leaving for Laramie tomorrow," he said. "I want you to tell me everything you can remember about the circumstances of the stagecoach robbery."

Just then, two little girls came running down the schoolhouse steps, giggling and squealing. Behind them was a boy, holding what looked like a frog. All three of the children were Caroline's students.

"Maggie," she said.

One of the girls stopped as she passed and looked at her with big eyes. The child wore an enormous satin bow at the back of her head, blue to match her party dress. "Yes, Miss Chalmers?"

Caroline handed her the punch cup. "Would you take this back inside for me, please?"

Maggie nodded, eager to please, snatched the cup and scurried off toward the schoolhouse.

With a sigh, Caroline hoisted herself out of the swing. For her, the joy of the night was over; reality had intruded, and there would be no ignoring it.

"Seaton was away on business when the robbery and killing took place," she said, starting toward the street, and Guthrie followed, one hand resting lightly, reassuringly, on the small of her back. He opened the gate with one hand and ushered her through.

Guthrie nodded thoughtfully. "Wasn't there anybody who could vouch for that?"

Caroline shook her head. "He went to Laramie, and the—the crime happened between here and there. The stage was stopped by half a dozen men wearing masks, and the leader was tall and dark-haired, like Seaton. A witness said he shot and killed the driver even though the man had already handed over the strongbox." She paused, shuddering, envisioning the scene and finding it impossible, as always, to picture Seaton there, doing such a cold-blooded, heartless thing.

"There must be a lot of tall men with dark hair between here and Laramie," Guthrie observed. "What made them identify Flynn?"

Caroline swallowed. "There was a man inside the coach —he said he saw the robber's eyes and that he'd never forget them, no matter how long he lived."

"That still doesn't explain why they arrested Flynn," Guthrie insisted quietly.

"The witness met Seaton in a saloon, a few days after the robbery and—and murder. He said he recognized him."

They stopped beneath Dr. Lendrum's maple again, but this time the mood and the reason were painfully different. Guthrie's hands cupped Caroline's elbows gently. "That's still the word of just one man," he said. "It isn't enough."

Seaton's innocence was a stone wall to Caroline, but she was beginning to see tiny chinks and cracks. Anger surged through as she realized tnat, even though Guthrie undoubtedly knew the story from the papers, he was cruel enough to make her tell it. "A man claiming to be part of the gang that robbed the stagecoach was arrested after a saloon brawl," she said stiffly. "He named Seaton as the leader."

Guthrie sighed and let go of her elbows to jam one hand through his hair. "Damn it, Caroline—doesn't that tell you anything?"

"The stage passenger was old and half blind," Caroline

cried, "and the other man was nothing more than a common criminal! One was mistaken, and the other was lying!"

"What if you're wrong?" Guthrie shot back.

"What if I'm right?" Caroline immediately retorted.

Guthrie swore and propelled her along the path toward her house.

"You'll hear from me in a few days," he said when they reached her porch. "I want you to sit tight until you do."

Caroline nodded, but she wasn't giving her word on anything. She was just trying to keep the tentative peace. She watched with her heart in her throat as Guthrie turned and strode down the steps and along the walk to the gate.

He untied his horse and swung into the saddle, watching her for a long moment before reining the animal away from the fence.

Caroline remained on the porch until he was out of sight, and then she hurried into the house.

Miss Ethel and Miss Phoebe had already retired to their rooms for the night, but there was a light burning in the parlor.

Her mind on the man riding into the night, Caroline turned down the wick until the lamp flickered out, then made her way quietly upstairs.

In her room, she hastily shed her shawl and the lovely pink dress and searched through her wardrobe until she found the divided riding skirt she'd made a few years before. She put it on, along with brown boots and a plain white shirt, then began flinging spare clothes and toilet articles into a carpetbag.

If Mr. Guthrie Hayes thought she was going to trust him with her whole future, he was sadly mistaken.

Caroline paused in the hallway, wondering if she should wake her guardians and tell them she was leaving. After standing there gnawing on her upper lip for several minutes, she decided against the idea. Such a scene would only upset everyone, and there was nothing that could have changed Caroline's mind.

Downstairs, in the kitchen, she wrote a hasty note and propped it in the center of the table, against the sugar bowl.

I promise I'll explain everything when I get home, she wrote. *Please don't worry about me.*

In a week or so, when the whole unfortunate misunderstanding was cleared up, she would return to Bolton with Seaton and apologize for her hasty departure. Her guardians were sure to understand.

At the livery stable, Caroline awakened Joe Brown, the night attendant, from a drunken sleep and asked for a horse. In return for a sizable chunk of the little money that remained to her, Joe turned over a swaybacked mare.

When she sneaked up on Guthrie's camp, barely an hour later, Caroline's suspicions were confirmed. The fire was out, and Tob wasn't barking to alert his master to another presence. That meant Guthrie had secured his belongings and ridden out almost immediately after returning from town.

Caroline intended to follow him, and she figured he was probably a good distance ahead by then. Still, he was on his way to Laramie, and that was all she needed to know.

She set out after him, hoping she was on his trail without being too close.

The night was long and, toward morning, it turned chilly. Caroline was shivering as she stopped in a lush meadow to let her elderly mare rest. A vista of sweeping plains lay ahead, bordered in the distance by more mountains.

A few doubts assailed Caroline as she ate a piece of the bread she'd tucked into her carpetbag and tried to think clearly. Laramie was probably a little farther away than she'd first thought, she admitted to herself.

By that night, she was ravenously hungry and cold clear through to the marrow of her bones. She saw a campfire ahead in the darkness and heard the exuberant bark of a dog.

Caroline knew she could be riding up on outlaws, or even Indians, but she was praying for another kind of reception, and she was too cold and hungry to hang back.

Her heart thudded against her rib cage when Tob came bounding out of the gloom, yipping happily. The old mare sidestepped and nickered, frightened, but Caroline spurred her on, toward the blazing light of the fire.

Guthrie's manner was clear as a first-grade primer. He wrenched Caroline off the horse, holding her so that her feet didn't quite touch the ground, and demanded, "What the hell are you doing here?"

Sweet misery filled Caroline. "Put me down," she said.

Grudgingly, Guthrie released her and stepped back. "Start explaining," he ordered.

Caroline sighed and raised the back of one hand to her forehead. "Guthrie, please—I'm so tired, and I'm starved, and we both know why I'm here."

He took her arm and dragged her roughly toward the fire, while the poor old mare stumbled along after them. Caroline sat down on Guthrie's saddle, next to the blaze, and drew up her knees. He led her horse away, speaking more soothingly to it than he ever had to her.

Presently, Guthrie stalked back to the fire, carrying her saddle, and set it down on the ground next to her. "Here," he said shortly, and produced a piece of jerky from the pocket of his coat.

Caroline accepted the dried meat and tore into it hungrily. Tob laid his graying muzzle on her knee and whimpered.

Cold fury was apparent in every line of Guthrie's body. "I ought to take you back to Bolton this minute, dump you on those old ladies' doorstep, and forget this whole crazy idea!"

Trembling, Caroline finished the meat and took the coffee he offered. The stuff tasted awful, but it gave her something to do while Guthrie delivered the inevitable tirade.

"You know," he went on, "you're not going to have a shred of reputation left by the time you get home. Everybody will assume we spent the night together."

Weariness and despair washed over Caroline. If Guthrie took her back and refused to help her, she didn't know what she'd do. Seaton was due to hang the first week in May, and time was running out. A tear zigzagged down her cheek.

To her surprise, Guthrie wiped it away with his thumb. The firelight danced over his features as she looked at him.

"I think you'd better get some rest, Teacher," he said huskily. "We'll talk about your shortcomings in the morning."

With that, he spread a single blanket out on the ground, then laid another one on top of it.

Caroline looked from the makeshift bed to Guthrie's face, which was hidden by the night and the brim of his hat. "You don't expect me to sleep with you?" she asked, her voice small and uncharacteristically timid.

Although she saw his jawline move in the shadow-streaked light of the moon, Caroline didn't know whether Guthrie was looking stern or amused. "I don't plan to sit up all night," he replied evenly, "and this is the only bed there is."

Reluctantly, Caroline poured out what remained of her coffee and stood. "I have to go to the bathroom," she said.

Guthrie was sitting on the blankets, pulling off his boots. "First door to your right," he joked. "And don't go far. You might find yourself passing the time of day with a Shoshone."

Terror filled Caroline, but nature was no less insistent. She went to the other side of the campfire and ventured about three feet outside its light.

When she returned, Guthrie was in bed and Tob was curled up at his feet. Awkwardly, Caroline removed her boots and wriggled in between the blankets.

"Guthrie?"

He sighed raggedly. "What?"

"Suppose there are Shoshone out there. Won't they see our campfire?"

"Unless they're blind, yes."

Against her will, Caroline moved a little closer to him. He chuckled and draped one arm across her middle. "Thank you for letting me stay," she said, and she hoped her voice sounded calm and even. In truth, there was a riot of emotion and sensation going on inside her.

"I didn't have much choice," Guthrie answered, in a sleepy rumble. "Good night, Caroline."

Five minutes later, he was snoring, but Caroline still felt as though her insides were doing battle with each other, and she strained to hear and identify every night sound. Then Guthrie shifted in his sleep and one of his hands came to rest possessively over her left breast.

Caroline's legs immediately stiffened, and her nipple pulsed to life against Guthrie's palm. She knew she should move away, but the sensation was pleasurable and besides, she was sure there were Indians lurking just beyond the edges of the blankets.

Guthrie groaned softly and rolled toward her, but Caroline knew he wasn't awake. His breathing was too deep and too even. He let go of her breast, but then he splayed his fingers over her stomach.

Caroline shivered, faced with a thousand scandalous curiosities and wants that wouldn't be easily put aside. She wanted something more from him, but what that something was eluded her completely.

"Mr. Hayes," she whispered, tugging at his sleeve.

"Go to sleep," was the grumbled response.

Caroline wanted Guthrie to hold her, even though she knew that would be a mistake, from a practical standpoint. The world seemed big and dangerous, and she felt small and confused. It took all the courage she possessed to whisper, "I need you to put your arms around me. I'm scared."

"Believe me, Caroline," he replied hoarsely, "I don't dare."

She began to cry softly, and Guthrie swore again, then turned over and positioned Caroline's back against his chest, spoon fashion. She thought she felt his lips touch her hair. "I think I might be just like my mother," she sniffled. Until that night, the fear had been an unrecognized one. Now that she was beginning to guess how powerful the pleasures of the flesh could be, it had come surging to the surface of her mind, demanding to be faced and accepted.

Guthrie's hand found hers and squeezed. "How do you mean?"

Caroline ran her tongue over her lips, full of misery. "It's the first time I've ever been close to a man when I wasn't standing up," she confessed, blushing even in the darkness, full of joy and despair. "And I'm afraid I like it."

He chuckled, and his hard chest moved against her back. "What's wrong with that?"

"Good women are modest," she said sadly. "They think having a man touch them is the worst thing that could happen."

At that, Guthrie laughed aloud, and Caroline elbowed him hard in the ribs.

"This isn't funny, Guthrie Hayes!" she cried. "Here I am, pouring out my heart, and what do you do? You *laugh!*"

His lips were so close to her ear that she could feel the warmth of his breath. "If you don't shut up and go to sleep," he vowed, "I'm going to show you everything there is to like about a man's touch. And I mean everything."

Caroline's mouth was open to argue, but she promptly closed it. Soon enough, Guthrie was sound asleep once more.

Caroline remained wide awake, despite her weariness, staring up at the sky. It seemed her whole being was at war with itself, body and soul—she felt plenty of fear and no small measure of pain—and yet the sensations weren't entirely unpleasant. There was wonder, too, and a gossamer sprinkling of joy.

A tear trickled down one dust-smudged cheek. With Seaton there had been no fear and certainly no pain, except for the grief so unfairly imposed by the outside world, of course. Neither, however, had there been wonder or true joy.

She wept in silence, alone even though she was tucked close against Guthrie, and finally slept.

The sun hadn't even risen over the mountains when Guthrie shook Caroline awake. When she sat up, he put a cup of coffee into her hands, but he didn't look cordial. His face was stubbled with two days' beard, and if the night before had meant anything to him, no one would ever have guessed it by his manner.

"I'm not going back," Caroline said firmly, after fortifying herself with a sip of his noxious coffee.

Guthrie flung the remaining contents of the coffeepot into the brush, and Caroline saw suppressed fury in every line of his body. That hurt, after the intimate way he'd held her the night before.

"You needn't be so ill-tempered," Caroline said, with shaky reason, pushing her tumbledown hair back from her face. "It doesn't become you."

He squatted in front of her to look directly into her face, and his green eyes were snapping. "Don't treat me like a slow first grader," he warned, in a gravelly undertone. "Out here, I'm running things. Is that clear?"

Caroline wriggled out of the blankets and stood, carefully balancing the coffee mug as she did so. "On the contrary," she said, with tremulous dignity, "you're working for me—remember?"

Guthrie rose and advanced ominously, forcing Caroline to take a step back. "Don't be too sure of that," he told her, and his nostrils flared slightly as he spoke. "You see, Teacher, I'd just as soon get on that horse of mine and ride straight back to Bolton. I've got a mine to work there and a house to build. There's a woman waiting for me to declare myself, and I'm thinking the sooner she and I tie the knot, the better I'm going to like it. So if you want me to take you the rest of the way to Laramie, you'd better not give me another moment's grief!"

Caroline bit her lower lip. There at the last, when Guthrie had raised his finger and shook it at her, she'd flinched, and that shamed her. "You weren't thinking about your precious Adabelle last night, when you touched me that way," she muttered under her breath, when Guthrie turned and strode away to saddle the horses.

He stopped, although he should have been too far away to hear, and turned to glower at her from under the brim of his disreputable hat. "What did you say?"

Caroline hugged herself. Her hair was falling down, her clothes were rumpled, she was out in the middle of nowhere with the most difficult man who had ever lived, and she had to go to the bathroom. "I said a lot of mosquitoes bit me during the night," she lied.

Guthrie glared at her for a moment, then went on about his business. Caroline found a bush to hide behind and took care of hers.

Chapter

❧ 6 ❧

*T*he grassy landscape stretched out around them, reaching like a carpet to the far mountains, and the sky made a canopy of cornflower blue, but Caroline had little opportunity to admire the view. Guthrie traveled at a fast pace, the dauntless Tob loping along beside his horse, and Caroline's swaybacked mare was at a distinct disadvantage. Finally, when the sun was at its zenith and Caroline was sure she would faint if they didn't stop to rest, her escort reined around to glare at her and slapped one thigh with his raggedy hat.

"If you can't keep up," he said impatiently, wiping his forehead with his sleeve before settling the hat back on his head, "then why don't you just go back to Bolton and let me handle this?"

Caroline stuck out her chin. Not for anything would she have let him see how relieved she was just to get a few moments to rest. "You'd like that, wouldn't you?" she challenged angrily. "Well, you're not going to get your way. I want to make sure this is handled properly."

Guthrie's eyes roved pityingly over her hired mare. "That animal is never going to make it all the way to Laramie, let alone back again. We'd better drop her off at the first homestead we see."

Patting the old horse's sweaty neck, Caroline nodded. At last, she and Guthrie finally agreed about something. "But what will I ride?" she asked.

"Nobody's likely to trade us a good mount for that poor old nag. You'll have to double up with me." He rode closer to gaze ominously into her face. "It's going to slow us down considerably, and I don't like that."

"What you like is of no earthly consideration to me," Caroline said stiffly.

Guthrie watched her for a moment longer, that obnoxious grin twitching at one side of his mouth, then he reined his gelding into a stand of whispering cottonwood trees. Caroline had no choice but to follow him.

Their horses' hooves made almost no sound on the soft, leaf-covered ground. Only the occasional snapping of a twig, the cautious songs of the birds, and Tob's panting broke the silence.

Finally, they came to a silvery stream and Guthrie dismounted. Both his horse and his dog hurried to the water to drink.

The balls of Caroline's feet ached fiercely when she got down and led her mare to the creek bank. She wasn't accustomed to riding; mostly, she walked everywhere she needed to go. Now, every muscle in her body seemed to be screaming for mercy.

"Why do you call that dog Tob?" Caroline asked, and there was an edge of insistence in her voice. The last time she'd inquired, Guthrie hadn't replied.

He sighed as he recovered his saddlebags from the gelding's back and carried them toward her. "It's nothing a lady should be interested in," he said.

Caroline flushed, remembering some of the thoughts she'd entertained concerning this impossible man. "Maybe I'm not a lady."

Guthrie produced more beef jerky from the leathery depths of his saddlebags and handed Caroline a portion, along with a wry look. "Tob is short for tits-on-a-boar," he answered, looking back at the canine with affection. "'Cause that's what that dog is as useless as."

Once again, Caroline's cheeks heated. "That's certainly crude," she remarked.

Guthrie shrugged and bit off a piece of his jerky, chewing with effort. "You asked," he replied. "So I told you."

Now he was talking with his mouth full. It was a mystery to Caroline why her spinster guardians thought this man was a gentleman. Of course, they'd had very limited experience with the opposite sex. She felt a pang, imagining how worried the gracious old ladies must be by now, even though she'd left them a note.

"You'd better get a drink while you can," Guthrie said, walking away and leaving Caroline standing there, gnawing on her ration of dried beef. The horses had drunk their fill and wandered away from the creek to graze on tender spring grass. Guthrie took off the canteen that had been looped over his shoulder by a long rawhide strap and squatted beside the flow of clean, icy water to fill it.

Caroline had been thirsty even before she'd eaten the heavily salted jerky, but she couldn't think of any way to drink gracefully. The mug Guthrie used for coffee was apparently stuck away in his pack somewhere, and her confidence didn't extend to plundering his things.

Finally, she just hunkered down at the creek side and scooped water up in her cupped hands. The taste was bracing and delicious, and she couldn't help giving a sigh of satisfaction.

Guthrie grinned at her as he stood twisting the lid back onto his canteen.

"What are you smiling about?" Caroline demanded. There was an arrogance in his amusement that made her scramble back to her feet.

"I was just thinking what sad shape you would have been in if you'd tried to make this trip on your own," he said. And then he turned and walked back toward the horses.

Caroline knew he was right, and that infuriated her all the more. She mounted her weary mare in stubborn silence and didn't say another word until hours later, when Guthrie spurred his horse toward an enclosed wagon and an enormous flock of dusty, muddy sheep in the distance. They'd heard the bleating of the animals even before seeing them.

The sheepherder's two collies came bounding at the sight of Tob, ready to defend their charges. With a plaintive yelp, Tob leaped up in front of Guthrie in the saddle and perched there, quivering, like a big, hairy bird.

Caroline was still getting over her surprise at that when the shepherd approached. He was a tall scarecrow of a man, wearing patched clothes and a top hat that must have been elegant at one time, and he carried a rifle easily at his side.

Guthrie touched the brim of his hat. "'Afternoon," he said, with a grin meant to put the other man at ease. Although he wore a .45-caliber pistol in a holster on his hip, he didn't reach for it or even lay his palm over the handle. Still, Caroline had a sense that the weapon would leap into his fingers in an instant if he summoned it.

"'Afternoon," replied the shepherd, studying the two visitors solemnly. His dogs kept their distance, but their teeth were bared and they were giving low, threatening growls.

Caroline knew their hostility was directed at Tob, but she was still afraid. These animals were not pets but valuable property, and they would be vicious if provoked.

Guthrie ran a gloved hand down Tob's shivering back while smiling companionably at the sheepherder. "We're looking for a place to leave this animal," he said, nodding toward Caroline's pathetic mount.

She rode up a little closer to her escort and said out of the side of her mouth, "Mr. Hayes, this horse does not belong to me. It's hired, and I shall be expected to return it at some point."

The man had the consummate gall to ignore her entirely. "You headed toward Bolton by any chance?"

The sheepherder rubbed his chin, considering. "Lot of cattlemen around those parts," he said thoughtfully. "They might not take kindly to me and my woolies."

Guthrie took two cheroots from his shirt pocket—very

slowly, Caroline noticed—and handed one to the shepherd. He lit his own, then handed the burning match to the man standing on the ground. "If you pass within seven or eight miles, I figure the mare will find the way home on her own."

"I could do that," the shepherd answered.

"Thanks," Guthrie replied.

Caroline got off the weary mare and climbed, with great difficulty and a hand from Guthrie, onto the back of his gelding. Considering that she was carrying her carpetbag, it was not a graceful process. "Shouldn't we offer him money?" she whispered into Guthrie's ear.

"It wouldn't hurt," Guthrie replied in an undertone, hardly moving his lips.

Caroline took a coin from the pocket of her skirt and tried to smile as she handed it down to the sheepherder. Soon, she was going to be broke, and all the funds she had at home in the Bolton City Bank were pledged to Guthrie for rescuing Mr. Flynn from jail. "Thank you," she said.

The shepherd bit the coin, then dropped it into the pocket of his ragged vest. After sparing a brief inclination of his head, the tall man turned and walked back toward his camp, leading the mare behind him.

Tob had leaped reluctantly to the ground, ever aware of the watchful sheep dogs.

"Suppose he doesn't take that poor animal back to Bolton at all?" Caroline fretted. She had one arm around Guthrie's muscular waist, but she felt sure she was going to slide off over the gelding's sleek rump anyway. The carpetbag was heavy in her other hand, and it thumped painfully against her thigh. "Suppose he just keeps her for himself?"

Guthrie made a clucking sound and spurred the horse slightly, nearly sending Caroline tumbling into the grass. "Then I guess you'll just have to pay the people at the livery stable whatever she's worth. Probably wouldn't be much."

Caroline clutched a handful of his shirt in an effort to keep her seat. That was easy for him to say, since the money wouldn't be coming out of his pocket. "I just hope he'll be kind to her."

"Anything's got to be kinder than forcing her to keep up with a gelding half her age," he commented, then urged his horse into a trot.

Caroline held on for dear life. Even if she'd been able to think of something to say, uttering the words would have taken effort she couldn't spare, so she rested her cheek between Guthrie's shoulder blades and endured.

When they finally stopped again, this time beside a narrow, tree-sheltered stream, Caroline was weak, and her hand ached from hours of clutching Guthrie's shirt. The insides of her thighs felt bruised and sore, as well. She let the carpetbag tumble to the ground before gratefully dismounting.

Guthrie didn't seem a bit the worse for wear and even Tob, who had trotted along beside the horse all afternoon, was hardly winded.

"See if you can find some twigs and chips of bark to start the fire." Guthrie gave the order offhandedly, while leading the gelding toward the water.

Although Caroline was annoyed at his tone, she had never expected to make the trip without having to do her part, so she searched the area until she had an armload of sticks and bark.

When she got back to camp, Guthrie had already made a circle of stones for the fire, and he was whistling as he constructed a crude spit from two forked sticks and one longer, sturdier one.

Caroline's stomach grumbled loudly, and her mouth watered. She hardly dared ask, "Are we going to have something besides dried beef for supper?"

Guthrie grinned as he got to his feet and shoved his bowie knife back into the scabbard hanging from his belt. "That'll depend on how good my aim is," he replied. He took a couple of wooden matches from the pocket of his shirt and held them out to Caroline. "Here. You get the fire going."

Caroline figured a campfire couldn't be that different from one on the hearth of the parlor fireplace at home. She dropped the makings she'd gathered into the circle of stones and accepted the matches.

Guthrie took his .45 from its holster and laid it gently on top of his bedroll, which rested on a high, flat rock. "You know how to use one of these?" he asked.

Caroline eyed the pistol and shuddered. "No. There isn't much call for bloodshed in my line of work."

He laughed. "I reckon there are a few teachers who'd disagree with that," he replied. He left the gun where it was and took up the rifle that had been in a special scabbard beneath his saddle. The inside of Caroline's right leg had practically been rubbed raw by the thing.

The fire blazed to life, and Caroline rose awkwardly from her knees, dusting her hands together and smiling in satisfaction. Now, she would have to bring back some of the larger pieces of wood she'd seen earlier, to keep the flames going.

Guthrie startled her by cocking the rifle loudly. "Don't get too far from that .45," he warned, "and if anybody comes into camp, point it straight at their gizzard." He paused and gave his lopsided grin. "Unless it's me, of course."

Caroline looked from Guthrie to the pistol and felt the color drain out of her face. Although she certainly didn't relish the prospect of handling something so lethal, these weren't ordinary circumstances. There were bandits, drifters, and Indians abroad. "Just don't be gone too long," she replied, with a gulp.

His green eyes moved over her in an appreciative, humorous sweep, and then he turned and went off into the trees, with Tob bounding along at his heels. He was whistling some audacious saloon song as he went.

Caroline gathered the rest of the wood, ever conscious of the .45, stockpiling enough to keep the fire going through most of the night. She flinched when she heard a shot in the distance, hoping Guthrie had brought down a rabbit or a grouse. It was just as possible, it seemed to her, that her traveling companion had fallen prey to a Shoshone bullet.

She was enormously relieved when, about twenty-five minutes later, Guthrie came into camp carrying a sizable rabbit carcass in one hand. Blessedly, he'd already cleaned the animal and skinned it, and Caroline was too hungry for something other than beef jerky to worry about the niceties.

She watched as Guthrie washed the meat thoroughly in the creek, then handed it back to her. While she held it, he carefully cleaned the blade of his knife.

Back at the campfire, Guthrie took the rabbit from Caroline and put it expertly on the spit. Tob yipped and yowled a few feet away, obviously anxious for his share of the feast.

The meat smelled heavenly as it roasted and, as the light of day faded, the three travelers drew closer to the fire by instinct. The cheerful crackling of the blaze raised Caroline's weary spirits and made her feel safer, but all her muscles were protesting the long day of mistreatment.

A sidelong glance at Guthrie reminded her that there were different kinds and degrees of safety. Tonight they would again share a bedroll, and there was no denying that her virtue was in his hands. If he chose not to behave as a gentleman, she feared she would not be able to resist him.

And she was certain he knew that.

She turned the rabbit patiently on its spit, and when Guthrie pronounced it cooked, she was as eager for her share as a cave woman after a long, lean winter.

Guthrie gave her a portion, took one for himself, and then tossed a generous piece to Tob.

By the time she'd finished eating the delicious meat, Caroline was well satisfied, and a little less shaky, but she was also covered with grease. She looked with longing toward the shadowy stream.

"I'd like to take a bath," she confessed.

Guthrie dismissed the idea with a shake of his head and a lusty sigh, leaning back against his saddle to fold his arms and watch the fire. He'd already wiped his fingers on his trouser legs, but there was a tiny glint of grease at one corner of his mouth.

"Water's too cold," he said.

Caroline ran her slippery fingers back and forth in the deep grass, but she still didn't feel clean, and she wasn't about to use her skirt for a napkin. After all, she had only one other set of clothes stuffed into her carpetbag, and she couldn't be sure how long it would be before she had access to her wardrobe again.

Overhead, stars twinkled into view, seeming to flicker against the twilight sky. Guthrie was staring contentedly into the fire.

"For all your talk about marrying and building a house," Caroline ventured, trying to settle herself, "I think you like sleeping under the stars and having to hunt for your supper."

Guthrie grinned. "It has its merits," he admitted, with another hearty sigh, "but I'm ready to have a roof and walls of my own and start making babies."

Caroline felt the heat of the fire even more intensely in that moment. She wasn't used to men—or women, for that matter—speaking so frankly in her presence, although long ago, while living with her mother in Chicago, she'd seen and heard worse. "I suppose Adabelle is just right for that, too," she said, wishing she could call the words back the second she'd uttered them.

He chuckled and shifted comfortably on the ground. "Exactly right," he agreed.

Feeling wounded, Caroline folded her arms and scowled. "She's not the only woman in the world who can have babies, you know. It's not some rare, spectacular achievement."

Guthrie's eyes glinted with knowing amusement in the firelight. "I never said she was the only woman who could bear a child," he said quietly.

Caroline planned to bolt, but Guthrie reached out and caught hold of her hand when she stood. With one deft jerk, he had her kneeling beside him, staring into his eyes. She was as helpless against him as that rabbit had been when it was looking into the barrel of his rifle.

"Will you be faithful to her?" Caroline asked. Again, she felt as though the words had come from somewhere outside herself; she hadn't willingly said them.

"When she's my wife, yes," Guthrie answered. He was only looking at Caroline, studying her as if she were a mystery he had to solve, and yet she felt as if he'd let her hair down from its pins, as if he'd touched her intimately.

Caroline was achy and moist where her legs met. She wanted to break away but, for the life of her, she couldn't move or even speak. A terrible combination of guilt and longing overtook her, like some raging fire of the spirit, and she could barely breathe.

Was this the way Kathleen, her beautiful, tragic mother, had felt when men touched her? she wondered. Were these the same dangerous feelings that could make a woman send her own children west on an orphan train, never to know what became of them?

The thought made Caroline cry out softly, in a misery of confusion, and to her surprise Guthrie made a low, comforting sound in his throat and drew her down to lie beside him. He sheltered her in his strong arms, and she felt his lips brush her temple, but he made no demands.

He wanted only to give her a hiding place, it seemed to Caroline, and she was all but overcome by that.

"It'll be all right," he said, and Caroline could feel the stubble of his chin against the side of her face. "Everything will be just fine, Teacher."

Caroline's eyes brimmed with tears. Everything would *not* be fine. Even if she managed to save Seaton from the hangman's noose and fulfill all her precious dreams of marrying and raising a fine family, there would still be one glaring problem. She was beginning to care for this man, Guthrie Hayes, in a way she'd never imagined possible. And she had a feeling that caring wasn't going to fade just because she willed it to be so, or even due to the natural wearing away process of time. No, this was the kind of love that settled deep in a person's heart, heavy as a stone, and stayed, blocking the passage of all other emotions.

Guthrie stroked her dust-filled, sweat-dampened hair, just as though the tresses were freshly washed in rainwater and perfumed by sunshine and morning air.

"I'm scared," she said. She hadn't planned the words, hadn't shaped them in her mind. They were just there, all of a sudden, like another entity at the campfire.

He shifted easily, as though they were lying on a feather-bed instead of the hard Wyoming ground. "Most likely, that's because you're riding ahead into tomorrow and the next day and the day after that, in your mind, I mean. Biggest secret to life, Teacher, is that you've got to keep your thoughts snug inside the day you're living."

"People need to plan ahead," Caroline protested, but not very strenuously. She knew she should pull free of Guthrie's improper embrace, but she couldn't bring herself to do that. She liked being held; it gave her a feeling she'd been searching for ever since she and Lily and Emma had been separated on that railroad platform in Lincoln, Nebraska.

"Planning for the future isn't the same as setting up homestead there," Guthrie replied, sighing the words, as though he were just barely awake. "Too many folks get so busy seeing to next month or next year, they don't even notice today. A person could miss a whole lifetime that way."

The words made sense to Caroline, but then, she suspected anything he said would have done that. She laid her head on the solid warmth of his chest, listened to his heart beating strong and steady under her ear.

It was thinking of lying in a real bed with Guthrie, feeling flesh beneath her cheek instead of a coarsely woven shirt, that brought Caroline back to the real world. She sat bolt upright and raised both hands to her face.

Guthrie's grin was impudently crooked, like always, and entirely too knowing. "What's the trouble, Teacher?"

Since Caroline could hardly reply that she was starting to like being held entirely too well, that she was beginning to entertain dangerous fantasies, she was at something of a loss for an answer. She watched the firelight flicker over Guthrie's features and marveled.

He was a saddle tramp turned miner, with heaven only knew what kind of dreadful secrets rattling in his past, and yet his appeal was vast.

"I guess I was just thinking of Mr. Flynn," she lied, blurting out the first awkward lie that bumbled into her mind. "He wouldn't appreciate our being so—close"

Guthrie stretched languidly, made a masculine sound, part weary sigh and part contentment, and closed his eyes. "I don't reckon he's in much of a position to be complaining," he said. "But if you want to sleep out there in the dark, where the Shoshone can get you, go right ahead."

Caroline was terrified of Indians, but she was even more afraid of the feelings she was having. In addition, she was dirty—she certainly wasn't used to that—and her muscles pulsed with a gnawing pain.

She got up, without a word, and made her way through the trees to the moon-washed creek nearby.

She undressed, Tob whimpering protectively on the bank beside her, and waded into the chilly waters of the stream, feeling slippery pebbles beneath her feet. Even though the water was cold, it was a comfort, for it quieted the peculiar sensations being close to Guthrie had inspired. She washed, as though she could somehow splash away what she'd discovered about herself, just a few minutes before, beside Guthrie Hayes's campfire.

Chapter

❧ 7 ❧

*L*ate the following day, Guthrie and Caroline arrived in Clinton. The robbery and murder Seaton Flynn was accused of perpetrating had taken place five miles outside this small cattle town.

Guthrie headed straight for the hotel, a two-story structure of weathered boards that leaned ever so slightly to the right. Large front windows gave the place an aspect of surprise.

Caroline looked at the building with concern. "Why are we stopping here?"

Guthrie swung one leg over the pommel of his saddle and slipped deftly to the ground, leaving Caroline staring down at him from the horse's back. He grinned and resettled his hat. "We can't go around asking questions about the stage robbery if we look like a couple of saddle bums," he pointed out. "We've got to clean up."

There was no denying that Guthrie needed a shave and a change of clothes, to say the very least, and Caroline didn't want to think how she must look. "You're right," she conceded reluctantly, allowing him to close his hands around her waist and lift her down. She was still appalled by the thoughts she'd had about him the night before, while they lay side by side, and she was careful to avoid his gaze.

When she stood on the ground, he curved his fingers under her chin and lifted. The glint in his eyes told Caroline he'd guessed what was troubling her. "Imagining something isn't the same as doing it," he pointed out quietly.

Caroline swallowed and blushed hard, and she was most relieved when Guthrie turned away to tether the horse to a hitching rail. Tob was already sitting in front of the swinging doors of the saloon down the street, making a low yowling sound.

"He needs a drink," Guthrie explained, as he stepped up onto the high wooden sidewalk and reached down to offer Caroline his hand.

Recalling how the dog had lapped up whiskey out of a bowl, Caroline reflected, "I think he has an unnatural fondness for liquor."

Guthrie nodded. "That he does. One time down in Texas, I won big in a poker game and three or four cowboys came to my camp to let me know they weren't happy about losing a month's pay. Tob just laid there, too hung over to help, while they beat hell out of me."

Caroline winced at the images that came to mind. "Were you badly hurt?"

He waited beside the open doorway of the hotel, so that Caroline could precede him. "I was sore for a while, and I had bruises ranging all the way from light green to purple, but they didn't break any bones."

She grimaced and looked around. The lobby was small and shabby, with a worn Oriental rug covering the floor. There was a row of pigeonholes on the wall behind the registration desk, and dusty plants towered in each corner, making the place seem even more constricted than it was.

Caroline drew in her shoulders, feeling cramped and uneasy, while Guthrie went to the desk. She hoped she had enough money left to pay for two rooms, hot baths for both of them, and good restaurant meals.

For the first time, Caroline sorely regretted the indulgence of the fancy pink gown she'd bought for the spring dance. It seemed like a frivolous and foolish purchase, now that she could view it with hindsight.

Guthrie spoke to the clerk stationed behind the desk, a trim man with a green visor jutting out from his forehead, then turned around and handed Caroline a key.

"How much did it cost?" she inquired, keeping her voice low.

He favored her with his curious, off-kilter smile. "Don't worry about it, Teacher. We'll square up when this is over."

Caroline hardly found his reply reassuring.

The door of her room was the first one on the right, at the top of the stairs. She unlocked it and stepped over the threshold, and Guthrie handed her the carpetbag that had pulled at her fingers with the weight of an anvil while they were traveling.

"Thank you," she said, feeling shy now that there were people around. In the night, miles from nowhere, it had been easier to let her guard down. Now, she must remember to acquit herself as a schoolteacher should.

He leaned toward her and kissed her lightly on the forehead. "I'll meet you downstairs in an hour, and we'll have some supper," he told her, and, after nodding, Caroline closed the door.

The room was tiny, with the ceiling sloping so low over the narrow bed that she could have reached up and touched it while reclining, and the window looked out on the noisy, bustling street below.

Opening her carpetbag, Caroline took out her favorite blue and white calico dress and spread it on the bed. She was trying to smooth away the wrinkles with her hands when a knock sounded at the door.

Caroline turned, and was startled by her own image. She hadn't realized there was a mirror, however cracked and cloudy, on the inside of the door. "Who's there?" she asked, and her voice trembled as she took in her tangled, unkempt hair, her dirty clothes and scuffed boots, her smudged face.

"It's Molly, ma'am, come about your bath."

Just the thought of soaking in a tub of hot water lifted Caroline's spirits. She turned the knob eagerly.

A plump young woman with curling brown hair waited in the hallway, twisting her apron in strong, work-roughened hands. "There's a tub down at the end of the hall, there," she said, gesturing. "We can fill it for you, or else you can use the water what's left from the last bath."

Caroline suppressed a shudder. "I'll need fresh water, please," she said, "and do be sure to wipe out the tub very carefully before you fill it."

The maid looked put out. "That costs extra," she warned, waggling a finger. "Hot water what ain't been used yet is five cents."

Caroline produced a nickel from the pocket of her skirt and offered it without further comment.

"I'll knock when your bath's ready," the maid replied, with a shrug. She examined the coin, then dropped it into her apron pocket. "Mind you don't take too long in there, neither. There'll be lots of folks wanting a dip tonight."

Twenty minutes later, Caroline stepped into a small room reserved for bathing. There was no lock on the door, so she dragged a chair in from the hallway and braced it under the knob.

A round laundry tub sat in the middle of the floor, the water steaming. She'd be all cramped up in that little space, but at least the bath looked sanitary. She hung her clean clothes from a hook on the wall and began stripping off her divided skirt, shirtwaist, and underthings.

Using soap of her own—indeed, Caroline was afraid to even *look* at the community bar provided by the hotel—she washed her hair and every inch of her skin. Then she climbed out, stood on the cold, bare wooden floor, and dried herself with a thin, grayish towel she'd found by the washstand in her room and put on her calico dress.

Back in her room, she stood before the mirror, brushing her hair. Since it would be a long time drying, and she was supposed to meet Guthrie for supper soon, she wound her long tresses into a single plait and tied the end with a blue ribbon.

Guthrie was waiting in the lobby, clean and shaved, and

Caroline's heart gave a little leap when she saw him. She gave herself an instant, if silent, reprimand for reacting the way she had. She was supposed to be engaged to Seaton Flynn, even if he hadn't actually gotten around to giving her a ring, and it was about time she started remembering that.

Or was it already too late?

"You've had a bath," she said. The effort to cover her embarrassment only resulted in more of the same.

Guthrie chuckled. "There's a tub next door, above the saloon. While Tob was quenching his thirst downstairs, I was making myself presentable." He offered his arm, just as he had the night of the dance, and Caroline accepted it.

He ushered her out onto the sidewalk, since the hotel had no restaurant of its own, and across the street to a dining hall with fly-specked windows and a sawdust floor.

"I'm afraid this is the best place in town," Guthrie whispered into Caroline's ear. His breath was warm, and it set her flesh to tingling.

Caroline looked around at the rough-hewn trestle tables and benches. The sawdust was speckled with tobacco juice and spilled food, and the walls could have used a good whitewashing. If this was the best Clinton had to offer, she thought, may God deliver her from the worst. "Very nice," she said.

Guthrie grinned and seated her at one of the empty tables, taking the place directly across from her and setting his hat down on the bench beside him. "I'll say one thing for you, Teacher—you do know how to roll with the punches."

Caroline met his eyes. "I suppose I am resilient," she said, shrugging one shoulder. In another part of the room, men laughed loudly at some joke. "This is almost like being in a saloon."

A harried waitress approached the table, hands resting on her hips. Her dingy hair was pulled back from her face, sleek as a layer of onion. "We got chicken and we got beef," she said bluntly. "What'll it be?"

"I wonder," Caroline began, sitting up very straight, "if I might have a look at the kitchen?"

Guthrie gave her a surprised glance before shifting his attention to the waitress, whose lips were stretched thin across her teeth.

"Fancy lady, are you? Well, maybe you'd rather take your supper down the street at Miss Brayson's rooming house. 'Least there, you'll know nobody spit in the soup."

Caroline's cheeks burned with temper as she rose from the bench. "I believe I'd prefer that," she said, with hardwon moderation. "Exactly where is this rooming house?"

"Caroline," Guthrie interceded, under his breath.

She paid no attention. "If you'll just give me directions, please," she said to the waitress, making sure she didn't slouch.

Guthrie rolled his eyes and stood, hat in hand. There was utter silence in the room while the other customers waited to see what would develop.

The waitress looked sheepish; probably, she would be reprimanded for driving off customers. "It's three streets to the west, on the corner. There's a sign in the yard."

"Thank you," Caroline said. She would have strode imperiously out of the dining hall on her own if Guthrie hadn't taken her arm and propelled her along as though leaving had been *his* idea.

"Did it ever occur to you," he demanded, giving her a little shake when they reached the sidewalk, "that I might have wanted to stay? You could at least have asked my opinion!"

Caroline found the setting sun and started off in that direction. "You're perfectly welcome to stay if you want."

Guthrie made a rolling motion with his shoulders, rather reminding Caroline of a rooster with his feathers ruffled. "Thanks to you, Teacher, I won't be able to set foot in that place again."

"Why not?" Caroline inquired, holding up her skirts as she crossed a side street.

"I don't want to talk about it," Guthrie grumbled.

Reaching the other side of the street, Caroline stopped,

her hands resting on her hips. "You're afraid they'll think you're a henpecked husband!" she trilled, delighted.

Guthrie looked around in anxious annoyance to make sure no one had overheard, and his neck went a dull red "I'm not anybody's husband," he reminded her crisply, "and if I was, I sure as hell wouldn't let any *woman* tell me where to eat!"

Caroline set off in the direction of the rooming house, leaving Guthrie with a choice. He could join her, or he could try his luck in some other eating establishment. He must have been as tired of beef jerky as she was, because he fell grudgingly into step beside her.

The food at Miss Brayson's was unimaginative and tasteless, but the place was clean. Caroline and Guthrie consumed their suppers, and Guthrie paid for the meals. Then they excused themselves and left.

Since twilight was falling, the stores were about to close. "What about Tob?" Caroline asked. "Has he eaten?"

Guthrie grinned, slowing his pace as they came abreast of the marshal's office. "He had half a dozen hard-boiled eggs while we were in the saloon."

Caroline shook her head. "And I suppose he's sleeping in your room?"

"After six hard-boiled eggs? Are you kidding? He's on the outside stairs." Guthrie pushed the marshal's door open and stepped back so Caroline could enter in front of him.

"How can I help you folks?" the marshal asked cordially. He was an older man, substantially built, with a bristly gray mustache.

"We'd like to ask a few questions about a stagecoach robbery," Guthrie said, opening the gate in the thigh-high railing that set the cells and the marshal's desk off from the entrance. Again, he let Caroline go through ahead of him.

"The one Mr. Seaton Flynn is accused of committing," she said.

Even while he was taking off his hat and smiling companionably at the well-fed lawman, Guthrie somehow managed to nudge Caroline in the ribs. The message he wanted to convey was clear enough.

Quiet.

"You members of Flynn's family?" the marshal inquired, studying them closely from beneath eyebrows as bushy and gray as his mustache.

"Miss Flynn here is his sister," Guthrie replied, before Caroline could explain her identity. "And I'm his cousin, Jeffrey Mason."

Guthrie and the marshal shook hands while Caroline bit her tongue to keep from protesting the lies Guthrie was telling.

"My name's John Teemo," the lawman said. Clearly, he'd sized Guthrie up and decided he was all right. Which showed what he knew. "The case against your cousin is pretty well settled, Mr. Mason, as you probably know. He's been convicted of murder, besides robbery, and sentenced to hang." His blue eyes stopped briefly on Caroline's face. "Sorry, ma'am."

Guthrie folded his arms and narrowed his eyes in an expression of friendly thoughtfulness. "I wonder if there's anybody around here who could show us exactly where the crime happened? We'd just like to see the place for ourselves."

"I understand," Mr. Teemo replied, with polite sympathy. "I could take you out there myself, come morning. You might want to talk with Rafe Binchly while you're here, too. He was on the stage when it was robbed and poor old Cal Walden was gunned down. Saw the whole thing." Again, he looked apologetically at Caroline. "Testified to it in court."

Caroline fought down the aching uneasiness inside her. She mustn't start losing faith in Mr. Flynn now, not when she'd come so far. She could no longer deny, at least to herself, that her feelings toward him had changed irrevocably, because of Mr. Hayes, but that didn't excuse her from her vow to see that justice was served. "My . . . cousin and I are convinced he was mistaken," she said evenly. "Seaton would never do such a thing."

"Seems like he went ahead and did, though, ma'am," Marshal Teemo said solemnly.

Guthrie took her arm in a grip that was firm enough to leave minor bruises, though he was turning a mannerly face toward the marshal. "Miss Flynn and I will be leaving now," he said. "We'll come back around nine tomorrow, if that's convenient for you."

The marshal nodded. "And don't forget about ol' Rafe Binchly. He could tell you just what happened."

"Where would we find him, please?" Caroline blurted. She knew Guthrie would have asked the same question, but she'd wanted to show him that he couldn't tell her when to speak and when to keep her silence. His say-so only went so far.

"This time of day," the marshal said, consulting the watch that hung from a chain stretched across his broad belly, "Rafe's usually down at the Golden Garter—begging your pardon, ma'am—bending his elbow at the bar."

Guthrie moved his hand from Caroline's arm to the small of her back. Somehow, he managed to propel her out of the marshal's office without revealing the fact that he was using force.

"I want to go to this Golden Garter place with you," Caroline hissed, once they'd reached the sidewalk again, "and I don't care whether you're for or against, Mr. Hayes!"

"I'm against," Guthrie said tautly. "And we're doing this my way or I'm putting you on the next stage back to Bolton and heading for Cheyenne."

Mr. Flynn was being held in Laramie, and Adabelle lived in Cheyenne. The message was not lost on Caroline. "As long as you help Seaton," she replied, "I don't care if you marry Tob's mother!" That last part was a lie, of course. Caroline had tender feelings for Mr. Hayes, much as she would have liked to squelch them. It followed quite naturally that she couldn't marry Mr. Flynn, of course, but following through on her plan to set the man free so he could prove his innocence was the least she could do.

Guthrie grinned, making Caroline wonder if he was somehow divining her thoughts again. "In order to help your—friend—I need your help, Teacher. And getting yourself thrown out of a saloon on your pretty little bustle isn't going to aid our cause any."

Caroline could see the establishment in the distance, at the end of the darkening street. Across the top of the facade, someone had painted the words *Golden Garter* in garish gilt. Light flowed through dirty windows, along with noise and music and raucous laughter.

"Just remember," she said, thinking of the saucy girls inside who liked to sit on a man's lap and whisper in his ear, "I'm not paying you to carouse."

"You're not paying me at all," Guthrie reminded her, "because I haven't agreed to take this job. So just go back to your room and wait for me. I'll come to you when I know something."

Caroline hated being shunted aside that way, like some worrisome child, but she knew she would accomplish nothing by storming into a place where ladies weren't welcome. So she nodded tersely and turned back toward the hotel.

She couldn't resist glancing over her shoulder, and when she did, she saw Guthrie grinning at her. He winked, then ambled through the double doors of the saloon.

Along the way, Caroline paused to admire a green velvet traveling suit and a matching feathered hat in a store window. She took her time returning to the hotel.

Too restless to wait in her room, she climbed the stairs behind the hotel instead and sat beside Tob, who was lying quietly on the landing, his long muzzle resting on his paws. He greeted her with a companionable whine.

She patted his head. The poor beast was probably exhausted, having kept pace with Guthrie's horse for so many hours. "One of these days soon," she told the animal, "Mr. Hayes will build that house of his, and you'll have a nice barn to sleep in. Maybe Mrs. Hayes will even let you inside to lie on the hearth, though I wouldn't depend on that. I have an idea the woman isn't so wonderful as your master would like us to believe."

Tob whimpered forlornly, and Caroline took immediate pity on him.

"Don't listen to me," she said, ruffling his loose hide.

"Just because I don't expect to take to the woman, I shouldn't be trying to influence you."

"You're right," put in a familiar masculine voice. "You shouldn't."

Caroline peered down through the spaces between the wooden steps and saw Guthrie standing there, gazing up at her with that insufferable grin on his face.

She ignored his needling words, moved to stand, and then reconsidered. Purposefully, she tucked her skirts in around her legs and cleared her throat. "That certainly didn't take long," she observed.

Guthrie was climbing the stairs. "How much time did you expect me to spend in the Golden Garter, Teacher?" he asked, arching one eyebrow.

Caroline's cheeks throbbed, but she lifted her chin and squared her shoulders. "Long enough to play poker, get yourself intoxicated, and—well—long enough, that's all."

He sat down on the step below hers with a sigh and gazed off toward the blazing sunset visible over the shoddy roofs of the ramshackle frontier town. The sky boiled with crimson, apricot, and gold.

It took a great deal of self-control on Caroline's part to keep herself from reaching out to massage Mr. Hayes's shoulders, the way a wife might do. She couldn't imagine where such an improper desire might have come from.

"I found Binchly right away," he said, after a few moments of rich silence had passed. "He'll show us the site of the robbery and shooting tomorrow, and tell us all about it, so we won't have to trouble the marshal."

"Good," Caroline agreed, because she didn't know what else to say. She was dreading visiting that place of death and greed, even though she was certain she would find proof of Seaton's innocence there.

Guthrie looked back at her over one shoulder. Evidently, he wasn't going to let what he'd overheard earlier pass unchallenged. "Adabelle wouldn't be mean to my dog," he said flatly.

His defense of the woman was unnecessary and, for that reason, it only made Caroline angrier. "I'm sure she's an absolute saint," she replied. She stood, but Guthrie grasped her skirt and pulled her back down. Her bottom struck the landing hard.

"How come you hate Adabelle so much, when you don't even know her?" he demanded.

"I don't hate her," Caroline insisted miserably. She couldn't admit to her true sentiments, of course. Mr. Hayes would surely laugh if he knew the schoolteacher was falling in love with him.

Guthrie's eyes narrowed for a moment, then went wide and filled with laughter. "You're jealous," he accused.

Caroline slapped her knees with the palms of both hands in her ire. "I most certainly am not."

He chuckled, full of masculine arrogance, then moved up to sit on the step beside her. She was sharply aware of his scent, his substance, his strength. "Yes, you are." He went right on talking to her after that, but something was different. He spoke in a low, mesmerizing voice, uttering magical words that seemed to fade from her mind like mirages an instant after they were spoken. His voice caressed her, doing the work of his hands, making her breathing quicken and her heart pound.

Caroline made a soft, despairing sound and still, with his mind, with those words that left no imprint on her memory, he stripped her of all resistance.

It was, in fact, as though he'd peeled away her clothes, garment by garment, kissing each patch of pale skin as he bared it. Caroline had never read about, or even imagined, that such intimacy was possible, and she feared what would happen if she didn't regain control of her senses.

She might as well have been intoxicated, so powerless were her muscles, while inwardly her body thrummed and pulsed with an acceleration of life. She let her head rest against Guthrie's shoulder, but both his hands still lay lightly on his knees. She could see them.

And yet she could feel them, too, moving over her flesh. Smoothing and shaping, teasing and tormenting.

He continued to speak, in that low voice only she could hear, and the sweet pressure inside Caroline rose like floodwaters. Still the phrases flowed, like a silvery river, and they might have been woven of another language, so indecipherable did she find them. They were like magical smoke curling around her, making its way inside.

"Oh," Caroline gasped, clutching the rough wooden step with both hands as a delicious explosion rocked her, unfolding into one violent tremor after another. Guthrie put his arm around her then, and held her lightly until the quaking stopped.

Chapter

✣ 8 ✣

*C*aroline closed her eyes and wrapped her arms tightly around her trembling knees, struggling to regain her perspective. Somehow, this man had bewitched her, cast some spell that had changed her feelings for Seaton Flynn forever. Dear God how she despised Guthrie for taking away her dreams and offering nothing in return but heartache and shame!

"Caroline."

She didn't open her eyes. "What?"

"Look at me."

She lifted one eyelid. The darkness had thickened to the point where she could barely see Guthrie's form in the stray light from a rear window below the stairs. "What?" she repeated, this time with a distinct note of impatience.

"What just happened here doesn't make you a bad person."

Caroline was still a bit dazed, and more confused than she'd ever been in her life. She leaned forward, glaring at Guthrie. "It's generous of you to say so, Mr. Hayes, considering that *you* were the instigator and I was, if anything, your hapless quarry."

He gave a chortling laugh, rose to his feet, and offered

Caroline a hand to rise after him. "If you'd wanted me to stop," he pointed out reasonably, "all you would have had to do was tell me so."

"How could I tell you to stop when you weren't actually touching me?" she blurted. After that, Caroline made a great business of smoothing her skirts, stalling while she searched her thoughts vainly for an acceptable reason. The sad truth was, she'd been swept up in the pleasure of Guthrie's words and it hadn't even occurred to her to protest.

Behind her, on the landing, Tob hinted to be invited inside the hotel.

Guthrie took Caroline's hand and led her down the stairs, and the dog followed, panting happily, his toenails making a rhythmic click on the wood.

"I could put you on a stagecoach back to Bolton first thing tomorrow morning," Guthrie offered, and desolation crushed Caroline as she realized how eager he was to get rid of her. "You'd be back with Miss Phoebe and Miss Ethel, safe and sound, in a couple of days."

Resolutely, Caroline shook her head. "I can't go home without freeing Mr. Flynn," she said.

Guthrie sighed. "You might have to, darlin'," he said gently, leading her through the little space between the hotel and the noisy saloon next door. Caroline hadn't noticed the name of the place. "After all, so far there's still no reason to believe that judge and jury were wrong about what happened."

Caroline shuddered, caught by a chill she attributed to the night breeze, as they reached the sidewalk and approached the door of the hotel. Tob still trotted along behind them, confident of his acceptance inside the building. "Have you ever been to a hanging, Mr. Hayes?"

"Guthrie," he corrected hoarsely. "And, yes, I saw a man hanged once for deserting. It wasn't a sight you or any other lady should be allowed to see."

Caroline felt like anything but a lady; her knees were still weak from that scandalous little episode on the back stairway when nothing and yet everything had happened. She lifted one hand unconsciously to her throat and swallowed hard as Guthrie pushed open the door for her.

"Good night, Mr. Hayes," she said, pausing at the foot of the stairs. She certainly hoped none of the people chatting and smoking in the lobby had guessed what she'd been up to. But then, she didn't really know that herself, so how could they?

Guthrie released her hand, but in some strange way his gaze held her just as effectively. "I hope you'll think over what I said about going home," he told her quietly. "Your guardians probably believe I kidnapped you."

Caroline didn't need to consider; she'd been over the problem from every angle, beginning on the dreadful day when word had reached her that Mr. Flynn had been arrested and thrown into jail. "I made my decision long since," she said. "And I left a note for Miss Phoebe and Miss Ethel."

He sighed and rested one elbow on the newel post at the foot of the banister. In his other hand, he held his battered hat. "They're probably convinced that I forced you to write the note, and you damn well know it. And as for your decision, it's the wrong one."

Caroline shrugged nonchalantly, even though she was weary inside, and full of fear and confusion. "Right or wrong, I'm standing by it. Wouldn't you want your Adabelle to believe in you if you'd been accused of a crime you didn't commit?"

Guthrie looked around uneasily, and there was anger in his eyes when he finally turned them to Caroline. He spoke in a low voice. "Unless you want to end up in Marshal Teemo's jail, charged with conspiracy, you'd better watch what you say!"

Properly chagrined, Caroline lowered her eyes for a moment. Guthrie took advantage of the fact that she was off-guard and gripped her arm, steering her up the stairs beside him. His faithful dog came along behind, unimpeded and apparently unnoticed.

Mr. Hayes waited, like the gentleman he most certainly wasn't, while Caroline unlocked the door to her room. The day had been a long and trying one, and her bumpy bed beneath the eaves looked inviting.

For a moment, it seemed as though Guthrie meant to say something. In the end, however, he just turned and walked away, slapping his hat against his thigh once in exasperation. But Tob skulked into Caroline's room, his belly brushing the floor as he crept along, and curled up at the foot of her bed with a low whine.

"I don't blame you," Caroline said, closing and latching the door. "I wouldn't want to sleep with him either."

With that, she began to undress. That night, she had the luxury of sleeping in a nightgown, instead of her clothes, and she took her time performing her evening ablutions. She was sitting on the edge of the bed, brushing her hair, when there was a knock at the door.

Caroline had heard stories about the misfortunes that could befall unwary women far from home and hearth, and she was grateful for Tob's presence, however ineffectual the animal might be. "Who's there?" she called, in a shaky voice meant to be firm.

"I want my dog back," came Guthrie's unmistakable drawl.

Caroline went to the door and opened it just a crack, peering around the edge. "He seems to prefer staying with me," she replied politely.

A muscle went taut in Guthrie's jawline, then relaxed again. He gave a soft whistle, and the dog whimpered, then rose to his feet and obeyed his master's summons.

Disappointed, Caroline closed the door after the feckless dog and turned the key in the lock. Then, hearing noise from the saloon next door, she put a chair under the knob.

She slept well that night, despite a confused state of mind that would have kept her awake if she'd been at home. Her adventures with Guthrie had exhausted her.

Early the next morning, before the sun was even up, she awakened to wash and dress. Knowing she would have to ride, she wore her dusty divided skirt and the soiled shirtwaist that went with it. She had just finished pinning up her hair when someone knocked at her door.

She opened it, expecting to find Guthrie standing there. Instead, she was confronted by Marshal Teemo and a man she didn't recognize. Her heart slammed against her rib cage and sent color flooding into her face as she considered the possibility that Guthrie had betrayed her true identity and purpose. It seemed likely that she was about to be arrested for conspiring to break Mr. Flynn out of jail.

"Mornin', Miss Flynn," the marshal said cordially, touching the brim of his impeccably brushed hat.

Caroline remembered with a second jolt that Guthrie had introduced her to the lawman as Seaton's sister. "Good morning," she said, barely able to squeeze the words past her throat.

"This here is Mr. Rafe Binchly, ma'am," the marshal continued. "He's the man that witnessed the robbery and killing."

Caroline sized up the man who had been partially responsible for Mr. Flynn's conviction—he was tall and slender and completely nondescript—but the look in his pale blue eyes was uncomfortably direct. "Good morning, Mr. Binchly," she said formally.

He shook her hand and nodded.

"Rafe and I figured you might like to join us over at the jail for some breakfast," Marshal Teemo went on. "We already invited your cousin, and he'll be along right away."

Caroline had never taken a meal in a jailhouse, and she hoped she wouldn't be making a steady habit of it in the future. She was hungry, though, and not much inclined to venture into the dining hall across the street. Besides that, she liked and trusted John Teemo. "Thank you," she said. "I'd like that very much."

A moment later, Guthrie joined them in the hall, minus his dog. He gave Caroline's elbow an eloquent little squeeze, but said nothing.

The sun was pushing away the night with slender golden fingers as Caroline and her three escorts reached the darkened street below. A smiling, cheerful woman was adding a chunk of firewood to the jailhouse stove when they came in.

Using her apron for a potholder, the woman lifted a huge

blue enamel pot from the top of the stove and poured coffee into waiting mugs. Her graying blond hair glinted in the cozy lantern light. "John," she reprimanded good-naturedly, "you might trouble yourself to introduce me."

"My wife," the marshal complied, with a slight smile.

Guthrie jumped in just as Caroline opened her mouth to speak, and it was a good thing, too. She would have offered her real name.

"This is Miss Caroline Flynn," Guthrie said. "And I'm her cousin, Jeffrey Mason." He put a slight emphasis on the first name, probably warning her to be careful how she addressed him.

After that, Caroline was afraid to say much. She was an honest person, and lies tended to snag themselves on her tongue. She enjoyed a hearty breakfast of hot blueberry muffins, fried sausage, and scrambled eggs with the men, thinking drifters and drunks must make a point of getting themselves thrown into the city jail just so they could eat Mrs. Teemo's cooking.

When the meal was done and the sun lit the sky, Caroline, Guthrie, and Mr. Binchly set out for the sight of the robbery and killing in Mr. Binchly's buckboard. Tob appeared at the last minute and bounded up into the wagon bed to ride with his tongue hanging out.

Caroline climbed back over the seat to perch beside her canine friend on a wooden toolbox. She ruffled his loose hide, and he made a sound of affectionate welcome.

Presently, Mr. Binchly stopped the wagon on a curve in the trail. There were enormous rocks up ahead, standing like giants on either side of the makeshift road.

Guthrie got down from the wagon seat and held his hands up, and Caroline let him lift her down, even though his touch sent shards of spiky fire surging through her veins. Tob jumped down after them.

Mr. Binchly gestured toward the rocks. "They was waiting for the stage on the other side of them boulders, five or six of 'em," he said, lifting one hand to rub the white stubble that covered his chin. The haunted look in his eyes tightened Caroline's throat and made it impossible for her to so much as glance in Guthrie's direction. "Two of 'em were up there," he said, gesturing toward the top of the outcropping, "and the rest were on horseback. That tall one, Flynn, he shot poor old Cal Walden dead."

"Did Mr. Walden go for his gun?" Caroline managed to ask, while Guthrie was already scrambling up the side of one of the rocks to stand in the robbers' perch.

"No, ma'am," Rafe answered sadly. "He handed over the strongbox with no trouble. Flynn just kilt him for the sport of it."

A shudder went through Caroline as she imagined the man she'd once loved and trusted shooting a man down in cold blood. *It couldn't be true,* she insisted to herself.

"How did you come to see all this?" Guthrie asked, standing on top of one of the rocks now, his hands resting on his hips. "Weren't you inside the coach?"

"I was riding beside Cal," Rafe answered, his voice quivering ever so slightly. "Didn't make no sense to stay inside when there was nobody to talk to."

Guthrie turned to survey the countryside, his face unreadable from Caroline's angle of vision. "How is it that they didn't shoot you?" he asked.

"The one with the dark eyes—Flynn—he hit me with the butt of his rifle. I reckon they thought I was dead, an old man like me. When I woke up, they was gone. I was bleedin' from my head, but I put poor Cal inside the stage and then I drove it back to Clinton."

Guthrie climbed deftly down from the top of the rock and he and Rafe paced off the scene, again and again, endlessly. Finally, Guthrie was satisfied.

He thanked Rafe for his time and lifted Caroline into the back of the wagon, where Tob immediately joined her. While Guthrie and Mr. Binchly talked quietly in the wagon seat, Caroline considered the Seaton Flynn she knew and tried again to imagine him robbing a stagecoach, killing the driver.

It proved impossible.

Guthrie was quiet after Rafe dropped them off at the hotel, and that troubled Caroline. She wished he'd look at her, tell her what he thought and, at the same time, she was afraid to read the expression in his eyes or hear what he had to say.

They checked out of the hotel and walked to the livery stable. Occasionally, Tob licked Caroline's hand, as if to reassure her, but Guthrie didn't speak until he came out leading two saddled horses, his own and a sprightly little black-and-white pinto.

Before Caroline could ask, Guthrie said flatly, "I traded my father's watch for it."

Caroline's mouth dropped open. "You can't do that," she protested, when she could speak again. "I won't let you."

In answer, he hoisted her up into the saddle. "You don't have a choice," he replied.

"But your father's watch!"

"Don't worry," Guthrie said, cordially enough, "I hated the bastard."

Caroline was silenced, at least temporarily. Guthrie had tied her carpetbag on behind her saddle, so she didn't have to carry it, and the morning was clear and bright. When Clinton was well behind them, she rode close to Guthrie and said, "You think Mr. Flynn is guilty, don't you?"

Guthrie shifted his hat on his head, and it ended up at exactly the same angle as before. "Yes," he answered, after a long moment.

Caroline felt as though she'd just taken a blow, even though she'd known from the first that Guthrie was inclined to take the dark view where Seaton was concerned. "Why are you here, then?" she asked. "Why did you trade your father's watch for a horse for me to ride if you don't intend to help me?"

He sighed and surveyed the surrounding countryside, which was largely flat and covered with grass and scrub. "If I thought you'd go home to your schoolhouse and your guardians and concentrate on finding yourself a good husband, I'd do that. But you're bound to see this thing through, no matter what, and I can't leave you on your own, knowing that. I'd never get another good night's sleep if I lived to be ninety-nine."

Caroline swallowed and gripped her saddle horn with both hands, the reins held firmly between her fingers. "I guess you probably wish you'd never met me," she said in a small voice. "That way, you could just get on with your life and marry Adabelle and everything."

"You guess right, Teacher," Guthrie answered gruffly, without meeting her eyes.

She drew in a deep breath and let it out again. "You must have found Mr. Binchly to be a credible witness."

Guthrie glanced at her, and a humorless smile curved his lips for just a moment. "He seemed to know what he was talking about."

Caroline swallowed and then bit her lip. "Yes," she said, finally. "But I still think he was wrong."

Guthrie sighed.

"Do you?" Caroline asked, feeling a necessity to make conversation.

"Do I what?" Guthrie retorted irritably.

"Do you wish you'd never met me?"

He gave her a sidelong glance and considered his answer for a long time. "No," he said. "But I probably will before this is over."

Caroline was jubilant. Whatever might happen later, Guthrie was glad he knew her. She didn't stop to ask herself why that was important. "Maybe you won't," she ventured. "Maybe you'll tell your grandchildren that you helped save an innocent man from the gallows."

His tone was wry, and he didn't look at her as he leaned forward, resting his forearm on the pommel of the saddle. "And maybe I'll never have any grandchildren, Teacher. Thanks to you, I might spend the rest of my life in a federal prison."

The thought chilled Caroline. "That would be ironic," she observed, "considering your reputation as a raider."

"I'm glad you think so," Guthrie responded dryly.

"Who did you kill?" The words were out of Caroline's mouth before she'd had time to consider their impact.

To her surprise, Guthrie answered the audacious question. "A man named Pedlow," he said. "He and I had a little encounter during the war. Afterward, he came looking for me."

Caroline was so filled with suspense that she could barely breathe. "And?"

"He found Anne instead. She was home alone."

A chill wove itself around Caroline's soul and closed in, threatening to smother her. The ordinary sounds—the horses' hooves on the road, Tob's panting, her own breathing—seemed to fall away in silence as she waited, not daring to prompt Guthrie in any way.

He spoke sparingly. "She died."

Caroline squeezed her eyes shut in a futile attempt to keep brutal images at bay. She knew without asking that this man Pedlow, whoever he was, had murdered Anne. "I'm so sorry," she said, reaching out to lay a hand on Guthrie's forearm.

She felt the muscles tense under her fingers, but he didn't draw away from her.

"You asked," he said, the words sounding rusty and harsh as they came from his throat. "Now you know."

After that, Caroline didn't try to make conversation. In fact, if she could have gone back in time somehow and chosen some other subject, she would have.

A little after noon, they came upon a water hole surrounded by hoofprints and stopped to water the horses Guthrie took his canteen from over his shoulder and handed it to Caroline.

"How long 'til we'll be in Laramie?" she asked, after swallowing two mouthfuls of tepid water.

Guthrie didn't look at her directly, and he took several drinks from the canteen before replying, "Three or four days, if we're lucky."

Caroline was disheartened, thinking of sleeping on the ground again. There was no telling what would happen if she had to spend that many nights sharing a blanket with Guthrie. She shielded her eyes from the bright midday sun and scanned the horizon. "Maybe there are some ranches between here and there . . ."

For the first time since before he'd admitted killing the

man who'd murdered his wife, Guthrie grinned. "We might be able to find a barn to sleep in," he predicted. "But there's still only one blanket."

Caroline looked away quickly, her cheeks hot. "I wasn't thinking about that," she lied.

Guthrie laughed. "The hell you weren't," he replied. Then he brought the inevitable beef jerky from his saddlebags and gave Tob and Caroline equal portions.

"Once this trip is over," Caroline muttered, after tearing off a bite of the dried meat, "I'm never going to eat this wretched stuff again."

Guthrie grasped her by the waist and thrust her unceremoniously back into the saddle. "Careful, Teacher," he warned. "You're tempting fate."

Privately, Caroline agreed, but she wasn't thinking about beef jerky.

Throughout the coming afternoon, dark clouds moved in, taking over the blue sky and finally obscuring it. Caroline and Guthrie traveled through the rising wind, stopping only once in the late afternoon to rest the horses, and came upon an isolated hay barn about an hour before sunset.

The structure had a roof but no walls, and it was half filled with musty-smelling baled hay. Caroline looked around, disappointed. She'd hoped for better accommodations, and maybe a woman to talk with.

"Isn't there a ranch house?"

Guthrie shrugged, holding his hat on with one hand so it wouldn't blow off and go tumbling across the prairie. "Probably. But it could be miles away, and it's going to rain like hell in about five minutes. Gather up whatever you can find for firewood while I see to the horses."

Caroline couldn't remember a time in her life when she'd been ordered about so much. Grudgingly, she searched the ground, finding only dried cow chips.

She brought back a stack and dropped them under one eave of the barn roof, her lip curled in revulsion. Guthrie chuckled as she wiped her hands on her skirts.

Thunder shook the ground, then lightning cracked the sky and came knifing down to stab at the verdant earth. The horses nickered and danced at the end of the lines that tethered them to a corner pillar of the barn, and Tob whined and tried to squirm under a haystack.

"Looks like we'll have to keep each other warm tonight," Guthrie said, his eyes dancing as he watched Caroline's response to his remark.

Caroline hugged herself and turned away. Rain pounded at the roof over their heads and poured off the edges, shutting them in behind a murky crystalline wall.

She felt Guthrie's hands come to rest on her shoulders and drew in her breath as he gently brought her around to face him.

"Caroline," he began reasonably, "stop worrying. I told you before that I'd never force you."

Her lower lip was trembling a little, and she couldn't seem to still it. Her response came tumbling out of her mouth before she could bar its way. "I'm not sure you'd have to," she confessed sadly. Behind them, just out of reach of the rain, the little cow-chip fire flickered bravely against the chill.

He took off his hat and tossed it aside to lie in the hay, then wrapped both arms around her waist. "The pull between us is mighty strong," he said, and now it sounded as if he were the one being forced. "By the saints, I tried to hold back." With a low groan of protest, he bent his head and touched his lips to Caroline's.

She was determined to stand against him, but that first warm contact brought her onto her tiptoes. She gave a soft whimper as he mounted a gentle invasion, his tongue entering her mouth to conquer. One of his hands came to rest just beneath her breast, and when his thumb swept across her nipple, a sweet, violent shiver racked Caroline.

"Sure you don't want to go back to Bolton?" Guthrie asked, in a husky voice, when the enchantment ended briefly.

Caroline rested her forehead against his shoulder, finding the fabric of his coat damp from the rain. "I'm sure," she choked out.

Guthrie's hand trailed down her back to her bottom.

Boldly, he squeezed her, following that with a painless little swat. "Don't say I didn't warn you, Teacher," he said

Then he turned and walked away.

There were pieces of fallen, rotting timber around the barn, and Guthrie added those to the blaze. They had the inevitable jerky for supper, and Guthrie made a bed for them high in the haystack.

Night came all too quickly

"I think I'll just sit by the fire for a while," Caroline said, staring down at what remained of the feeble blaze. She was freezing, and she felt pulled toward Guthrie just as surely as if he'd taken a grip on her hair

She heard his yawn from up near the roof somewhere "Rain's letting up a little," he said. "The wolves will be out soon to hunt."

Caroline rose to her feet with dignity and smoothed her skirt. Guthrie had a gun, and he knew how to use it. If she encountered any wolves, she wanted to be close to him when it happened. She climbed awkwardly up the stacked bales until she reached the little nest of dryness and warmth Guthrie had made for them.

She couldn't see his face clearly, but she sensed that he was smiling, at least inwardly. When his hand came out and closed around hers, she let him pull her down into the bed he'd made

The straw felt soft beneath her as she stretched out beside Guthrie, then curled close to him.

His hand cupped her face, the thumb stroking her cheekbone. Caroline thought she was prepared for the feel of his mouth against hers, but she wasn't. She gave a little cry and entwined her fingers in his hair.

Guthrie laid one strong leg across both of hers, and she felt his manhood against her thigh, hard and powerful. Even as her body prepared to receive him, she wondered how she could possibly accommodate his size without suffering serious injury.

He left her mouth to nibble at her neck, and all the while his fingers were undoing the buttons of her shirtwaist

Instinctively, she arched her back, offering herself. "Guthrie?"

He laid aside the fabric of her blouse and untied the ribbons of her camisole. She gasped with pleasure as he shaped a nipple with his fingers. "Yes?"

"I've never done this," she blurted, in an anxious, breathless whisper. "And I'm—I'm scared."

He bent his head and circled the taut, straining peak of her breast with the tip of his tongue before answering, "I won't lie to you, Caroline. When I take you, it's going to hurt a little, just this first time. But the things I'll do to you before that, and after, will make it all worthwhile."

Caroline thought of that other time, on the stairs behind the hotel. He'd made love to her with words then, and she'd been swamped in pleasure so deep she'd fully expected to drown in it. What would it be like to actually give herself to him?

She cupped her hand under the breast he was sampling and held it for him. "Love me, Guthrie," she pleaded, in a strangled voice. "Love me."

He took her greedily, brazenly into his mouth and suckled hard, and Caroline gave a cry not of pain, but of welcome. She felt as though her breasts had been made to nurture and please this man, and in some hidden part of her soul, she grieved that they would not nourish his children as well.

Caroline had no fear of becoming pregnant; she'd heard once that it never happened the first time a woman lay down with a man.

Needing desperately to make Guthrie feel what she was feeling, she found the crux of his thighs with her hand and spread her fingers over his manhood as it strained against his trousers. A fevered groan against her breast told her she'd found the way to power, and she fumbled with his buttons, enjoying his torment as he waited to be set free.

He raised his head and moaned when she clasped him in her fist and moved her thumb across the tip of his shaft, and Caroline was instantly intoxicated. She moved her hand up and down, and Guthrie made sounds like a man in delirium.

Finally, he clasped both her wrists and pressed them into the hay, wide of her head. He gasped like a man near to drowning as he tried to speak and ultimately gave up on the effort.

Caroline freed one hand to stroke the nape of his neck and urge him gently back to her breast.

One by one, Guthrie took away Caroline's boots, her skirt, her drawers. Her blouse lay beneath her back, and he slid her arms out of the camisole. She shivered as a cold breeze blew between her body and his, raising her nipples to eager peaks.

Guthrie braced himself above her, and his breath came in low gasps as she pushed back his trousers to touch him still more freely. "Caroline," he ground out, "say no now, if you're going to, because in another couple of minutes it will be too damn late."

Caroline knew she ought to forbid him, but she couldn't bring herself to speak or twist away. She arched her neck, and he fell to her breast with a groan, drawing at the nipple with an almost frantic hunger. He brought Caroline's hands high above her head and held them there, gripping her wrists, and the vulnerability increased her pleasure tenfold.

Finally, Guthrie released her and began kissing his way down over her rib cage and belly, and every touch of his lips excited Caroline more. When she felt the silken curtain part, she cried out and grasped Guthrie's powerful shoulders, and he lowered his mouth to her.

She tensed, not knowing that to expect, and gave a strangled moan when he flicked at her with his tongue. Her fingers delved deep into his hair. "Oh, Guthrie," she whimpered, and she didn't know whether she wanted him to stop or go on. She only knew she was pleading.

He set her legs over his shoulders and muttered against her pulsing flesh, "I want everything, Caroline. Everything." Before she could absorb that, he had claimed her again, and this time he was in earnest.

Caroline heard the calls of night animals in the darkness, wolves or coyotes, and her own cries of pleasure and finally release echoed with theirs. Guthrie lowered her gently back to the blanket on the straw, kissing the inside of her thigh before he parted from her.

She had been satisfied, but not fulfilled, and this time Caroline could not settle for just a sample of what Guthrie offered. Like him, she wanted everything.

She caught her hands behind his nape and pulled him into a kiss spiced with musk. He was lying between her legs now, and she could feel the hard heat of his shaft waiting without, like the Trojan horse outside the walls of Troy.

Caroline opened the gates to her conqueror willingly and, with a raspy exclamation, he entered her, though just barely. She moved beneath him, urging him with frantic whispers, but he would not be hurried. Her body heated by degrees, and she felt it expanding to harbor him.

"I don't want to hurt you," Guthrie said hoarsely, weaving his fingers into her tumbledown hair and stroking her high cheekbones with the pads of his thumbs.

"The needing hurts," Caroline told him. "Please, Guthrie, don't make me wait."

He bent his head to give her a light, frenzied kiss. "Caroline—"

The lack of him was a consuming, bitter ache, spreading from the center of her femininity to every part of her body and soul. Instinct sent her hips surging upward, and Guthrie could no longer restrain himself. He gave a powerful thrust, tearing through the last barrier that kept them apart, and Caroline cried out, startled by the ferocity of the pain.

Guthrie lay still within her, but his lips moved against her temple, and she held on to the soothing words he was whispering until the hurting had ebbed. Only then did he begin to move inside her, withdrawing, then gently filling her again.

As the friction increased, Caroline's responses grew more and more heated. Soon she was twisting and writhing beneath him, her hands clutching at his back, her head tossing from side to side on the blanket.

Beyond the roof and the clouds that hid the sky, the stars raced in crazy streaks and circles, pulling Caroline toward them. The pleasure, when it peaked, was so intense that she couldn't bear it, and her soul fled toward the heavens even as her body buckled beneath Guthrie's in their bed of straw

She was back inside herself in time to stroke and soothe Guthrie as he threw his head back and stiffened in her arms with a satisfaction that seemed powerful enough to tear him apart.

After several deep, desperate thrusts, he gave a loud cry his powerful body convulsing atop hers, then sank down beside her on the blanket, trembling

Chapter

❧ 9 ❧

Caroline lay close to him, her fingers lightly plowing the dense mat of hair on his chest as she waited for her insides to stop quivering. Her body was covered in a fine mist of perspiration, and so was Guthrie's

"I warned you," he said, after a very long time had passed. He'd pulled away to right his clothes

Caroline couldn't see his face, and his tone had revealed exactly nothing. "Don't spoil it, Guthrie," she said. "I'll have to deal with the truth soon enough. For now, just let me pretend that everything is the same as it was before."

It was too late. Reality was closing in around Caroline like a pack of wolves, ready to rip her to pieces. She was wanton and thoughtless, no different from her mother, and worst of all, she'd betrayed a man who loved and trusted her.

She turned onto her side with a low wail of despair and drew her knees up. Her hands covered her face, and her shoulders and back trembled painfully with the force of her grief

"Caroline," Guthrie whispered, and the name was a tender reprimand. He sat up, and drew her onto his lap, and wrapped the blanket around her to keep away the chill of a rainy night. One of his hands moved lightly over her hair. "Sweetheart, don't cry. Please." His lips touched her temple. "Everything's going to be all right, I promise."

"You p-promise!" Caroline sobbed, afraid to believe him. Her hands made fists and rested ineffectually against his chest because she couldn't make herself strike him. "H-how could you promise s-such a thing?"

He held her close, rocking her slightly. "It wasn't your fault," he assured her gruffly, "it was mine. I guess I've been set on seducing you since that day you walked into the Hellfire and Spit. One of these days, you'll marry a good man, and you'll put me right out of your mind." He dried her cheek with three fingers. "Fact is, you probably won't even remember tonight at all."

Caroline wouldn't forget that momentous night in a thousand lifetimes—she didn't even have to desire to forget, God help her—but she was too proud admit as much straight out. Furthermore, she was wounded that Guthrie could share such a shatteringly beautiful experience with her and then say the memory would fade soon, like the words of a bad poem or the events of a dream. Clearly, she was no more to him than any of the whores he'd visited over the years, but he would always be tragically special to her.

"Mr. Flynn won't want me now," she sniffled miserably. "No decent man will." Never mind that she no longer wanted Mr. Flynn either; that was none of Guthrie's business. She was going ahead with the rescue, that was the least she could do, but once Seaton was safe from the noose she would have to tell him their engagement was off. "I'll be a spinster with a past!"

Guthrie chuckled and pressed her head to his shoulder. "Shhh," he said, and there was a smile in the sound. "He's out there somewhere, this man of yours. He's decent all right. And he's going to be pleasantly surprised when he discovers he's brought a wildcat to his bed."

Caroline stiffened, insulted. "A what?"

He laughed and held her all the more tightly, and that felt almost as good as his loving had. Caroline couldn't consciously remember anyone holding her in their arms. "A wildcat," he answered. "Too many women just lie there under a man, stiff as a board, and wait for him to finish."

Heat suffused Caroline's face at the reminder, and self-doubt filled her soul. Real ladies didn't kick and claw and writhe and shout; they endured, closing their eyes and thinking of other things until it was all over. She began to cry again, this time softly. Forlornly.

Guthrie laid her gently on the straw and tucked the blanket around her, then he left without saying a word. And even though he was the man who had spoiled Caroline forever, she ached for the strength of his arms around her and the warmth of his shoulder under her cheek.

He returned after several minutes and, by then, Caroline's eyes had adjusted enough that she could see he was carrying the canteen and what looked to be a handkerchief. He moistened the cloth, parted her legs, and began washing away the traces of their lovemaking with light, sure strokes.

Caroline bit down on her lower lip, horrified that she was becoming aroused again. She prayed he couldn't sense what she was feeling, but soon he gave a hoarse chuckle and spread his hand over her belly. His thumb burrowed through the moist curls at the junction of her thighs to ply the hidden rosebud.

"A wildcat," he said again, with a certain raspy smugness. "Miss Caroline, Miss Caroline, what a little wanton you are."

A moan squeezed its way between Caroline's teeth, and she clenched her eyes shut tight. Her knees drew up and fell wide, and still Guthrie toyed with her, making her skin glow with perspiration again. And the sound of his voice stroked her sensitive place just as surely as his thumb did.

She reached up, clawed at his shoulders, tried to speak and couldn't. All that came from her throat were strangled, nonsensical sounds, primitive and raw with need.

Guthrie chuckled. "Umm, Sweet thing, you do keep a man busy." He shoved several fingers inside her, this time making no effort to be gentle, for that was not what she needed then and he knew it.

Caroline cried out in welcome, the sweet tension within

growing tighter and tighter, like the spring of a watch wound to the breaking point, and then came undone in a rapid, humming spiral. At its height, she followed Guthrie's hand high off the blanket; at its depths, sleep was waiting to claim her.

When Caroline awakened, the sky was a bright blue and she thought she must be imagining that the scent of coffee filled the crisp spring air. She scrambled into her clothes and found her hairbrush in the carpetbag Guthrie had thoughtfully left nearby. After grooming her tresses, she braided them into a single plait and climbed gingerly down from the stack of hay bales.

Guthrie handed her a mug of steaming coffee and the inevitable piece of jerky.

"Thank you," she murmured, not quite able to meet his eyes. After all, he'd made love to her the night before, not once but twice, and he'd called her a wildcat straight out. Now she had no idea how to talk to him.

"Are we going to pretend it didn't happen?" he asked, and there was no condemnation or anger in his voice, only honest curiosity.

Caroline made herself look at him, perhaps as penance. Though he needed a shave, he was every bit as disturbingly attractive as he had been the night before.

This would never do.

She took a sip of her coffee and regarded him thoughtfully for a long time before answering, "Yes. And we're going to see that nothing like it ever occurs again."

His lips slanted in a delighted smile, and his eyes danced under the brim of his hat. A person would think someone with a copper mine could afford decent headgear, Caroline reflected.

"What about Flynn?" he asked presently. "Do you plan to casually mention to him that you and I—"

Caroline reached out and pressed her fingers to his soft lips, unable to listen to the rest. "Yes," she said miserably "I'm going to tell him exactly what happened. It would be wrong to deceive him."

This time, it was Guthrie who averted his eyes. He watched a couple of deer grazing in the distance as he raised his cup to his mouth.

He wasn't getting off that easily, not after what he'd done. "What about Adabelle?" Caroline demanded. "Will you tell her?"

"Probably not," he replied, sometime later, with a long sigh.

Caroline could barely believe her ears. "What?"

Guthrie shrugged. "It will only hurt her. And it isn't as though you and I mean anything to each other."

His words, as quietly as they were delivered, crushed Caroline's spirit beneath them like the wheels of an oncoming locomotive. She rose and turned away, her hands trembling as she used them both to raise her mug to her lips. He'd put her into the same class as the whores he dealt with, and that bruised her in tender places.

She felt him behind her, even before he laid his hands on her shoulders and turned her to face him.

"What's wrong?"

She made herself smile as she shook her head. "Nothing. You're right—we mean nothing to each other. We're completely unsuited."

Her lips curved gently at that, and he touched her face with the tips of his fingers. "Um-hmm," he replied. And then he kicked dirt over the fire he'd made with pieces of wood found around the floor of the barn the night before.

"That settles it, then," Caroline said.

Guthrie nodded, but his eyes seemed to be focused on her mouth.

She retreated a step. "Naturally, I'll expect you to honor your word as a gentleman and keep your distance at night."

He chuckled and caught her chin lightly in one hand. "I'm no gentleman," he warned, his eyes twinkling, "and I haven't given my word on anything." With that, he turned and walked away to saddle the horses.

Caroline was right behind him. "Just one moment, Mr. Hayes," she said, in her best schoolteacher voice. "I'm afraid I must demand your promise—"

He turned and met her gaze with a level stare. "You're in no position to demand anything, Teacher," he interrupted. "In case you've forgotten, I'm doing the leading and you're doing the following."

Caroline raised her chin a notch. "That may be true," she replied, with dignity, "but it doesn't entitle you to the use of my body. I'm not one of your prostitutes, Mr. Hayes, and I'll thank you to remember that."

His grin was smooth and quick as mercury, and he sketched a very Southern bow. "I'd never impune your character by comparing you to lowly women," he assured her. "But you're not exactly a lady, either."

Caroline whirled, flushed and uncertain whether she'd been slandered or praised. She hurried around to the other side of the barn to tend to private business. When she returned, Tob was barking, eager to be on his way, and Guthrie had already mounted his gelding. Although Caroline was anything but an experienced rider, she would have died before asking for help.

She gripped the saddle horn, planted one foot in the stirrup, and hoisted herself up.

Guthrie waited until she was settled to ask, with exaggerated innocence, "Aren't you forgetting something?"

Only then did Caroline remember her carpetbag. After glaring at her companion for a moment, she swung down from the saddle and climbed up into the hay to find her valise. By the time she was mounted on the pinto mare again, Guthrie was way out ahead of her. Tob lingered, waiting for her, his agitated bark bidding her to hurry.

Gritting her teeth, Caroline spurred her mount to a gallop and closed the distance between herself and Guthrie.

Stopping only for brief breaks, they rode until late afternoon, when they came upon an isolated ranch.

The sole inhabitant, an elderly man wearing a derby hat and coveralls with no shirt underneath greeted them at the front door of the cabin. He was scowling and pointing a double-barreled shotgun at Guthrie's chest.

"State your business!" he barked.

Guthrie smiled in that leisurely way of his and leaned

forward in the saddle. "Take it easy, old-timer," he said. "All the missus and I want to do is water our horses."

The rancher squinted at them from beneath the dusty brim of his hat, and his scowl gave way to a toothless grin. Evidently, his desire for company outweighed his sense of caution. Caroline knew that some of these ranchers didn't lay eyes on another human being for months at a time.

"Well, see to the horses and come on in," the old man said, propping his shotgun against the wall of his cabin. "Name's Efraim Fisk."

"Guthrie Hayes," responded Caroline's escort.

"Since when am I 'the missus'?" Caroline hissed, keeping one eye on the beaming Mr. Fisk.

"If he knew you were just my woman," Guthrie whispered back, grinning as he lifted her down from the saddle, "he might expect me to share you."

Caroline trembled with fury, but there was nothing she could do. " 'Just your woman' indeed," she breathed, through her teeth.

He let her slide down the length of him before waggling a finger in front of her nose. "Don't press me to prove my point, Teacher," he told her in a jovial undertone. "There are a lot of long, lonely miles between here and Laramie."

"You got any chewin' tobaccy?" Mr. Fisk wanted to know. He was standing in the flow of a breeze, and the smell of him made Caroline's eyes water.

Since Caroline had never seen Guthrie chew tobacco, she was surprised when he produced a tin of the stuff from his saddlebags and tossed it to the rancher with a friendly smile.

Mr. Fisk opened the lid, dipped in a finger, and filled one cheek with tobacco. His eyes wandered over Caroline's frame just as though they had a perfect right, and that made her stiffen.

"Like to come inside and set a spell?" he asked.

If he smelled this bad in the open air, Caroline could well imagine what he'd be like in the confines of a ten-by-twelve-foot cabin. She declined with a polite smile and a shake of her head. "I'm fine, thank you," she said.

Guthrie was busy drawing water up from the well. He

filled the canteen first—Caroline's face ached at the memory of him washing her so intimately the night before—then let Tob and the horses drink their fill.

"I got a nice mutton stew in the house there," Mr. Fisk cajoled and, while Caroline sympathized with his loneliness, she wouldn't have eaten anything he'd cooked to save herself from starvation.

Guthrie scanned the western sky. The land unfolded into the horizon like a bumpy brown blanket. "I reckon we have time to stay a while," he said.

Mr. Fisk beamed with delight, turning and hobbling back into the cabin, and Caroline fixed Guthrie with a desperate stare. "Why?" she whispered balefully. "He probably cooked that poor sheep hooves, wool, and all."

Guthrie's eyes laughed, though his lips only quivered slightly. "Don't forget the tongue and eyeballs," he replied, propelling her toward Mr. Fisk's gaping front door

The inside of the tiny cabin smelled even worse than Caroline had expected it to, but she couldn't help being touched by the way their host scrambled about picking up shirts and boots. He wanted the place neat for company.

"The missus is carrying," Guthrie said confidentially, as Mr. Fisk took a kettle from a hook inside the fireplace and set it in the middle of the table. "That makes her a little fussy about what she eats"

Carrying? Caroline thought. Then she realized he meant carrying a child, and embarrassment made her drop her gaze.

Somehow, Guthrie managed to spoon and chew and convince Mr. Fisk he was eating the half-spoiled stew without ever putting a bite into his mouth. When the rancher went out to fetch a jug from the barn, Guthrie set the bowl on the floor and Tob gobbled up the contents.

"You'd be welcome to bed down in the barn tonight," Mr. Fisk said, when he returned, uncorking the earthenware jar he carried and handing it to Guthrie

Guthrie raised it to his lips and drank—Caroline saw him swallow—then expelled a huffing breath and dragged one arm across his mouth. "Thanks," he answered. "That's mighty kind of you."

Caroline kicked him under the table. Even though night was coming, and there were probably Indians and other menaces abroad, she felt uneasy in that depressing place and eager to move on.

She smiled warmly at Mr. Fisk. "Don't you have to get back to your cattle?"

"Sheep," Mr. Fisk corrected her, after taking a healthy swig from the bottle. The tiny red and purple veins on his nose seemed to writhe like little snakes when he reached to pass the jug back to Guthrie. "I got sheep. Right now, my brother Feenie is mindin' 'em."

Feenie Fisk. Caroline savored the name for a moment and widened her smile. "We wouldn't want to put you out," she said earnestly. "The—mister and I, we'll just be moving on—"

"We'll stay," Guthrie interceded.

"Believe I'll see if that ole hound dog of your'n is diggin' in my rutabaga patch," Mr. Fisk said diplomatically, rising from his chair and faltering out the door.

"I don't like it here," Caroline whispered to Guthrie, the moment the older man disappeared. "I want to leave!"

He aligned his nose with hers, and she could smell the moonshine on his breath. "Then you just go right ahead and leave, Teacher. And when you catch up with that Shoshone hunting party we've been trailing, you tell them hello for me."

Caroline's eyes went wide, and she felt the color drain from her face. "You saw them?"

"I saw their tracks and what was left of their campfire. We're just lucky they didn't stop by last night and roast Tob for supper."

"You're just trying to scare me," Caroline protested. But she was thinking of the distance they still had to travel, and of all the terrible stories she'd heard about Indian attacks. "Aren't you?"

He regarded her solemnly. "What do you think?"

131

Caroline shifted on her upturned orange crate, which was doubling as a chair. "I'll stay," she said, in a generous tone.

Guthrie gave her braid a gentle tug. "Good. Then you'll probably get to keep this. Now, don't give me any more trouble or I'll suggest that you clean the cabin from top to bottom to thank Mr. Fisk for his kind hospitality."

"You don't have the nerve."

He raised his eyebrows in silent question as he stood. Pausing at the door, he said, "I'm going to settle the horses in the barn. While I'm gone, I'd like you to reflect on how a good wife comports herself."

Caroline shot to her feet, her fists clenched at her sides, and then sank disconsolately back to her orange crate again. There was no way she could retaliate, since she depended upon this man for safe passage to Laramie. Poor Adabelle, she thought. The woman's life was going to be a misery.

Except at night, of course. That just might make up for everything.

When she was sure Guthrie was gone, Caroline stood and went outside, where she shaded her eyes with one hand and scanned the horizon for signs of Indians. Satisfied that a massacre wasn't imminent, she proceeded to the barn at what she hoped was a circumspect pace.

Guthrie was grooming his tired horse when she walked in, and although he acknowledged her arrival with a grin, he didn't speak or stop his work. Mr. Fisk was tending the pinto mare, and he was doing enough talking for everybody.

Caroline sat down on a musty bale of hay and pretended to be reflecting on how a good wife comports herself.

After the horses had been taken care of, Mr. Fisk announced that he felt festivelike and slaughtered a hen that had stopped laying. Smiling demurely and batting her eyelashes at Guthrie whenever he looked at her, Caroline dutifully cooked up a dinner of chicken and dumplings, mashing a panful of boiled rutabagas for good measure.

Mr. Fisk allowed as how it was the best meal he'd had since Christmas of '68 and offered to sleep out in the barn himself, so that Caroline and Guthrie could have his bed.

Caroline was certain the barn was cleaner, but she didn't want any more trouble with Guthrie, so she kept her opinion to herself. Guthrie smiled and thanked the old man and said he liked to sleep where he could keep an eye on his horse when he was away from home.

Mr. Fisk was gracious and provided them with a kerosene lantern to light their way through the darkness to the barn.

Tob, who had dined on the remains of the mutton stew, trotted along beside Caroline, nuzzling her palm every now and then with a cool, wet nose. Her mind was on the dilemma of how to spend another night with Guthrie Hayes without giving in to his practiced charms and making a wanton of herself all over again.

Inside the barn, he steered her toward the rickety ladder leading into a hayloft. "I tossed the blanket up earlier," he said. And then he turned down the wick in the lantern and the barn was pitch dark, except for a few stray beams of moonlight coming in through the cracks in the wall. "After you, Mrs. Hayes," he added, giving her a brazen little pat on the bottom.

Caroline's choices were limited, so she climbed the ladder, but she was fuming inside. In the hayloft, she found the blanket easily, since there was a window to let in the light of the moon, and began making a bed in the straw.

"That was a fine supper you made in there," Guthrie said, plunking down on an upended bucket to pull off his boots. "That stage-robbing, trigger-happy beau of yours doesn't deserve a woman like you."

Caroline wasn't about to tell Guthrie she'd decided not to marry Seaton. She didn't want to have to explain the reasons. She sat down on the blankets and kicked off her own boots, "He probably won't even *want* a woman like me."

"He will if he has any sense," Guthrie replied, making a distinctly masculine sound as he stood up and stretched. "Wildcats are rare, and they're precious."

Caroline settled herself as close to the edge of the make-shift bed as she could. She lay with her back to Guthrie,

133

praying he wouldn't touch her, because she knew if he did, she'd be lost. For all that, she couldn't resist asking, "Is Adabelle a wildcat?"

Guthrie made a production of getting into bed and making himself comfortable. "I hope so, Teacher," he yawned. "I really hope so."

Something skittered out of the straw, just a few feet from where Caroline lay, and stared at her with close-set crimson eyes. She inched a little nearer to Guthrie. "You'd think Mr. Fisk and his brother would be nervous, living clear out here all alone, wouldn't you?"

Guthrie yawned heartily and stretched again. His arm came to rest lightly across Caroline's hip. "Go to sleep, Wildcat," he said. "We'll be getting an early start tomorrow."

Caroline ran her tongue over her lips. That thing with the red eyes was still looking at her—speculatively. "I'd appreciate it if you wouldn't refer to me as Wildcat," she said primly.

He chuckled and drew her into the curve of his body. "I know," he answered. "But I like the sound of it, so I'll probably go right on doing it."

Caroline closed her eyes, hoping the watchful creature would go on about its business. The next thing she knew, dawn was breaking and the straw around them glowed as though it had been spun into gold during the night.

And Guthrie was poised over her, his eyes smiling.

Caroline knew what he wanted, and she knew she should refuse him, but somehow, the words just didn't come. She arched her neck and bit down hard on her lower lip as Guthrie opened her blouse and her camisole to find her breasts.

He suckled slowly, gently, until Caroline was whimpering deep down in her throat and her hips were twisting beneath his, seeking any contact he would allow her. With her own hands, she unbuttoned her skirt and pushed it down, along with her drawers.

Guthrie entered her smoothly, in one long, gliding stroke,

and she welcomed him by lifting herself high to receive him. He cupped his hands under her bottom and groaned into the flesh of her neck as he nibbled there.

"Have mercy, Wildcat," he breathed

But there was no mercy in Caroline. Not for Guthrie Hayes, anyway.

Chapter
10

Release wrung a series of throaty cries from Caroline, and Guthrie muffled them by laying a hand over her mouth. A moment later, he gave up his seed, muttering a raspy exclamation as his body arched repeatedly against Caroline's.

He lay entwined with her until his breathing returned to normal. Then, without a word, Guthrie rose, fixed his clothes, and climbed down the ladder.

Caroline knew despair awaited her beyond the lingering shimmer of pleasure that enclosed her like a cloud, and she held it off as long as she could. Guthrie returned with a bucket of warm water and her carpetbag just as she was beginning to hurt.

He said nothing. He just set the bucket and the valise where Caroline could reach them and climbed back down the ladder.

Caroline took a handkerchief from the bag and gave herself an impromptu bath. Once she'd washed, she put on clean drawers and camisole, then the same old shirtwaist and skirt. It would be grand, she thought distractedly, to get back to a civilized way of life.

When she reached the cabin, her hair was freshly brushed

and braided and her face and body had been scrubbed. She felt equal to another day on the trail, if not enthusiastic.

Guthrie was frying eggs at the cabin stove when she came in, and his eyes moved over her once in intimate affection before he said, "Sit down, Wildcat. Breakfast is ready."

Caroline looked around even as she took a seat on the upended crate she'd used the night before. "Where is Mr. Fisk?"

Guthrie shrugged one shoulder as he peppered the eggs from a metal shaker. "He's around somewhere."

The timbre of his voice touched things deep inside Caroline that were still tender from his lovemaking, and she shifted on the crate. "Will we be moving on today?"

He scooped two eggs onto a surprisingly clean plate and set them in front of her. They stared up at her like two enormous golden eyes.

"Yes," Guthrie answered.

Caroline picked up her fork and examined it carefully before starting in on her breakfast. "What about the Indians?"

Guthrie sat down next to her with a plate and fork of his own, and she sensed mischief in him, rather than saw it. "I could probably swap you and the dog for safe passage to Laramie."

Before Caroline could think of a comment on that, Mr. Fisk came limping into the cabin. He'd plainly made an effort where his appearance was concerned, for his face and hands glowed with cleanliness and the chill of well water, and his bushy white hair stood out crisply under the brim of his derby hat.

"Mornin'," he said cheerily, taking eggs from the pan on the stove and dumping them onto his plate. The yolks were clearly visible in his mouth when he went on. "When Feenie finds out he missed them dumplin's of your'n, ma'am, he's goin' to spit green nickels."

Caroline muttered a modest thank you and continued to eat, knowing she'd need her strength for the day ahead. Besides, unappealing as they were, the eggs had one thing in their favor: they weren't beef jerky.

"You and Feenie ought to get yourselves some wives," Guthrie said, in the same tone he might have suggested that they buy wire for a chicken pen or curtains for the cabin's one window.

Mr. Fisk chuckled at the notion. "I reckon one could probably do for the both of us, since one of us is gone most o' the time."

Caroline choked and Guthrie gave her an indulgent pat on the back.

"Two women would be twice the trouble all right," he agreed thoughtfully, though Caroline saw an imp dancing in his eyes.

She glared at him disapprovingly. He was in dire need of some civilizing, and she didn't envy Adabelle Rogers the job.

After breakfast, Caroline cleaned up the dishes while Guthrie went back to the barn to saddle the horses. Although she would be glad to put Mr. Fisk's ranch behind her, she wasn't unmoved by the delight he'd taken in their company.

"We slept comfortably in your barn, Mr. Fisk," she said formally, when she and Guthrie were about to leave. "We're obliged."

For the first time in their acquaintance, Mr. Fisk removed his hat, revealing a bald pate dappled with large freckles. "You come back and visit again, ma'am," he said earnestly.

On impulse, Caroline kissed his grizzled old cheek, and he flushed with pleasure at the small intimacy.

When she and Guthrie and the dog were well away, Guthrie turned in the saddle to grin at Caroline. "That was a kind thing you did back there. Old Fisk probably can't rightly recall the last time anybody touched him with affection."

Caroline was abashed by his praise and by the wild, disproportionate pleasure it brought her. When it came to this man, she had about as much dignity as Tob. "That remark he made about sharing a wife with his brother nearly sent me running for the hills," she admitted. "I do believe it was the most scandalous thing I've ever heard anyone say."

Guthrie chuckled and brought a cheroot from his shirt pocket. After lighting it and taking a deep draught of the smoke, he finally answered, "You take life too seriously, Teacher. It wasn't as though he was going to rush out and drag some woman home, you know."

Caroline couldn't help smiling at the picture that came to her mind. Whatever her regrets about making love with Guthrie, she was suffused with a sense of well-being and general happiness, and she decided to enjoy it while she could.

That night they camped beside a stream, and Guthrie caught trout for their supper. Although Caroline had sworn she wouldn't let him make love to her again, he bent her over a waist-high boulder and glided into her femininity from behind, and she welcomed him with a primitive shout of pleasure.

The following day, long about midmorning, they rode into Laramie.

Now that she was within mere minutes of facing Seaton Flynn, the man she had once believed she loved, Caroline's newfound joy in the mysteries of womanhood was replaced by a sense of shame. She was, she reminded herself, no better than her strumpet of a mother. Perhaps in a few years she would be reduced to drinking hard liquor and bringing strange men to some shoddy little room somewhere, just as Kathleen had done. Would she even give up her own children, because some man who could give her pleasure and brandy told her to?

"What in hell are you thinking about?" Guthrie demanded irritably, interrupting the gloomy progress of her contemplations. "You look like somebody just dipped you in flour."

The noise and energy of Laramie clamored all around Caroline, distracting her. She heard shots in the distance, and piano music, and men and women laughing together inside the numerous saloons. "What if we made a baby, Guthrie?" she asked, barely able to push the frightening words past her throat. She loved Guthrie and she hadn't been able to resist him, despite the risk. Now, however, the fairy tale was ending and reality was pressing close.

He didn't answer her question, maybe because he didn't hear, and maybe because he didn't know what to say. He spurred his gelding a little ahead of Caroline's mare and dismounted in front of the marshal's office.

Seaton was thinner than Caroline remembered, and his knuckles were white where he gripped the bars of his cell. Caroline looked into his eyes and was frightened by the fact that all she felt was numbness.

"I knew you'd come," he said, reaching out for her with one hand. His dark eyes, so expressive and bright, seemed to caress her.

Caroline kept her distance, though she did manage a faltering smile. Her first impulse was to confess that she'd given herself to Guthrie, not just once but several times, but she checked it. This was neither the time nore the place for such confidences, but she couldn't delay breaking off the engagement for another moment; her conscience wouldn't let her.

"There's something I have to tell you," she said, in a breathless rush. "We can't be married."

Behind her, in the marshal's office, she could hear Guthrie talking quietly with the lawman.

Seaton's voice was plaintive, his skin waxen. "What?"

"I still mean to help you," she whispered, taking a step closer in her earnest desire to make reparation for sins she'd thought better of confessing.

Without warning, he reached out and caught hold of her braid, pressing her close to the bars, wrenching her head back a little too roughly. All of this took place before she could catch a breath, let alone cry out.

There was something urgent in the way his lips crushed hers, devouring them. When his tongue invaded her mouth, her secret places didn't flower the way they did with Guthrie, and she laid both hands to Seaton's chest and pushed him back.

He looked at her in anger and wounded surprise.

"No, Mr. Flynn," she said, speaking to him in the formal way he'd always preferred. "Things will have to be different between us from now on." She knew her cheeks were flaming, knew he believed her chagrin stemmed from virginal innocence. And she thought the glorious disgrace of her behavior with Guthrie would finish her off.

The door to the office opened, and Guthrie stood beside her.

"Flynn," he said. That single word was at once a question and a statement and a summing up.

Seaton's beautiful dark eyes narrowed. "Who are you?" he demanded.

Caroline braced herself for an explosion, but it didn't come. Guthrie's voice was icily cordial. "My name is Guthrie Hayes," he said.

Seaton's gaze moved for Caroline to Guthrie and back again, and she told herself it was impossible for him to know they'd been intimate just by looking at them. "What's your business, Mr. Hayes?"

"We'll discuss that when we're alone," Guthrie replied, catching Caroline in a sidelong glance. She lingered, since she'd already determined that the other two cells were empty.

Finally, Guthrie cleared his throat pointedly.

Caroline laid a hand to her chest. "You don't mean—but this was my idea—"

"Out," Guthrie said.

Caroline hesitated, but then she remembered that Seaton's fate was essentially in Guthrie's hands. She couldn't afford to flout his orders, however much she might want to do that. Keeping her chin high, and being careful not to make eye contact with either man, Caroline left the jail as though it had been her own choice to do so. She proceeded regally through the marshal's office, but the moment she reached the sidewalk, she ran around to the back of the building.

Since there was no glass in Seaton's window, just bars, Caroline could hear well enough through the opening.

"—why I'm innocent," came Seaton's voice. His tone was at once accommodating and bristly.

141

"I'm afraid it's going to take more than your word to convince me," Guthrie responded quietly. "The territory has a good case against you."

Caroline thought she heard the cell bars rattle and, in her mind, she saw Seaton's strong hands tightening around them again. "Damn it," he rasped, "I want to know what you're doing, traveling with Caroline."

Her heart practically stopped beating while she waited for Guthrie's answer. "Let's just say I work for the lady," he replied, after a long time, and Caroline let out her breath. "She seems to think you're husband material."

Seaton didn't sound reassured. "Still, a man and a woman, alone on the trail—"

"Caroline's a woman all right," Guthrie said evenly

Caroline closed her eyes. Her own wanton cries of the night before echoed in her ears, and she could feel the smooth boulder beneath her breasts and her belly, and the fiery strokes of Guthrie's shaft as he pleasured her. Just before the final thrust, he'd clasped the undersides of her knees in both hands and pressed them up and wide apart, and the universe had splintered before Caroline's eyes.

"If you've touched her," Seaton said, "I'll kill you."

There was a smile in Guthrie's voice, a slow and insolent smile. "Considering that I'm probably the only thing standing between you and a noose, you might want to be more diplomatic in the future."

Tob appeared at Caroline's side just then and whimpered, nudging her thigh with his nose. He probably wanted whiskey, the shameless sot.

"Be that as it may," Seaton countered seriously, "I meant what I said."

Guthrie passed off the threat—and Caroline—with an idle chuckle. "Don't worry, Flynn. Skinny schoolmarms with tongues like cross-saw blades don't appeal to me. I like my women soft and sweet and warm."

Stung, Caroline rushed around to the front of the building again. She was just stepping onto the sidewalk when Guthrie came out the door.

His gaze came unerringly to her, and his lips tilted as he

noticed her flushed face and flashing eyes. "If you don't want to hear things that might upset you, Wildcat," he said flatly, "you shouldn't eavesdrop under jailhouse windows."

With that, he slapped his hat against one thigh and he and Tob disappeared into the saloon next door.

Caroline went a few steps toward the swinging doors herself, then stopped. She wouldn't be any help to Mr. Flynn if she was in jail herself, and in many towns it was illegal for a woman to enter such an establishment.

She crossed to the other side of the street and angrily paced back and forth along the wooden walk, heedless of the stares she drew.

After Fisk's moonshine, and the headache it had left him with, Guthrie didn't care if he never saw another glass of whiskey as long as he lived. He bought a drink for Tob and set it in the sawdust so he could lap it up right out of the glass.

Leaning back against the bar, Guthrie assessed the clientele. Business was slow; there were two cowboys at the pool table, and the railing edging the upstairs mezzanine was lined with exotic wildlife in brightly colored dresses.

Guthrie chose a sturdy redhead, because she was the least like Caroline, and she sashayed down the stairs, the pea green feathers in her hair bobbing over her painted face. Her dress was a vivid shade of blue and, coupled with the feathers, its effect was jarring.

Reaching him, the soiled dove cuddled up close to his chest and purred, "My name is Cozy. What's yours?"

Guthrie couldn't help chuckling. "Did your mama name you that," he drawled, "or did you make it up yourself?"

She wriggled against him. "It was give to me," she said. "I liked it, so I kept it. Don't you think I'm cozy?"

He was still weak in the knees from last night's session with Caroline, but Guthrie had never been one to purposely hurt a lady's feelings. "Cozy as hell," he replied. He sure hoped Caroline hadn't gone and spoiled fleshy women for him with her wildcat ways. "Listen, darlin', for right now I just need some questions answered."

She linked her arm through his and led him behind a

curtain into a shadowy enclosure containing a chaise and a big, dusty potted palm. "Ask away, honey," she said, sitting down on the velvet upholstered lounge and patting the place beside her.

Guthrie removed his hat and leaned forward, resting his forearms on his knees. His head was turned toward Cozy, and his smile was affable. "You know a man named Seaton Flynn?"

Cozy's big white shoulders, bared by her low-cut dress, moved in a shudder. "He's that handsome bastard with the dark eyes—the one that killed the stagecoach driver."

"You seem pretty sure he's guilty."

"I am. And I'm pretty sure he's a bastard, too."

Guthrie turned his hat by the brim. Before he stood up with Adabelle, he was going to have to get himself a new one. He took a silver dollar from the pocket of his vest and tossed it into Cozy's broad lap. "Tell me about him."

"None of the girls like to take him," Cozy sighed, smoothing her satin skirt and palming the dollar in the same motion. She warmed the coin in her hand for a moment, then tucked it into the bodice of her dress. "He's mean. Likes to make a lady holler a little, and not because she's wanting more, neither."

Guthrie's stomach twisted as he imagined Flynn hurting Caroline and, for the first time since he'd found Annie all broken and bruised, he wanted to kill. He calmed himself with the silent reminder that many men were gentle with wives and rough with whores.

Cozy wasn't bothered by his stillness. "Flynn killed that driver, all right. And he gambled away some of the gold right here in the Green Goat."

Guthrie frowned. "He had a law office up in Bolton. People looked up to him, thought he was making a good living." *People?* Guthrie scoffed to himself. *Caroline.*

"He's no more a lawyer than I am," Cozy said. "But he's talked about some woman he knew up there. Made some of the girls answer to her name whilst he was with them."

It wasn't necessary to ask the name; Guthrie knew it only too well. He patted Cozy's hand, with its big, cheap rings.

"Thanks, darlin'," he said, rising from the lounge and putting his hat on again.

He scanned the shadowy interior of the saloon once, out of old habit, before stepping past the curtain, half expecting Caroline to be peering at him through one of the murky windows.

Instead, she was pacing up and down the sidewalk on the other side of the street.

There was something about her that made Guthrie want to grin, even in the damnedest circumstances. He composed his face, summoned the dog with a slap to one thigh, and stepped out of the Green Goat Saloon.

Caroline stopped her pacing, arms folded, and waited while Guthrie crossed the street. "Well?" she snapped.

"Well, what?" Guthrie countered, leaning forward so far that his nose was practically touching hers.

"I'm not paying you to dally around in saloons!" Caroline hissed.

"As I've told you before," Guthrie pointed out, "you're not paying me at all. And you're not going to have to, Teacher."

Caroline would have sworn she felt the sidewalk buckle beneath her feet. "Y-you're leaving?"

Guthrie straightened, his hands resting on his hips. "I told you I'd make my decision after I'd talked to the marshal and Flynn himself, and I've done that. He's guilty, Caroline."

She was already shaking her head. Seaton couldn't be guilty, she wouldn't accept it. She would have known. "Guthrie, please—"

He took her arm and propelled her down the walk. Although his jaw was set tight as a bear trap, he dispensed a few grimacelike smiles to passersby. "Wire home for money, Wildcat," he said, when they stopped in front of the doors to the bank, with their green shades. "You're going to need a stagecoach ticket back to Bolton."

Caroline stopped him when he would have strode away. "That's it?" she said miserably. "You're just going to leave?"

Guthrie was as cold and expressionless as if they'd been strangers. "Yes."

To her mortification, Caroline could feel tears burning behind her eyes. "I see," she said, holding them back

"Good," he replied, turning to walk away.

"Give my regards to Adabelle."

He stopped, his back stiff, then looked at Caroline over one shoulder. "I imagine you'll meet her, once I've brought her home."

Not for anything would Caroline have let him see how those words injured her. "I imagine so," she said.

"You will go home, won't you?"

Caroline knew there was only one way to truly let go of Guthrie and make some sort of life for herself from the ruins of her dreams. "Yes," she said quietly. "I'll go home."

She saw mingled pain and relief in his face. "As for what happened between us—"

Caroline stopped him because she couldn't bear to hear him out, knowing what he'd say. "There's no need for either of us to think about that again, I guess," she said. "Or talk about it."

Guthrie nodded. "Good-bye, Caroline," he said hoarsely. And then he had his back to her, and he was striding down the sidewalk, and this time he didn't turn around.

Caroline stood in front of the bank, sucking deep breaths in and blowing them out until she was sure she could speak without breaking down and weeping. Then she went into the building and asked a clerk to wire the bank in Bolton for a part of her funds.

After that, she hurried across to the general store and bought herself a pair of denim trousers, as well as a set of men's long-handled underwear, a broad-brimmed hat, a derringer, and bullets.

With all her purchases wrapped in a paper bundle and tied with string, she proceeded to the hotel, where she secured herself a room and asked that fresh, hot water be brought up for a bath. Once she was clean, Caroline dressed in the trousers and shirt, saving the underwear for the trail, and put on her own boots. Then she took the clothes she'd brought along on the trip to a Chinese laundry to be washed and pressed.

She drew her share of stares, being clad like a man, but Caroline didn't pay them any mind. She had more important things to think about than Laramie's opinion of her personal appearance.

She was dining in the hotel's small restaurant when, as luck would have it, Guthrie ambled in. He glanced at her once in passing, then whirled around and gaped.

"Caroline?" he demanded, in a disbelieving whisper, narrowing his eyes at her.

She smiled. "Hello, Mr. Hayes," she said warmly "Won't you sit down?"

He had already been dragging back a chair when Caroline began to speak. Now, he dropped into it. "Why the devil are you dressed like that?"

Caroline took a bite of her steak and chewed thoroughly before answering in dulcet tones, "I can't imagine why my clothes would matter to you, one way or the other "

"They don't," Guthrie barked. There was a window beside the table and Tob was on the other side of the glass, his paws on the sill, his expression pitiful. "It's just that, well, no lady ever goes around in men's clothes."

She arched an eyebrow and ignored the remark. "Don't you ever feed that poor dog?" she asked, as Tob began to whine and slobber.

"He eats better than I do," Guthrie grumbled. "Caroline, I want to know what you're up to."

"I'm minding my own business," she replied, cutting another piece of steak. She was only too aware of Tob watching its progress from her plate to her mouth. "It's an approach I highly recommend, Mr. Hayes. You really ought to try it yourself."

Guthrie swore, though it was not clear whether he was annoyed with Caroline or the dog. Pushing back his chair, he stood, stormed into the kitchen, and returned a few minutes later with a large soup bone. He went outside and tossed it to Tob before rejoining Caroline at the table.

"You are going home?" he demanded, narrowing his eyes at her again.

Outside, Tob was chewing ecstatically on the bone. Caroline had finished her dinner, and she pushed her plate away. "Yes," she said. "I am going home." She just didn't add that she meant to take care of a few details first. She sighed. "And you're going to Cheyenne."

"Yes." Guthrie sounded almost defensive, as though he expected her to protest. "But I'll be back in Bolton in a week or two."

Caroline had a sip of her tea. She had decided to leave Bolton, once Seaton was cleared, and start an active search for her sisters. Only that knowledge made the prospect of Guthrie's arriving with Adabelle bearable. A waitress came to the table before she had to say anything, and Guthrie ordered a bowl of beef stew and some fresh bread.

"You're not planning anything stupid, are you?" he asked plaintively, when the waitress was gone again.

Caroline smiled. "Of course not," she assured him. *Just a little jailbreak,* she added mentally, as she pushed back her chair and stood. "If you'll excuse me, I'd like to get some rest. Tomorrow's going to be a long day."

Guthrie reached out, quick as a snake striking, and caught hold of her wrist. Without apparent effort, he forced her back into her chair. For all of that, the expression on his face was a contrite one. "Caroline," he said quietly, "I'm sorry. About making love to you, I mean."

He might just as well have stabbed her with a fork as apologized for that, but she managed to smile as though it didn't hurt. "Don't worry, Mr. Hayes. I'm not planning to greet Adabelle at the edge of town with an account of our time together."

"Damn it," he rasped, looking around to make sure none of the other diners could hear, "that isn't what's bothering me. I took advantage of you when I knew nothing could come of it, and I'm sorry."

"I was there, so you used me," Caroline agreed in a bright undertone, pushing back her chair again. "Believe me, I never once thought I meant anything to you, Guthrie, so kindly keep your bumbling apologies to yourself. And if you try to stop me from leaving again, I'll scream so loud your eardrums will split."

Color stained Guthrie's neck, and he set his jaw, but he didn't move when Caroline rose to walk away.

She went straight to her room, which was on the second floor of the hotel in the rear, and got out her derringer and the printed leaflet that came with it. She practiced loading and unloading the small weapon and became so caught up in the process that when she saw something move outside her window, she nearly pulled the trigger.

Tob was standing on the fire stairs outside, his muzzle squished against the glass.

Caroline put the derringer on the bedside stand and went to raise the window. The moment she did, the dog plunged into the room and cowered at her feet, making a companionable yipping sound.

"I thought you'd be off to Cheyenne by now," Caroline said, squatting down to pet the dog fondly. She hoped Adabelle would be good to Tob, though the woman was welcome to treat Guthrie any way she wanted.

Tob squirmed on the floor, enjoying the attention. A few minutes later, Caroline tried to shoo him back out the window, but he wouldn't go. Finally, she lowered the sill again and locked it. Laramie was a strange, noisy town, and she was glad of the company.

She'd just pulled the shade and was about to undress and get into bed when there was a knock at her door. Thinking Guthrie had come to collect his dog, she folded her arms and chimed, "Who's there?"

"Message, ma'am," said an unfamiliar voice. A piece of paper slid under the door, and Caroline hurried to unfold it.

She knew the forceful, oversized handwriting was Guthrie's. *Nothing will ever change the fact that you're a lady,* he'd written. *Good-bye, Wildcat. Warmest regards, G.H.*

Caroline held the note close to her heart for a moment, then she crumpled the paper and tossed it to the floor. Guthrie was a part of the past, and she had to think about the future.

Chapter

❧ 11 ❦

*T*ob reappeared, just as he always did, when Guthrie was ready to ride out the next morning. But he kept whimpering and running back toward Laramie, before reluctantly trotting along beside Guthrie's horse for a few minutes. Long after the town was out of sight, the dog was still repeating the process.

"Fool mutt," Guthrie grumbled, reining in his horse. "Caroline's gone and wrapped you right around her little finger, hasn't she? Well, damn it, just go back to her, then. I can always get another useless, no-good dog!"

Tob yipped apologetically and stretched out on the ground, his muzzle resting on his forelegs, his hindquarters quivering.

"Go on," Guthrie ordered, "get out of here. I don't have any use for an old hound like you anyway."

After one parting yowl of dismay, Tob turned and loped back toward Laramie. Guthrie waited five minutes, but the animal didn't return.

"Damn skinny schoolteacher," Guthrie groused, as he spurred the gelding and rode away. "I've heard of some low things in my life, but stealing a man's dog—"

He opened his canteen, took a long draught of fresh water,

150

and wiped his mouth on his sleeve. To hell with Caroline *and* the dog. He had sweet Adabelle waiting for him in Cheyenne.

She'd press those oversized breasts of hers to his chest and he'd forget all about Caroline. Anyway, Adabelle was the kind of woman a man wanted for his wife. You wouldn't catch *her* running all over the countryside in pants and trying to persuade total strangers to help her set up a jailbreak.

Not only that, but he probably would have gotten skinny, saucy, contentious children from Caroline, given the theory that such traits tend to run in families. Adabelle, on the other hand, was likely to give him a dozen sturdy babies with placid dispositions and musical voices.

Guthrie frowned. For the first time, the dream seemed a little, well, dull. Still, it sustained him, even though there was a strong pull toward Laramie, too. Laramie and Caroline. Guthrie told himself he was only feeling that because he missed his dog—and he didn't turn his horse around.

Against both his personal will and his better judgment, he thought of Caroline lying naked and pliant beneath him, her lithe body responding gracefully to his every command. Skinny or not, he had to concede, there in the privacy of his mind at least, Caroline had a shape a man could learn to like, with some study.

A whole lot.

After making a brief stop at the bank, Caroline proceeded to the livery stable, where she bought back the little mare that Guthrie had traded for his watch, and selected a fine horse for Mr. Flynn, too. If her daring plan was going to work, she and Seaton would need fast mounts.

Tob came barking down the road to greet her as she led the two horses out of the stable and, for one glorious moment, Caroline thought Guthrie had returned. Then, with her heart taking a little dive, she realized the dog had come alone.

Glad to have at least one friend in this uncertain world, Caroline stopped by the butcher counter at the mercantile and bought a meaty bone for Tob before squaring her shoulders and marching on toward the jailhouse. She had the little derringer tucked into the pocket of her trousers, and it was loaded. She just hoped it wouldn't go off accidentally and hurt somebody.

Like herself, for instance.

Reaching the jail, Caroline was pleased to find Mr. Flynn there alone, eating his breakfast. When he saw her, he rose off his cot so quickly that he nearly overturned his tray. His eyes bulged at the sight of her clothes.

"Good God, Caroline! Have you actually let people see you dressed like that?" If Seaton was at all unsettled by her previous announcement that their engagement was off, he gave no indication of it. Probably, she reflected charitably, he hadn't yet come to grips with the disappointment and needed time to rally his wits.

For her part, Caroline was most relieved that she wouldn't have to threaten anyone with the tiny pistol in her pocket. Later, when the danger was past, she would say farewell to Seaton, return home and begin preparations to leave again, on her quest to find Lily and Emma.

"Never mind my clothes," she said tersely. "I've got horses outside, and I've come to set you free so you can prove you're innocent."

Seaton gripped the bars and pulled at them in his haste to be liberated. "You'll have to get the keys from old Charlie—he keeps them with him all the time."

Caroline brought out the derringer and frowned at it. "Couldn't we shoot the lock off somehow?"

Before she'd had time to work the idea through, Seaton's hand shot out unexpectedly and grasped her wrist. His hold was cruel, and the surprise of that widened her eyes. He wrenched her against the bars with bruising force.

"Where's Hayes?" he rasped, prying the derringer free of her fingers with his other hand as he spoke.

Caroline blinked at him in confusion. Although she had seen hints of unseemly behavior in the lawyer before, it was only now that she consciously recognized their source. "Mr. Flynn, I must insist that you let me go—"

His grip tightened, causing Caroline to utter a little cry of pain.

"He's gone," she whispered. "He said you were guilty."

"Did he, now?" Seaton breathed, still holding her against the cold bars and pressing the end of the pistol barrel to her temple as someone came clattering into the outer office. "Charlie!" he yelled, making Caroline start violently and then shut her eyes.

The realization that Guthrie had been right all along was brutally painful.

Seaton was a thief and, worse, a killer.

"Just keep your pants on," the old man muttered, and Caroline heard the sound of keys jingling as he approached. "Damn it, this ain't a hotel, you know, and you ain't nobody fancy neither."

Regaining her senses, Caroline started to shout a warning, but Seaton must have felt her tense for the effort, because he slapped the hand that had been gripping her throat over her mouth. When she tried to bite him, she thought the strength of his fingers would break her jaw.

Charlie's small eyes nearly popped out of his head when he saw Caroline standing there against the cell bars, with the little derringer held to her head.

"Take it easy, now, Flynn," the old guard muttered wearily. "You don't want to shoot a lady."

"Unlock the door and she won't get hurt," Seaton rasped.

Caroline's mind was spinning, and she was sick with fear and disgust. She wondered wildly how she could have been so naive as to believe in this man, to *love* him.

Then, despite the dizziness and distraction induced by her terror, she realized the truth. She had never loved Seaton, but only the man she'd thought he was, the potential husband and father she'd invented in her own mind.

Charlie was holding out the key ring. "See?" he said reasonably. "I got the key right here. I'm goin' to let you out. Just don't pull that trigger."

The moment Charlie had opened the door, Seaton flung Caroline into the cell with such force that she struck the inside wall and fell. Then he stepped out and clubbed the old man hard in the side of the head with the pistol butt, and Charlie toppled, bleeding, to the floor. Seaton stood and pointed the barrel directly at Charlie's head. Caroline knew by the hard set of his jaw and the gleam in his eyes that he meant to kill him.

"Seaton, no!" she shrieked, bile rushing into her throat after the words, flinging herself across the tiny cell and covering the wounded jailer as best she could. "I beg of you—don't kill him!"

Seaton glared at her for a long moment, during which Caroline devoutly prayed for the marshal's return. He was a much younger man than Charlie, competent and strong, and if he came in time, he could prevent an escape and perhaps a murder.

Caroline thought quickly. "If you fire a shot," she burst out, "people will hear. They'll know something's wrong and come running!"

Only then did Seaton lower the gun to his side. There was sweat on his forehead now and along his upper lip. "You said there were horses outside?"

Caroline swallowed, absently patting old Charlie's big shoulder. "Two." She sighed, with resignation. It didn't look like the marshal was going to return soon enough to stop Seaton, and Caroline was annoyed. Little wonder there was so much crime in the modern world, with lawmen taking their jobs so lightly.

Seaton was poised to flee, but suddenly he came toward Caroline, where she lay on the filthy floor of the cell, still trying to shelter Charlie. Seaton gripped her chin hard and bit out, "Hayes has had you, I know he has. I swear to God, Caroline, both of you will pay for that."

Caroline just stared at him, stunned.

He deepened her shock by bending his head and kissing her tenderly, then nipping at her lower lip with his teeth and drawing back. "My time will come, Caroline. And when it does, I'll teach you what it means to give yourself to a man." He rose gracefully to his feet, still brandishing the derringer. "Have you got more bullets for this?"

Dazed by the events of the minutes just past, Caroline never thought to lie. She nodded numbly and reached into her pocket for the handful of ammunition she'd bought; all she wanted now was for Seaton Flynn to go, to leave her and Charlie in peace. The old man was gasping for breath and holding one hand to his chest as it was.

"Soon," Seaton said, touching his fingertips to his mouth and smiling. "Scream, sweet thing," he warned, in parting, "and I'll not only shoot this old coot, I'll take you with me as a hostage."

Caroline swallowed, horrified by the prospect of either event. "I won't scream," she promised.

And she didn't.

The moment she heard the outer door close behind Seaton, she ran for the marshal's gun rack and helped herself to a rifle. She just hoped it was loaded, that's all.

Running outside onto the sidewalk, she saw Seaton riding away on the back of one of the horses she'd bought with her hard-earned money. She trained the rifle sights on his left arm and pulled the trigger, and the gun went off with such thunderous force that it sent her sprawling backwards onto the wooden sidewalk.

The marshal chose that moment to appear. "What the hell?" he demanded, jerking the rifle out of Caroline's hands and dragging her to her feet in the same motion.

"He's getting away!" Caroline cried, bruised and filled with frustration. Seaton was just a speck in the distance now.

Charlie came stumbling out of the jailhouse at that moment, holding one hand to his bloody head. "Flynn broke out," he said. His eyes touched Caroline with kindly recalcitrance. "Looked to me like the little lady here brought him a gun, and she probably provided the horse for his git-away, too."

"Lock her up," the marshal said, thrusting Caroline toward Charlie and turning to mount his horse. A half dozen other men joined the impromptu posse and rode off with him.

"You're not really going to put me in *jail?"* Caroline asked in horror, as Charlie gently took her arm and squired her back inside. "I saved your life!"

"It was 'cause of you that my life was in danger in the first place," Charlie reasoned. He escorted Caroline into the very cell Seaton had occupied, closed the door with a clang, and locked it soundly.

Caroline rushed forward to grip the bars. "You don't understand!" she wailed. "I thought Mr. Flynn was innocent!"

"Don't make no never mind what you *thought,* Miss. Fact is, the man was convicted of robbery and murder, and you let him go. You'll have to stand trial for that."

She felt herself blanch. And outside her cell window, she heard a commiserating yowl that could only have come from Tob, her faithful friend.

Despondently, she turned away from the cell door and crossed to the window. Then, standing on the edge of the flimsy cot where she might be sleeping for a very long time, she peered out through the bars.

Sure enough, Tob was sitting out there among empty barrels and other refuse, staring up at her with soulful eyes. Caroline took the food that remained on Seaton's breakfast tray and tossed it out to the dog, then climbed down from the cot.

"Oh, Mr. Charlie!" she called pleasantly.

"What?" came the terse reply. The outer office was evidently full of curious townspeople who wanted to hear Charlie's account of the morning's incident.

"May I speak with you privately?"

Grumbling, Charlie appeared. His demeanor plainly showed that, in view of the fact that he'd nearly been killed, he felt entitled to a little peace and even a measure of glory. There was a huge bandage on his head, putting Caroline in mind of a painting she'd once seen of several soldiers in the Revolutionary War. "What do you want?" he snapped.

Caroline dropped her voice to a confidential level. "I need to use the facilities," she said, pained at having to speak to a man of so personal a subject.

Charlie pointed a beefy finger toward the cot. "The chamber pot's under there," he answered, and then he turned and walked out.

"Mr. Charlie!" Caroline immediately called. Somehow, she had to make the jailer listen. Using a chamber pot right there in her cell simply wouldn't afford her the required privacy.

"I said use the thunder mug under the bed!" Charlie bellowed from outside, and Caroline was so mortified that she put both hands over her face and turned away with a moan.

She waited as long as she could, but presently she was forced to take care of her business. She had barely finished when the office door swung open and a young man holding a pencil and a pad of paper appeared.

He regarded her solemnly from under the green brim of his visor. "Your name, madam?" he asked politely.

She gripped the bars, staring at him. "Why do you want to know?" she countered.

He smiled, revealing a wide gap between his front teeth. "I'll be writing about you in the newspaper."

Caroline sighed and let her forehead rest against the bars. She could just imagine Hypatia Furvis reading the account of her descent into shame, and Miss Ethel and Miss Phoebe would be positively beside themselves at the scandal. "Is that necessary?"

"You'll be famous," the eager reporter promised. "Sort of a lady outlaw."

"That's what I'm afraid of," Caroline responded dismally.

"Your name?"

She sighed. "Caroline—Hayes."

The reporter wrote busily. "Miss or Mrs.?"

"Mrs.," Caroline lied, figuring it served Guthrie right that a criminal, however inadvertently she'd run afoul of the law, was claiming to be his wife. After all, none of this would be happening if he hadn't abandoned her. "My husband is Mr. Guthrie Hayes." She was warming up to the idea. "And that's my dog right outside the window."

"Your husband lets you break other men out of jail?" the young man asked, in scandalized wonder.

Caroline sighed. "My husband left me," she said tragically. "And I only released Mr. Flynn because I sincerely believed he had been wrongly accused. Now, of course, I find myself in difficult straits."

Before the newspaper fellow could ask another question, the marshal returned.

"Get out of here, Vince," he said. He was a big, imposing man with graying hair and a dark handlebar mustache, and Caroline instinctively took a step back from the bars. His arms were akimbo as he regarded his prisoner. "You'll be happy to hear that we lost him."

Caroline's cheeks throbbed with chagrined color. "I'm not happy at all," she huffed, folding her arms. "The man is a murderer and a thief!"

"Too bad you didn't consider that before you helped him escape," the marshal replied, his voice a low, throaty rumble.

Tears rose in Caroline's eyes, but she kept them at bay. This was all a misunderstanding, and if she could just make the marshal see her side, he would surely release her. One thing was for certain: she couldn't allow herself to fall apart. "As I have explained to your assistant, Charlie—whose life I saved, by the way—I would never have brought the derringer here if I'd known what Mr. Flynn was going to do."

"You thought he'd take you with him, I reckon," the marshal said disparagingly.

Caroline drew a deep breath and let it out slowly, the way she did when she was dealing with a difficult student. Then, slowly and carefully, she explained what had happened, though she left Guthrie out of the matter of course.

When she'd finished, she fully expected the marshal to release her, but he didn't. He just shook his head and said, "Somebody ought to take you over their knee and whack some sense into you."

With that, he was gone, leaving Caroline to stare after him, incensed and helpless. She was alone with a cot and thunder mug for her only comforts and, just beyond the window, a whimpering dog for her one friend.

She sat down on the cot and buried her face in both hands. Even Kathleen had probably never stooped so low as to end up incarcerated, she thought miserably. How disappointed Emma and Lily would be if they saw her now.

Guthrie was camped well outside of Laramie when Tob bounded out of the darkness to nuzzle him and whine.

"Finally came to your senses, did you?" Guthrie asked, ruffling the dog's loose yellow hide. He'd been feeling lonely, and the animal's presence helped a little.

Tob drank the water Guthrie poured into a bowl for him, and ate the leftover grouse meat he gave him, then started nipping at his master's shirt sleeve and pulling.

Guthrie was sitting on the ground, his saddle supporting the small of his back, and he folded his arms stubbornly and gazed into the fire. "She's gone and gotten herself in trouble, has she?" he asked.

The dog practically wept, he was so anxious, and Guthrie felt his teeth through the material of his shirt.

With a sigh, Guthrie hoisted himself up from the ground, kicked dirt over the fire, and began saddling his horse. He didn't give two hoots and a holler for Miss Caroline Chalmers, he told himself, but he couldn't stand to see a dog suffer.

Fifteen minutes later, he'd broken camp completely and was on his way back to Laramie, while Tob bounded tirelessly ahead of him. He wondered what that two-timing canine saw in the Wildcat, anyhow. In all his born days he'd never known a woman more in need of masculine guidance.

Guidance, hell, he thought, turning his head to spit. She needed a good talking to for starters, and then a few strenuous hours in a man's bed, so she'd know who was boss.

After a couple of hours, he saw the roofs and walls of Laramie standing like shadows in the moonlight. He spurred his tired horse into a slightly faster pace, unable to hold his real fears at a distance any longer.

Deep in the privacy of his heart, he offered his first prayer since Annie's funeral, when he'd essentially told God, "You go Your way, and I'll go mine." *I know You like to do most things after Your own fashion, Lord, but You've got to admit I don't trouble You with my concerns very often. And I figure, after taking Annie like that, You owe me one. So here it is, God: keep Caroline safe. Please keep Caroline safe.*

Marshal John Stone's pretty little wife, Amy, had come by at suppertime to bring Caroline clean sheets and blankets, and Charlie had grudgingly fetched her a chicken dinner from the dining hall down the street. And the pastor from the Presbyterian Church had stopped in to warn her that the fires of hell were licking at her heels.

All in all, she thought dismally, lying there on her cot, with the moonlight and the chill of a spring night flowing in through the barred window, it had not been a productive day.

She sighed, pulling the blankets up to her chin, and a sniffle escaped her. She'd been all kinds of a fool, first giving herself to a drifter who intended to marry another and made no bones about the fact, then releasing a dangerous killer from jail. If Mr. Flynn murdered someone else, it would be at least partly her fault.

A tear welled up and trickled over Caroline's temple and into her hair. In both cases, she'd had the most noble of designs, which only went to prove that the road to hell really was paved with good intentions, just like Miss Phoebe had always said. Miss Ethel had steadfastly refused to use the word "hell" at all, even in a theological context.

Beyond the wall that separated the cells from the marshal's office a clatter arose, and Caroline lay rigid in that narrow, hard cot, terrified that Seaton Flynn had come back to collect her. She'd been wrong about so many things, but she knew for sure and for certain that Mr. Flynn's threats were not idle ones.

However, when the outer door slammed against the inside wall, and Caroline sat bolt upright on the cot, it was Guthrie's shape she saw in the glow of the marshal's lantern.

Caroline needed a rescuer, but in Guthrie Hayes she saw an avenging angel. She gulped and clutched the edge of the cot with both hands, almost glad of the bars that separated them.

"Guthrie," she said, with a polite little nod.

In the moonlight streaming in from the window, Caroline saw his clenched jawline and narrowed eyes. "Do you realize that bastard could have killed you?" he breathed. "Or taken you with him?"

Caroline trembled at the reminder, then offered up a brave smile. "But he didn't."

The marshal remained behind Guthrie, listening and watching, holding the lantern high. He clearly didn't trust visitors, and after the events of recent hours, Caroline didn't blame him.

She bit down on her lower lip. "G-Guthrie, you've got to bail me out. I can't stay here."

"Bail you out? Woman, this is the safest place you could be, at least until we find Flynn. Besides, if you were out right now, I'd probably throttle you like a supper chicken!"

Caroline's cheeks flamed at the insult. "There is no need to be coarse," she said indignantly.

"I'll be back in the morning," Guthrie told her in a weary voice, and when he turned to go, Caroline flew off the cot to grip the bars.

"Guthrie, please don't go!" she cried. "You can't leave me here!"

His back was rigid and, for a moment, Caroline truly thought he was just going to walk out without speaking to her again. Instead, he glanced back at her over his shoulder. "Like I said, Wildcat, until we find your Mr. Flynn, I wouldn't want you anyplace else. Besides, a few days in here might give you some time to meditate on the error of your ways."

With that, he went out, the marshal behind him.

"*Guthrie!*" Caroline screamed, clutching the bars.

Outside the window, Tob whimpered sympathetically.

"Guthrie!" Caroline yelled again.

The door opened, but it was Marshal Stone who appeared

161

in the chasm. "My policy is to douse a pesky prisoner with cold water," he announced. "So I'd advise you, Mrs. Hayes, to shut up."

Caroline swallowed a shout of outrage and whirled away from the bars to hurl herself down onto the cot. Covering her head with the pillow, she sobbed, as much from fury as from hurt, until she had no strength left.

Then, at last, she slept.

In the outer office, Guthrie reclaimed the pistol and gunbelt the marshal had demanded he leave on the desk.

"She really your wife?" Stone inquired, looking horrified that any man would consider claiming such a spitfire as Caroline.

Guthrie chuckled, recalling how Caroline carried on when he made love to her. "She's my woman," he replied, well aware that the words constituted a non-answer.

Stone sank into his creaky chair and scratched the back of his head. He had a posse out looking for Flynn, but both the marshal and Guthrie knew the men probably wouldn't have any luck. Finding the outlaw would take a man with a certain quiet affection for the sport. "Woman like that would keep a man mighty busy," he said.

Guthrie nodded. "You're right there, Mr. Stone," he agreed with a philosophical sigh. "If I bring Flynn back, will you let her go?"

The marshal sat back in his chair, frowning as he pondered the idea. "I could have her thrown into a federal prison, you know. In fact, though I haven't mentioned it to her, she could even hang for what she did."

"I didn't ask what you could do to her, Marshal," Guthrie said evenly, bracing his hands against the edge of the desk and leaning in a little. "Caroline isn't an outlaw, and she doesn't belong in prison. She honestly thought that son of a bitch had been accused of a crime he didn't commit. She believed she loved him."

Stone looked up at him in surprise. "Your wife believed she loved another man?"

Guthrie didn't react to the unaccountable pain the words caused him. At least, not visibly. "I'll straighten her out when I get her away from this place," he replied.

The marshal smiled approvingly. "These women," he marveled. "Give 'em the vote, and they think they can do anything they want to. I honestly don't know where it's going to end."

"They're out of hand, all right," Guthrie agreed. "But personally I think it's too late to do much about it." With that, he nodded a farewell and left the jailhouse.

After settling his horse at one of the livery stables, he rented a room in a hotel and had himself a cigar and a bath. He considered sending for a woman, then decided he was too tired. Besides, he probably wouldn't get his money's worth because he'd be worrying about Caroline the whole time.

Damn that little hellcat. If she wasn't lousing up his life one way, she was lousing it up another. At the rate she was going, he wouldn't be able to stand the sight of her in another day or two.

He frowned, settling back in the hot, clean water he'd paid a premium price for. He might stop liking her in the space of a week or so, but a month of blue moons would probably go by before he stopped wanting her.

There was a soft hiss as cigar ashes fell into Guthrie's bathwater. The solution to his dilemma was simple, and he didn't know why he kept forgetting it. All he had to do was marry Adabelle.

Five minutes into the honeymoon, that troublemaking schoolmarm would be forced out of his mind forever. With a contented sigh, Guthrie turned his thoughts to his wedding night. Trouble was, it was Caroline who appeared in his mind's eye, Caroline who made his manhood jut out of the water like a flag pole.

Cursing, Guthrie clamped his cigar between his teeth and began to wash with angry sudsings and splashings. A man couldn't even take a bath without that woman deviling him.

* * *

Linda Lael Miller

When Caroline awakened the next morning, she was shocked to realize she'd been asleep. She'd never expected to close her eyes in that awful place, let alone get any rest.

Amy Stone brought her a pitcher of hot water, along with a metal basin and a clean bar of soap first thing, promising to stand guard at the door while Caroline performed her ablutions.

She was feeling almost human by the time her breakfast was brought in, and her spirits were rising steadily. Guthrie had had the whole night to think, and by now he surely realized he couldn't leave a decent woman in jail.

When he arrived, she smiled at him, patted her tangled hair self-consciously, and then tucked her shirt into her trousers. "I knew you'd come to your senses," she said.

The expression on his face dashed all her hopes. "My mind's made up, Caroline," he said flatly. "I'm going to find Flynn and bring him back. Then I'm going to marry Adabelle. And you're going to wait right here in this cell the whole time, so I know you can't make any more trouble."

164

Chapter

❧ 12 ❧

Caroline was careful of her behavior in the days to come and, because she seemed so contrite over her crime, the marshal finally agreed to let her take her meals and a biweekly bath at Miss Lillian Springer's Boardinghouse, just down the street. The hated chamber pot became a thing of the past after a week, when Charlie began marching her to the privy out back of the jail.

It was on her third visit to this place of horrific smells that Caroline saw her avenue of escape, a cobwebby gap between the back wall of the toilet and its ramshackle roof that was just big enough for her to squeeze through. She quietly returned to her cell with Charlie, her eyes lowered, her mind traveling as fast as a runaway wagon on a buttered slope.

Caroline hadn't heard a word from Guthrie Hayes in a full week. While she would have liked to believe he was out hunting down Mr. Flynn, it seemed far more likely that her erstwhile rescuer had married his prized Adabelle and was lost in the sweet spheres of wedded bliss.

Locked in her jail cell again, Caroline sat down on the cot and sighed. There was no one to vindicate her; she would have to do that herself. In order to right the wrong she had done with such pure intentions, she must find Seaton Flynn personally, and somehow bring him to justice.

She balanced her elbows on her knees and her chin in her hands. The task looked impossible from where she sat, and yet she had to undertake it. She couldn't let her life and freedom depend on Mr. Hayes, who might never come back.

Because of Amy Stone's good-natured lobbying, Caroline had finally been allowed to keep her extra clothes in the cell with her. She put her one calico dress on over her denim trousers and shirt and, when Charlie took her to Miss Springer's for supper, she picked at her food even though the landlady had prepared meat loaf, one of her favorites.

On the way back to the jailhouse, looking as peaked as she could manage, she asked Charlie to make a stop at the privy and went in, purposely catching her skirts in the door so that a good part of them would be visible from outside. Then, as swiftly and quietly as she could, Caroline squirmed out of the dress, stepped up onto the bench, being careful to avoid stepping in the hole, and climbed through the opening under the roof.

She was covered in spider webs when she landed in the soft, grassy dirt behind the privy, and she flailed at them as she ran for her freedom. When Tob came loping after her, barking joyfully, she thought all was lost, but poor old Charlie was apparently fooled by the scrap of cloth caught in the door, for he didn't pursue her.

Of course, time was still crucial; Caroline knew if she didn't ride out of Laramie within the next few minutes, the marshal would apprehend her. If that happened, she wouldn't get another chance to escape—nor would there be any more baths or boardinghouse meals.

Stealing her own horse proved easy, since the livery stable attendant was nowhere around. Caroline found the mare, saddled it as she had seen Guthrie do, and rode out of the large barn at a sedate pace. It wasn't until she reached the edge of town that she spurred the little mare into a dead run.

Jubilation filled her as she raced toward the mountain range that lay between Laramie and Cheyenne, with Tob bounding along ahead.

Because she had read her share of dime novels, Caroline knew enough to keep to the forest itself and avoid the trails, where the marshal and his men would look for her. She hoped it wouldn't take long to find Seaton and overcome him, because she had no food and no blankets, and she surely wouldn't last long in the wilderness on her own.

Caroline rode along behind Tob all that night, afraid to stop, the sound of her horse's hooves muffled by the deep carpet of pine needles on the forest floor. By morning, she was frightened, cold, and ravenously hungry, and she still hadn't come up with a plan for capturing Mr. Flynn. After all, he was twice her weight, and much taller, and she didn't even have a gun.

She was beginning to think she'd made another error in judgment by escaping when the sound of a pistol shot shattered the early morning peace and sent the birds flapping and squawking into the skies.

With her heart wedged into her throat, Caroline got off her horse and led it behind her as she crept through the woods, trying to follow the sound. The elevation was high, and the wind was bitingly cold. Through the fragrant branches of the fir trees, she could hear the rushing sound of a spring or a creek.

Rounding a rock ledge, she instinctively put out a hand to touch Tob's muzzle, instructing him to be silent. Below, on the slippery brown rocks beside a misty waterfall, Guthrie stood facing Seaton, his .45 trained on the outlaw's chest. Seaton's pistol lay on the ground several feet away.

Caroline was so delighted to see justice prevail that she threw up both hands and gave a shout. "Christopher Columbus!" she shouted, echoing her favorite literary character, Jo March of *Little Women,* in her exuberance. "I call that splendid!"

Unfortunately, Guthrie glanced in her direction, obviously stunned by her appearance, and in the next instant Seaton sprang at him. There was a struggle, while Caroline abandoned her horse and went scrambling down a rocky hillside with Tob, and then Seaton somehow knocked Guthrie's pistol into the grass and found his own. Using the butt, he struck Guthrie on the side of the head and sent him crumbling to the ground.

Caroline was practically choking on horror and outrage, and her mind was frozen. Her body, however, seemed to be operating under an entirely different directive. She lunged for Guthrie's fallen pistol and, kneeling there in the wet grass and pine needles, trained it on Seaton.

Mr. Hayes was moaning on the ground, only half conscious, his mouth bleeding.

The scene was frighteningly similar to their last encounter, when Seaton had been ready to shoot Charlie, only now it was Guthrie who lay helpless in his sights. There was one other important difference this time, though; Caroline had a gun, too.

"Fire that pistol, Seaton Flynn, and you'll pay with your life," she said evenly, and she meant every word as devoutly as any prayer she'd ever said.

He glared down at her, slowly lowering the pistol to his side. Then, in the space of a second or two, his face underwent a change that was terrifying purely because of its simple incongruity. Seaton smiled. "Come with me, Caroline," he pleaded reasonably, holding out his empty hand to her. "I have plenty of money. We'll live like royalty in Mexico or South America . . ."

Guthrie's heavy .45 trembled in Caroline's hands, but she kept it aimed squarely at Seaton's breastbone. "You have to go back to Laramie," she said, as though he hadn't spoken. "You've got to pay for what you did."

Seaton laughed as though she'd said something uproariously funny. "And hang? Not on your life, pretty Caroline. Now, stop acting like a goose and put away that gun. You don't have the courage to shoot me anyway."

Caroline bit her lower lip and closed her eyes for a moment, rising higher on her knees and stiffening her arms. When she looked again, Seaton was several feet farther away, and he was white as biscuit batter. "Stop," she said, as Guthrie groaned fitfully beside her and tried to rise. "Put down your gun."

At that, Seaton laughed again, albeit nervously. "Sorry,

sweet thing, but I'm not stupid enough to do that." He slipped the pistol deftly into its holster at his hip and backed away, both hands raised at his sides. "I guess maybe you would shoot me to save that no good bounty hunter of yours," he said, "but I'm banking that you won't pull the trigger just to keep me from getting away. You loved me once, Caroline. And if you shot me, your conscience would torment you from now until the day you drew your last breath."

He was right. She couldn't shoot him, but it wasn't just because the act would haunt her for the rest of her days. She wasn't sure how many bullets remained in the chamber of Guthrie's .45, but Seaton might know. She couldn't risk firing and missing and then having to face him with an empty weapon.

"We'll find you," she warned, and her arms were beginning to ache from the effort of supporting the gun. She wished Guthrie would wake up and take over, instead of just lying there like a lump and being no help at all. It's was God's own wonder that he'd ever been able to get anybody out of a Yankee prison, let alone earn a reputation as a raider.

Seaton smiled. "No, I'll find you," he replied, following that with a low whistle through his teeth. A horse ambled out of the woods in answer to the call. "And when I do, you won't have any defenses against me—no down-on-his-luck Rebel drifter, no mangy dog, no .45 to aim at my head. I'm going to kill Hayes when that time comes, Caroline, and you'll be traveling to Mexico with me whether you want to or not."

"You flatter yourself, Mr. Flynn," Caroline replied, operating on sheer bravado. "Mr. Hayes caught you once, and he'll catch you again. Probably before the sun goes down."

Seaton chuckled and shook his head, mounted his horse, and touched the brim of his hat with his pistol barrel in an insolent gesture of farewell. Then, mercifully, he turned and rode away.

Caroline knelt there, holding the gun straight out from her body, for long, agonizing minutes before she felt safe in dropping her guard. The instant she did, she crawled around Guthrie's other side, dipped her cupped hands into the racing stream, and splashed the icy water over his bruised and bloodied face.

No warm greeting or grateful endearment passed Guthrie's lips when his thoughts cleared again. He burst out with a string of swear words, sprang upright so rapidly that he nearly sent Caroline toppling into the water, and wrenched the pistol out of her hands.

"Where is he?" he rasped, blinking against obvious pain, and running one sleeve across the gouge above his temple.

Caroline winced, not because she was afraid of Guthrie's wrath but because she saw dirt and pine needles clinging to his bloody cut. "He got away," she said resolutely, pulling a bandanna from the pocket of her trousers and dipping it into the water.

Guthrie pushed her hand away when she would have wiped the wound clean. "Don't touch me, damn it!" he barked, rising awkwardly to his feet. "Which way did the bastard go?"

Caroline remained calm, because she knew what Guthrie apparently did not: he was in no condition to go chasing after Mr. Flynn on the back of a horse. When he took a faltering step, his knees gave out and he rolled back to the ground.

Once again, Caroline dipped the bandanna in the water, and this time Guthrie allowed her to clean the wound. The look in his eyes as he glared up at her, however, was hardly consoling.

"Are there any fish in that creek?" she asked, ignoring his rancor as she inspected the wound. "I haven't had anything to eat for the longest time, and I'm starved."

Guthrie's eyes widened, then went murderously narrow. "Of all the scatterbrained, pesky, *interfering* females . . ."

Caroline smiled, rinsed the bandanna, and gave it to Guthrie to hold against his wound as a compress. "I must say, I was pleasantly surprised to find you here, tending to business and capturing Mr. Flynn," she remarked. "I thought you had probably gone straight to Cheyenne, married Miss Adabelle Rogers, and forgotten all about my unfortunate situation."

"I spent a week looking for that son of a bitch!" Guthrie raved, opening his pistol with one hand and spinning the chamber with a practiced thumb. Caroline saw that she'd been right to be cautious, since there was only one bullet. "I was a damn *week* tracking him down, and what do you do? You get out of jail and ride right to us, just at the exact worst moment! Now I ask you, what kind of damnable, chickenshit luck is that?"

"I simply followed the dog," Caroline answered, with cool logic, "and I'll thank you to watch your language. I've always believed that profanity is the hallmark of a weak vocabulary."

Guthrie set his teeth and made a sound that was a cross between a growl and a muffled shriek, and thrust himself back to his feet again. This time, although he was wobbly and he had to blink a few times, he didn't topple over.

Caroline stood at a little distance from him, biting down hard on her lower lip. There seemed no point in talking when anything she said would have been wrong.

He found his horse, removed the saddlebags with a difficulty that made Caroline want to leap to his assistance, and flung them at her. "There's jerky inside," he said.

Since Caroline was so hungry that even jerky sounded good, she quietly opened the leather bags and rummaged until she found the dried meat. She also found a small photograph—the oval frame was of tarnished silver, no bigger than the palm of her hand—and a fair-haired woman gazed serenely back at her from behind the cracked glass.

Caroline tossed a piece of jerky to Tob, then took a bite for herself. She'd forgotten her hunger, for the moment, all her attention being focused on the photograph. "Is this Adabelle?" she asked.

Guthrie crossed the grassy space between them and summarily snatched the picture out of her hand. Unconsciously, he polished the glass against the front of his shirt before tucking it back into his saddlebags. "No," he answered, not meeting her eyes. "It's Annie."

Sadness filled Caroline. "Oh."

Guthrie put the bags back in their place behind his saddle and secured them with rawhide strings. "Get your horse, Wildcat," he said. "We're headed back to Laramie."

Caroline forgot everything but the shock she felt at Guthrie's offhand remark. "What did you say? Guthrie, I can't go back to Laramie. I'm a wanted woman."

He turned away from his horse to face her. "Caroline," he said, "I've made up my mind. It's just been plain, dumb luck that Flynn hasn't already either killed or raped you—or both. The Laramie jail is the safest place for you right now."

"I won't go back, Guthrie!"

"You will," Guthrie replied, "even if I have to tie your hands and feet and drape you over the back of my horse."

Caroline took a step backwards, her eyes round, her mouth going at top speed. "Please, Guthrie—I could *help* you—why, just a few minutes ago, I saved your life—"

"If you hadn't come along just when you did," Guthrie interrupted, "I'd be on my way back to Laramie with Flynn by now. And I wouldn't have this gash in my head. Now, get on that damn horse and shut up!"

A blush heated Caroline's cheeks. "There's no need to be rude," she pointed out. Then, because she knew she'd been beaten, she mounted the mare. She told herself she wasn't *really* obeying Guthrie's arbitrary commands; she just needed some time to come up with a plan.

Guthrie rode ahead of her all that day, his mood watchful and wary. Caroline knew he half expected Mr. Flynn to ambush them, and she was nervous herself.

"So, you didn't get time to marry Adabelle or anything?" she asked, when they stopped to rest the horses beside a stream. Laramie was visible in the distance, and Caroline still didn't have a plan.

Guthrie chuckled, and it was the first pleasant response Caroline had had from him all day. "No, Wildcat," he said. "I didn't get around to that yet."

She turned away, so he wouldn't see the sweeping, magnificent relief in her face. "I see. Well, that's too bad."

172

"Caroline," he said, and his tone had a bewildered sound, as though he'd spoken a word he didn't recognize. "Come here."

She was stepping into Guthrie's arms before it came to her that she didn't want to obey. When he brought his mouth down to hers, she tilted her head back for his kiss.

He shaped her lips with his own, then tempted her mouth open with his tongue, and Caroline whimpered. She knew she should rebel, not submit, but Guthrie had long since trained her body to ignore the dictates of her mind. As always, she responded to him on a purely primitive level, acting first and thinking later.

His strong hands cupped her bottom, lifting her slightly and pressing her hard against him. His manhood burned like a pillar of fire against her, and she felt herself expanding to receive him into her aching warmth.

"I've missed you, Wildcat," he said, and his lips were against Caroline's neck now, nibbling between words. He opened her trousers and pushed them down, chuckling when he discovered that she was wearing nothing underneath. "You're ready for me," he teased, and she stiffened and tilted her head back as he began to caress her.

Guthrie took advantage of her position and bent to nip at the peak of one of her breasts, which was still hidden away under the flannel of her shirt and the thin muslin of the camisole beneath. With her own hands, Caroline unbuttoned the shirt and bared a breast to Guthrie, and he took the nipple greedily, suckling hard. And all the while he made her dance at the tips of his fingers.

This was not a time or a place for civilized coupling, with linen sheets and firelight, and the threads that bound them together were not woven strictly of affection or even passion. They were made of anger, too, and rebellion, and a strange compulsion to do battle.

Guthrie was a warrior, Caroline was his woman, and their vital young bodies demanded that they mate.

Gasping for breath, he turned her away from him and, at the same time, pulled the sides of her shirt off her breasts.

The camisole he simply tore, and then her bounty throbbed in his palms. He held her reverently for long moments, his thumbs shaping her nipples for the nourishment he would take later, and Caroline could barely stand, so weak were her knees.

With a groan, Guthrie swept her up and carried her to where an elm branch stretched out like a giant arm, thick and low to the ground. After taking off his coat and laying it over the rough bark as a cushion, Guthrie leaned Caroline against it, facing away from him, and whispered hoarse, senseless words as he took her trousers the rest of the way down.

Caroline gave a little cry of acquiescence when he gripped the tender undersides of her knees and spread them far apart, then lifted her so that she could feel him at the portal of her womanhood. He did not take her tenderly, he conquered her, and that was exactly what Caroline wanted him to do.

The friction grew faster and keener and sweeter with every thrust of his hips, until Caroline was delirious. Eyes tightly shut, she gripped the sturdy tree limb to anchor herself to earth as Guthrie took her from one level of ecstasy to another. Then, at the exact moment that he cried out and stiffened against her, it seemed to Caroline that both their bodies dissolved for an instant, freeing their souls to fuse in a spray of golden fire.

She stood clinging to the branch when it was over, as though a high, sheer cliff loomed beneath her feet. It was a struggle just to breathe. She was only dimly aware of Guthrie washing her tenderly and righting her clothes, and when he turned her into his arms, she sagged against his chest.

"Oh, Mr. Hayes," she managed to get out, "it *is* a pity we don't like each other much, isn't it?"

His chuckle was a rumble beneath Caroline's ear. "Yes, Wildcat," he answered, running his hands up and down her back, "but it's probably for the best. A steady diet of that would kill us both."

Caroline drew back a little and looked up into his face. The blood had dried over his wound, but he was still a little pale. "You mean it isn't the same for you with—with every woman?"

Guthrie kissed the tip of her nose. "No. It's nice, don't get me wrong. But when I'm with you—well, it's like being dipped into hell three times and then tossed into heaven."

She wrapped her arms around him and rested her forehead against his shoulder. "You're still going to make me go back to Laramie, aren't you?"

"Yes," he answered, holding her no less tenderly for the firm conviction in his voice. "This time, damn it, stay put until I come back for you."

"You have no idea how angry the marshal is going to be," Caroline fretted, her words muffled by the fabric of Guthrie's shirt. "He's bound to see my escape as a personal reflection on his abilities as a constable."

Guthrie laughed. "Don't worry, Wildcat. Stone's a good man. If he weren't, I wouldn't trust him with you."

Caroline tilted her head back to look up into Guthrie's face. "I thought you weren't coming back," she told him. "I truly believed that you'd forgotten all about me and gone off to marry Adabelle."

His eyes were incredibly tender as they caressed her in that next moment. "I'll see this through," he said quietly. "You have my word on it."

Still, the thought of being incarcerated again was almost more than Caroline could deal with. She backed away a step, wondering what her chances of success would be if she bolted for her horse and rode off as fast as she could go.

She sighed. Guthrie would catch her before she'd gone a hundred yards. "Suppose I promise—"

He laid his fingers over her lips. "No, Caroline," he said.

Dispiritedly, she righted her hair and clothes the best she could and swung deftly up onto her mare's back. For all her mistakes, she was becoming a good rider; the soreness was gone from her legs and thighs, and she hardly bounced in the saddle anymore.

When they reached Laramie, and the jailhouse, Marshal Stone was only too happy to arrest Caroline and put her behind bars again.

Guthrie watched her with a sort of amused fondness as she walked into her cell, moving as augustly as Anne Boleyn being brought before her accusers, and sat rigidly upright on the edge of her cot.

"It won't be long, Caroline," he promised.

She looked at him with solemn, accusing eyes and spoke not a word.

Guthrie sighed. "I'll send Miss Phoebe and Miss Ethel a telegram and let them know you're all right—"

Caroline bolted off the cot and flew to the bars, gripping them so hard her knuckles showed white against her skin. "Don't you dare!" she hissed. "They'd die of shame if they knew!"

"But—"

"Guthrie Hayes, if you say anything to my guardians about me, I swear I'll tell Adabelle Rogers everything that's ever happened between us!"

Grudgingly, Guthrie agreed to keep his peace, at least where the Maitland sisters were concerned. He warned Caroline once again to stay where she was until he returned for her, and then he was gone. As glad as she was to see him go, Caroline was desolate in his absence.

The marshal was surprisingly polite, considering all the trouble Caroline had put him to, but he made it clear that he would brook no more nonsense. Caroline's meals were to be brought to her from then on, and she would no longer be allowed to leave the jail for baths and trips to the privy.

That first night, she lay on her cot, tossing and turning, remembering the soul-splintering way Guthrie had made love to her, reliving every caress, every muttered exclamation. Before long, her skin was hot to the touch and a fine mist of perspiration covered her from head to foot. She closed her eyes and, mercifully, drifted off into a deep and instant sleep.

Tob's whimpering and the rattling of keys awakened her to a gloomy new day of rain and wind.

"'Morning," said Charlie the jailer, sounding insincere. He was carrying a tray covered with one of Amy Stone's red-and-white checked table napkins.

Caroline sat up and, with as much dignity as she could manage, smoothed her tangled hair back from her face. She was still wearing her trousers and shirt, and she longed with all her heart and soul for a hot bath. "Good morning," she replied coolly.

The old man unlocked the cell door, after giving Caroline a warning look, and brought the tray in. Outside, Tob's whine grew to a shrill crescendo. "What's that dog carryin' on about?" he grumbled.

"I imagine he's hungry," Caroline answered. "And since it's raining, he's probably wet and cold as well. I don't suppose he could come in and lie down by your stove?"

Charlie pondered the question while he backed out of the cell and locked the door. At the same time, Caroline went to the window and dropped one of the buttermilk biscuits through the bars along with a plump piece of sausage.

"I reckon he could come in for a while," the jailer finally conceded. "You ain't got him trained to steal keys or anything like that, have you?"

Caroline smiled ruefully as she climbed down off the end of her cot and began to eat her breakfast. "Unfortunately, all he knows how to do is whine and drink whiskey."

Charlie left and, a few minutes later, Tob came in, wet and shivering, to put his muzzle through the bars of Caroline's cell and give a single mournful yip.

She patted the dog's head and gave him what remained of her breakfast. It seemed to her that Guthrie could have learned a few things about loyalty from his canine companion.

The day remained dreary, wet and cold, and when the marshal's wife arrived, she looked like an angel of mercy to Caroline. She was a pretty woman, with glossy brown hair and blue eyes, and she treated her husband's prisoner with amazing respect and courtesy, considering the circumstances.

"I thought you might like a bath and some fresh things to

wear," Mrs. Stone said brightly, handing soap, a towel, and some folded clothes through the bars. She shivered delicately. "It's such a nasty day out."

"A bath?" Caroline echoed, confused. The marshal had sworn on his mother's grave that he wouldn't let her step out of that cell again unless the jailhouse caught fire.

Amy nodded. "Mr. Stone is bringing our own tub down here, and I'll heat the water on the stove out front and keep watch for you."

The sheer generosity of the act tightened Caroline's throat and brought the sting of tears to her eyes. She looked down at the starched calico dress in her arms, and the soft muslin underthings, to hide her emotion. "Why are you being so kind?" she asked.

"Because I don't believe you're guilty of anything, that's why. You wouldn't have let Mr. Seaton Flynn go if you hadn't truly thought he was innocent." Amy reached through the bars to pat Caroline on the hand. "Don't you worry, now. After you've had your bath, and brushed out your hair, you and I will have a nice cup of tea and play a game of hearts."

And so it was that Caroline had her hot, luxurious bath, changed into fresh clothing, brushed and braided her hair, and sipped tea from a delicate china cup. She smiled once or twice as she pondered her cards to think what a picture she and Amy must make, conducting their tea party with a wall of iron bars between them.

Chapter

❧ 13 ❧

*I*t was just like old times, Guthrie thought, as he sat at a corner table in the Red Duck Saloon, a cigar clamped between his teeth, four aces and a queen in his hand, and Tob lapping up whiskey from a dish on the sawdust floor. If he had a lick of sense, Guthrie told himself, he'd take tonight's winnings and head straight for Cheyenne.

Trouble was, he'd given the Wildcat his word, and he knew if he went back on it, he'd be haunted by the image of those velvety brown eyes for the rest of his life.

He'd just taken another pot, much to the disappointment of the other four players at the table, when he saw Marshal Stone approaching. Guthrie thought he and the peace officer might have become friends, given the time.

Stone pulled a chair away from another table, turned it backwards, and sat astraddle of it, his arms draped over the back.

"What's she done now?" Guthrie asked, counting his money as the other men at the table made their excuses and vanished.

The marshal smiled ruefully. "Actually, Miss Caroline's been behaving herself. Makes me wonder what she's up to "

179

Guthrie grinned and took a puff on his cigar. "If I were you, I'd check for a secret stash of dynamite." He regarded the lawman solemnly for a moment. "You're a busy man, Stone—not the type for an idle chat. What is it?"

"The circuit judge came through this afternoon," Stone answered uneasily. "He set bail for Mrs. Hayes."

Guthrie didn't correct the improper reference to Caroline as his wife. Mrs. Hayes. He liked the sound of it. "How much?"

"One hundred dollars."

The money was lying in Guthrie's palm, thanks to the string of poker games he'd won that night, but the decision wasn't quite that easy. Up to this moment, he'd believed the Laramie jailhouse was the best place for Caroline, until Flynn was caught again, at least. But now he was forced to consider his true feelings.

He didn't want to leave Caroline behind; that was the real reason he was still hanging around town instead of out picking up Flynn's trail again. If he was to be entirely honest with himself, he had to admit he had the same uneasy feeling he'd had the day he rode away and left Annie alone on their small homestead in Kansas. When he'd returned, she was dead.

On the other hand, the trail was no place for a hellcat like Caroline Chalmers. Guthrie just flat out didn't need the aggravation.

The marshal seemed to understand Guthrie's quandary all too well. "Damned if you do, damned if you don't," he said.

Guthrie laughed. The statement summed up the way things had been between him and Caroline ever since their first meeting back in Bolton. Although that had taken place only a few weeks before, it seemed like a century had passed since those simple days when everything was so clear cut.

"I guess I'd better take her with me," Guthrie said, tamping out his cigar and pushing back his chair.

Marshal Stone stood, realigned his hat, and led the way out of the saloon.

Caroline looked amazed when Charlie brought her out of her cell. She blinked at Guthrie as though she thought she might be hallucinating and shifted her tattered valise from one hand to the other.

The sight of her filled Guthrie with an aching tenderness the likes of which he hoped he'd never feel again. It was too poignant, and it made him far too vulnerable. "The marshal and I have decided that the taxpayers of Laramie have enough trouble without you on their hands," he said, in an effort to hide the fact that she mattered to him.

"Mr. Hayes has posted your bail," the marshal explained. "You're free to go, but you've got to be back in Laramie in sixty days so a judge can decide what's to be done with you."

Caroline's throat moved visibly as she swallowed. "I could still go to federal prison," she said.

Glumly, Stone nodded. "Yes, ma'am." His gaze linked with Guthrie's. "Unless, of course, you manage to bring Flynn back. That would weigh pretty heavy in your favor. In fact, I might just drop all the charges if you did that."

As simply as that, without so much as a handshake, the agreement was made. Guthrie would bring in the prisoner, and the marshal would forget that Caroline had been instrumental in his escape.

Guthrie took the valise from Caroline's hand, spread his fingers at the small of her back, and propelled her toward the door. "Come on, Wildcat. We've got some tracking to do."

It was the strangest thing, Caroline reflected, as she walked along the dark street with Guthrie, how sometimes God would answer a person's prayer before it had left their lips and sometimes He would ignore the prettiest pleas and reasonings.

"You're actually taking me along? I'm going to help you find Flynn?"

Guthrie chuckled humorlessly. "I don't know how much help you'll be," he answered, "but at least I'll be able to keep an eye on you."

Tob was trotting along at Caroline's side, and she touched

his furry head just to reassure herself that she was really out of jail. Maybe she'd never have to go back. "Are we leaving tonight?"

Guthrie nodded. "We'll ride back to the place we lost Flynn and start from there."

Caroline's cheeks heated at the memory Guthrie's words brought to mind. It was generous of him to say "the place *we* lost Flynn" when in truth Caroline had been the one to bungle the situation. "That'll take all night, won't it?"

"Probably," Guthrie agreed. He glanced up at the sky. "But there's a moon tonight, so we should make good time."

They reached the livery stable, where Guthrie reclaimed their horses. The attendant knew Caroline as the illustrious woman prisoner who had helped Seaton Flynn escape, and then climbed out of a privy and made a run for it herself, so he had to be shown a release paper signed by Marshal Stone.

The sense of freedom Caroline felt as she rode along beside Guthrie through the moonlight was so trenchant that she very nearly couldn't bear it. And she certainly didn't trust herself to speak.

Guthrie seemed content with just the night sounds himself, though occasionally he whistled tunelessly through his teeth for a few minutes. Even when they stopped to rest the horses Guthrie didn't speak; he appeared to be in a state of deep concentration.

Finally, just as the moon and stars were beginning to fade in the first glimmers of daylight, they reached the waterfall where Guthrie had had his last confrontation with Mr. Flynn.

"I'm sorry," Caroline said hoarsely, as she climbed down out of the saddle and stood watching the sun rise over the peaks of the mountains.

Guthrie was already busy leading the horses downstream, away from the small waterfall, so they could drink. "For what?" he asked, in an offhand tone of voice, when he realized Caroline had followed him.

"It was my fault Seaton got away." She came around to face Guthrie, reached up tentatively to touch the healing wound on the side of his head with gentle fingers. "And I'm to blame for this, too."

Guthrie treated her to one of his crooked grins. "You do have a gift for showing up at the wrong time," he conceded, spreading his hands in a magnanimous gesture. "But I'm willing to forgive you as long as you promise not to try to help me again."

Caroline laughed. "You *are* generous."

He touched her cheek with one hand, then thought better of the action and withdrew. "Gather up some firewood," he said, breaking off a stick and testing it between his hands for flexibility. "I'll see if I can't catch us a few fish."

Although it hurt, the way he'd distanced himself from her all of the sudden, Caroline understood. There was something very volatile in their relationship, something treacherous. The flames could leap up and consume them both at any moment, marking their souls with scars that might never heal.

She and Guthrie would be going their separate ways soon, Caroline reflected sadly. He would have his mine, and that fancy house he planned to build—and Adabelle.

She turned and walked blindly away, in a pretense of searching for firewood. She still hoped to find her sisters, of course, but the West was a big place and she knew her chances of success were puny at best. At that weary, discouraged moment, it seemed to Caroline that there would be nothing for her but a lifetime of spinsterhood, spent teaching other people's children.

She bent and picked up a good-size chunk of wood, having noticed it only because she'd stumbled over it. Her longing to find her sisters, always running beneath the surface of her thoughts like an underground river, rose up to pierce her heart.

She gathered wood until she had an armload, then returned to the campsite next to the stream. Guthrie had already garnered four sizable trout with his makeshift spear, and he looked pleased with himself as he started a little pile of dried twigs burning.

Caroline let her burden fall from her arms with a clatter, and Guthrie looked up at her in concern. His voice was so gentle that it made Caroline want to cry.

"What's wrong, Wildcat?"

She knelt beside the fledgling fire, the splayed fingers of both hands spread across her abdomen. Only a split second before, the true implications of her situation had come home to her. "Suppose I'm—suppose I'm expecting, Guthrie?"

He regarded her steadily. "We'd get married."

"But we don't love each other. And there's Adabelle—"

Guthrie's jawline tightened for a moment. "If you're carrying my baby, we'll take the matter up with a preacher. And that's the end of it, Caroline."

"I won't marry a man who doesn't love me!"

"And *I* won't see a child of mine raised as a bastard. Your woman-time—is it late?"

Caroline swallowed hard and tried to calculate, but in the end she was so confused she couldn't remember the last time she'd flowed. She knew it hadn't happened since she met Guthrie. "I don't know," she said pitiably.

Guthrie got his small, lightweight frying pan from his gear and set it in the fire, unceremoniously adding the freshly cleaned fish.

"What would Adabelle say? If you had to marry me, I mean?"

He didn't look at her. "Wouldn't be much she could say, it seems to me. At least, not much that was ladylike."

"But you'd never be happy. You'd always be thinking about how it would have been with her."

At last, Guthrie lifted his eyes, and Caroline was stunned to see a glint of mischief in their depths. "I figure just keeping you out of dutch would take up most of my time What was left over we could spend making love."

Caroline's cheeks burned. "Oh, but we've got to stop doing that."

He grinned. "I saw a brushfire once up in Kansas—wiped out about fifty acres of grass in half an hour. I figure putting that fire out by spitting on it and stopping our lovemaking are in about the same category. As long as the flames have something to feed on, they're going to keep right on burning."

Caroline climbed awkwardly to her feet and stepped back a little way. "That's all well and good—for you. But I'm the one who would have to bear the shame of conceiving a child out of wedlock. Things like this are very different for women, you know.

"Men are secretly admired for making a conquest, as though it were some kind of spectacular accomplishment, but women are looked down upon and even ostracized."

A delicious aroma began to rise from the fish, causing Caroline's mouth to water and her stomach to grumble.

"People will base their opinions of you on what you think of yourself," Guthrie answered quietly. He stood, his gaze solemn and direct. "You're not like your mother, Caroline."

She lifted her chin a notch. "What makes you so sure of that? You never knew her."

"Maybe not, but I know you. You've never willingly abandoned anybody in your life—not even that sorry excuse for a man you thought you wanted to marry. And it still tears at you that you had to get off that train and let your little sisters go on without you." He stepped close and took her shoulders gently into his hands. "They're all right, Wildcat. Wherever your sisters are, they're just fine."

"How can you possibly know that?" Caroline fretted, but she wanted to believe he was right.

Guthrie grinned. "Because they're your sisters. My guess is, they're both looking for you, and each of them is driving some man crazy."

"The fish is burning," Caroline said, to distract him from the fact that her eyes were watering.

He went back and pulled the pan expertly from the fire. They ate off metal plates from Guthrie's gear and then Caroline washed the utensils in the stream. When she'd finished that, she turned and saw her traveling companion stretched out on his stomach in the sweet grass beyond the reach of the waterfall's mist.

Caroline felt herself being drawn toward him just as

surely as if there was a rope tied around her waist and he was pulling at the other end. "Guthrie?"

He didn't lift his head from its resting place on his arms. "What?"

"Aren't we going on?"

"Later. We'll rest a while first." At that, Guthrie rolled onto his side and looked up at her. "All I want to do is hold you," he said, in answer to a question Caroline hadn't had the courage to ask.

"Promise?"

"Yes."

She believed Guthrie and lay down beside him in the bruised grass, drawing in its clean, summery scent. He draped one arm around her waist and pulled her close, and they fitted together like two spoons in Miss Phoebe's chest of silverware. "What if Mr. Flynn comes back to wreak vengeance?"

Guthrie chuckled. "Damn, but I wish he would, Wildcat. Then I could grab him by the short hairs and take him back to Laramie to hang. Unfortunately, he's probably halfway to Mexico City by now."

"You wouldn't actually chase Mr. Flynn into *Mexico?*" Caroline marveled.

"I'd chase him into hell," Guthrie replied. "Now close your eyes—not to mention your mouth—and try to sleep."

Sleeping was easy, since Caroline was exhausted. When she awakened hours later, the sun was low in the sky and Guthrie was crouched by the fire again, cooking something that smelled wonderful.

She sat up, yawning, feeling strangely safe. It was as though this isolated, mystical place belonged only to the two of them. "What is that?" she asked, sniffling the air.

Guthrie smiled. "Rabbit."

Caroline took herself off to the woods, then came back to the stream to wash her hands and brush and rebraid her hair. She sat on a dry rock, her feet bare, watching Guthrie turn their dinner on an improvised spit. "Are we staying here tonight?"

He turned to look at her, and an expression of enchantment flickered in his eyes, though it was gone so quickly that Caroline decided she'd imagined it. "Yes. Flynn's so far ahead of us by now, another day isn't going to matter."

Caroline frowned. "I'm not so sure," she said thoughtfully, wriggling her toes in the icy water of the stream. "That he's all that far ahead of us, I mean. Seaton meant it when he said he was going to kill you and take me to Mexico with him, Guthrie."

Guthrie paused to study her somberly for a long time. "You may be right," he said, and his tone was low and grave. "Caroline, if anything happens, don't worry about me. Just get the hell away from him, any way you can."

A shudder passed through Caroline as she thought of how close she'd come to marrying Seaton Flynn. To think she'd actually looked forward to sharing his bed and bearing his children. "You said it yourself," she answered, forcing herself to smile. "I've never deliberately abandoned anyone. And I'm not going to start with you, Guthrie Hayes."

"Damn it, woman, if I tell you to leave, you'll leave!" He picked up a stick from the wood he'd gathered to replenish the fire and flung it angrily. Tob went bounding after the twig, barking in delight. In that moment Guthrie looked so much like a small, obstinate boy that Caroline had to smile.

"Did you hear me?" Guthrie demanded, advancing on her.

Caroline looked up at him, batted her eyelashes, and did her best to imitate his southern drawl. "Yes, sir, Mr. Hayes, I heard you," she said sweetly.

He glowered at her, his expression as ominous as a bank of storm clouds gathering in a summer sky, then suddenly laughed. "I swear when a Yankee mama takes her baby on her knee, the first thing she teaches him is how to talk through his nose."

Pretending offense, Caroline rose from the rock. "Northerners, sir, do not speak through their noses."

He laughed again, clamped a thumb and forefinger over both his nostrils, and mimicked what she'd said.

Haughtily, Caroline swept around him, as though she were wearing a ball gown instead of trousers and a man's shirt, and opened her valise. "You're just put out because you lost the war," she said, taking out her calico dress.

Guthrie turned her to face him, his eyes dancing, and kissed her lightly on the mouth. "We didn't lose, Miss Caroline," he told her. "We're just taking some time out to plan our next campaign."

Caroline put her hands to his chest to keep him at a distance because she could feel herself succumbing to his unquestionable charm. "While you're doing that, General Lee, our food is scorching."

Guthrie didn't even bother to glance back at the fire. "It's not quite done," he said, and his lips were so close to Caroline's that her mouth started to tingle in anticipation. "In about the time it takes to make love to you, it'll be perfect."

"You promised," Caroline protested weakly. His hands were resting on either side of her narrow waist now, gently pulling her into the whirlpool of sensation his kiss would create.

Unexpectedly, he set her away from him. "You're right," he said, in a decisive tone of voice. "If you want me to make love to you, you'll have to do the asking." And he went back to tending the roasting rabbit.

Nothing could have made Caroline admit to the disappointment she felt. She went into the woods a little way, took off her trousers and shirt and quickly put on the dress. She passed Guthrie without speaking to rinse the garments out thoroughly in the creek. After that, she hung them over the lowest branch of a birch tree to dry.

When the rabbit was fully cooked, Guthrie cut it deftly into manageable pieces and gave Tob a generous portion before serving Caroline her share.

"I would never ask a man to make love to me," she said, however belatedly, sitting sideways on Guthrie's saddle with her plate balanced on her knees.

The meat was juicy and delicious. After several minutes of silent eating Guthrie reached out and took Caroline's hand in his, running his tongue slowly along the length of one of her fingers, then kissing her palm. "Of course you wouldn't," he agreed. It took Caroline a moment to remember what it was he was agreeing with.

When she did, her cheeks flamed. "Well, I wouldn't," she insisted.

He broke off a succulent piece of meat and teased her lips with it until they opened. Then he laid the morsel on her tongue and lightly traced her mouth with a fingertip. "Certainly not," he replied.

"Don't patronize me, Guthrie Hayes," Caroline said, incensed because heat was surging through her system and there were so many other parts of her that wanted his touch. "I'm perfectly serious!"

Guthrie finished his meal and tossed the leftovers to Tob, offering no response. He took a handkerchief from Caroline's valise and carried it to the stream.

When he came back, he knelt beside her and gently washed her face and hands. It was a simple, ordinary act, and yet it left Caroline trembling. She watched in a state of delicious misery as Guthrie unrolled his blanket and spread it out on the ground beside the fire. After that, he kicked off his boots and then began unbuckling his belt.

The sun had long since set, and a bright sliver of moon had risen, bathing the land in an eerie silver light. Guthrie unbuttoned his shirt and slipped out of it, then took off his trousers.

Caroline stared at him, unable to look away. Although they'd been intimate on more than one occasion, she'd never really seen Guthrie without his clothes, and she was unbearably curious. Her eyes widened as his manhood rose to its full magnificence, and she wanted to touch him so badly that she had to knot her fingers together in her lap.

He found the handkerchief and took it back to the stream. When he returned, he handed the cloth to Caroline without a word.

She stared up at him for a long time, marveling at his power over her, and then, very gently, she washed him. When that was done, she simply held him, and his shaft strained warm and hard against her fingers.

When she touched him with her tongue, he moaned, and

that was all the encouragement Caroline needed. She took him full in her mouth and enjoyed him shamelessly, revelling in the sounds he made.

Finally, though, Guthrie stopped her. Pulling her after him, he went to the blanket and stretched out on it, gloriously naked in the moonlight. Wanting more of him, Caroline knelt between his legs and bent her head to him, her thick, dark braid lying across his belly like an ebony rope.

Guthrie's back arched as his hands wandered from Caroline's shoulders to the sides of her face, urging her on even as he pleaded aloud for her to stop. "Wildcat, you—don't understand—I can't—*oooooh,* Caroline—"

She teased him mercilessly with her lips and tongue, somehow sensing when he was on the brink of an uncontrollable response and pulling back. "Ask me," she said, remembering his challenge, his vow that she would ask for his lovemaking.

He groaned and stiffened beneath her as she tempted him, but he wouldn't give in to her demand. Instead, he groped for her with his hands, undoing the buttons of her dress, pushing it down so that her breasts were freed.

He caught them in his palms and held them as Caroline punished him with a teasing nip, and his thumbs moved over the nipples, taming them, preparing them to serve him. Now it was Caroline who moaned as fiery sensation throbbed in her breasts and spread like molten gold into every part of her body.

Guthrie gripped her waist and thrust her forward, holding her above him and capturing a taut pink nipple in his mouth. Caroline found herself sitting astraddle of his manhood as she nourished him, but she still wasn't willing to concede defeat.

Releasing his hold on her waist, he pulled up her skirts, found the inner seam in her worn drawers, and split it wide with one tug of his hand.

Caroline trembled as she felt him teasing her, felt her body prepare itself to receive him, but she still wouldn't give in. While he suckled noisily, greedily on her breast, she reached back to caress him.

He broke away from her nipple with a desolate groan. "Caroline, in the name of—"

She bent to nibble at his lower lip, drawing it briefly into her mouth, then kissed him thoroughly, in the way he'd taught her to do.

He was breathless when he finally broke away. "Caroline—"

She began to move downward over his chest, letting him anticipate what she meant to do.

At the last possible moment, Guthrie gasped out, "Make love to me."

Exaltation filled Caroline as she rose to center herself upon him and then take him slowly inside her. With a sudden motion of fierce strength, he turned her onto her back and plunged deep, his head thrust back like a stallion's as Caroline ran her fingers over his bare chest, his back, his buttocks.

Then he put his hand between them, spreading his fingers over her belly, dipping his thumb into the place where the rosebud was hidden and stroking it. Caroline gave an involuntary shout of response as her slender body arched like a bowstring under Guthrie's, quivering as he clasped her bottom in one hand and held it high. There was no way of retreat now; she had to experience the pleasure fully, and it was so powerful, so devastatingly sweet, that Caroline cried out like a wild thing of the forest.

At that, Guthrie shuddered, gave a guttural cry of his own, and delved deep. She felt his warmth spilling inside her and the unbearable beauty of that made her body climb toward another response, this one unexpected and even more urgent than the first.

Guthrie clasped her wrists in his hands, held them high above her head, and bent to take suckle at her breast. This caused him to withdraw almost completely, and Caroline pleaded senselessly while he teased her with an inch, two inches, an inch again.

Gasping, her body on fire, Caroline finally realized what he was demanding of her. "Guthrie," she whispered, as he shaped her nipple with his tongue. "Make—make love to me."

In one powerful stroke, he gave her the friction that ignited the dynamite within her, and her head moved wildly from side to side as she gave herself up to a release of primitive proportions. When it was over, Caroline lay transported beneath Guthrie, her arms tight around his sturdy middle.

A long time passed before either of them spoke.

Guthrie laid a warm hand over her naked abdomen in a territorial, claiming gesture. "I hope my baby is growing inside you right now," he said.

Caroline turned her head, stricken. She'd just realized she was in love with Guthrie Hayes, and that her situation was hopeless. "Don't say that. You're going to marry Adabelle. You belong to her."

He curved his hand under her chin and made her face him again. "Caroline—"

A painful, hiccuping sob passed her throat. "I wish I'd never met you—I wish I'd never heard your name!"

Guthrie pulled Caroline close and settled her against the warm strength of him, covering them both with the spare blanket from her bedroll. "Shhh," he said, his lips soft against her temple. "I told you I'd marry you if you're expecting."

"You don't love me," Caroline reminded him, filled with despair.

She felt his smile against her skin and heard it in his voice. "Maybe not, Wildcat. Truth is, I don't know exactly how I feel about you. But having you in my bed every night would sure as hell make up for a lot."

Chapter

❧ 14 ❧

*G*uthrie awakened Caroline at first light. She rose, grumbling, and made her way to the stream, where she splashed cold water over her face. Birds were chirping in the birch trees that lined the banks, and the air was chilly.

There was coffee, Caroline found, when she went back to the campfire, but breakfast consisted of beef jerky. She gave Guthrie an accusing look over the rim of her mug. "No rabbit? No fish?"

Guthrie's beard was growing in and his clothes were rumpled, and Caroline tried to resign herself to the fact that she'd given her heart to another rascal. "Sorry, Your Highness," he answered, with a grand bow. "I didn't have time to hunt."

Caroline looked around at the trees and the waterfall and the soft, fragrant grass where they'd lain together in the night. In those moments, she almost wished she and Guthrie could stay there forever, just the two of them, living like Adam and Eve in the garden. "Speaking of hunting, do you have any idea which way Mr. Flynn might have gone?"

Guthrie was saddling Caroline's horse. "None at all," he replied, without turning to look at her. "Yesterday, I would have said he'd gone south, but now I think you might be right. Flynn's just enough of a bastard—and a fool—to stay in Wyoming Territory and wait for a chance at the both of us."

Finished with her coffee, Caroline went to the stream and rinsed out her mug and Guthrie's, then tucked them back into his gear. It made her nervous to think of Seaton lying in wait somewhere, ready to ambush them. And the idea of his touching her in an intimate fashion sent bile surging into the back of her throat.

"Don't look so scared, Wildcat," Guthrie said, hoisting her up into her saddle. His eyes were intent and amused as he met her gaze. "I'm not going to let anybody hurt you."

Caroline looked away. It obviously hadn't occurred to Guthrie that *he* might be the one to hurt her. All he'd have to do, really, was marry Adabelle Rogers and bring her to Bolton to live. Then Caroline would encounter his pretty wife in the mercantile and at church, and later she would teach his children in the town's one-room schoolhouse. And every moment would be agony, because, for better or worse, Caroline was desperately in love with Guthrie.

He swung up into his own saddle, after tossing a curious glance in her direction, and set off through the trees. Caroline followed, hoping her affection for Mr. Hayes would pass, like a case of the grippe, but all the while she knew it wouldn't. What she felt for him was far deeper and more complex than the silly infatuation she'd borne for Seaton Flynn.

The really terrible thing was that she suspected nothing Guthrie could do would be bad enough to make her stop loving him. Even if he turned out to be a murderer, every bit as cold and cruel as Seaton was, Caroline knew her feelings wouldn't change. She might avoid Guthrie Hayes for the rest of her life, but her love for him would live in her heart until the day it stopped beating, and in her soul until the end of eternity.

She bit her lip in an effort not to cry and rode stoically along behind. Of course, there was a very good chance that she was carrying Guthrie's child even now, and that would mean a whole different set of heartaches. Being married to

Guthrie and knowing he loved and wanted someone else would be worse than having to say "Good morning, Mrs Hayes" to Adabelle every single day for the rest of her life.

In Caroline's opinion, the future looked bleak indeed. If she was to have any hope of happiness, she would definitely have to leave Bolton behind forever. She would buy herself a simple gold wedding band and tell everyone she'd been widowed if there was a child. Yes. And she'd go straight to Chicago and visit the orphanages and adoption agencies until she found the one that had sent Lily and Emma and herself west on the orphan train. Maybe someone there had received a letter from one of her sisters or from the people who had adopted them.

Caroline hoped Guthrie was right about Lily and Emma, hoped they wanted to find her as much as she wanted to find them. Her need to connect with her sisters had never been stronger.

All morning, Caroline and Guthrie traveled in silence. Guthrie was watchful and alert, Caroline was introspective and distracted. When they stopped at noon to rest the horses and consume their quota of beef jerky—by now it seemed just so much salty shoe leather—Guthrie cupped his hand under Caroline's chin and ran his thumb lightly over her lower lip.

"You haven't said a word in three hours," he pointed out. "What's the matter, Caroline?"

She wondered what would happen if she told Guthrie she'd fallen in love with him, but she didn't have the courage to find out. To be rejected, and maybe pitied in the bargain, would be more than she could bear. "I was just brooding about my sisters," she said, and that was at least a partial truth. "I think I'll go back to Chicago after we've found Mr. Flynn and try to find out where they ended up."

"Was anybody on the train keeping records?" Guthrie reached out and smoothed a tendril of dark hair back from her cheek.

Caroline shook her head sadly. "I don't think so. The only person who showed any interest in us was this mean old conductor, and he only wanted to make sure we didn't disturb the other passengers." She paused and sighed. "I was determined to remember where Lily and Emma got off the train and go back looking for them as soon as I could, but I was chosen first."

Sympathy flickered in Guthrie's green eyes, and his smile was gentle. "What do you think they would be like now?" he asked, and Caroline was grateful for the opportunity to talk about her sisters some more. It made her feel closer to them.

Wearing her jeans and flannel shirt, which were stiff from last night's washing and very wrinkled, Caroline sat down in the deep grass and plucked a brilliant yellow dandelion from its stem. Guthrie joined her.

"Lily—she was the smallest of the three of us—had large brown eyes and very pale blond hair. I imagine she's still quite fair. When she was little, she was stubborn and a bit willful, so I suppose she's a woman of distinct opinions."

Guthrie grinned. "Stubborn and willful?" he teased. *"Your* sister? Impossible."

Caroline threw the dandelion at him and reached for another. "Emma was the middle child, and her eyes are a very dark blue. Her hair was the color of a new penny when I saw her last, and she always had the best singing voice of us all. She's probably very beautiful, with a formidable temper and the tendency to do impulsive things."

"Sounds like a blood relative of yours," Guthrie agreed, and that mischievous light was still cavorting in his eyes.

"Of course," Caroline reflected, avoiding Guthrie's gaze, "they could both be dead. The West isn't always kind to women."

"It isn't always kind to men, either," Guthrie pointed out reasonably. "But I'd bet my horse and two weeks' take from my mine that Lily and Emma are alive and well. The people you just described to me are survivors, Caroline. Like you."

Caroline sighed. "There's so much I want to ask them," she said.

Guthrie rose to his feet and pulled Caroline after him. "You'll get your chance, Wildcat—provided we find Flynn and keep you out of prison, I mean."

The reminder bruised Caroline's tenderest hopes. "Will

you take me back and turn me over to Marshal Stone if we don't find Mr. Flynn?" she asked solemnly, searching Guthrie's face.

He met her gaze squarely. "No," he answered. "But I'd just as soon settle this right now, so you don't have to change your name and hide out from the law for the rest of your life. We're going to find Flynn, Caroline, and when we do, things will be normal again."

Normal? Caroline's world would never be the same. Just knowing Guthrie Hayes had turned it upside down. She let him lift her up into the saddle just because she liked having him touch her, though she would have denied that if questioned.

"Tell me about Annie," she dared to say, as they rode on up the mountainside. Now, the path was wide enough that they didn't have to ride single file.

Guthrie sighed and readjusted his hat. "I guess I owe you that much," he said, "after all that's happened between us. Annie was my wife—she waited for me when I went to war, and when I came home, I married her and we went to Kansas to homestead.

"We didn't have a damn thing besides that piece of land, a couple of horses and a cow, and a sod hut, but we were happy. By winter, Annie was carrying our child.

"We were running low on provisions, so I put on snow-shoes and went out to hunt. When I got back that night, the fire was out and the lamp wasn't lit. I found Annie lying on our bed—" He paused and swallowed. "She'd been raped, and then strangled."

Caroline's eyes stung with tears. "Oh, Guthrie, I'm sorry."

"The man who did it," he went on, "was a sergeant I'd tangled with during the war, while I was in prison. He left the Union insignia from his cap on the pillow to let me know he was the one."

"W-what did you do then?" Personally, Caroline didn't want to hear any more of the tragic story, but she sensed that Guthrie needed to finish telling it, now that he'd started.

"The first thing I did was bury Annie," he said. "It took

hours to dig a grave—the ground was frozen solid—but I was so crazy with grief that I must have had the strength of several men. Once I'd said good-bye to her, I left with just my rifle, the clothes on my back, and Annie's picture. Then I tracked Pedlow down."

Caroline felt a chill, even though the May afternoon was warm and sunny. "Where did you find him?"

"He was in Abilene, drinking the saloons dry. He wore a lock of Annie's hair under his hatband, and he laughed when I kicked over the table he was sitting behind and told him to go for his gun.

"He said he'd settled his score with me, and he wasn't about to get himself shot."

Guthrie rode in silence for a few minutes, and Caroline said nothing, respecting his need to gather his thoughts. She couldn't even begin to imagine what it must be like to try to put such a horrendous experience into perspective.

Finally, he went on. "I put the barrel of my rifle to Pedlow's—in his lap and told him he didn't have a choice. He was scared all right, but probably not as scared as Annie was when he forced himself on her, and I wanted him to sweat."

At last, Guthrie's eyes met Caroline's, and she saw the shadows of the torment he'd endured.

Again, she waited, wishing there were some way to lighten Guthrie's burden. In the end, though, all she could do was listen.

"For the next five weeks, I followed Pedlow everywhere he went—a whore's room, the outhouse, it didn't matter to me where he was. I was there. Finally, he couldn't take it anymore and he broke and drew on me. I emptied my rifle into him."

Caroline closed her eyes against the images that had been flipping through her mind ever since Guthrie started talking. "Dear God," she breathed. "Did they arrest you?"

Guthrie scratched the back of his neck. "Let's just say I'm not particularly welcome in that part of Nebraska anymore."

She swallowed. "What made the sergeant hate you so much? And why did he attack Annie, instead of you?"

"Pedlow hated every Reb. Back in the prison camp, he branded men just like they were animals. I suppose he took a particular dislike to me because I engineered an escape, and he probably caught hell for that from his superior officers. As for what he did to Annie, well, Pedlow was no genius, but he was smart enough to know that nothing he could do to me would hurt as much as knowing he'd made my wife suffer. From now 'til my dying day, I'll never forget for more than an hour that I wasn't there when Annie needed me."

Caroline gulped a few times, in an effort not to throw up. Although the war had been over for more than a decade, she still could hardly bear to think of the terrible misery it had wrought on both sides. "You said he—he branded people. Surely Union officers didn't permit such brutality."

"Most of them wouldn't have," Guthrie admitted grimly. "But the Yanks needed their best men in the field, just like we did. I don't guess they had time to stand around making sure people like Pedlow were kind to the prisoners."

Guthrie reined in his horse at the top of a ridge. Below in a gully was a cluster of ramshackle buildings and rickety fences.

"What's that?" Caroline asked, frowning.

"It's a way station for the stage line," Guthrie answered, in a tone of indulgence. "We'll spend the night there."

The thought of sleeping in a real bed and eating something that hadn't been rolling around in the bottom of Guthrie's saddlebags buoyed Caroline's flagging spirits. "What will we tell them? About us, I mean?"

"As little as possible," Guthrie answered wryly, spurring his horse toward a trail that led down off the ridge. Tob raced ahead, barking like a fool and scattering a flock of squawking chickens in every direction.

A heavy woman came out of one of the buildings, even more upset than the chickens, waving her apron and yelling. Poor Tob skulked back toward Guthrie and Caroline, whimpering.

The woman smiled and smoothed her calico skirts when she saw company coming. "You folks in need of a place to put up for the night?" she asked cordially.

Caroline looked to Guthrie to answer, her cheeks flushed.

He grinned at their hostess in his charming, off-kilter way and touched the brim of his seedy hat. To look at him, Caroline reflected, anybody would have thought he was an outlaw. "Yes, ma'am," he said. "We'll need a room if you have one. And the use of a bathtub, too."

A toothy smile was the woman's response, and she said, "I'm Callie O'Shea. I run this place, with my husband, Homer."

Caroline lowered her eyes and said nothing when Guthrie introduced her as Mrs. Hayes.

"Your missus is surely a shy one," Callie boomed to Guthrie, as Homer came out of a barn to take charge of the horses. "I don't believe she's said a word yet."

Guthrie untied Caroline's valise from the back of her saddle and winked once at his 'missus.' "Once she's had some food and a hot bath, there'll be no shutting her up," he said.

Callie laughed uproariously at that and led them through a crowded kitchen with four big wooden tables lined with benches and then down a dark hallway. "Best room in the house," she said, pushing open a creaky door. "You're lucky you got here before the four o'clock stage."

Guthrie set Caroline's valise on the foot of a large four-poster bed covered with a worn but still colorful quilt. "How much?" he asked, hanging his hat on one of the bedposts.

"Two bits," Callie answered, looking curiously at Caroline's trousers and shirt, as if she'd just noticed them. "Four bits if you each want a bath. You have to go out back for that, by the way. Homer done curtained off a place for bathin'."

"We'll share one," Guthrie said nonchalantly, and Caroline stared at him. He handed Callie two coins and she went out, promising to start the bathwater heating right away.

"Suppose I don't want to share a bath with you, Mr.

Hayes?" Caroline inquired pointedly, arms akimbo, when they were alone.

He shrugged, sitting down on the edge of the bed and pulling off one of his boots. "Then I guess you'll just have to go without one."

Caroline looked at the bed with longing. "It isn't proper, our sleeping together," she whispered.

Guthrie grinned. "Hypocrite," he said. "I've had you in the grass, on a rock, and draped over a tree limb. Seems to me it's about time we made love in a real bed."

Caroline folded her arms. "I want you to take another room. Or sleep in the barn."

He reached out suddenly, caught her by the waistband of her trousers, and flung her down onto the mattress beside him. He moved his hand from her waist to the crux of her womanhood, cupping her shamelessly. "Shall I prove to you, right now, that you don't want that at all?"

Caroline felt her nipples jutting against the inside of her shirt, and the place Guthrie was holding was growing achy and moist. "No—yes—damn you, I don't know!"

Guthrie chuckled and bent to scrape one flannel-covered nipple lightly with his teeth, at the same time opening the buttons on her trousers and putting his hand inside. "You know," he breathed, "if you are carrying my baby, and we do get married, you're going to have to work on being more obedient." His fingers parted Caroline, and she gasped at the resultant shock of pleasure as he thrust them inside her. At the same time, he worked her expertly with his thumb.

Caroline was writhing helplessly, needing what he was giving her too badly to break away. "Oh, Guthrie—*damn* you—"

He chuckled at her predicament and told her to open her shirt. As much as she longed to defy him, she couldn't; she fumbled with the buttons and bared her breasts.

For long, torturous moments, Guthrie just admired them, his fingers and thumb driving Caroline slowly and rhythmically toward madness. Then he took one pink tip into the warmth and wetness of his mouth and began to suckle.

Caroline made a low, growling sound in her throat as

Guthrie made her ride his hand, first at a trot, then a gallop. She was vaguely aware of a loud clatter, but she didn't know whether it was the stage arriving or the bed springs creaking, and at the moment she was too desperate to care.

Guthrie led her into a place of light and fire, covering her mouth with his own to muffle her cries, and for a few moments, she actually thought she'd die of the pleasure. When the dazzling brightness faded and her sated body at last lay still, she realized she was weeping.

She was emotionally drained, and the many uncertainties of her life encircled her, like wolves just outside the glow of a campfire.

With a tenderness Caroline had never suspected he possessed, even in his most endearing moments, Guthrie kissed the moisture from her eyes. Then, very gently, he undressed her and put her beneath the covers. "Sleep," he said.

Caroline closed her eyes, and when she opened them again, the room was dark and there was a fire flickering on the stone hearth. She sat bolt upright. "Guthrie?" There was no answer, though she could hear laughter outside the room. "Guthrie!"

The door creaked open and his form appeared in the doorway. "It's all right, Wildcat," he said gently. "I'm here."

She swallowed. "I thought you were gone. I thought you'd left me."

He crossed the room and kissed her forehead. "I'm not going to do that, Wildcat. I promise." He lit the lamp on the bedside table and turned the wick so that it burned brightly. "Are you hungry?"

Caroline felt foolish for carrying on so, now that she was fully awake. Just moments before, she'd been a child again, riding west on an orphan train and praying for a way to keep her sisters with her. "Yes, as long as we're not having jerky," she answered.

Guthrie chuckled. "Callie made venison pie," he said.

Caroline's mouth watered, but she narrowed her eyes and looked at him suspiciously. "How come you're being so nice to me, Guthrie Hayes?"

"Maybe I like you," he answered, with a shrug. She noticed then that he'd shaved, and his hair and clothes were clean.

"You took my bath!" she accused.

He grinned. "Well, in that case, I guess you'd better take mine," he replied. "I'll bring the tub in after you've had your supper."

"I thought Callie said we had to bathe outside."

"She'll make an exception." With that, Guthrie got up and left the room. When he returned, just minutes later, he was carrying a plate on a rustic wooden tray, along with a glass of milk and utensils.

Caroline reached eagerly for the tray, being careful to keep the covers over her breasts with one hand. Callie's pie was hot and succulent, filled with carrots and potatoes and big, savory chunks of meat. "These people must think I'm nothing but a layabout," Caroline said, after taking the edge off her hunger with a few large bites and several sips of milk.

Guthrie, seated on the foot of the bed, grinned. "They think you're a tired woman who's been on the trail for too long," he replied.

Just looking at him, Caroline was filled with a dangerous tenderness. It was frightening, the way he could make her so angry at one moment, and melt her with his smile the next. And then there was the unbelievable passion. "You've been very kind," she told him, her voice wobbling slightly.

He acknowledged the compliment with an almost imperceptible nod, then rose from the bed. "I'll see about that bath I promised you," he said.

Caroline watched as he left the room, then settled back against her pillows. She'd eaten every scrap of her pie, and drained her milk, and now that she was rested, she felt much better.

Almost half an hour passed before Guthrie returned carrying the bathtub. Callie was right behind him with two huge buckets of steaming hot water.

Once Callie had poured the water into the old, scarred wooden tub and left the room, Guthrie built up the fire and sat down on the raised hearth to smoke one of those thin cigars he liked so much.

Caroline knew it would be a waste of time to ask him to leave, so she got out of bed, draped in the quilt, and made her way regally to the middle of the room. She stepped into the deliciously hot water and sank down, the patchwork coverlet billowing around her.

Guthrie grinned and shook his head. "Don't you think it's a little late to start acting modest?"

"I suppose you're right," Caroline said, flushing and lowering her eyes as she remembered the incident before she'd fallen asleep. She let the quilt fall away and nodded toward her valise. "There's a bar of soap in my bag. Would you get it for me, please?"

He pondered the question for a few moments, then tossed the cigar into the fire and crossed the room to comply with her request. Instead of just handing her the soap, however, he knelt beside the tub and began to lather her back with it.

Caroline closed her eyes and enjoyed the utterly luxurious sensation. When Guthrie continued to bathe her, she didn't protest. She let him lather and rinse every part of her, and then she stood in the warm crimson light of the fire and allowed him to dry her.

By the time he lifted Caroline and carried her to the bed, resisting him was the furthest thing from her mind. She watched as he put the door latch in place, then turned toward her, unbuttoning his shirt. By the time he crossed the room, he had shed the last of his clothes.

He laid the covers back and slid in beside Caroline, reaching out to turn down the lamp so that the only light in the room was the romantic glow of the fire. Then he lay on top of her, raising himself on his forearms so that he wouldn't crush her. With a sigh, he bent his head and kissed her.

It took so little, where this man was concerned, to ignite all Caroline's senses. Tearing his mouth from hers, he trailed his lips gently down her body, stopping to nibble at her neck, to taste each of her breasts, to set her satiny belly a-quiver.

And then he put Caroline's legs over his shoulders and she was lost.

He loved her at a leisurely pace, no matter how she urged and begged, and when he was through making her arch her back and alternately curse and praise him in breathless gasps, he lowered her to the mattress and sheathed himself in her.

She'd thought she had nothing left to give, but soon she was moving wildly beneath him, her hands roaming over his back and buttocks, her entire body moist with the effort of pursuing something he kept just out of reach. When he gripped Caroline's bottom and lifted her so that he could delve into her depths, however, her body suddenly buckled in the throes of a savage release.

Through her own cries, muffled by the palm of Guthrie's hand, she heard him surrender. When his body stiffened and then shuddered violently, she felt a love so woundingly poignant she was certain her heart was breaking.

Guthrie collapsed beside her, when he was spent, his head cushioned on her breasts, and she held him, her fingers deep in his rich, soap-scented hair. She wanted to say, "I love you, Guthrie," but she didn't dare. She was too afraid of what his response might be.

Presently, when he'd regained his composure, he took one of her nipples again, and she could feel him growing hard against her thigh. She welcomed him when, minutes later, he entered her a second time.

Now their coupling was slow, with none of the desperation that had driven them before. Caroline's climax unfolded in delicious stages, each new height bringing a little moan of surprised pleasure from her lips. Guthrie came long after she'd finished, groaning huskily as she flicked at his earlobe with her tongue.

Perfectly content, Caroline cuddled close to him and fell asleep. When she woke up again, the fire had gone out, the room was cold, and she was alone.

Despite Guthrie's assurances that he wouldn't leave her, Caroline was alarmed. She climbed hastily back into her trousers and shirt and crept toward the door of the room.

Chapter

⊰ *15* ⊱

*E*ven though she moved as quietly as possible, the boards creaked under Caroline's feet when she made her way down the hallway and peered around the corner into the kitchen.

Guthrie was sitting at one of the trestle tables, a fan of cards in his hand, one of his thin cigars between his teeth. Two men sat across from him, with their backs to Caroline, carefully studying their cards. Her eyes rose to the clock ticking loudly on the wall behind Guthrie; it was nearly midnight.

Disgusted, but nonetheless relieved that he hadn't ridden off and abandoned her, Caroline went back to the room and exchanged her clothes for a nightgown from her valise. Then she stirred the ashes in the fireplace until she uncovered glowing embers. Once she'd added a few pieces of kindling from the neat little stack of wood to one side of the hearth, a happy blaze crackled.

She was sitting in a rocking chair in front of the fire, brushing her hair, when the door opened and Guthrie came in.

"Did you win?" she asked, without looking at him.

She heard him chuckle, heard the bedsprings creak and the thumps of his boots as he tossed them onto the floor. "I broke even. Unless you count finding out Flynn is headed for Cheyenne as winning."

At that, Caroline turned to meet Guthrie's eyes. He was sitting on the edge of the bed, unbuttoning his shirt, looking for all the world like a tired husband at the end of a long day. "Those men know Seaton?"

"They talked to a man who fit his description," Guthrie replied with a yawn.

Caroline got out of the chair and moved slowly toward the bed. Despite all her intimacies with this man, it still came as something of a shock to find herself sharing a room with him. She didn't even want to think of what Miss Phoebe and Miss Ethel would say if they knew. "When?"

"Yesterday, along the trail." Guthrie divested himself of the rest of his clothes and crawled blithely into bed, stretching and then cupping his hands behind his head. "You look like a gypsy princess, with the firelight shining in your hair."

Caroline scrambled over the foot of the bed and crawled under the covers, careful to keep to her own side of the mattress. "When was the last time you encountered a gypsy princess?" she asked reasonably.

He laughed, then lost himself in a cavernous yawn. "I admit I haven't actually met one," he said, a few moments later, turning onto his side to face her. The expression in his green eyes was solemnly tender, or so it seemed to Caroline. The firelight could have been playing tricks. "We'll be in Cheyenne in a couple of days."

Caroline turned onto her back and looked up at the ceiling, where shadows played tag with fragments of light. "I guess you'll be paying a call to Adabelle as soon as we arrive," she said, trying to sound as though the idea didn't matter.

Guthrie caught her chin gently in his hand and made her look at him. "Yes, Caroline," he said. "I will be."

She closed her eyes for a moment, and when she opened them again, Guthrie was regarding her steadily.

"I'm going to tell her we can't be married," he said.

Caroline was certain she'd only imagined his words. "What did you say?" she asked, her cheeks warming.

"I said I'm going to tell Adabelle the wedding's off," he answered gravely. Now he was looking at the ceiling, and that gave Caroline leave to watch his face.

"Why?" Her voice was soft, uncertain.

He withdrew one of his hands from behind his head and thoughtfully rubbed his clean-shaven chin. "Because I've got to figure out what the hell it is I'm feeling for you before I go promising to spend the rest of my life with somebody else."

Caroline had no answer for that. She was still afraid to tell Guthrie she loved him and, besides, if they didn't find Mr. Flynn, she might spend the rest of her life in federal prison or even hang. She moved close to him, more by instinct than by willful choice, and laid her head on his shoulder.

He put an arm around her, combing her long, loose tresses with his fingers once or twice, then holding her against his side. "Caroline," he breathed, as though the name embodied everything in the universe that was too mysterious for a mere man to comprehend. And then he closed his eyes.

When a long time had passed, and Caroline was sure Guthrie was asleep, she raised herself up on one elbow to look into his face. He really was remarkably handsome, in a rakish sort of way, and even in sleep his mouth had a look of mischievous amusement to it, as though he knew some funny secret and wasn't about to tell.

Because the future was uncertain, and the past had been difficult in so many ways, for all the generosity and love of the Misses Maitland, Caroline allowed her mind to stray into a time that would probably never exist.

She imagined herself as Guthrie's wife, living in a big house at the edge of Bolton, her stomach protruding with his baby. This wasn't their first child, but the second—no, the third.

It was winter, and snow sprinkled the rosebushes Caroline had planted in spring and outlined the points of the picket fence in iridescent white. As she gazed out the window of her warm parlor, where a fire was blazing and an evergreen tree stood in the corner, resplendent with Christmas decorations, a carriage of the sort she had only read about drew up at the front gate.

The driver, wearing a top hat and an ulster, climbed gracefully down from the box and opened the door. A beautiful woman with coppery hair and dark blue eyes climbed out, with his help, followed by a graceful, brown-eyed blonde.

Her sisters! Caroline flung open the door without bothering to reach for her cloak. "Lily," she cried, barely able to contain her joy. "Emma!"

But before the three sisters could embrace, the lovely image faded. Caroline felt Guthrie's arm tighten around her briefly.

"You'll find them," he promised, in a quiet voice, and Caroline knew then that she'd said the names aloud.

"Please God," she answered, and then she closed her eyes.

In the morning, Caroline sat up in bed, blinking, to see Guthrie standing in front of a small mirror affixed to the wall. His face was covered with lather, and he was singing a bawdy saloon song as he shaved.

"It's about time you woke up, Wildcat," he commented cheerfully, dipping the blade of his razor into a basin of water and scraping away another section of beard and lather.

Caroline scrambled out of bed and ferreted through her valise for her divided riding skirt and plain blouse. The garments were hopelessly rumpled, but they were still better than wearing those dratted trousers again. "I didn't realize you were one of those people who feels cheerful in the morning," she commented critically. "And keep your back turned, please."

Guthrie chuckled and went right on shaving, while Caroline looked for a part of the room where she wouldn't be visible in the mirror. There wasn't one.

She turned her back and exchanged her nightgown for the riding skirt and blouse as modestly as she could. It seemed vitally important to keep the conversation away from the things that had been happening between them.

"Why do you suppose Mr. Flynn would go somewhere like Cheyenne, when Marshal Stone has probably already wired the marshal there to be on the lookout for him?"

"Why did he go to Laramie after robbing the stage?" Guthrie retorted. "Flynn likes taking chances. And, of course, there's the obvious possibility that he's hoping we'll follow him so he can avenge himself."

Caroline had to pause in the act of buttoning her blouse to shudder as she remembered Seaton's threats. In the jailhouse, and later, when she'd happened upon him and Guthrie by the waterfall, Mr. Flynn had sworn he'd have her and pay her back for her supposed betrayal. "How did he know?" she wondered, her voice hardly more than a whisper.

Guthrie tossed the water from his basin out the window, refilled it from the pitcher on the washstand, and splashed his face thoroughly before replying. "It was natural to think we'd been intimate, given the fact that we'd been traveling alone together for days," he said, holding a white damask towel in both hands. "Flynn may be a murdering son of a bitch, but he's no fool."

Caroline sighed, took her brush from her valise, and began to groom her hair. When she'd freed it of tangles, she braided it and wound it on top of her head in a coronet. Then, when Guthrie had left the room, she used the last water in the pitcher to wash and to brush her teeth.

Callie was serving a hearty breakfast of sausage patties, eggs, and fried potatoes when Caroline came out. Although she would normally have been hungry, that morning the mere smell of food was almost her undoing. She accepted a cup of coffee and went outside to drink it while Guthrie ate.

Tob, who had probably slept on the porch or out in the barn, since Callie disliked dogs, came whimpering and whining to meet her. Smiling, Caroline petted him, but her gaze was fixed on the mountains looming all around her, covered with pine and fir and birch trees, seeming to touch the sky.

She wondered if Callie and Homer stayed on here in the

winter, when the snow was probably several feet deep and the stagecoaches couldn't get through.

The barn door creaked and Homer appeared, a thin little man with a narrow face and a good-natured expression. "'Mornin', Mrs. Hayes," he said. "You feelin' poorly? Not many folks like to miss one of Callie's meals."

Caroline shook her head, even though she was a little queasy. There was absolutely no sense in troubling Homer with her maladies. "I'm fine," she answered. "I had some venison pie last night, and it was the best I've ever tasted."

Homer beamed at the compliment to his wife. "She's got a way with food, my Callie." He patted Tob idly. "You like to cook, missus?"

She thought of her well-equipped kitchen back in Bolton. Guthrie had certainly seemed to favor her fried chicken and pie. "Yes," she answered. "When I get the opportunity, that is. Do you and Callie stay here all year around?"

To her surprise, the small man nodded. "We get snowed in, long about the end of October," he said. "Sometimes we don't see another soul all the way 'til the last of April."

Before Caroline could make a comment on that, the door opened and Guthrie came out. He gave Homer a friendly nod and threw some scraps to Tob, who gobbled them up eagerly.

"Ready to leave?" he asked, and his voice was gentle.

Caroline knew he was probably wondering if she was pregnant or not, and she would have given just about anything to know whether he hoped she was or wasn't. "Any time," she answered.

Guthrie went back into the way station and came out a few minutes later with her valise. Homer entered the house, and Caroline walked to the barn with Guthrie.

"Callie and Homer are snowed in from October to April," she marveled. "Sometimes they don't see another human being in all that time."

Pulling open the barn door, Guthrie shrugged. "I wouldn't mind that, if I could have you and plenty of food and firewood."

"You wouldn't miss your poker games?"

"I could play poker with you," Guthrie answered, opening a stall gate and giving a low whistle to his gelding. The animal nickered and came to him.

Caroline folded her arms. "I don't know how to play."

Guthrie grinned. "Fine. That means you'd lose a lot, and every time you did, I'd make you hand over some of your clothes."

"You are reprehensible," Caroline scolded, but there wasn't much conviction behind the words and they both knew it.

Guthrie saddled the gelding, whistling through his teeth again, while Caroline led her mare out of its stall and stood patting its neck. Fifteen minutes later, they were riding through the woods again, avoiding the muddy stagecoach trail.

They climbed all morning, reaching a grassy meadow in the early afternoon. The grass was deep and richly green there, and dandelions, blue bells, daisies, wild violets, and tiger lilies encircled the clearing like a crown of flowers made of a princess's head.

"Oh, Guthrie," Caroline breathed, gazing around her in wonder as she slipped down off her horse's back. "It's so beautiful—to think all this splendor was sleeping under the snow!"

He led the horses to a little stream bubbling its way down from the top of the mountain, making a silver ribbon to compliment the wildflower crown. When he came back, he brought the inevitable jerky and a surprise—a slice of white cake wrapped in a piece of oilcloth.

Caroline was moved by this small treat, however crumbled and squashed it was. Her hands trembled a little as she reached out to accept it. "Thank you, Guthrie."

He grinned, looking pleased. "Feeling better?"

She took a bite of the delicious cake, savoring the sweet white icing. "Much," she answered.

Guthrie touched her lip and then laid his finger to his tongue. "Annie used to be sick in the mornings," he said.

And Annie had been pregnant. Caroline felt sad all of the sudden. "You needn't feel obligated if there's a baby—"

"Obligated?" Guthrie frowned. "Of course I'd be obligated. A man doesn't just walk away from a situation like this, Caroline."

"My father did," she said. "And so did Lily's and Emma's."

Guthrie sighed, broke off a corner of the cake, and popped it into his mouth. "I'm not any of those men, Wildcat, and the sooner you get that straight in your mind, the better. I have my own set of rules, and one of them is that I take responsibility for what I do."

She and the baby, if there was one, would be mere responsibilities to him, then. He'd look after them because it was the right thing to do, not because of any feeling so sentimental and silly as love.

"I hate you, Guthrie Hayes," Caroline muttered, turning away. She finished the cake in two bites and was thus mightily embarrassed when he turned her to face him and grinned because her cheeks were bulging out like a squirrel's.

The grin turned to a chuckle, then an uproarious laugh.

Caroline chewed and swallowed hastily, her face red. "Don't you dare laugh at me!" she shouted, spewing crumbs.

Guthrie dragged in a few breaths in an effort to compose himself, but his eyes were still dancing with amusement long after the laughter had stopped.

Irritated, Caroline approached a cluster of tiger lilies and picked one exotic orange blossom. After a few moments, she'd regained her temper, and was about to turn around and speak to Guthrie when she saw six mounted Indians lining the next ridge. They held spears in their hands and Caroline could see something that looked disturbingly like blood spread over their chests in some ritual design.

Swallowing, she stepped back, and her voice came out as a squeak. "Guthrie!"

He was right behind her; Caroline felt herself strike the

solid wall of his chest. His hands came up to grip her upper arms, and his words and tone steadied her. "I see them, Wildcat," he said evenly, his breath touching her ear as he spoke. "They're Shoshone, probably a hunting party. And unless we give them reason, I don't think they'll bother us."

Caroline had heard and read about the things that happened to women who were stolen by savages, and she was appropriately terrified. "What, exactly, would they consider a reason?"

Guthrie chuckled. "A couple of shots from my .45, or any sudden move." He paused and gave that familiar low whistle through his teeth, and Caroline heard the jingle of bridle fittings as his horse trotted obediently toward him.

"Are we going to make a run for it?" Caroline whispered, still staring up at the Indians, who were staring back.

"No, Wildcat," he answered easily. "I just want my rifle within reach, in case we need it."

The most colorfully decorated of the red men gave an invisible signal to his painted pony, and the other Shoshone filed along behind.

Guthrie squeezed Caroline's arms once, then pressed his .45 into her hand. "Whatever you do," he told her, in the same pleasant tone he might have used to ask for punch at a garden party, "don't panic, and don't pull the trigger unless they attack."

He stepped up beside Caroline as the riders came closer, the powerful rifle from his scabbard resting lightly in his hands, a companionable smile on his face. He greeted the visitors with a nod of his head and, while his manner was easy, Caroline could sense the restrained power in him. For the first time, she had an idea of what a formidable opponent this man could be.

The first Indian spoke in a tangle of words that was part Shoshone and part English and, to Caroline's utter surprise, Guthrie answered in the same unintelligible tongue.

Caroline smiled at the visitors with a fierceness she usually reserved for the school board. "What is he saying?" she asked, through her teeth, when the conversation had gone on for some time.

"They want the dog," Guthrie answered.

"The dog?" Caroline turned and looked into Guthrie's face, certain he must be baiting her. All she'd read and heard had convinced her that she would either be scalped or carried off to some isolated camp to serve as a slave. "Why would they want Tob?"

Guthrie elbowed her and then went on chatting with the Shoshone. "I imagine they'd like to roast him for supper," he replied, after more time had passed.

Caroline was horrified. *"No!"* she cried, kneeling down beside Tob and wrapping her arms around his furry neck. The .45 was still in her right hand, and pointed straight at Guthrie's big toe.

"Caroline," Guthrie said evenly, "if you shoot me in the foot, it isn't going to do our cause a hell of a lot of good."

Carefully, Caroline maneuvered the pistol so that Guthrie was no longer in imminent danger. "I will not allow them to cook this wonderful dog. Of all the barbaric ideas! Why, when I think of . . ."

Guthrie interrupted her tirade in a firm but still friendly tone of voice. "Shut up, Caroline."

The Indians were talking animatedly among themselves now, and, finally, the ringleader looked straight at Caroline, then he glared at Guthrie, burst out with what was probably a profanity, and spat on the ground. In the next instant, the little band of hunters was riding rapidly back up the ridge.

Caroline rose slowly to her feet. "What happened? Why are they leaving?"

Guthrie sighed, shoved the rifle back into its scabbard, and snatched the .45 somewhat impatiently from Caroline's hand. "Believe me, Wildcat, you wouldn't have wanted them to stay for supper."

She folded her arms. "I want to know what made them ride away, Guthrie."

He holstered the .45 in an annoyed motion. "The gist of it was, they figured I had enough trouble, with a stubborn woman like you on my hands, and they decided not to add to it."

Caroline opened her mouth, then closed it again. Guthrie

215

hoisted her up into the saddle, and handed her the reins. "Will they be back?" she dared to ask, after a long time had passed, and the flowery meadow was far behind them.

"Probably not," Guthrie answered, "unless they have bad luck hunting, of course. Tob might start looking pretty good to them if they don't find a deer or two."

"They would really eat him?" Caroline's mouth filled with acid and, being too ladylike to spit, she swallowed.

"Fried, roasted, or boiled," Guthrie answered, narrowing his eyes as he scanned the surrounding terrain for possible danger.

"You had quite a long conversation with them," Caroline remarked. She wanted the reassuring sound of another human voice. "And I think you were talking about me."

Guthrie grinned at her. "As a matter of fact, Wildcat, we were. I told them that while you looked pretty good on the outside, underneath those clothes you were covered with running sores. They have a horror of white man's diseases, with good reason. When you put your arms around the dog, they probably figured he was contaminated."

Caroline swallowed again. "That was a clever, if disgusting, tactic," she conceded.

He touched the brim of his hat. "Thank you, ma'am," he replied. "I was gambling that they wouldn't put a spear through me and strip you to see for themselves."

Another shudder rocked Caroline's slender frame. "I suppose I should be grateful to you," she said thoughtfully. "Some people would say you saved my life."

"Some would," Guthrie agreed, and after that, the subject was closed. They rode on, climbing higher and higher into the mountains, where patches of ragged, dirty snow lay on the ground and the wind was still frigidly cold.

Caroline shivered when they stopped for the night, in a rocky, godforsaken place where the only visible shelter was a cave in the side of the mountain. Heaven only knew what might be in there, just waking up from its winter slumber.

Guthrie got off his gelding, handed the reins to Caroline, and pulled the rifle from its scabbard beneath the saddle. He cocked the weapon, then strode purposefully toward the cave.

Standing in her stirrups, Caroline called after him, "Isn't there another way station where we could stay?"

Guthrie tossed her a look of wry impatience over one shoulder, then proceeded into the cave. Moments later, he came out again. "It's clear," he said, leaning the rifle against the trunk of a birch tree near the mouth of the cavern. "Gather some firewood."

Caroline got down from her horse. "Suppose that's the den of some vicious animal?" She walked toward Guthrie, who had removed his jacket and was rolling up his shirtsleeves. "Just imagine what will happen if it comes home from hunting to find us trespassing."

Guthrie grinned and shook his head. "Don't worry, Wildcat. There's nothing living in there except for some spiders and a few rats."

"You're deliberately making this harder for me," Caroline accused coldly, already scanning the ground for pieces of wood suitable for a fire.

He shrugged and spread his hands. "I told you the trail was no place for a lady, but you wouldn't listen."

Caroline turned away from him and went on with her work, wondering why she felt so angry. She wanted to pick a fight with Guthrie, a loud and rousing one.

When she came back to the camp with the first armload of twigs and broken branches, he had finished taking the saddles and bridles off the horses and staked them out to graze. He was sitting on his heels like an Indian, his back to a birch tree, and the muscles in his right forearm corded as he whittled a pointed end onto a stick.

Caroline dumped the firewood practically in his lap and stood looking down at him with her hands on her hips. "Here," she said, her tone one of pure challenge.

He set the stick and the knife aside and stood. But instead of anger, his eyes showed a strange, gentle compassion. "It's all right, Caroline," he said. "You're safe now. Nobody's going to hurt you."

That was when she realized she'd mistaken anger for fear. She began to cry softly, and Guthrie took her into his arms and held her.

Presently, she recovered herself and sniffled, "It's just that I've read such horrid things. And Miss Phoebe's own fiance was shot dead by a Shoshone brave . . ."

Guthrie cupped a hand under her chin. "I'll protect you, Wildcat," he said. And then he bent his head and kissed her gently, lightly, on the lips. It was just enough contact to make her yearn for more, and she put her arms around his neck.

He gave a low groan and then set her away from him. "More firewood," he ordered, averting his eyes.

Caroline was hurt, but she was also proud. She lifted her chin and went off to seek more fallen branches and pieces of deadwood. When she returned, the camp was set up and a nice fire was burning, but there was no sign of either Guthrie or the horses.

At first, Caroline's old fear of being abandoned came up, but then she realized he'd probably found a water hole somewhere nearby and taken the mare and gelding to drink there. Flinching at the sound of a shot, she dropped the firewood and went back to the woods for another load.

Why gathering the wood was always her job she didn't know. She brought back three more armfuls before Guthrie returned to the camp, leading the horses and carrying the carcass of a small animal. Fortunately, he'd already cleaned and skinned it.

Caroline was still injured because Guthrie had rebuffed her earlier, so she didn't speak. Still, Guthrie's eyes were warm with understanding and humor as they touched her, making promises for the night to come. He got out the small frying pan he carried in his saddlebags, along with the little coffeepot and a flat tin of grounds, and started supper.

Caroline paced, trying to hold in the question, but in the end it escaped. "Don't you want me, Guthrie?"

He filled the coffeepot from his canteen, added grounds, and set it in the fire to brew before looking up at her. "Always," he answered gruffly, deftly cutting up the meat and laying the pieces in the pan. "You might be in a delicate condition, Wildcat. And if you are, you need good food and shelter and rest. What kind of man would I be if I spent the last hours of daylight making love to you, then let you go hungry?"

Caroline swallowed. The Maitland sisters had always been very generous with her, but she'd never really experienced caring from a man. Not even Seaton Flynn, she realized now. "You must think I'm dreadfully forward."

He laughed and rose from his haunches, leaving the meat to cook over the low flames of the fire. "It's a quality I admire in a woman," he replied, rubbing his hands down his thighs.

Caroline felt unaccountably shy, considering all she'd done with this man. And she had a poignant sense of urgency, as though her association with Guthrie was destined to end soon. The incident with the hunting party had brought home to her how easily the two of them could be separated. Perhaps next time it would be forever.

"Hold me," she said, trembling, and Guthrie took her into his arms. She laid her cheek against his chest and heard his heart beating strong and steady beneath her ear. *I love you, Guthrie Hayes,* she thought, as a sweet sadness filled her.

It was the same feeling she'd had just before she'd been forced to leave Emma and Lily behind on the orphan train.

Chapter

⇘ 16 ⇙

Guthrie gave Caroline a thorough, leisurely kiss that left her with wobbly knees and a heart that was pounding away at double its normal speed. When he pulled back, his hand lingered under her chin, the calloused thumb moving over her lower lip.

"We'll make love later, Wildcat," he told her. "After supper. Once we start, I don't want to have to stop for anything short of total exhaustion."

Anticipation made Caroline's flesh tingle. Her nipples stood out against the fabric of her shirt, and she was warm and moist, ready for him. He dropped his hand to her breast and caressed it gently, then turned, with a heavy sigh, and walked away.

Caroline was so excited through dinner that she barely tasted her food. "There's water nearby?" she asked, once the leftovers had been tossed to Tob, who had waited patiently with only the occasional whimper.

"About fifty yards beyond those trees," Guthrie answered, with a nod in that direction. His eyes smoldered as he looked at her.

Nervous as a bride, Caroline tore her gaze from his, stood, and got her soap from the bottom of her valise. Then she made her way through the birch, cedar, and fir trees, hearing the murmured poetry of the creek long before she actually reached it.

The water was unbelievably cold—Caroline was certain the slightest drop in temperature would freeze it solid—but she stripped and washed herself thoroughly, nonetheless. When she went back to camp, she was shivering and her skin glowed pink all over from the chill.

"You'll be lucky if you don't catch pneumonia," Guthrie scolded, but he didn't sound angry. His eyes were smiling and his mouth was set at that lopsided angle that always twisted a tiny muscle buried somewhere deep in Caroline's heart. He wrapped a blanket around her, took her hand, and led her inside the cave.

There, he'd made a bed of sorts by piling fresh clover and grass on the dirt and covering that with a blanket. Since the fire was near, some of the heat drifted toward them, but Caroline knew it wasn't the blaze that was warming her as Guthrie slowly took away every stitch of her clothing.

When she was naked, he laid her down and covered her with a new blanket, probably bought in Laramie, then began taking off his own clothes. Caroline couldn't help noticing that the rifle was within easy reach, and when he unbuckled his gunbelt, he put the .45 close at hand, too.

The firelight flickered over his naked skin, giving him a savage magnificence; he stretched out beside her, and the fragrance of bruised grass and clover blended with his scent, a distinctly masculine mingling of musk, fresh air, and sweat.

With one hand, he unplaited Caroline's hair, then combed it with splayed fingers, and in all this time his eyes never left hers.

The night seemed enchanted somehow, and Caroline's voice came out husky because her throat had tightened with emotion. "We'll be in Cheyenne tomorrow?" she managed, and she was humiliated to realize tears had gathered on her lower lashes. She wanted to find Mr. Flynn and clear herself with the law, but at the same time, she hated the thought of sharing Guthrie with the world again.

He touched her lips with his own. "The day after, if we don't meet up with any trouble." He kissed both her eyelids, and his mouth came away wet with her tears. His voice dropped lower, until it was hardly more than a husky rumble. "If those Indians hadn't come along when they did, I would have made you a bed of wildflowers and taken you then and there."

Caroline caught his lower lip lightly between her teeth and pulled at it. "Ummm. You have a poetic soul, Guthrie Hayes, though nobody would ever have guessed it to look at you."

He chuckled. "Was that a compliment or an insult?"

"You decide." With a saucy smile, she put her arms around his neck, only to have him reach up and catch her hands together at the wrist, then press them down high over her head. The motion made her breasts totally vulnerable, their tips jutting toward Guthrie, and he bent to sample her with a groan of pleasure.

Caroline's back arched, and a soft whimper escaped her. Guthrie's hand moved from beneath her breast to her thigh, gently urging her to part her legs.

Trembling, she obeyed, gasping with pleasure when he took her boldly into his hand. Then, suddenly, he thrust his fingers inside her, while the heel of his palm moved against her in a rhythmic taming that made her breathing quick and harsh and set her hips to rising and falling.

She sobbed out his name, too desperate to wait, too deeply in need of the most intimate contact. He must have felt the same urgency because he mounted her immediately and plunged deep inside her.

Caroline cried out in triumph as she raised her hips high to receive him, her hands roaming wildly up and down his back. Their loving was rapid and fierce, ending with the cataclysmic collision of two universes, and the deafening silence drowned out their cries of release.

Long minutes after they'd fallen to their bed in exhaustion, their arms and legs still entwined, Guthrie raised his face from Caroline's neck and gasped, "Much more of that, Wildcat, and I'm bound to die a young man."

She kissed his damp, hairy chest. "Young but happy," she teased.

He laughed and called her a name that would have been an insult under any other circumstances, and then he fell to her mouth and the whole lovely battle began all over again. It was well toward morning before they ran out of strength and passion and let sleep overtake them.

Tob awakened Caroline by licking her face. She pushed him away grumpily and sat up, holding the blanket pressed to her bosom. Guthrie was no longer in bed, but she could hear him whistling somewhere nearby.

Remorse filled Caroline as she recalled the night before, and the motions of her hands were angry as she snatched her clothes from the floor of the cave and dressed herself underneath the blanket. "You'd think I'd learn," she muttered to herself, as she scrambled out from under the covers and got to her feet.

Guthrie was cooking something by the fire, and he looked up and grinned when he saw Caroline approaching. "Don't say anything," he warned good-naturedly, pouring coffee into a mug and holding it out to her. "Just drink this and keep your thoughts to yourself until you can be civil."

Caroline took the mug from his hand and lifted it to her mouth, wondering how it was that she could be so swept up in Guthrie's lovemaking when it was going on and regret the contact so heartily in the bright light of day. She took a noisy sip and glared down at this man who was at once her champion and her nemesis.

He turned pieces of what looked like fish with an improvised spatula onto two metal plates and handed one to Caroline. She accepted it, then turned and stomped away to sit on a fallen birch log.

Guthrie remained where he was, eating his own portion in silence. When he was finished, he washed the plate and fork with canteen water and shoved them back into his saddlebags.

Caroline, who was feeling a bit queasy, picked at her fish, pushing it around and around on her plate. She was relieved when Guthrie finally came and took it from her, giving the leftovers to Tob, cleaning the utensils, putting them away.

He saddled the horses while Caroline finished her coffee and shook out the blankets.

Later that morning, they spotted the same Shoshone hunting party they'd met up with before. Mercifully, the Indians kept their distance, but there were chills spinning up and down Caroline's spine long after the red men had disappeared from view.

As Caroline and Guthrie climbed higher into the mountains, the air grew colder and more difficult to breathe. When they reached the pass Guthrie had been seeking, Caroline didn't know whether to be exultant or disconsolate.

They would be in Cheyenne soon and, good Lord willing, they'd manage to capture Mr. Flynn and turn him over to the authorities. After that, there would be no reason for Guthrie to remain with Caroline—unless, of course, she could honestly tell him she was carrying his baby.

She sighed as her mare patiently plodded along behind Tob and Guthrie's gelding on the rocky path. White-capped peaks rose on each side, lined with trees, and in some places there was still snow on the ground.

They stopped around noon for jerky—Caroline didn't even taste that anymore—and something special Guthrie had saved as a surprise, a chunk of Callie's savory wheat bread wrapped in cloth.

Caroline eagerly snatched her share from Guthrie's hand, and he grinned at her.

"As soon as we get to Cheyenne," he said, "I'll buy you a real dinner."

Since Caroline's nausea had passed and she was over her attack of chagrin, she smiled at him. "I think I should do the buying, since we wouldn't be here if it weren't for me."

Guthrie's grin faded to a frown. "Caroline," he said, putting his hands on his hips, "I'm the man, and you're the woman. That means I pay."

Caroline was enjoying Callie's bread, which was only a little dry, and she was not particularly inclined toward an argument. "That's silly," she said, amused. "If you hadn't met me, you wouldn't even be here. You'd be back in Bolton, working your mine. Why should you have to pay for things when this trip wasn't your idea in the first place?"

He sighed and rubbed the back of his neck in an exasperated motion. "I've already told you. I'm the man. I do the paying, and I give the orders and make the decisions."

Suddenly, the conversation wasn't funny anymore. "Now just one minute," Caroline interrupted, finishing her bread and dusting her hands together to get rid of the crumbs. "We're not married, Mr. Hayes, and even if we were, I certainly wouldn't allow you to dictate every little detail!"

Guthrie was face-to-face with Caroline now, his nose within a half inch of hers. His index finger tapped her chest. "If you're expecting my child, you *will* be my wife."

"You're saying I won't have a choice?" Caroline retorted, and the toes of her shoes and Guthrie's boots were touching.

He thought for a moment. "That's right," he said resolutely.

Caroline narrowed her eyes and leaned toward him. He was looming over her, but she wasn't about to retreat. "Well, if that's the kind of husband you're going to be, I wouldn't marry you for anything!"

"The hell you won't!" Guthrie yelled. "If you think you're going to raise *my* child by yourself, you're crazy. Making a baby is just about the most important thing a man can do, and *by God*, I won't let you bring this kid up to be a prissy schoolmaster!"

"What's wrong with being a schoolmaster?!" Caroline shouted back, but her argument lacked a certain spirit because of something Guthrie had said. *Making a baby is just about the most important thing a man can do.* She'd never encountered or even read about a man who thought that way.

Now, Guthrie's finger was tapping his own chest, instead of Caroline's. "My son will help me run the mining company."

Caroline arched an eyebrow. "Suppose 'your son' is a girl? Suppose there's no baby at all?"

Guthrie was quiet for a moment, and he looked as stunned as if she'd slapped him or stomped on his toe. But then, typically, he recovered. "I wouldn't want any daughter of mine teaching school, either. And if there's no baby, Wildcat, we won't have a problem, because we won't be getting married."

It was Caroline's turn to feel shocked, though she couldn't think why his statement had surprised her. He'd made it clear enough that the only reason he would be even remotely interested in marrying Caroline was to give his child a proper name. "Oh," she said quietly, and she stepped back.

Guthrie had won that round, and she hoped he found the victory sweet. When she turned to walk away, meaning to get back on her mare and press on toward Cheyenne, however, he reached out and grabbed hold of her arm.

His grasp was firm, but not painful. "I'm sorry," he said hoarsely. "I shouldn't have raised my voice to you that way."

Once again, Caroline was taken aback. What an enigma this man was, giving her dictatorial orders one moment, the next apologizing for shouting. And she still couldn't get over his belief that fathering a child was one of the most important things a man could do.

She almost told him, in her confusion, that it wasn't the hollering that had injured her, but in the end she couldn't bring herself to do that. She couldn't let him know how much it hurt that he wouldn't consider marrying her unless he was forced to by some moral code. "Let me go," she said and, yet again, Guthrie surprised her. His compliance was immediate.

They mounted their horses and rode on in silence, not speaking until they came to the top of a canyon and looked down on a small log cabin nestled among pine, fir, and birch trees, smoke curling from its chimney. There was a barn, and a well, and the beginnings of a vegetable garden, carefully fenced off with chicken wire. Sheep and cattle grazed together in a grassy meadow nearby.

Outside of the cabin, two saddled horses stood patiently in the sunshine, a paint and a sorrel. It all seemed very innocent, and Caroline was looking forward to a chat with someone besides Guthrie, but when she would have ridden down the hill, he reached out and caught hold of her horse's bridle, stopping her.

"Quiet," he ordered, and even Tob, who normally would have been barking, was silent.

The sound of raucous laughter drifted up the dandelion-scattered slope, and Caroline frowned as she realized the cabin door was open. That was odd, since most women didn't like to let the flies in. And there *was* a woman living in that cabin; Caroline could see her bloomers and petticoats drying on the clothes line.

"What's the matter?" she whispered.

Guthrie shook his head. "I don't know. But something isn't right."

No sooner had he said the words when a woman screamed and two shots were fired inside the cabin. The paint and the sorrel nickered and tossed their heads, frightened by the noise.

Caroline drew in her breath and raised one hand to her throat in an agony of suspense.

Guthrie pulled the rifle deftly from his scabbard and cocked it. Without even looking at Caroline, he commanded, "Stay here."

Caroline was frozen in the saddle, watching as Guthrie rode rapidly down the hill. There was more loud masculine laughter from inside the cabin, and the woman screamed again.

Squeezing her eyes shut, Caroline prayed. *Dear God, help that poor woman. And please, don't let Guthrie be hurt.*

Before his horse had even come to a complete stop, Guthrie was dismounting. He ran through the tall grass toward the cabin, the rifle gripped in both hands.

Reaching the door, he kicked it the rest of the way open with the heel of one boot.

Immediately, a shot was fired from inside, and Caroline watched in horror as Guthrie stumbled backwards. He'd been hit!

Warnings be damned, Caroline was already on her way

down the hill when Guthrie got back to his feet, aimed the rifle through the cabin doorway, and fired twice. The outlaws' nervous horses bolted and ran.

She hit the ground running or, more properly, stumbling, her braid flying behind her. "Guthrie!" she screamed. Now that she was nearer, she could see the bloodstain spreading to encompass the whole front of his shirt.

"Damn it," he rasped, "stay back!"

Caroline ignored him entirely, and when he stepped cautiously inside the cabin, she was right behind him.

Two men lay dead on the bare wood floor, while a blond woman of about Caroline's age crouched in the corner by the fireplace. The front of her simple calico dress was torn, and she looked at Guthrie with huge, hollow eyes.

Caroline stepped over the dead outlaws to go to the woman and kneel beside her. "It's all right now," she said gently, putting her arm around the quivering, slender shoulders. "We're not going to hurt you."

Guthrie had set the rifle aside. Gripping his wounded shoulder with one hand, he looked down at the men he'd killed with an expression Caroline couldn't read. She knew well enough that it wasn't the first time he'd taken another human life.

She patted the silent woman's hand and stood. "Let me have a look at that wound," she said to Guthrie.

He stared at her in a strangely disoriented way for a few moments, as though he didn't recognize her, and then wavered slightly on his feet. Caroline hurried forward and gripped him by the shoulders, and her hands were stained with his blood.

He pushed her away distractedly, grasped one of the corpses by the shirt collar, and dragged it outside. Not until he'd done the same with the other body did he stagger back into the cabin. He was deathly pale now, and Caroline feared he'd already lost too much blood to survive.

She pulled back a chair from the oak table in the center of the cabin and pressed him into it. Biting her lower lip, she unbuttoned his shirt and laid it aside.

The sight of his torn flesh made her sway slightly and sent

vomit rushing into the back of her throat. Caroline swallowed hard and closed her eyes for a moment, praying for strength. Then, determinedly, she turned to the woman, who had risen from her place in the corner and pressed both hands to her mouth.

Caroline knew just by looking at the woman that she was screaming silently, but she couldn't take the time to offer comfort now. Guthrie was bleeding to death.

"I need hot water," Caroline said to her hostess, speaking in a firm and even voice. She forced her attention back to the wound. "Whiskey, too, if you've got it, and a good, sharp knife. And some clean cloth for bandages."

Woodenly, the woman picked up an old metal bucket and walked outside.

Caroline bent to look into Guthrie's eyes, her hands resting on either side of his face. He was only half conscious, and she was sure he didn't know her. "You hold on, Guthrie Hayes," she ordered, fighting back tears of frustration and fear. "Don't you dare go and die now. If you do, I'll spend the rest of my life in prison and Mr. Flynn will get away scot-free!"

He smiled stupidly, though Caroline was sure he hadn't the first idea what she'd said, and she kissed him soundly on the forehead before straightening again and beginning to look around the cabin for the things she needed. She couldn't depend on the lady of the house; the poor woman was on the verge of collapse.

But she returned with the bucket, set a large kettle on the stove, and poured water into it. Then she opened the fire door and shoved in more wood. "My name's Penny Everett," she said. Her voice had a peculiar, singsong quality to it.

"I'm Caroline Chalmers," Caroline answered distractedly. She'd found a clean dish towel and was doing her best to stanch the flow of Guthrie's blood. "And this is my—friend, Mr. Hayes."

Once the water was heating on the stove, Penny brought out a paring knife and sharpened it against a whetstone.

"Don't let him fall," Caroline said moments later, and

229

while Penny held Guthrie in the chair, she went outside to get her valise. Once the water was hot, she used her soap to scrub her hands, then lit the kerosene lamp in the center of the table and held the blade in the flame. "I'll need a needle and thread, too," she continued, pulling the lamp close and bending down to probe the wound with a cautious finger.

Guthrie flinched at that, and Caroline's eyes filled with tears. She instantly blinked them back, but inside she was still weeping.

The process was long, arduous, and bloody, but Caroline finally found the bullet and maneuvered it to the surface. Once she'd done that, she poured whiskey onto another clean dish towel and pressed the cloth to the injury as a compress.

Penny, who looked as though she was about to topple to the floor in a swoon, had already laid out the needle and a spool of white thread. She watched, gripping the back of a chair, while Caroline held the needle in the lamp flame, the way she'd done with the knife, then threaded it with crimson fingers.

Carefully, she began to close the wound, and every time the needle bit into Guthrie's flesh, she felt it herself. Each low moan he gave tore at her like an animal's teeth.

When she'd finished the gruesome task, Penny had a basinful of hot water ready for her. Gratefully, Caroline washed her hands and forearms until they were white again. Then she washed Guthrie's shoulder, doused it with whiskey and prayers, and bandaged him with strips torn from a sheet.

Together, Caroline and Penny moved him onto the one bed the cabin boasted. While Caroline smoothed his hair back and whispered words of comfort, Penny dragged his boots from his feet and covered him with a colorful quilt from the cedar chest in the far corner of the room.

There was coffee brewing and, while Penny scoured the table, Caroline went outside to drag in breaths of fresh air.

Instead, she caught sight of the two dead outlaws, lying neatly side by side on the ground, their bodies covered with their own blood and probably some of Guthrie's. Feeling sick, she went back inside and not only closed the door but latched it.

"What happened?" she asked, collapsing into a chair at the table and reaching for her coffee with one hand and the whiskey bottle with the other.

Penny joined her, adding a generous dollop of whiskey to her own coffee, along with plenty of sugar. "My husband's away, helping a neighbor of ours put up a new barn. Th-those two men showed up about an hour after he left this morning. Said they just wanted to water their horses." She paused, drew a quivering breath, and let it out again. "They did that, all right. Then they kicked open the cabin door and—and came after me."

Caroline reached out and closed her hand over Penny's, silently encouraging her to go on when she was ready.

"They pushed me down on the table and held me there." Bright tears filled Penny's eyes. "And—and they pulled up my skirts."

Caroline gave Penny's hand a squeeze.

Penny began to sob, apparently oblivious to the torn bodice of her dress. "They touched me all over. One of them put—did something awful. I was so scared, I thought I'd die of it. Then your friend came and there was shooting—"

"It's all right, Penny. It's over now."

"It isn't all right!" the young woman cried bitterly. "My William won't want me now!" She bounded out of her chair, hugging herself, her eyes wild with remembered revulsion and terror. "A bath! I've got to have a hot, hot bath!"

Caroline rose wearily, put an arm around Penny, and eased her back into her chair. "You just sit right there and drink your coffee." She paused to add another slug of whiskey to Penny's mug. "I'll get the water for your bath."

She carried in buckets of water to heat on the stove in every pot and pan Penny owned and, finally, the woman was able to slip into a round washtub next to the fire and begin to wash.

"You must be hungry," Penny said. Caroline didn't have

231

to look at her to know she was practically scrubbing off the top layer of her skin, trying to wash away the feeling of those men's hands touching her.

The last thing Caroline wanted was food, and Guthrie certainly was in no condition to take nourishment, but Tob was probably ravenous, not to mention confused and frightened. "Is there something I could give my dog?" she asked.

"There's what's left from last night's stew in the warming oven," Penny answered. "I kept it to have for my midday meal today, but I imagine it's about to go bad by now."

Caroline took the cast-iron kettle from the warming oven with potholders to protect her hands and carried it outside. Tob met her immediately, whining and wagging his tail.

Touched, Caroline sat on the step while the dog ate, petting his head and silky back. She was startled to see that it was getting dark out; she'd been too busy with Guthrie's wound to notice the passing of time. She just hoped she'd done everything right.

One thing was for sure: Guthrie wasn't out of danger. She'd cleaned the wound, removed the bullet, and stitched up the gaping hole it had left, but there had surely been damage to his muscles, and infection could still set in. Or the bleeding could start up again.

Caroline patted the dog and went back inside. By that time, Penny was dressing modestly in the shadows by the stove, while Guthrie lay fitfully on the bed, his body drenched in sweat.

Although she was exhausted and barely able to function, Caroline nonetheless carried and heated more water. Then she stripped Guthrie of every garment, knelt beside the bed, and gently bathed him. He seemed more settled when she'd finished, and she covered him carefully and kissed his forehead.

When she turned around, Penny was scrubbing the table again, this time with a brush and soapy water. Her expression was grim, her jawline set with determination, and Caroline's heart went out to her.

"Penny," she said softly. "You need to rest."

232

Only then did Caroline realize that there was only one bed, and her face must have clearly reflected her thoughts.

"Don't worry," Penny told her, still scouring. "I can put the chairs together for a bed, and William won't mind sleeping in the barn, given the circumstances. You could lie down with your friend."

Caroline went to Penny and stopped her incessant cleaning by gripping her forearm. "You can't wash away what happened," she said quietly. "You've got to accept it and go on."

Penny's eyes filled with tears, but her fingers relaxed and she let go of the scrub brush. "I've got two babies buried up on the hillside, and there aren't going to be any more. Those awful men came into my house and—and touched me. You tell me, just how much is one woman supposed to accept?"

Gently, Caroline put her arms around Penny and held her close. Since there was nothing to say, she was silent.

"Shouldn't your husband be coming home soon?" Caroline asked, later, as she and Penny set the table by lamplight for a simple meal of fried eggs and toasted bread. Guthrie was resting, though his flesh had a hot, dry feel to it.

Penny looked away. "I reckon he'll be here any minute," she said. "I don't know what he'll say when he sees those bodies lying outside."

The two women sat down to eat, though Penny didn't seem to have much of an appetite. She kept watching the door, and at every sound she started. Caroline began to wonder just what sort of a man William Everett would turn out to be.

They finished supper and Penny went out to tend to Caroline and Guthrie's horses and do the other evening chores while Caroline washed the dishes and kept her vigil beside Guthrie.

When he opened his eyes, she felt a surge of hope, and when he clasped her hand, she was jubilant. But the name he whispered wasn't Caroline's.

"Annie," he said, and then he lapsed into unconsciousness again.

Chapter

❧ 17 ❧

*I*n the morning, Guthrie was still unconscious and his flesh was hot as a stove lid. Caroline bathed his face with cool water while Penny dismantled the bed she'd made by putting three chairs in a row and dressed for the day.

"I can't imagine where my William is," she fretted, going to the cabin's single window and peering out past the gingham curtains. "He promised he'd be back by last night."

Caroline thought of Seaton Flynn, out there on the loose somewhere, and hid a shudder. "I'm sure the work on your friend's barn just took longer than expected," she said.

Penny's eyes were grave when she turned away from the window. "We've got to do something about those bodies," she said. "We can't leave them lying out there."

The reminder of the two corpses killed what little appetite Caroline had had in the first place. Now she didn't suppose she'd even want coffee. "Where can I find a shovel?"

Penny told her, and Caroline's eyes strayed to Guthrie. She didn't want to leave him, especially for the grim task of digging graves, but something had to be done.

"You call me if he wakes up or seems to be getting worse,"

Caroline instructed Penny, then she went out to the barn to find the tool cabinet that had been described to her.

Tob joined her with a joyful yip the moment she emerged from the cabin and followed her to the barn. There she found the shovel and a large canvas tarp that was probably used to cover hay.

She draped the bodies with the tarp, then went in search of a suitable burial place. She picked a grassy meadow well away from the house so Penny wouldn't be confronted with a constant reminder of her ordeal, and began to dig.

The work was hard, and the shovel handle wore away layers of flesh on the insides of Caroline's hands, but she was determined to finish the task. She'd dug about three feet of dirt out of the first grave when Tob barked, alerting her to the approach of a rider.

Caroline climbed out of the hole and balanced the shovel against the side of a tree. Then, dusting her hands together in a hopeless effort to get them clean, she hurried toward the cabin.

Penny burst through the cabin door and flung herself into the man's arms the moment he dismounted, and Caroline smiled. William was home.

Her smile fell away when she saw him draw his pistol. Guthrie was in the doorway, wearing just his trousers, leaning against the jamb. His skin was gray with exertion, but his hand was steady where it gripped the .45.

"No!" Caroline and Penny cried in unison.

"I'd be dead if it weren't for these people, William," Penny pressed, while Caroline ran to Guthrie.

She was alarmed by the look in his eyes; he was like a walking dead man, with no expression and no emotion. There were no thoughts behind his actions, they were pure reflex.

"Guthrie," she whispered, slipping under his arm to lend support. "It's all right. This is Penny's husband."

Slowly, Guthrie lowered the gun, and Caroline took it carefully from his hand.

William, a tall man with rich brown hair and eyes of the

same color, lifted the edge of the tarp and grimaced when he saw the bodies beneath. Then, seeing Guthrie's knees buckle, he hurried over to help Caroline get him back inside and onto the bed.

"What the hell happened here?" he asked, looking curiously at his wife.

Caroline set Guthrie's gun gingerly on the table and averted her eyes. Penny needed privacy to explain the events of the previous day to her husband, but Caroline wasn't willing to leave Guthrie again. There were signs of infection in his wound, and he was out of his head with fever.

Only God knew what had given him the strength to put on his trousers, find the .45, and stagger to the doorway in an effort to protect the household.

"I'll help you tend your horse," Penny said, taking her husband's arm. She glanced at Caroline in a silent bid for support, and Caroline nodded.

When Penny and William had left the cabin, Caroline removed Guthrie's bandages entirely and found the flesh surrounding the wound inflamed. He was going to die if a doctor didn't attend to him soon, and there probably wasn't one within fifty miles.

"What am I going to do?" she whispered, resting her forehead against Guthrie's. His flesh was blistering hot.

The answer was painfully clear. If she couldn't persuade William to go for a doctor, and she had no idea what kind of man he was because she'd just met him, she would have to make the trip herself. Alone.

She'd made up her mind to do just that when Penny and William came in. He looked shocked and sick, and his wife was little better, but the expression in his eyes was kind when he hung up his hat and approached the bed.

"Mr. Hayes needs a doctor," Caroline said, barely able to force the words past the thickness in her throat.

William nodded. "That he does," he said, with a long sigh. "Penny told me you were digging graves up in the meadow. I'll finish the burying, then ride for Doc Elkins. I don't think he's a real doctor, but he's been looking after horses and men for a long time."

Caroline wanted to weep, to scream a protest, to demand the best physician in the world. But she knew Doc Elkins would be better than nothing, even if he was a horse doctor.

Guthrie grew worse by the hour. He was drenched in sweat, and he kept twisting from side to side, tearing at the stitching in his wound. Now and then, he cried out in a burst of desperate words, and the only one that ever made sense was Annie's name.

It was early afternoon when William finished burying the outlaws—they would probably never know their identities —and saddled his horse to go for Doc Elkins. He ordered the women to stay inside the house, with the door bolted, until he got back. He'd made sure both Guthrie's rifle and pistol were loaded and ready to fire.

When evening came, and Penny and Caroline had consumed a small supper of salt pork and biscuits in disconsolate silence, Guthrie's fever rose. Since Miss Phoebe and Miss Ethel had always maintained that more people died at night than in the daytime—and they'd had years of nursing experience to back up their theory—Caroline was scared.

She found a clean piece of cloth and was about to bathe Guthrie's fevered flesh again, in an attempt to bring his temperature down, when she realized that there was no water left.

Resolutely, she picked up the bucket and started toward the cabin door.

"William said to stay inside," Penny warned her, looking worriedly up from the sampler she'd been stitching on.

"I won't be long," Caroline replied, and then she unlatched the door and went out into the chilly twilight, leaving Tob inside in front of the stove. The moon and stars weren't visible, and she could feel an icy wind coming down from the mountain peaks. She shuddered and made her way toward the well.

Humming an old hymn to keep up her courage and stave off the angel of death, Caroline hurriedly cranked the bucket down into the well and up again. When she turned to carry the water back into the house, she practically collided with Seaton Flynn.

Her heart actually stopped beating as she looked up at him, recognizing his shadowy features even in the dim light that flowed out through the cabin window.

He smiled and grasped her shoulders, and the water bucket fell to the ground, spilling over Caroline's shoes and wetting the hem of her dress.

"I'm glad to know you're so enamored of me that you'd follow me to Cheyenne," he said.

Caroline screamed, as much from frustration and rage as from fear. She struggled, but he held her fast, so she turned her head and bit him on the side of the hand, clamping down until she tasted blood.

Seaton howled in pain and anger and drew back his hand to strike her, but at the last instant, he changed his mind and hauled her against him for a bruising kiss instead. Caroline squirmed and managed to kick him hard in one shin, but when she tried to run away, he entangled his fingers in her hair and pulled her back.

She cried out again, terrified, knowing he meant to take her away with him, or else rape and kill her right then and there.

He hurled her against the rock wall that surrounded the well, his hand still in her hair. "You little bitch," he rasped. "By the time I'm through with you, you're going to wish you were never born!"

Seaton was about to kiss her again, in the same brutal, punishing way as before, when a shot sounded. He stiffened, cursed, and grasped his upper thigh and, in that moment, Caroline broke away and ran for the cabin.

Penny was standing in the doorway, holding Guthrie's pistol in both hands, and there was still smoke spiraling from the end of the barrel.

Caroline shoved Penny inside, bolted the door behind them, and grabbed for Guthrie's rifle. Peering cautiously around the edge of the window, she saw Seaton mount a horse, still clutching his bleeding thigh, and ride off.

"He's leaving," Caroline said.

Penny was white with fear. Now that the immediate danger was past, she could afford to collapse, and she sank into a chair and rocked back and forth, back and forth. "Who was that?" she whispered, after a long time.

Wearily, Caroline explained about Seaton, how he'd robbed a stagecoach and killed a man, and how she'd mistakenly helped him to escape and gotten in trouble with the law herself. Penny's eyes grew wider with every word.

"Then you're an outlaw," she marveled, when Caroline had finished telling the story, bringing mugs of coffee to the table for both of them.

Caroline sat down, but she kept an eye on the window, afraid Seaton would come back. There could be no doubt now that he was a cruel and vengeful man. "I guess you could say that, but I honestly never intended it. Mr. Flynn claimed he'd been wrongly accused, and I believed him. The rest just sort of—happened."

Penny was looking at Guthrie, who lay fitfully on the bed, his flesh pale and glistening with sweat. Caroline realized that he was in direct line with the window and went to sit at the foot of the mattress, the .45 resting in her lap.

"What about him? What does Mr. Hayes have to do with all this?"

Caroline was careful not to incriminate Guthrie. "He's a friend," she said, filled with remorse. "He wouldn't have been hurt if he hadn't tried to help me."

"He's more than a friend," Penny persisted, lifting her coffee mug to her lips and taking a sip. Once again, she'd added whiskey to both their cups in the hope of steadying their jangled nerves. "I know by looking at your face that you'd change places with him in a moment if you could, just to save him from the pain."

Caroline's eyes glistened with tears, blurring the crude little cabin and its furnishings, as she imagined burying Guthrie in some mountain meadow. She sobbed, caught herself, and sobbed again. "Oh, God, if only I could," she wept. "If only I could give him my strength and health, I would!"

"You must love him very much," Penny reflected, going to the window and looking anxiously out at the night.

"I do," Caroline said, realizing that this was the first time she'd ever made the admission out loud. "I love him desperately."

Penny moved away from the window, but Caroline noticed she was careful not to turn her back to it. "I love my William, too," she said. "I told him what those men were about to do, how they touched me and everything, and he just put his arms around me and held me close. He said he was sorry he wasn't here to protect me."

Caroline smiled, drying her eyes with the back of one hand. "He's a good man, then. You'll want to hold on to him."

Penny looked infinitely sad. "If only I could give him a baby—but I guess the good Lord doesn't mean for that to be." She sat down at the table, next to the one Caroline had just left. "William's sister Belinda wrote that she was widowed, and can't keep her children together much longer. William thinks we ought to take her two boys and raise them ourselves. That way, they'd still be in the family."

Sympathy for the widow's plight filled Caroline. If Guthrie died, she might find herself in similar straits. The thought of giving up his baby was almost as devastating as imagining his death had been. "I think that's a fine idea. But what about school? And you and William must get snowed in every winter."

"William could teach the boys, he's a right smart man," Penny said, a little defensively. "And we don't mind a little snow."

Caroline shrugged wearily as Guthrie arched his neck and writhed in some agony he couldn't express. A deluge that could virtually imprison a person from October to April wasn't her idea of a little snow, but her friend had a right to her opinion.

She thought with a blush of how she and Guthrie would probably pass the time, then felt an ache plunge through her soul like a huge icicle dropping from an eave. She might never know that same sweet, consuming intimacy again.

"Don't you die," she whispered brokenly, grasping one of Guthrie's big toes through the blanket and giving it a little pull, and Penny pretended not to hear.

It was another hour before a fist pounded at the door and a masculine voice yelled, "Open up! It's me, William!"

Caroline and Penny both rushed for the door, and Penny reached it first.

"There was a man here," Penny burst out, hurling her arms around William's neck, "and he attacked Caroline when she went to the well. I shot him!"

William looked baffled, but Caroline didn't spare him much attention. She was more interested in the stooped, white-haired man who came in behind him, carrying a reassuringly battered black bag.

"This is Doc Elkins," William said, closing the door with one hand and keeping his free arm wrapped around Penny's waist.

The old doctor nodded an acknowledgement and immediately approached Guthrie's bed.

"Not good," he said, peeling back the bandages. "Not good at all."

Caroline pressed close, ready to protect Guthrie if she had to and, at the same time, desperately hoping the doc could save him. "Will he be all right?"

The doctor sighed, dragged up a chair, and sat down. He put a practiced hand to Guthrie's forehead and said, "Hello there, young fellow." Then his kindly blue eyes shifted to Caroline's face. "I can't answer your question one way or the other, ma'am. I'm going to try my damnedest to pull him through, and that's all I can promise."

Caroline nodded numbly.

"Heat me up some water so I can wash," the doc said to William, who immediately rushed to do his bidding. "First thing we're going to have to do is clean out this wound, and then we'll close it up. He's going to have a nasty scar to remember this by—provided he makes it through the night, that is."

Caroline swallowed. "He's got to live," she said, talking to herself, the doctor, and God. "He wants to work his mine, and build his house, and father children—"

The doctor's smile was kindly but sad. "I'll do my best," he assured her. After he'd washed his hands—Caroline considered his bent toward cleanliness a positive sign—Doc Elkins once again sat down next to Guthrie's bed.

"There's gonna be some pain, I'm afraid," he warned his unconscious patient quietly, "but it'll remind you that you're alive, and that's something."

Caroline hovered nearby, wanting to hold Guthrie's hand but afraid of getting in the way.

Doc Elkins moved his chair slightly. "There now, young lady," he said. "You can talk to him while I work if you want to, tell him all the reasons why he's got to stay right here with the rest of us instead of going on."

Caroline knelt and held Guthrie's head gently in her arms. "I love you, Guthrie Hayes," she said softly. "Do you hear me? *I love you.* I want to cook for you, and darn your socks, and have your babies. But I can't do any of those things if you go floating off to lie around on some cloud and play a harp." Her commentary was interrupted by a chuckle from the doctor. "They've got lots of nice people up in heaven," she continued, "but sometimes we run short down here on earth. You've got to stay, Guthrie." She kissed his forehead. "Please stay. I swear I'll let you pay for everything, and I won't argue with you unless I absolutely can't help myself."

Guthrie groaned as the doctor cut away Caroline's careful but inadequate stitches and began to clean the wound. It was a painful process, both for Guthrie and for Caroline, but if the infection was left to flourish, the patient would surely die.

Finally, after what seemed like hours, the tear in Guthrie's flesh began to bleed cleanly. Caroline lifted her head from his shoulder and looked up at the doctor's face, sensing something.

"Now we come to the worst part," the old man said with a sigh. "We've got to cauterize this wound, and he's going to feel it. The shock of the pain will either stop his heart or make him mad enough to fight for his life."

Caroline's throat constricted so that she could barely breathe. She watched with wide, horror-filled eyes as Doc Elkins took a bottle from his medical bag.

"What is that?" she demanded.

242

"It's a type of acid," the doctor answered, and he had the decency to look at Caroline directly when he spoke. "The stuff'll burn like the fires of hell, but it's our best hope of keeping the infection from coming back."

Caroline swallowed hard. "He's not conscious," she managed to say, her voice small and hopeful. "Surely he won't feel the pain."

"I'm afraid he will," the doctor disagreed.

"Can't you give him something? Morphine or laudanum?"

Doc Elkins shook his head. "I've known morphine to blow a man's heart apart like a blast of dynamite," he said. "But I'll leave some laudanum for afterwards."

Caroline cradled Guthrie's head in her arms and rested her forehead against his, braced for the ordeal ahead, wishing she could take it upon herself.

The instant the acid made contact with Guthrie's open flesh, he screamed in agony, and the sound echoed in Caroline's soul long after it had died away.

The doctor laid his hand on her trembling shoulder. Her clothes were wet clear through with sweat, as though she'd been chopping wood instead of keeping a vigil by a sickbed. "There now, miss. The worst is over. We'll give him a good dose of laudanum and let him rest."

Caroline kissed Guthrie's forehead and rose awkwardly to her feet. "How much do I owe you?" she asked.

The doctor stated his fee, and Caroline fetched the correct amount of money from her valise. Doc Elkins had whiskey with William and then went out to the barn to sleep. Only then did Caroline notice that Penny was slumbering soundly on a makeshift bed near the stove.

"What time is it?" she asked.

William consulted his pocket watch. "Three-thirty," he replied. "You'd better get some rest yourself, or you won't be much use to your man come morning."

His kindness warmed her heart. "I'm sorry for taking your bed, and for all the problems our being here has caused."

He looked embarrassed. "God only knows what would

have happened to Penny if the two of you hadn't come along when you did. I figure I'm the one that owes the debt, not you."

Caroline glanced at Guthrie, who appeared to be resting peacefully for the first time since he'd been shot, then met William's clear eyes again. "Thank you," she said softly. "And good night."

William extinguished the lamp and went to lie down beside Penny, and Caroline removed her shoes and crawled into bed with Guthrie. She couldn't help smiling, even though she was still very much afraid of losing him, when his hand rose unerringly to her breast and remained there.

She put her lips close to his ear and whispered. "I love you, Mr. Hayes, more than any woman ever has, and when you get better, I'm going to prove it."

He made a low sound in his throat that might have been a moan and squeezed her breast, and she cuddled close to him, resting one arm across his waist.

She awakened to blinding sunshine and a string of curse words that would have mortified the saltiest sailor.

"What the hell happened to my shoulder?" Guthrie demanded.

Caroline sat up, tousled and bleary-eyed, to see his green eyes glaring at her. After a moment, it struck her that the man she loved was awake, albeit complaining, and jubilation rushed through her. "You were shot!" she cried joyously.

"Whoopee," grumbled Guthrie, frowning at her enthusiasm. "I guess if I'd been horsewhipped in the bargain, you'd be *really* delighted!"

Caroline tried to stop smiling, but she couldn't. She bent and kissed his pouty mouth. "Stop being such a baby," she scolded. "I'm just happy that you're awake. We thought we were going to lose you."

Guthrie was fumbling with the covers, struggling to sit up.

"Just where do you think you're going?" Caroline demanded, gently pressing him back down.

"Guess," he glowered, rolling stubbornly back to an upright position and then getting out of bed.

"There's a woman around here, so just watch yourself," Caroline said, a little primly.

He made his way slowly across the room and out the doorway. When he returned, he was buttoning his trousers.

"I remember now," he said, looking down at the still angry wound on his shoulder with a frown. "Those two bastards had a woman down on the table—"

"She's all right, thanks to you," Caroline said, guiding him back to the bed, then going to the stove to get him a cup of coffee. "It was her husband who went for the doctor."

Guthrie sat propped up on the pillows, barefoot, sipping the hot coffee. His hair was rumpled and his beard was growing in, and Caroline couldn't remember when he'd looked better to her.

She turned her back so he wouldn't see the emotion in her eyes and offered a silent prayer. *Thank you, God.*

"Flynn must be a hundred miles away by now," Guthrie fretted.

Caroline faced him, having gotten her feelings under some control. "I don't think so," she said, keeping her distance from the bed because she knew Guthrie was going to go up like a geyser. "He was here last night, and if it hadn't been for Penny, he'd have taken me with him."

Guthrie swore roundly and tried to get out of bed, but he'd expended all his strength earlier, when he'd gone outside. He sank disgustedly back against the pillow, his eyes closed.

"We'll catch Mr. Flynn," Caroline assured him. And she really believed it. Guthrie was still alive, and that was proof that miracles could happen. She even had hopes of finding her sisters one day soon.

"Hell," Guthrie spat.

"Stop swearing. It doesn't help."

"Damn it all to perdition, woman, my shoulder is on fire, I feel as weak as an old lady, and that son of a bitch is out there somewhere, planning his next ambush! Don't tell me not to swear!"

Caroline set her coffee mug down with a thump, put her hands on her hips, and glared at him. "I doubt if he's laughing. Penny shot him in the leg, and that's bound to slow him down."

Just then, William came in, followed by Doc Elkins. "Looks like your doctoring worked," he observed, grinning at Guthrie.

The physician approached his recalcitrant patient. "Let's have a look at that wound of yours, son. Lie back."

Grudgingly, Guthrie did as he was told. "How soon can I get out of here?" he demanded.

Caroline was standing at the end of the bed, and she made it plain she didn't like his attitude. "A thank you would seem to be in order, Mr. Hayes, since the doctor here single-handedly saved your life."

Guthrie returned Caroline's sour look, then favored the doctor with one of his endearingly crooked grins. "I hate admitting it, Doc," he whispered, "but she's right. Thanks."

The doctor laughed, setting aside the soiled bandages and reaching for his bag. "Best way you can thank me is by getting well," he said, taking out a bottle of some sort of antiseptic. "You'll be up and around by tomorrow, I reckon, but you'll have to take things real easy for a while."

Guthrie flinched and set his teeth as the medicine touched his raw wound.

Doc Elkins rebandaged Guthrie's shoulder, then made up a sling from an old pillowcase Penny gave him. "There," he said, stepping back to admire his handiwork. "Now you're as good as new."

With that, the doctor said good-bye to Caroline and the Everetts and left for Sweet Home, a little town that lay just at the foot of the mountain. William said the place was about ten miles away.

William dragged a chair up beside the bed, turning it backwards and straddling it, his arms resting across the back. Soon, he and Guthrie were deep in a discussion of the war between the states, which Miss Ethel always referred to as "the Late Unpleasantness."

Caroline felt a pang of guilt at the thought of her gentle guardians. They were probably desperately worried about her, but she couldn't bring herself to face them until everything was settled and she was cleared of any unlawful behavior. If they ever found out she'd not only been arrested but actually spent time in jail, the shame would kill them.

After washing and brushing and braiding her hair, Caroline went outside. She found Penny pulling weeds in her vegetable garden, with Tob watching in fascination through the chicken wire.

With a smile, Caroline opened the little gate, went inside, and began helping her friend with the task.

"You've got blood all over you," Penny said matter-of-factly, and Caroline looked down at her clothes and was horrified that she hadn't even noticed.

"I have some things you can wear while we wash your clothes," Penny went on kindly, rising and dusting her hands off in a sideways clapping motion. "We'll make a fire in the yard and heat up the wash kettle. And I'll shoo William outside, so you can have a bath by the stove."

Caroline was moved. "Thank you. That would be wonderful."

Penny smiled and put her arm around Caroline's waist as they went back to the house. "You have folks somewhere, Caroline?" she asked.

"I have guardians—Miss Phoebe and Miss Ethel Maitland," Caroline answered. "They looked after me from the time I was eight years old." She swallowed. "And somewhere, I have two sisters."

"Somewhere?" Penny asked, frowning.

Caroline nodded, reminding herself that she had a lot to be grateful for, and that would be true even if she never saw Lily and Emma again. "It's a long story," she said, and while she and Penny heated the water for laundry and a bath, she told it.

Chapter

❧ 18 ❧

We're going," Guthrie said stubbornly. He was sitting upright in bed, with pillows behind his back, and there was a very stubborn set to his jaw.

"We're staying," Caroline countered, just as firmly. She'd laundered her clothes and Guthrie's, washed her hair, and taken a bath, and now she was sitting by the fire, brushing her hair dry. She felt as though she'd been resurrected.

Guthrie's nostrils flared. "Fine, damn it," he bit out. "You stay, and I'll go. It's better that way anyhow!"

Caroline continued to groom her dark tresses. "You're not going anywhere," she replied blithely. "You couldn't stay in the saddle for five minutes, and if you didn't have the temperament of a mule with a toothache, you'd admit it."

He swore and gazed despondently out the window. "All the time we thought we were tracking Flynn," he said, after a long time, "he knew we were there. He was watching. Waiting."

Heat pulsed in Caroline's cheeks. Watching? Dear heaven, she hoped not. "I know it's a blow to your pride," she said, trying to smooth things over. "Since you regard yourself as an expert of sorts—"

"Damn it," Guthrie broke in, "I *am* an expert!"

Caroline sighed. "Anyway, Mr. Flynn was shot. I'm sure he didn't get far."

"Give me my pants."

She reminded herself that she loved this man, that she was grateful he hadn't died. "Mr. Hayes, please address me politely. Simple courtesy makes all the difference, you know."

He glowered at her. "All right, then, *please* get me my damn pants!"

Caroline smiled. "I can't. I did laundry today, if you'll remember, and your things are hanging on the clothesline with mine."

Guthrie's neck turned a dull red. "You did that on purpose," he accused.

"Washed your clothes? Yes, Mr. Hayes, I did that on purpose."

"How do you expect me to go outside and pi—relieve myself?"

She remembered her time in jail, when she'd had to use a chamber pot and no one, including Guthrie, had seemed to be in any rush to obtain her release. With another smile, she went to his bedside and pulled the lidded pot from underneath. "Here," she said cheerfully.

Guthrie made no effort at all to speak politely. "I'm not going to piss in this!"

"Your choices seem rather limited," Caroline replied, and then she went outside, clad in one of Penny's dresses, to see if her own garments were beginning to dry.

Penny and William had taken their wagon and driven up the hillside, carrying hay for their livestock. Shading her eyes with one hand, Caroline watched their distant figures and felt a moment or two of pure envy. Whatever their problems and personal disappointments, the Everetts had each other, until death chose to part them.

Caroline lowered her hand and proceeded to the clothesline. She loved Guthrie, there was no question of that in her mind. The silly infatuation she'd felt for Seaton Flynn was a sad joke by comparison.

And she couldn't afford to forget that Guthrie hadn't

called her name when he was suffering, or even Adabelle's. He'd wanted Annie, the delicate bride he'd lost so long ago in Kansas.

The clothes on the line were still damp, so Caroline turned from them, her eyes on William and Penny again. As she watched, William took Penny into his arms and kissed her.

Embarrassed, Caroline averted her eyes and went to the well for the first of several buckets of water she meant to draw. If Guthrie was going to have clean clothes, he might as well have a bath, too. And a shave.

He was lying back against his pillows when Caroline returned to the cabin and poured the first bucket of water into the big kettle to heat.

"I'm going to remember this, Caroline," he warned.

Caroline couldn't help smiling in amusement, despite her dark thoughts about the feelings Guthrie still had for his lost wife. "I should think so," she answered brightly. "A person doesn't get shot every day."

"That isn't what I mean and you know it!"

She brought the washtub inside before answering. "We're even, Mr. Hayes. It isn't very pleasant, being forced to stay somewhere where you don't want to be—is it?"

He let out a long, raspy sigh. "If you're talking about the fact that I took you back to jail after you escaped, you've made your point. I thought that cell was the safest place you could be, under the circumstances."

Caroline went to him and bent to kiss his forehead. "And this is the best place for you right now, Guthrie. Your injury was serious—you could have been killed."

With his good hand, he caught hold of her wrist and pulled her down to sit beside him on the mattress. His finger touched the peak of one of her breasts, causing it to bud beneath the gingham of her borrowed dress. "I need you, Caroline," he said, in a husky voice.

Caroline blushed. "We can't. William and Penny might come back from feeding the cattle at any time."

Guthrie favored her with a sideways grin, now shamelessly caressing her breast. "We've been in their way for a while

They're probably rolling around in the tall grass, doing the same thing we'd be doing if we were up there."

She shifted slightly, but couldn't quite bring herself to slap his hand away. "Nonsense."

"Go and look," Guthrie challenged.

To spite him, she rose on wobbly legs and went to the door. Stepping outside, she could see the wagon in the same place on the hillside, but there was no sign of William and Penny. And the grass did look pretty high.

"I can't see them," she said, frowning, as she stepped through the doorway again.

Guthrie patted the mattress. "Come here, Caroline."

She couldn't stop herself from going to him; it was as though he'd lassoed her and was drawing her in, hand over hand. Once again, she sat down on the bed beside him.

"Open your dress," he commanded lazily. "I want a breast."

A shudder of need went through Caroline; her fingers fumbled and failed as she tried to obey. Finally, Guthrie undid the line of buttons at the front of her dress and laid the fabric aside. Underneath, her breasts pushed at the thin muslin of the camisole she'd borrowed from Penny, their nipples dark and taut.

Guthrie untied the worn little ribbons that held the garment together in front and sighed contentedly as he admired her bare, shapely bosom. Then, very gently, he put one hand to her back and pressed her forward, capturing a throbbing nipple lightly between his teeth.

Caroline groaned involuntarily and tilted her head back, her eyes closed as the beginnings of ecstasy washed over her in shallow waves.

While Guthrie suckled the one breast, he caressed the other, and when he turned to it, Caroline laid her hand to his nape and pressed him closer. In the meantime, he was raising her skirt, finding his way inside her drawers, cupping her feminine mound in his hand to let her know she was about to be conquered.

She whimpered. "Guthrie, the Everetts . . ."

But he didn't stop. He parted her with his fingers, making

251

his touch that much more intimate, all the while sucking hungrily on her nipple.

Caroline began to writhe as a consuming heat grew within her, degree by degree. He pushed her drawers down until she could kick them off, then set her astraddle of him. By that time, she was beyond all protests; she needed Guthrie too desperately to think about propriety.

She arched her back when Guthrie boldly entered her, his hand still beneath her skirts, splayed over her bare bottom, skillfully setting the pace.

Caroline rode him faster and faster as the friction grew sweeter and keener, and Guthrie lay still beneath her, letting her be the aggressor. She watched in a daze of increasing pleasure as he closed his eyes and tilted his head back in final surrender, and the knowledge that she'd just taken Guthrie, in the way he usually took her, drove Caroline straight over the edge.

Guthrie teased her nipples with his fingers while she convulsed on top of him, a long, low, primitive cry of ecstasy pouring from her lips. But she had no time to languish in satisfaction because she heard William and Penny's voices outside the cabin.

Hastily, she dismounted, straightened her bodice and skirts, and covered Guthrie. She didn't get a chance to pick up the drawers she'd shed earlier, so she kicked them underneath the bed.

There was a fetching flush in Penny's cheeks when she entered the cabin, and William was whistling. Guthrie grinned and pinched Caroline's bottom subtly, as if to say, "I told you so."

Caroline went back to heating Guthrie's bath water, while William hung a quilt from nails on the cabin's cross beam to afford him some privacy. He and Penny were at the opposite end of the little house, talking in low voices, when Caroline helped Guthrie into the tub.

He sighed contentedly while she washed his hair—it needed cutting—and then his back.

"Try not to get your bandages too wet," she said, when

those tasks were done, handing him the soap. He was kneeling in the small tub, his body glistening with cleanliness, when Caroline heard the cabin door open and close.

William and Penny had gone to the barn to attend to their nightly chores.

Caroline's eyes drifted down the broad expanse of Guthrie's chest, following the inverted V of light brown hair. His manhood stood proudly under her abashed perusal, and when she met his gaze again, he was watching her with a sort of solemn tenderness.

He gasped when she closed her fingers around him, and when she leaned forward and clasped the backs of his thighs, she felt them cord against her palms. She touched him with the tip of her tongue, and he drew in a sharp breath and murmured her name.

He was so beautiful, like one of the gods portrayed in Miss Phoebe's books about ancient Greece, and, for this brief time at least, he wasn't Annie's man, or Adabelle's—he was hers. She meant to enjoy him.

In the next minutes, Caroline exalted Guthrie, and humbled him until he pleaded with her. To her surprise, his response alone brought her to a deep climax. After soothing him with light kisses and soft words, Caroline took a towel and dried Guthrie.

He went back to bed willingly and slept as soundly as Rip Van Winkle. Caroline had to wake him up to give him some of the delicious chicken and dumplings Penny had made for supper. He ate distractedly and then fell asleep again.

Caroline lay beside him in the darkness later that night, her hand resting beneath the covers on his hard belly. He slid downward, opened her nightgown, and found a breast, promptly taking the nipple into his mouth. He suckled briefly, then fell asleep, waking up later to suckle again. All through the night, he repeated the process, and each time Caroline welcomed him.

When she awakened in the first gray light of dawn, he positioned her on top of him again and entered her in one smooth thrust. Being quiet with Guthrie inside her, and lying damnably still, was almost impossible for Caroline. She bit her lip as he clasped her hip with his one free hand and raised her along the length of him, then pressed her down again, very slowly.

Satisfaction came unexpectedly, savage in its force. Caroline's eyes rolled back in her head and inward cries of release rocked her. Guthrie grinned up at her when she'd finished, but then his eyes took on a glazed expression and he breathed an exclamation as he hurled his hips upward.

Caroline caressed his face and chest as he spasmed beneath her, then bent to kiss him. He returned the kiss, and when she offered him his favorite breakfast, he took it hungrily. She stroked his hair as he drank of her, her body feeling loose and heavy with satisfaction.

As soon as William had gone off to the barn, and Penny to the chicken coop to gather the eggs, Guthrie threw back the covers and sat up. He was fully dressed almost before Caroline had managed to button up the bodice of her nightgown.

"Guthrie Hayes . . ."

"We're leaving today, Wildcat. Or, I should say, I'm leaving. If you want to come with me, you're more than welcome."

Caroline reached for her trousers and shirt. She didn't say anything because she didn't trust herself not to nag and plead with Guthrie to rest for at least one more day.

After hurriedly washing herself with water Penny had graciously heated for her and poured into a plain crockery pitcher, she dressed and brushed and braided her hair. Guthrie was outside, scanning the countryside with eyes narrowed against the bright sunshine, when she joined him.

"Why are you in such a hurry to go, Guthrie? Don't you like it here?"

He smiled and rubbed his beard-stubbled chin. Caroline had never gotten around to shaving him. "I like sleeping in a real bed with you, and I especially like the way you bathed me last night," he answered. "I could do without the bullet hole in my shoulder, though."

Caroline adjusted his sling. "If you're really determined,

then I'll go with you, of course. But I still think you should rest for at least another day."

Guthrie was looking toward Cheyenne again, and Caroline felt a tug in her heart. "It's time to move on," he said distractedly. "I don't want to spend the rest of my days chasing Flynn all over the territory."

The tug became a twist of pain. Guthrie was probably yearning for the peaceful life he'd had before he'd encountered Caroline, and who could blame him?

"Caroline?" Guthrie curved his fingers under her chin, and his gaze was no longer wandering. He stared straight into her eyes. "What's wrong?"

She swallowed, searching her mind for a way to tell him she loved him, but the effort failed. "You called Annie's name when you were unconscious," she said instead. The statement sounded lame, but she couldn't help that.

His answer startled her completely. "I saw her, Caroline," he said. "She was standing at the foot of the bed."

Caroline's eyes were wide. "You were delirious."

"Maybe so," Guthrie agreed. "But she was as real as you are."

She reached up to touch his face, subtly testing for fever. "Guthrie, you know you just imagined . . ."

He shook his head abruptly. "No. I didn't imagine her, Wildcat. She was there—she even spoke to me."

The pain of knowing Guthrie still loved his lost wife so much, still needed her so badly, was incomprehensible. Caroline turned to walk away, not wanting him to read her emotions in her face.

But he reached out and caught hold of her arm, gently forcing her to face him again.

"She said we're still in danger, you and I," he told Caroline solemnly. "She also said we belong together."

Caroline looked into his eyes and shivered, despite the sunny warmth of the day. "I believe you," she said, although she really wasn't sure whether she did or not.

One side of Guthrie's mouth quirked upwards in an unexpected grin. "You don't," he replied. "But that's all right."

Caroline still gazed at Guthrie, her love stretching before and behind her into infinity. "You belonged to Annie first," she said, in despair. "Maybe you'll always belong to her."

He smiled sadly and gave her a light, nibbling kiss. "No person belongs to another, Caroline."

She wasn't satisfied; she wanted Guthrie to say he no longer loved Annie and, at one and the same time, she knew he wouldn't. In a corner of his heart, he would always care for the bride of his youth.

"I can tell you this much, Guthrie Hayes," she blurted, on the verge of tears, "I won't marry a man who loves another woman. Baby or no baby!"

His jawline tightened, and then he sighed heavily. "I think we'd better drop this subject before we end up yelling at each other. Get your things together, Wildcat. We're heading for Cheyenne."

"You won't be able to saddle the horses," Caroline pointed out, folding her arms.

"William will do it for me," Guthrie replied.

Deciding it was no use talking to the man at all—and he was probably loco anyway—Caroline stomped into the house and began packing her things. She had so few that it didn't take long.

Soon William had prepared the horses to travel and tied Caroline's valise on behind her saddle.

Caroline and Penny embraced.

"You stop by here if you ever come this way again," Penny warned, with tears glimmering in her eyes. "William and I will be building on a room for his sister's boys, so there'll be plenty of space for company."

Caroline kissed her cheek. "Thank you. And I want your word that you'll look me up if you're ever in Bolton. Miss Phoebe and Miss Ethel Maitland will know where to find me."

With that, Caroline nodded and turned to mount her horse. She'd never dreamed it would be so difficult to say good-bye to Penny Everett, but the two women had formed a lasting friendship during their short time together.

William and Guthrie shook hands, and then Guthrie and

Caroline were riding the trail again, with Tob trotting happily along beside them.

They rode until nightfall, when they reached the tiny town of Sweet Home. Caroline remembered that Doc Elkins lived there.

Since there was no hotel, Caroline and Guthrie took rooms at a ramshackle boardinghouse. Caroline didn't feel up to convincing some suspicious innkeeper that she and Guthrie were married, since they weren't, and Guthrie's mood was obviously much the same. They ate solemnly and went off to their separate bedrooms.

Caroline couldn't sleep, even though all her limbs ached with exhaustion, so she ventured back downstairs hoping to borrow a book from the prim landlady.

Instead, she was just in time to see Guthrie leaving the house, freshly bathed and shaved and wearing clean clothes.

While Sweet Home had no hotels, it boasted half a dozen saloons, and it was fairly obvious to Caroline that Guthrie meant to visit one. He was probably going to drink and smoke and play poker, and maybe he'd even fraternize with one of the loose women who worked in places like that.

Caroline sighed. Considering the way she'd been behaving with Guthrie, she had no room to call any other woman loose. And Guthrie had made no vows before God, for all his pretty words. If he wanted to gamble and carouse, he was well within his rights as an unmarried man.

Sadly, Caroline made her way into the front parlor. She'd spotted a well-stocked bookshelf there earlier, and now Mrs. Beeker, the landlady, was seated on the horsehair settee, crocheting a doily. She was a sturdy-looking woman with red hair streaked with gray and an ample bosom, which she was probably attempting to minimize with the frothy lace froufrou she wore at her throat.

Caroline hesitated in the doorway, waiting for Mrs. Beeker to become aware of her, and sure enough the middle-aged woman looked up from her handwork.

"Good evening," she said stiffly.

Caroline nodded. "I was wondering if I might borrow a book—just for tonight, of course."

Mrs. Beeker looked her up and down with disapproving eyes, and Caroline wondered how much the woman had guessed about her association with Guthrie. "Help yourself," she said, at last, gesturing toward the bookcase.

Caroline hurried across the room and eagerly scanned the titles, most of which were familiar and beloved. She selected a thin volume entitled, *The Life of Robin Hood.* "Thank you," she said, pausing again in the doorway.

Mrs. Beeker didn't look up from her doily. "Don't read anything but the Good Book, myself. Those frivolous things belonged to my daughter, Ruby."

As so often happened with Caroline, curiosity won out over reason and even discretion. "Ruby. What a pretty name. Did she leave the books behind when she married?"

The landlady made a disgusted sound. "Ruby didn't marry anybody. And she died giving birth to a peddler's brat."

Caroline shivered at the vindictive, heartless way the woman had spoken of her own daughter and grandchild. And she pitied the unfortunate Ruby, whose great sin had been that she'd fallen in love. "The baby?" Caroline dared to ask, holding her breath for the answer.

"He died with her. It was the Lord's vengeance."

Caroline's face heated with enraged conviction, but she didn't argue with Mrs. Beeker's view of the Lord, because she knew it would be hopeless. The God Caroline knew would never take vengeance against a helpless little baby. "I'm sorry for your loss," she said. *And I'm even sorrier for poor Ruby and her child.*

Mrs. Beeker made another noise, and Caroline fled up the stairs. Returning to her room, with its slanted ceiling and drab wallpaper, she found herself wondering if this bed had been Ruby's. Maybe the pitiable girl had dreamed of her peddler and borne her baby and died, all within those four walls.

"You're being fanciful," Caroline scolded herself, sitting cross-legged in the middle of the bed and determinedly opening the book about Robin Hood. She didn't want to think about Ruby Beeker or the fact that her own experiences might run disturbingly parallel to the dead girl's.

Resolutely, Caroline read the first line of the book, but her mind wasn't on the whispering leaves and fragrant evergreens of Sherwood Forest. She was reflecting on how easily she could end up bearing a child alone, and her fate might very well be the same as Ruby's.

"No," she said aloud, shaking her head. She would go to Chicago, tell people she was a widow, find herself a job as a governess or a nurse.

Out of desperation, Caroline forced her attention back to the book. Soon, mercifully, she was lost in the adventures of Robin Hood and Maid Marian and Friar Tuck. She read the scene where Robin lifted Marian onto his horse with him and kissed her three times through. It was so romantic, she thought with a sigh.

But she'd finished the book and gone through a thousand hells imagining herself bearing Guthrie's baby alone when she heard his boot heels on the stairs.

Throwing prudence to the winds, she bounded off the bed, unlocked the door, and wrenched it open. Guthrie paused and grinned at her, his hat in one hand. His other arm was still in a sling, of course.

"Evening, Wildcat," he said, and his eyes were dancing with mischief. He knew she was jealous, damn him, and he was enjoying it.

"Good evening, Mr. Hayes," she replied coolly. "I was wondering what time you and I would be leaving for Cheyenne tomorrow."

"Bright and early," Guthrie replied. "I'd advise you to get a good night's sleep—Miss Chalmers."

Caroline drew a long breath and let it out slowly to show that she held him in the purest contempt. "Your advice means nothing to me," she said haughtily. She dropped her voice to a near whisper. "I'm merely concerned with staying out of prison."

He had the temerity to grin. "I'm well aware of what you're concerned with," he replied, and the fact that she was

aroused when he ran his eyes briefly over her figure only
annoyed her more.

Blushing, she stepped back and closed the door smartly in
his face. But she could still hear him chuckling as he
proceeded to his own room.

Caroline not only locked the door, she propped a chair
under the knob, too. Guthrie Hayes needn't think he could
come sneaking in by moonlight and have his way with her
after what he'd said.

Half the night she lay there listening for him, hoping he'd
knock, hoping he wouldn't. Dawn came and there was no
sign of him.

Caroline's mood was black as she washed and dressed
that morning, putting on her riding skirt, boots, and blouse.
It was certainly no surprise that Guthrie hadn't come to
her—he had probably satisfied his appetites upstairs at one
of the town's saloons the night before.

At breakfast, he greeted her with a knowing grin. Caroline
ignored him, thanking Mrs. Beeker politely for the loan of
the book and dutifully consuming her food, which came
with the price of the room.

Half an hour later, she and Guthrie were ready to leave,
much to Caroline's relief. When she said good-bye, the
landlady reminded her that God's fury had destroyed the
Egyptian army when they pursued the Israelites and that
Lot's wife had turned to a pillar of salt.

Stifling a sigh, and quite unsure of what message Mrs.
Beeker had meant to convey, Caroline shook the woman's
hand and promised to remember.

"She thinks you're a fallen woman," Guthrie remarked,
when they were well away from the grim boardinghouse.

Caroline shrugged dismally. "And she's right, isn't she?"

Guthrie reached out and grabbed Caroline's horse's bridle, bringing her to an immediate stop. *"What?"*

She couldn't meet his eyes. "Last night, I was worrying
that you were with a saloon woman. And I realized that I'm
no better than any of them."

"Look at me," Guthrie ordered sternly.

Caroline's eyes went straight to his face, though she would have given everything to be able to disobey the command.

"Any man with a lick of sense would be proud to call you his own," Guthrie said evenly. "And I wasn't with any damn saloon woman. I was asking questions about Flynn."

Caroline barely managed to hold back a whoop of joy. "Did you find out anything?" she asked, after several moments of struggle with herself.

By that time, they were riding along the street again. "Nothing I didn't already know," Guthrie sighed, uneasily scanning unpainted storefronts and houses lining the road on both sides. "A man answering Flynn's description paid Doc Elkins to take a bullet out of his thigh early yesterday morning."

Caroline remembered the attack by the Everetts' well and closed her eyes for a moment, while fear closed around her spirit like a mist.

Chapter

❧ 19 ❧

*C*aroline and Guthrie had barely left Sweet Home when he pulled off the sling he'd been wearing and tossed it into the scrub alongside the trail. After a glance in Caroline's direction that dared her to comment, Guthrie began bending and unbending his right arm. As he did this, he grimaced with pain.

She took the challenge. "Dr. Elkins expressly said—"

"Be quiet, Caroline." Guthrie continued to stretch the muscles in his arm. "Catching Flynn is going to be one hell of a job, and I'll need both hands for it."

Caroline let out her breath. Nobody knew better than she did what a waste of time it was to argue with Mr. Hayes once he'd made up his mind. "Will we be in Cheyenne soon?"

"Probably sometime this afternoon," Guthrie answered distractedly. He was clearly more interested in the surrounding countryside than anything Caroline had to say and, as he rode, he practiced drawing his pistol. When that ritual was completed, he lit a cheroot and clamped it between his teeth.

"I guess I'll send a wire to Miss Phoebe and Miss Ethel when we get to Cheyenne and let them know I'm all right,"

Caroline said. Something about Guthrie's watchful silence made her uneasy.

"No matter what you tell them," Guthrie replied, "they're going to think I kidnapped you."

Caroline thought he was probably right, but she meant to send the telegram anyway, in hopes of sparing the elderly ladies any unnecessary worry. She would make it all up to her guardians, somehow, when this whole thing was settled and she could return to Bolton. She sighed. "I seem to have an uncertain future," she remarked.

Guthrie grinned around the cheroot. "It looks pretty clear to me. You'll be in one kind of trouble or another from now until the day you draw your last breath. The thing about women like you, Wildcat, is that you've always got to have some kind of crusade to go on. First it was Flynn, and when he's dangling at the end of a rope, it will be finding your sisters."

"Seeking Mr. Flynn's release was obviously a mistake," Caroline conceded indignantly. "But there's nothing wrong with my wanting to find Emma and Lily. They're the only blood relations I have in the world."

"I never said there was anything wrong with looking for your kin. It's what you'll be up to afterwards worries me."

Caroline sighed. "After I've found my sisters, Mr. Hayes, I shall be content to raise children and keep a home." She was suddenly embarrassed by the implications of that. "O-or teach school, of course."

Guthrie didn't comment, and Caroline wasn't sure whether she should be relieved or indignant. It would have been nice if he'd assured her that she'd be keeping *his* home and raising *his* children but, looking at him, she knew he probably hadn't even heard what she'd said.

After a morning of steady riding, they finally reached Cheyenne. It was a lively place, with lots of saloons sending out their raucous laughter and bawdy piano tunes, but there were stores, too, and several small hotels and restaurants. Buggies and wagons lined the streets, and people strode purposefully along the sidewalks.

Caroline, reminded of Bolton, felt a whisper of homesickness, but she smiled when Tob trotted up to the doors of the Diamond Lady saloon and sat there whimpering for a drink.

"I'll get the dog a whiskey and talk to a few people while you're sending your telegram," Guthrie informed her, dismounting and tying his gelding to the hitching rail in front of the Diamond Lady.

Although Caroline didn't approve of this strategy, she knew there was little or nothing she could do to change it. "I'll be around town somewhere," she told him offhandedly.

To her surprise, Guthrie took exception. "I don't want you wandering all over Cheyenne by yourself," he said, taking hold of her horse's bridle when she would have ridden away. "Send your telegram and then wait for me over at the Statehood Hotel. It's a respectable place."

Since an argument would only extend this unpleasant scene, Caroline nodded. "Shall I rent a room for you while I'm there, or do you want to do that yourself?"

His hand touched her leg once, lightly, and under the denim of her trousers, Caroline's flesh tingled. "We'll only need one room, Wildcat. After I've seen Adabelle, you and I are going to pay a visit to a preacher."

Caroline's heart soared, then plummeted. Guthrie wanted to marry her only because he thought she was carrying his child, and that wasn't reason enough. "We can talk about that later," she said.

Down the street, at the Western Union office, she dictated a telegram to her guardians, telling them not to worry about her and that she'd explain everything when she got home. That done, she proceeded to the Statehood Hotel and asked for accommodations for one. Guthrie could get his own damn room.

Having made this decision, Caroline carried her valise upstairs to her quarters while the desk clerk sent a boy to the livery stable with her horse. She unpacked her things, counted her dwindling store of money, and then went back down to eat a modest luncheon in the dining room.

After that, she went back upstairs and stretched out on her bed for a badly needed nap.

When she awakened, Guthrie was standing at her feet, freshly shaved and barbered and wearing a new suit of clothes. He looked like a different man.

"That's a pretty narrow bed," he said, one thumb tucked into his watch pocket, "but I guess we won't need much room considering that I plan to keep you either under me or on top of me most of the night."

Caroline blushed so hard that her face hurt. And she hadn't rested well. "I have no intention of sharing these covers with the likes of you, Mr. Hayes," she said, sitting up and smoothing her hair back from her face. "Have you been to see Adabelle yet?"

Guthrie came to sit beside her on the thin, lumpy mattress. "No," he said gently, taking her hand. "I'm going there now." He smelled pleasantly of bay rum and peppermint.

"Oh." Aching at the knowledge that he'd gone to so much trouble to look good for Adabelle, Caroline made no attempt to smile. Despite his promises, she knew that men were fickle creatures who could not be depended upon. Just the sight of the woman would surely bring back all the reasons he'd been so enamored of her in the first place.

He sighed and straightened his string tie nervously, then he took Caroline into his arms and gave her a kiss that started out gentle and then grew progressively more intimate until it rocked her soul.

Caroline found herself reclining when the kiss was over, though she remembered distinctly that she'd been sitting up when it began. When Guthrie opened her trousers, there was nothing she could do to stop him.

"When I come back," he said, caressing her, "I mean to finish what I've started. Be ready for me."

Caroline was trembling. "Guthrie—"

The skilled motions of his fingers made her buck against his hand. "Be ready," he said again. Then he withdrew and left her lying there on the side of the bed, aroused but unsatisfied and most definitely furious.

* * *

Outside the room, Guthrie straightened his tie again. God knew, he would have preferred to remain on the bed with Caroline for the rest of the day, but he had serious business to take care of.

He knew Cheyenne, having worked for six months on a cattle ranch just a few miles out of town, and he proceeded toward Adabelle's place in long, deliberate strides. She and her mother ran a respectable boardinghouse three streets to the east.

The familiar sign was still hanging from the limb of the big maple tree in the front yard, and the fence was freshly painted to a stark white. The grass was well kept and the flowerbeds burgeoned with colorful blossoms even though it was relatively early in the season.

Guthrie opened the gate—it still creaked on its hinges—and straightened his tie again as he advanced toward the front porch.

Both to his horror and relief, the screen door opened just as he reached the bottom step, and Adabelle came out. Her cheeks were flushed, her eyes feverish, and she reminded Guthrie of a skittish filly.

She was pretty, with her dimpled smile, her shiny blond hair, her lush and ample figure. But Guthrie didn't feel the complex tangle of emotions that always beset him whenever he laid eyes on Caroline.

He stopped, unsure how to begin.

"Hello, Guthrie," she said, and her warm, husky voice quavered a little. She clasped her hands together and forced another smile. "I'm glad you're here because there's something I must tell you."

Guthrie gulped back explanations and excuses of his own and waited, curious.

Adabelle flushed prettily and averted her eyes for a moment. "Guthrie . . . Mr. Hayes . . . I've . . . well, since I saw you last . . . I've . . ."

A shaky hope began to rise in Guthrie. Could it be that he was to be spared hurting this good woman who deserved only kindness and love? It seemed too much to expect.

"Yes?" he prompted gently, keeping his distance.

Her eyes shone bright with tears. "I've met someone," she said. "A railroad man named John Dennis. He and I are to be married next month."

Guthrie's reaction must have surprised her mightily—he let out a whoop of joy, picked Adabelle up with his one working arm, and swung her around once in celebration. Then he gave her a smacking kiss on the forehead.

She looked up at him, stunned, a cautious smile forming on her mouth. He was a lucky cuss, this John Dennis, just as Guthrie himself was.

"You don't mind?"

Guthrie chuckled. " 'Course I mind, darlin'. But the irony of the situation is that I met someone else, too. Her name is Caroline Chalmers, and she's a little skinny spitfire of a schoolmarm with the temperament of a scorched rooster."

Adabelle laughed and sniffled, both at the same time. "Guthrie, that's wonderful," she said. Then she embraced him, kissed him lightly on the cheek. "Be happy. Please?"

"You too," he responded, with gruff tenderness. Even though he realized now that he had never truly loved Adabelle, he also knew that she would have made an ideal wife. With her, he could have expected peaceful days, pleasant nights, and a whole dooryard full of apple-cheeked children.

She held his hands for a long moment; they said good-bye with their eyes; and then Guthrie was turning, walking away, toward a woman who would probably provide him with his share of trouble and Job's too.

Sometimes, Guthrie reflected, things just didn't make sense.

Caroline paced in front of the window, the tip of one fingernail caught between her teeth, her body still quivering in readiness like the strings of an instrument that had been tuned but never played. She'd taken a sponge bath and changed into the best garment she'd brought along, her simple calico dress. Her hair had been braided and then pinned up at the back of her head, and she'd pinched her cheeks repeatedly to make them rosy.

When a knock sounded at her door, she turned and said shyly, "Come in."

Guthrie stepped into the room, and he was smiling at her, though there were signs of weariness in his face. "You look beautiful, Wildcat, but for a wedding you're going to need something a little fancier than that."

Her face felt warm, and she raised the fingers of both hands to cool it. For one dreadful moment, she thought he was going to say he'd decided to marry Adabelle after all and wanted her to stand up as a witness. And in the moment after that, she was purely confounded. "What?"

"I want you to wear something—floaty," he said, frowning as he assessed her. "Something white."

Caroline's cheeks actually ached. "Some people would say it wasn't suitable for me to wear white."

"I don't give a damn what people say."

"But we don't know for sure that I'm—expecting. And besides that, Guthrie Hayes, I've already told you I don't plan to marry a man who doesn't love me."

Guthrie sighed. "You're expecting, all right," he said, as though it were a foregone conclusion. "And if I'm willing to marry a woman who doesn't love me, why can't you return the favor?"

Caroline hadn't expected him to take this tack. And she wasn't about to admit to her tender feelings when she knew Guthrie didn't hold any for her. She clasped her hands together in anxiety. "Perhaps, given time, you might come to love me . . ."

He approached and pulled her into his arms. "I'd say there was a real good chance of that, Wildcat."

Her heart was fluttering, eager and hesitant at the same time. "Guthrie, I could still go to prison. Then what would you do?"

He curved his fingers under her chin and lifted. "You won't end up in prison," he promised. "Now, let's go and buy you a dress." Then a look of consternation came over his face, and he edged her toward the bed. "Of course, I did say I'd finish what I started, and I'm a man of my word."

Caroline's tense body grew tenser at the prospect of sweet

relief. But she laid the palms of both hands to his chest. "No, Guthrie," she said, her voice husky with conviction. "If we're going to be married, I want to wait."

He chuckled and bent to nibble at her lips. "All right, Wildcat. Now, let's go and find a dress and a judge in that order."

A woman in a daze, Caroline allowed Guthrie to take her hand and lead her out of the room and down the stairs. They found a proper dress, gauzy as an angel's gown and just as white, in the first shop they visited.

Guthrie bought it with what Caroline presumed were poker winnings, and then they proceeded to search out someone to marry them. According to the marshal, the circuit judge happened to be in town, staying over at Mrs. Rogers's boardinghouse.

Caroline recognized the name, and her gaze went swiftly to Guthrie's face.

Her future husband simply thanked the marshal and ushered her toward the door. "Go back to the hotel and change into your dress," he said. "I'll send somebody for the judge."

All the problems, real and potential, came to the forefront of Caroline's mind, but she loved Guthrie too much to call off the wedding. She agreed with a brisk little nod and, "All right, Mr. Hayes, I'll do as you say. But in the future I'll thank you to phrase your requests politely instead of issuing them as orders."

Guthrie smiled. "I'll try, Wildcat," he agreed. And then he turned Caroline around and gave her a little push toward the hotel.

When she looked back over her shoulder, she saw him handing a coin to a young boy. She picked up her pace, wanting to be ready when the judge arrived.

Outside the hotel, Caroline encountered Tob, who whined when he saw her. Shuffling her dress box to her other arm, she bent to pat the dog's head. "There now," she said, "one of these days, we're going to stop dragging you all over the territory and you'll have a hearth to lay beside and plenty of soup bones to chew on."

Tob gave a little whimper, and Caroline left him, knowing the desk clerk would never let her take the animal through the lobby to her room.

Once she was behind her own door, however, she tossed her dress box onto the bed, opened the window, and whistled. After several summonses, Tob came bounding up the fire stairs, panting with the effort, and leaped through the chasm to join his mistress.

"Shhh," Caroline warned, as the dog settled himself laboriously onto a hooked rug in front of the dresser. "If anyone hears you, we'll both be thrown out on our ears."

Tob laid his muzzle on his front legs with a contented sigh and closed his eyes.

Caroline, in the meantime, unpacked her dress and hastily put it on. Since she couldn't do up the buttons in the back, she waited for Guthrie.

When he arrived, he brought a handful of buttercups and bluebells. "Sorry, Wildcat," he said, "but these were the best I could do on short notice. I picked them in the lot behind the feed and grain store."

The little nosegay of wildflowers delighted Caroline, as did the image of Guthrie picking them for her. Holding the blossoms gently, she smiled up at him, her eyes glazed over with tears. The words were so close, so close that she almost said them. *I love you, Guthrie.* But she caught them in time.

"Thank you."

He frowned. "What's the matter with your dress?"

Caroline laughed and then sniffled. "Nothing," she said, turning her back to him. "It just needs fastening."

Guthrie managed the buttons with his usual dexterity and, by the time he turned her to face him again, her tears were gone. "Well, Wildcat, the judge is waiting to make an honest man out of me. Shall we go?"

It seemed that Caroline's heart wedged itself into her throat. She nodded because she couldn't speak.

Downstairs, in a corner of the lobby, the judge stood waiting. He was a large man with a rounded belly, and he was clad in a pin-striped suit. He favored Caroline with an admiring smile and then led the way into the hotel manager's office, where there was a little more privacy.

He brought an ornate license, decorated with birds, flowers, and golden script, from the pocket of his coat, and both Guthrie and Caroline signed it. Then the judge took a book from his pocket and struck an authoritative pose. Two housemaids served as witnesses.

Caroline and Guthrie stood in front of the windows facing the street, a little distance apart, and a sidelong glance told Caroline her groom was every bit as nervous as she was, despite his attempts at aplomb. He had to be wondering whether such a marriage could possibly work or not, just as she was.

The judge began reading the sacred words, although Caroline could tell he knew them from memory, and somehow, she managed to make her responses at the appropriate time. Outside, she could hear the sounds of wagons and horses going by.

When the time came for the exchange of rings, Caroline didn't have one. To her surprise, though, Guthrie produced a gold band from the pocket of his coat and slid it onto her finger.

"By the power vested in me by the territory of Wyoming," the judge wound up, his voice rising as he neared the crescendo of the ceremony, "I now pronounce you man and wife. Mr. Hayes, you may kiss your bride."

The feel of Guthrie's lips on hers was familiar, and yet Caroline was as jarred by the contact as she had been the first time he'd kissed her. She swayed slightly and had to grip her husband's suitcoat to steady herself.

Merciful heavens, she reflected with an inner smile, people would think she was drunk.

Guthrie paid the judge and collected the marriage license and it was all over, as quickly and simply as that. Caroline marveled that Fourth of July speeches by pompous politicians could go on for upwards of two hours, while a wedding lasted no more than ten minutes.

She stretched out her hand to admire her wedding ring,

thinking how pleased Miss Phoebe and Miss Ethel would be to learn that she'd finally landed a husband. And one she loved, no less. Involved as she was in these thoughts, it came as a surprise to Caroline when Guthrie suddenly swept her up into his arms.

"Now, Mrs. Hayes," he said, "I have the right to bed you, and that's exactly what I'm going to do."

There were cowboys in the lobby when Guthrie carried Caroline up the stairs, and they all cheered. Reaching the first landing, Guthrie turned and she tossed the now bedraggled bouquet of bluebells and buttercups.

A grizzled old cowpuncher with big, mournful eyes and a handlebar mustache caught the flowers, and his friends laughed and slapped him on the back.

Guthrie chuckled and proceeded to the room Caroline had rented earlier. Tob was still lying on the hooked rug, and he opened his eyes when the bride and groom entered and gave his tail a half wag, but he didn't lift his muzzle from his forelegs.

"You'll have to put that dress back on tomorrow," Guthrie said, setting his wife gently on her feet. "We're going to have our picture taken, provided the photographer's sobered up by then."

Caroline laughed. A cowboy had caught her bridal bouquet and the daguerreotypist was too drunk to take wedding pictures. For all of that, she wouldn't have changed anything about it, except to have her sisters and the Misses Maitland there with her.

Guthrie laid his hands on either side of her waist. "I could stand here and look at you for the rest of the day," he said hoarsely.

She smiled. "Have you developed a taste for skinny schoolmarms, Mr. Hayes?" she asked, recalling opinions he'd expressed earlier in their acquaintance.

He gave her a light, nibbling kiss, and there was a look of wonder in his eyes, as though he were seeing something in her that he'd never noticed before. "Just for one in particular," he answered, and then, with an awkwardness that was unusual for him, he reached up to pull out her hairpins. He unbraided her dark tresses and spread his fingers to comb them.

She slowly undid his string tie, and Guthrie swallowed visibly.

He sat her down on the edge of the bed and crouched to remove her shoes, then stood to kick off his own boots.

It became a ritual then, slow, methodical, and tender. Guthrie would remove one of Caroline's garments, then she would take away one of his. Presently, they were naked, and there was no shame in Caroline's heart, only awe.

Guthrie smoothed Caroline's long, silken hair away from her breasts and then pulled her close for his kiss. She was careful of his wound, which was healing but still tender.

Before, their lovemaking had always been fiery and tempestuous, possessing a certain urgency. That day, it was gentle, leisurely. When Guthrie laid Caroline on their narrow bed and took her, it was with the same reverence and caution that he had taken her virginity.

She loved the feel of his hairy chest against her soft, smooth breasts, his hard thighs against her more fleshy ones, and she reveled in the sweet intrusion of his shaft as he moved it rhythmically in and out of her.

With all its gentleness and lack of haste, the culmination of their union caught them both unaware, for it was shatteringly explosive. Caroline flung back her head and shouted with triumph and pleasure while her body buckled helplessly under Guthrie's and, the moment the last of her cries had faded away, he stiffened on top of her and clasped the brass railings in the headboard in both hands. His eyes were glazed, and he moaned as her hidden muscles drew on him, making his seed erupt within her.

When he could give nothing more, Guthrie collapsed beside Caroline, gasping for breath. He rested his right leg across her thighs and held her breast in his hand, chafing the nipple with the side of his thumb.

Caroline rolled onto her side and moved up on the pillows, brushing his lips lightly with the peak of her breast. He took the morsel eagerly into his mouth and suckled, and Caroline groaned. Her body, so thoroughly appeased only minutes before, was already tightening again, and there was a warm ache in the depths of her, where only Guthrie could reach.

Gripping her bottom in one hand, he pressed her close against him, continuing to enjoy her breast. She arched her back as he moved her up and down against the flesh of his hip, and he left that nipple only to conquer the other.

Caroline whimpered softly, and a light film of perspiration dampened her skin from head to foot, and still he worked her, turning her on a fiery pivot.

"Oh, Guthrie," she sobbed out, and though he must have known the words were a plea, he was ruthless.

At the last moment, he turned Caroline so that she lay with her back to his chest, found her feminine sheath with his shaft, and thrust it into her. His hands fondled her breasts as she exploded in instant response, her hips grinding against his as she sought relief, her cries echoing unchecked against the walls.

Caroline wanted to watch Guthrie's face as he responded to her, so she turned in his arms and lifted one hand to touch his cheek. His eyes were hooded, his flesh damp, and he looked like a man in delirium.

She wrapped one leg around him in order to be closer, and when their joining inevitably deepened, he rasped out a senseless plea and emptied himself into her. They were still joined when Caroline bent her head and lightly touched her tongue to his nipple. It hardened instantaneously.

She squeezed his buttock as she tongued and teased his nipple and, after about twenty minutes of that, he was hard again, jutting within her like a ramrod. But this time Caroline meant to take her pleasure purely from pleasing her husband.

Kissing the underside of his chin, she began to move against him, very slowly, taking him in and out, in and out. With a muffled shout of frustration and need, Guthrie rolled onto his back, taking Caroline with him, and she sat impaled on his manhood, her hands clutching his powerful shoulders.

She was the warrior princess, claiming her spoils, and she

put Guthrie through his paces as she took him from one level of savage delight to another. Finally, he cried out and arched his back, and Caroline toyed with his nipples as she drained him of every essence. When it was over, he drew her down beside him, pressed her close, and fell into a sound sleep.

Presently, Caroline slept, too. When she awakened, the room was full of shadows and Guthrie was washing her gently with a soft, cool cloth. After he'd finished, he set her astraddle of his mouth and repaid her thoroughly for the way she'd conquered him earlier. She gripped the railings of the bedstead, just as he had, and surrendered, crooning as his hands rose to cover her breasts.

Her sobs of release were lusty—again, she could not restrain them—and the bedsprings creaked as she thrust her knees wide apart.

Guthrie made no effort at all to quiet his bride. Indeed, the more noise she made, the better he seemed to like it.

Chapter

❧ 20 ❧

*T*he first full day of Caroline's marriage dawned sunny and bright, but it didn't take long for clouds to appear in the relationship. She and Guthrie were sitting at a corner table in the hotel's small dining room, having breakfast, when he announced, "I'm leaving today."

Caroline put down her fork. "What?"

"I'll be able to track Flynn a lot faster if I don't have to worry about looking after you."

It was her fury that made her speak softly, not an attempt at cooperation. "Well," she began, leaning forward, "you could simply have me thrown in jail. That would probably keep me out of your way."

Guthrie sighed. "Caroline."

"Have you ever read the Bible, Mr. Hayes?" she pressed, her voice a rapid-fire hiss now. "There's a verse in the Book of Ruth that begins, 'Whither thou goest, I will go'!"

He looked implacable. "I *said* you're staying."

Caroline saw a lifetime of such arbitrary statements looming ahead and, suddenly, she couldn't face it. She pulled the golden band she secretly cherished from her finger and set it on the blue-and-white checked tablecloth, between her plate and Guthrie's.

His eyes widened, then narrowed. "Put that back on," he ordered.

Caroline shook her head. "Mr. Hayes, it is time you learned, once and for all, that you cannot order me about like you do your dog."

Guthrie sighed, obviously conscious of the other diners and how interesting they would find the exchange if they should happen to overhear. "You are my wife."

"And that puts me in the same category as your dog?"

"Of course not!"

"Then I will thank you not to make grand pronouncements concerning my life!"

Guthrie tossed down his napkin, even though he was only half finished with his bacon and eggs. "There are certain things that a husband just decides . . ."

"Things that concern only himself, perhaps," Caroline interrupted crisply. "But whether I go with you or stay here in Cheyenne and twiddle my thumbs for weeks or months is certainly my affair!"

"Damn it, Caroline, Flynn is dangerous. And we've just been lucky so far that we haven't had trouble with the Shoshone . . ."

"A few days ago, you were convinced Mr. Flynn had come to Cheyenne, that he was just waiting to pounce." She sat back in her chair, spreading the fingers on both hands and touching them together at the tips. "It seems to me that Cheyenne is the *last* place I should be."

Guthrie's jaw clamped down, then relaxed again. "He's not here, Caroline."

"How do you know?"

"I've asked the people who would have made his acquaintance," Guthrie answered, and his taut politeness had a sharp sting to it. "Besides, I'm not going to leave you here in the hotel. You'll be staying with a friend of mine—a Mr. Roy Loudon."

"Roy . . . ?"

"Loudon," Guthrie finished for her. And if the tone of his voice was anything to judge by, he was as resolute as before. "He's the rancher I worked for—a widower. I ran into him in the Diamond Lady when we first arrived, and he said he could use a tutor for his boy."

Caroline was amazed. Guthrie had never even *mentioned* this man to her. Now he apparently expected her to be pleased at the prospect of going to live in a stranger's home. "What kind of man spends his daylight hours in a saloon?" she demanded. "Besides, it wouldn't be proper for me to live in a masculine household unchaperoned."

"You won't be unchaperoned," Guthrie argued flatly. "Roy has a housekeeper, Jardena Craig. She'll look out for your virtue, believe me."

Caroline felt her heart tighten within her until it ached. Guthrie actually meant to leave her, after less than one day of marriage, to chase after Seaton Flynn. Mr. Flynn was deadly and of course there were numerous other perils that could befall a lone rider. She looked away for a moment. "Suppose I tell you I'll follow you?"

"If you try to trail me, Wildcat," he warned, in a grave undertone, "I'll catch you. The first thing I'll do is turn you across my knee. The second thing is take you back to Laramie and hand you over to Marshal Stone for safekeeping. That would take up valuable time but trust me, I'll do it if I have to."

Caroline could feel her face heating. She was beaten, but she kept her peace because it would have wounded her pride to say so. As subtly as she could, she reached out for the wedding band Guthrie had given her, tucking it into the pocket of her divided riding skirt.

Guthrie closed his hand over hers. She felt a sweet jolt, as though he'd somehow sent a charge up her arm and into her heart. "Caroline, if we're going to have any chance at happiness, we have to get Flynn back to Laramie. And you know I'll find him faster if I'm on my own."

She took her wedding ring from her pocket and squeezed it tight in her palm, like a talisman. She wouldn't wear it again, she decided, until she and Guthrie could be together permanently, like a real husband and wife. "I'll miss you very much," she admitted, averting her eyes.

Although Caroline wished with all her soul for some

poetic avowal of love and fidelity from Guthrie, all she got was one of his crooked smiles and, "I plan to see that you don't forget me."

They went back to their room then, Guthrie gripping Caroline's ringless hand, and he kept his word. He stripped her and made such tender, thorough love to her that she knew his mark was branded on her soul for all time.

When it was over, she slowly lowered her hands from the bed rail, which she'd been grasping in a fever of ecstasy, and rested them on his shoulders. "Oh, Guthrie, if you don't come back . . ."

He silenced her with a light, nibbling kiss, his breath still coming hard. His voice was raspy when he spoke. "I'll be back, Wildcat. You and I will go back to Bolton and explain everything to Miss Phoebe and Miss Ethel, then we'll see about going to Chicago to start searching for your sisters."

Caroline's eyes brimmed with tears. "Guthrie, I lo . . ." she began, but he lowered his mouth to hers and swallowed the tender words she would have said.

In the early afternoon, they rode out to Roy Loudon's ranch and, with each mile they traveled, another piece of Caroline's bruised heart fell away and shattered on the hard reality of her circumstances. Despite what he said, Guthrie could easily be killed, or simply decide he didn't want to be burdened with a wife after all.

The Loudon place was huge; Guthrie told Caroline that Roy owned the land as far as they could see in any direction. In fact, they'd been on his property almost from the moment they rode out of Cheyenne.

The frame house was modest, sturdy and white, with green painted shutters and windows that sparkled in the sun. Grass grew in the front yard, and there were pink tea roses climbing the brick fireplaces at both ends of the structure.

A substantial woman with dark hair pulled tightly back from her face came out onto the porch, smoothing her apron. This, no doubt, was Jardena Craig, the housekeeper who would see to the preservation of Caroline's virtue.

As if, Caroline thought dryly, Guthrie had left anything to be preserved.

Mrs. Craig came down the front steps, a cautious yet hopeful expression on her moon-shaped face. Her skin was pock-marked, her eyes small and dark, but her mouth was wide and generous.

Caroline was only too aware of her own divided skirt, rumpled blouse and hastily braided hair. She stood close to Guthrie after he helped her down from her horse.

"Well, Guthrie Hayes," Mrs. Craig boomed, her bright smile making her almost pretty. "I thought sure the devil woulda caught up with you by now and left nothing but bone and gristle."

He gave Caroline a brief, fond glance. "I'm not sure it would be fair to blame the devil," he answered, and Mrs. Craig laughed and extended a big, workworn hand to Caroline.

"Jardena Craig," she said, in her thundering voice. "It'd be real fine to hear a woman's voice call me by my Christian name."

Guthrie made introductions before Caroline could speak. "Miss Caroline Chalmers," he said.

She looked up at him, surprised he hadn't presented her as his wife, and then swallowed the lump of humiliation that rose in her throat. Guthrie obviously didn't want Jardena to know he'd married Caroline, although the fact was probably common knowledge in town.

"How do you do?" she said to Jardena, to fill in the ensuing conversational lapse.

"Look at you," Jardena said, taking Caroline's arm and propelling her through the gate and up the walk toward the front porch. "Just a *skinny* little thing. Hasn't Guthrie been feeding you?"

Caroline was still in something of a daze, trying to make sense of the fact that Guthrie had virtually disavowed her. "Yes," she answered, "but it was mostly just beef jerky."

At that, Jardena laughed and shook her head.

Minutes later, Caroline was settled in the housekeeper's big, warm kitchen, with a steaming cup of tea before her.

Guthrie had gone to seek out Mr. Loudon without so much as a fare-thee-well to Caroline.

"How did you happen to hook up with the likes of Guthrie Hayes?" Jardena asked, setting a plate of molasses cookies in front of Caroline.

She reached for one of the soft brown cookies sprinkled with coarse white sugar, stalling for time to think of an acceptable answer.

Jardena slapped her big thighs with both hands. "There I go again, buttin' in where I don't have no business. Mr Loudon's real pleased to get a teacher for his boy."

"When can I meet this child?" Caroline asked.

There was a mountain of dough resting on the worktable, and Mrs. Craig set to kneading it with a vengeance. "Ferris'll be along soon. He's out on the range with his pa right now."

Although Caroline loved children, she wasn't looking forward to the task ahead. All she could think of was that she wanted to stay by Guthrie's side—she wanted to *know,* firsthand, that he was all right. "Mr. Loudon has textbooks, I hope."

Jardena sighed. "A whole library full of 'em. Would you like something else besides them cookies?"

Caroline shook her head and pushed back her chair. "If you could just tell me where to find my room," she said, picking up the valise she'd left sitting on the floor at her feet. "I'd like to freshen up a little before I meet Mr. Loudon and Ferris."

The woman gestured toward a rear stairway rising beside the huge iron cookstove, with its hot water reservoir and warming ovens. The chrome trim gleamed with cleanliness, as did what Caroline had seen of the rest of the house. "Third door on your right," the housekeeper said.

Carrying her valise, Caroline set out for the second floor. Her room was small but immaculate, like the rest of the house. The bed was white iron, but there was a colorful quilt adorning it, and the curtains at the windows were a crisp, cheerful yellow. A washstand with a crockery pitcher and bowl stood in one corner, and Caroline knew without

281

looking that there would be a chamber pot in the cupboard
beneath. From the window, she had a sweeping view of the
range, which seemed to race away from her, losing itself in
forever.

Glumly, Caroline shook out her clothes and hung them
from the pegs aligned neatly along one wall. Then she
washed her face and hands with her own soap, after pouring
fresh water from the pitcher to the basin.

When she came downstairs again, sometime later, her
face glowed with cleanliness and her hair had been brushed
and wound into a loose knot at the back of her head. Jardena
immediately directed her to Mr. Loudon's study.

Caroline felt nervous as she approached that room, which
sat at the front of the house, opposite the parlor. She
knocked softly and heard a gruff, "Come in," from beyond
the door.

Guthrie was standing next to the fireplace, while a giant of
a man rose from his chair behind the desk, his hair dark, his
eyes a piercing blue. He seemed to look right inside Caroline
and read all her innermost secrets.

Standing respectfully next to the desk was a handsome lad
about nine or ten years old. He had blue eyes, like his
father's, and golden hair, and Caroline knew in an instant
that she was dealing with that most mischievous of creatures, a motherless boy.

Guthrie made introductions, again leaving out the fact
that Caroline was legally his wife, and she began to wonder
if he'd already set her aside in his mind. Heaven knew, it
wasn't an uncommon occurrence in the West for a man to
abandon a tiresome wife.

Only later, when Guthrie was preparing to ride away,
taking Tob with him, did Caroline get a chance to confront
him.

"Why didn't you tell these people that I'm your wife?" she
demanded, her whisper rendered sharp by her fear that she
would never see Guthrie again.

He lifted her left hand and kissed the place where his
wedding band had been. "You were the one who made the
decision to keep the wedding a secret, Wildcat, not me."

Caroline's yearning to go with him was so intense that she nearly couldn't bear it. "Please, Guthrie, don't leave me here. I can't bear the thought of conjugating verbs and working out mathematical problems and reciting poetry."

Guthrie sighed philosophically. "You're a teacher," he reminded her. "So teach. Right now, Ferris needs you."

She gripped his hand when he would have lifted it to the saddle horn and mounted. "Guthrie, when will I see you again?"

He touched her forehead lightly with his lips. "Pretty soon I'll be underfoot so much that you'll be thinking up ways to get rid of me," he answered hoarsely. And then he swung up into the saddle and touched the brim of his seedy hat. "Mind what I said before, Caroline," he warned in parting. "I've never laid a hand on a woman in anger before, but I'll make an exception if I catch you tagging along after me, and it'll be a long time 'til you feel disposed to sit down."

Caroline hated his officious manner but, deep down, she knew he was right. She would only hinder him on the trail, and it was unlikely that Seaton would dare breach the borders of the Loudon ranch to molest her in any way.

"Good-bye," she said brokenly.

Guthrie nodded remotely and rode away. Not only hadn't he told her he loved her, he hadn't even bothered to say farewell.

After composing herself, and collecting a supply of paper and some pencils from the house, Caroline sought out her student. It wasn't hard to find Ferris, for he was sitting on the front step and she nearly tripped over him.

"Could we go to the pond?" he asked eagerly.

"Not today," Caroline replied formally. "We're staying right here, on the porch, and you're going to show me what you've learned." She handed him some paper and a pencil, along with a book to put underneath for a hard surface, and sat down in one of the two rocking chairs that graced the spacious veranda. "I'd like you to write two paragraphs telling me whether or not you think Wyoming Territory should become a state and why."

Ferris looked at her blankly. "I don't much give a damn one way or the other," he said, in a forthright manner.

"Pretend you do," Caroline replied instantly, already caught up in writing down a series of mathematical problems for the young Mr. Loudon to solve.

"I saw Mr. Hayes kiss you," he said. Again, there was no malice in his voice, only that incredible directness, and Caroline found herself liking the boy. "Do you mean to marry him or something?"

"My relationship with Mr. Hayes is none of your business, young man," Caroline told the child pleasantly. "Now, if you would please write those paragraphs . . ."

Ferris bent his head and wrote diligently for a long time. The breeze ruffled his light hair, and Caroline thought sadly of Lily, whose tresses had been just that color, the pale yellow of cornsilk, when she'd seen her last.

Finally, Ferris looked up. "You could marry my pa if you wanted to, I reckon. We could use a wife around here."

Caroline was touched. Obviously, the little boy missed his mother. "You have Jardena," she pointed out, in the firm yet gentle tones a good teacher masters early.

"She already had one husband, and she doesn't want another," Ferris said. "She says it's only by the grace of the good Lord that she never kilt the one she had."

Caroline hid a smile. "I see."

Ferris turned his attention back to his assignment without being bidden, but when he'd scribbled out the second paragraph, he came right back to the subject at hand. "My pa would make some woman a good husband," he said earnestly. "He's got money in the bank and lots of land and cattle."

Caroline moved to sit on the step beside Ferris. She put an arm around him, embraced him briefly, then took the paper he offered. "Your father is clearly a fine man," she said. "No doubt, he's wise enough to choose his own wife, with little or no help from you and me."

The child's clear blue eyes reflected stoic disappointment as he looked up at her. "I really miss my ma," he confessed.

Caroline would have kissed his forehead, but there were bounds and she didn't want to overstep them. "I know exactly how you feel," she said. Then she read the paragraphs Ferris had written.

He would be a promising student, Caroline thought, but she must take great care not to become too attached to him.

Chapter
❧ 21 ❧

Guthrie had been clever in choosing a place to leave her, Caroline thought, that evening after supper, when she was alone in her room on the second floor of the ranch house. Under any other circumstances, she would have followed him, but she couldn't bring herself to leave Ferris so abruptly, and Mr. Hayes had known that full well.

After that, things fell into a natural pattern. Caroline worked with Ferris in the mornings, and in the afternoons he swam and did his chores around the ranch. There were no more hints that his father would make a good husband, but sometimes she caught the boy watching her with a yearning that tugged at her heart.

Each day, she hoped for a letter from Guthrie or, better yet, his reappearance. And each day, she was disappointed.

When a month had passed, she began to fear that he was never coming back. She hadn't bled in all that time, and her abdomen was definitely beginning to swell, though it wouldn't have been noticeable to anyone else.

Caroline wrote long letters home to Miss Phoebe and Miss Ethel, letters she didn't dare mail. She wrote to her sisters, too, separately and together, telling them everything about her life, her hopes, her dreams. What she said to Lily and Emma, knowing they might never read the words, was what she longed to say to her guardians, who had mothered her in their sweet and spinsterly way.

After another month went by, however, Caroline was beginning to panic. A doctor in town had confirmed that she was indeed expecting, and it wouldn't be long until her condition was obvious to anyone who looked in her direction. What was she going to do if Guthrie hadn't come back for her by then?

She was sitting by the swimming pond one hot summer afternoon, pondering those questions, when she heard a twig snap behind her. Thinking it was Ferris, who liked to pretend he was a red Indian after a scalp, she stood and whirled, her hands resting on her hips, a lecture waiting on her tongue.

But the visitor was Tob, and behind him, just barely visible through the trunks of the birch trees, was Guthrie.

Caroline flew at him, hurling herself into his embrace, closing her eyes in a rush of emotion as his strong arms closed around her. His chin was bristly with maple-brown whiskers, and his hat and clothes were as disreputable as ever.

He swung her around in his arms and then kissed her soundly.

As her quicksilver emotions changed course, Caroline broke out of his clasp to beat at his chest with both fists. "Damn you, Guthrie Hayes," she blurted out, when he gripped both her wrists and smiled down into her face, *"where have you been?"*

He let go of her wrists to cup both hands under her now plump bottom, lifting her slightly and pressing her against him. His blatant physical desire made her cheeks heat. "It would take too long to tell you, Wildcat," he sighed. "Suffice it to say, I've chased that ring-tailed mother—son of a bitch clear to the Mexican border and back. So far, he's always managed to stay one jump ahead of me."

Tears filled Caroline's eyes as her mood made another

abrupt turn. Her hands clutched the back of Guthrie's shirt and she gave him a little shake. "I thought you'd had our marriage annulled and left me for good," she managed to say.

Guthrie shook his head. "Once a marriage has been consummated, Wildcat, you can't annul it. Practically all I've thought about for the last two months is consummating it *again.*"

The birch trees and the pond made a sort of Eden, and Caroline felt no shame as she replied in a whisper, "Right here, Guthrie. Right now."

He laughed and shook his head again. "I've been on the trail for ten days straight, Caroline."

She was leading him toward the pond, having forgotten there was a ranch surrounding them, populated with people and cattle. It truly seemed to her that she and Guthrie were alone in the world.

The smile left Guthrie's face and his green eyes smoldered as he watched Caroline sit down on the fallen log to begin removing her shoes. Although there must have been ten feet of space between them, she could feel his desire as distinctly as if he'd been holding her close.

A little thrill went through her as she made a ceremony of lifting the skirts of her gingham dress and rolling down the white stocking beneath. Because she used a straight razor on her legs when she bathed, the flesh there was smooth as alabaster.

Guthrie's Adam's apple bobbed in his throat, and he took a stumbling step closer. "Damn it, Caroline," he protested in a hoarse croak. "Stop that."

She laid the stocking on the log beside her and began rolling down the other one.

He seemed propelled toward her by some unseen hand. "Caroline," he growled, narrowing his eyes.

She stood and unbuttoned the front of the dress she'd made for herself, along with others, to keep herself busy during the long evenings. Her saucy, sidelong look dared him to object further.

Guthrie tossed his hat aside with a muttered curse and sat down on the ground to pull off his boots.

Laughing, Caroline finished stripping off her clothes and ran toward the sun-warmed, shimmering water of the pond, moving far out into the middle to watch Guthrie as he undressed and stomped into the pond. He was gloriously, furiously naked.

"If half the ranch isn't looking on," he grumbled, splashing up beside her, "it'll be no thanks to you!"

Caroline approached him and put her arms around his neck. The water came to just above her breasts, even in the center of the pond, and the bottom felt squishy under her feet. "Kiss me again," she crooned.

Her husband scowled at her for a long moment, then hauled her against him and kissed her hard. When it was over, she fell back from him, dazed. One of her hands moved beneath the water, seeking him, wreaking sweet vengeance.

He groaned as she caressed him, enjoying his magnificence.

"Caroline," he pleaded, "this place isn't private. Half the hands on this ranch could show up at any minute, naked as jaybirds."

She laughed. "They're all out on the range," she said confidently. She traced his lips, which seemed a little swollen from the kiss they'd just shared. "There's nobody around to see me without my clothes except you."

Guthrie's sturdy frame stiffened. "That's a very good thing," he told her gruffly. "It means I won't have to shoot some poor bastard."

Caroline laughed, still bedeviling him with her hand.

"Oh, God," Guthrie groaned, as she worked him more and more industriously. His head drifted back, and Caroline tasted his neck and then his earlobe. "If you don't stop . . ."

"I'm not about to stop," Caroline assured him, in a lazy tone. "I want to see how much you've missed me."

Guthrie laid his hands lightly to the sides of her waist, his thumbs moving over the swelling place where their baby was growing. "I've missed you a whole lot," he said. "But I want to be inside you when it happens."

They moved into the shadows of an overhanging willow tree, where they were hidden from all but each other.

Gently, Guthrie lifted her, and she automatically wrapped her legs around his hips, needing the intimate contact that gave. When he began kissing his way down over her collarbone and the rise of breast beneath, Caroline moaned and tilted her head back.

His access to her breasts was unimpeded, and he took full advantage, taking a nipple hungrily into his mouth and sucking hard. At the same time, Caroline could feel him at the entrance to her body, pulsing against the tender, aching flesh hidden there.

"I'm sorry, Wildcat," he said, drawing back from her nipple just long enough to speak, "but I can't wait anymore."

Caroline buried her face in his neck as he slowly lowered her onto him, making her work for every inch. She didn't even need the friction; when he was fully inside her, Caroline came, her body buckling against his, his name tumbling from her lips in a long, joyous sob.

He whispered soothing words as she settled into a languid state of satisfaction, then began raising and lowering her, seeking the same fierce delight from her body that she'd just taken from his. Caroline clung to him, her hands entangled in his hair, her lips moving over his neck and ear.

When she told him how she was going to please him in bed that night, he gave a rumbling groan and stiffened, his shaft buried deep within her, his warmth sending her tumbling into the throes of another release. This one was unexpected, and it left her sagging against him.

He spread his hand over her belly when they'd both had some time to recover. "We were right, weren't we? There is a baby?"

Caroline's heart was full as she nodded. "Oh, yes. There's a baby, all right. He'll be born this winter."

She couldn't tell whether the moisture in Guthrie's eyes

was pond water or tears, but he was smiling. Without a word, he bent his head and kissed her, this time tenderly.

"If I'm going to take you to bed tonight, like a proper wife," he said, when he was finished, "you'll have to break the news to Roy that we're married. Otherwise, he'll shoot me for dallying with a female member of his household."

Caroline smiled and held up her left hand, revealing the golden ring gleaming on her finger. "I imagine he's guessed," she said. "I've been wearing your wedding band since about a week after you left."

He kissed her forehead. "I can't wait until all this is over and we have a place of our own. I'm going to keep you in bed for the first six weeks."

She laughed. "You won't accomplish much that way," she scolded.

Brazenly, his hand cupped her beneath the water, the palm massaging her most sensitive place. "Oh, no?" he teased.

Caroline's fingers sought his shoulders and tightened there, and she bit her lower lip for a long moment before bursting out with a whispered, "Guthrie, stop—I need a few minutes . . ."

His finger plunged inside her and began to tickle and tease. "Ooooooh," she crooned.

He leaned down to take the breast she brazenly offered him, all the while continuing the rubbing motion of his other hand.

Caroline felt herself tightening around him, and her eyes rolled back as the pleasure caused her to spasm repeatedly. By the time she'd gone still, with a little whimpering sigh, Guthrie was ready for her again. He turned her, his hands covering her breasts, and glided into her feminine channel from behind.

Soon, although she would have sworn it wasn't possible after the pinnacles he'd taken her to before, Caroline was slamming herself against Guthrie, puffing like a steam engine as she strained toward release. The achievement wrung a low cry of triumph and surrender from her throat, and Guthrie caressed her breasts and spoke softly and wickedly to her while she writhed in grinding, impossible pleasure.

Distant sounds of laughter and approaching horses gave them little or no time to recover from their explosive contact. Guthrie and Caroline had just barely finished dressing when Ferris burst through the trees, letting go with a soul-rendering Rebel yell.

Obviously, he'd won some sort of race, but when he saw Caroline and Guthrie standing there, uneasy and wet in their awkwardly donned clothes, all the triumph drained from his eyes.

"You're back," he said to Guthrie, sliding deftly off the back of his painted pony and leaving it to wander home on its own.

Guthrie nodded, reaching for his hat and settling it on his head. "Hello, Ferris," he said.

Distractedly, Ferris petted Tob, who butted his head against the boy's thigh until he got the attention he clearly considered his due. Ferris's gaze shifted to Caroline's face, and she saw such misery there that she wanted to cry for him.

Guthrie set one hand against the small of her back, and it was a proprietary, intimate gesture. "We'll leave you to your swimming," he said, and then he was propelling Caroline through the trees toward the ranch house.

Half a dozen cowboys arrived at the pond just as they were leaving, and Caroline wondered if Ferris was really such a fast rider or if the ranch hands had simply let him win the race. Guthrie responded to the men's greetings with a grin, but he didn't slow his pace.

Ahead, Caroline could see his gelding standing patiently in front of the barn.

She put her arm around his waist. "When are we leaving?"

He looked down at her and frowned. "Maybe we'd better talk about that later," he sighed.

Caroline stopped, forcing Guthrie to stop, too. "We'll talk about it *now,*" she said firmly. "You're planning to ride off and leave me again, aren't you?"

Guthrie swept his hat off in a gesture of weary frustration

and ran his sleeve across his forehead. "I've still got to catch up with Flynn," he told her impatiently. "His trail led right back to Cheyenne."

"So *that's* the only reason you're here? Because you were coming this way anyhow?!"

"Caroline—"

"Don't you 'Caroline' me, Guthrie Hayes. I won't spend my whole life waiting here for you to favor me with your presence!"

"Would you rather spend it in prison, Caroline?" he countered, gripping her upper arms and looking straight into her eyes. "Do you want to have our baby there?"

"I'm not going to prison. You said so yourself."

"All right, so I did. But you don't want to spend the rest of your days looking over your shoulder and running from the law, do you?"

Caroline swallowed and shook her head. If she and Guthrie had to flee to Mexico, she would never see her guardians again, and there would be no hope at all of finding her sisters.

"Then I have to go. But I swear to you, Caroline, I'll be back. We'll raise this baby together and make half a dozen more while we're at it."

Caroline's eyes filled with involuntary tears. "You could be killed," she reminded him.

"If that happens," he told her seriously, still gripping her arms, "I want you to stay right here. Roy is a good man. He'll protect you and give you a good home."

"You make me sound like a stray puppy!" Caroline protested. "I don't *want* to stay here forever, Guthrie. Besides, even Roy couldn't protect me from the law."

"He's a powerful man," Guthrie responded immediately. "He could do more than you think."

"I don't want to be married to anyone but you," Caroline insisted, and Guthrie let her go with a heavy sigh.

Later, while Guthrie was making use of the Loudons' fancy bathtub, Caroline washed his other clothes and hung them out on the clothesline in the backyard. When she returned to the kitchen, Ferris was standing by the counter, drinking lemonade and eating Jardena's oatmeal cookies. His blond hair was wet and his eyes were full of curiosity and hurt.

"That's Mr. Hayes's ring on your finger," he accused.

Caroline was stunned. "Ferris, whose ring did you think it was?" she asked gently.

"Pa's, maybe," the boy admitted. "I hoped you two might have gotten married in secret or something."

Her heart ached. So that was why Ferris had stopped campaigning for a wedding. "Surely your father would tell you a thing like that," Caroline said softly. She wanted to touch his shoulder, but she didn't quite dare.

"He didn't tell me Mama was dying," Ferris replied, with an offhand shrug that didn't fool Caroline for a moment. "He doesn't tell me nothin', except to feed and water the cows or pick up my boots or pay attention when you're teaching me."

Caroline resisted the urge to correct his grammar. "When did your mother pass away?" she asked gently, pulling back a chair at the table, sitting down, and reaching for a cookie she didn't want. She knew they should have talked about Mrs. Loudon before, but she'd avoided the subject, knowing it would be a painful one.

Ferris glared at her for a moment, then sank into a chair opposite hers. "Three years ago. She's buried on that little knoll west of the house, where the cherry tree grows. Pa and I planted it there because she loved the way cherry trees look when they blossom in the springtime."

Caroline's throat thickened as she thought of all the sadness in the world. She reached out and took Ferris's small, grubby hand in hers, and he didn't pull away from her. "I don't think you really want me for a mother, do you, Ferris?" she asked, with a gentle smile. "I'd be forever making you do sums and diagram sentences."

He grinned wanly, ran a hand through his still damp hair, and shook his head. "No, ma'am, Miss Chalmers. If I was a few years older, and you weren't Guthrie's wife, I reckon I'd be inclined to marry you myself."

She couldn't resist. She leaned forward and kissed his

forehead, her eyes shining. "One of these days you're going to grow up big and tall like your father. You'll meet a pretty girl at some dance and your cranky old teacher will be the farthest person from your mind."

Ferris's eyes took on a look of resolution, though, and he shook his head again. "No, Miss Caroline. I won't ever forget you," he said solemnly.

Just then, Guthrie came down the rear stairway, wearing clean clothes he'd evidently bought in town. He was freshly shaved and his hair was a shade or two darker than usual because it was still wet.

Ferris gave his father's friend a meaningful glance and then left the kitchen without a word.

"What's bothering him?" Guthrie asked with a frown.

Caroline sighed. "Nothing a little time won't cure."

A troubled expression lingered in Guthrie's eyes for a few moments, but it was gone when he came to the table after pouring himself a cup of Jardena's hot, fresh coffee.

"Why didn't you write to me?" Caroline demanded, studying her husband. Now that he'd shaved and his longish maple-colored hair was glossy with cleanliness, she was struck once again by his remarkable looks.

"I'm no letter writer," he answered, taking a sip of his coffee. "But I brought you a present."

Caroline's eyes widened with pleasure. "What?" she demanded.

He took a small package from his shirt pocket and handed it to her. Inside, Caroline found a delicate gold chain and an oval locket. She was so overcome that she couldn't speak for a few seconds.

Guthrie got up to fasten the chain around her neck, and his hands lingered, warm, on the flesh revealed by her summer dress. "Caroline," he began gruffly, "I—"

But before he could finish the sentence, the back door opened and Jardena came in, carrying a basket full of sun-dried laundry. She beamed at Guthrie and demanded, "What are you doing back in these parts, you black-hearted rascal?"

He laughed and crossed the room to kiss her forehead and

take the laundry basket out of her arms. "I couldn't stay away from you any longer, Jardena."

She hooted with amusement at that, but Caroline noticed the flush that pinkened the woman's coarse cheeks and was touched. "I'd sooner take up with a polecat or that scarecrow out there in the pea patch than with you, Guthrie Hayes," the housekeeper boomed. "So just you keep out from under my feet, you hear?"

Guthrie chuckled, set the clothes basket aside, and dropped back into his chair at the table. "I hear," he said.

Later that evening, Guthrie and Caroline shared a quiet dinner with Roy Loudon and his son in the formal dining room. Caroline excused herself soon after the meal ended, choosing not to help Jardena with the dishes for once, and Guthrie remained downstairs, probably to smoke and drink brandy with his friend.

It was almost midnight when he entered the bedroom, sat down on his own side of the mattress, with his back to Caroline, and pulled off his boots.

She reached out and touched his back. "What were you doing all this time, Guthrie?" she asked softly. "Offering me to Roy Loudon?"

"As a matter of fact, I did explain the situation."

Caroline sat bolt upright. *"You told him I could be sent to prison?"*

Guthrie stood and slipped his suspenders off his shoulders, then began unbuttoning his shirt. "Yes. And he promised me he'd take care of you and the baby if I don't come back."

"I don't want any man but you," Caroline said stubbornly, pulling the covers up to her chin. "And I'm warning you, Mr. Hayes, if you try to abandon me, I'll come looking for you."

He bent and kissed her, and he smelled of cheroots and good brandy. "Roy wouldn't let you," he said. "He's a strong-minded man, for all his quiet ways."

Caroline put Roy Loudon forcibly out of her mind. She was Guthrie's woman, and she always would be.

When he stretched out beside her in bed, wondrously

naked, she laid a hand on his hard chest, fingers splayed, and rested her head on his shoulder. But when another thought came to her, she raised herself to look straight into his face.

"While you were gone, did you . . . did you take your comfort with any other woman?"

Guthrie chuckled and drew her back down beside him. His arm was under her now, and his hand clasped her hip. "No," he said forthrightly.

Caroline wasn't satisfied. "When you were still planning to marry Adabelle, you acted as if you believed a man had a right to visit a whore, even when he was promised."

He rolled her on top of him, pulling on the blankets so that they lay flesh to flesh. "That was before you cast your spell over me, Wildcat. I haven't been with anybody else since you and I took up." He wound an index finger in a tendril of her dark hair. "When a man's been that good, he deserves a reward."

"He does indeed," Caroline answered, and she began kissing her way down over his chest and belly.

A few seconds later, Guthrie was being . . . rewarded.

Chapter

❧ 22 ❧

*I*ndignation filled Caroline to the back of her throat, like a bubbling, bitter liquid. She remained in bed, watching Guthrie dress, too angry and hurt to speak.

"I told you I'll be back," he said, coming to stand beside the bed and cup her chin in one hand. "And I meant it."

She twisted away from him and glared at the yellow curtains on her window, which were fluttering prettily in an early-morning summer breeze. "You've only been here one day," she pointed out.

"Caroline, if I don't go after Flynn right now, today, I'll lose him again. Hell, maybe I already have."

Beneath the blankets, she spread her hands over her stomach and grieved. The baby deserved a proper home, with a mother and father in residence. "It had better not be two and a half months before I see you again," she warned, but that was only bravado. Deep down, she knew there was little or nothing she could do to sway Guthrie. He'd made up his mind to capture Seaton Flynn, and he was not a flexible man.

He leaned down and kissed her lightly on the mouth. "Don't worry, Wildcat, I won't be able to stay away that long."

"You did before."

"Caroline, I'm closing in on Flynn. He's nearby. I can feel it."

His certainty alarmed her, and she caught hold of one of his hands with both of hers and held on tight. "Promise me you'll be careful, Guthrie. If anything happens to you . . ."

He sat down on the edge of the bed, his eyes gentle. "If anything happens to me," he said firmly, "do your grieving and then make a new life."

She clung to his hand, even though that normally wasn't her way. "I'd grieve forever," she said, "and I wouldn't marry another man, if that's what you're suggesting. I couldn't stand to feel someone else's hands on me."

"I'm not exactly on peaceable terms with the idea myself," Guthrie agreed. "But if I can't have your promise to let my friend protect you, at least, then you can't have mine to be careful."

"You wouldn't actually be reckless . . ."

Guthrie drew gently away from her and bent to pull on his boots. "I'm getting tired of playing cat and mouse with this bastard," he said obliquely. But she knew he was tempted to do something bold and thus force a confrontation with Seaton Flynn.

A mental image of Guthrie falling to the ground, fatally shot, filled Caroline's mind. She squeezed her eyes shut against the picture, but it was still there. "Dear God," she whispered miserably, "I wish I'd never met that man. I wish I'd never heard his name!"

Guthrie opened her eyes with a kiss, like a storybook prince, sliding his hand beneath the blankets to lay it against her warm, bare stomach. "No, you don't. You wouldn't have come looking for me at the saloon that day if it hadn't been for him," he said, "and my baby wouldn't be growing inside you right now."

"Guthrie, please—stay."

He shook his head. "Give me your promise, Caroline," he said, "and I'll give you mine."

It was one of the hardest things she'd ever done, but she swallowed hard and gave her word. "All right," she told him, in an anguished whisper. "If—if you don't come back—I'll do as you asked."

He touched her lips with the tip of one index finger. "By Christmas," he clarified. "If I'm not here before Christmas."

Miserably, she nodded.

Guthrie sighed like one who has just prevailed in a struggle. "I'll be careful," he said. And then he tossed the covers back and moved downward to kiss the quivering flesh of Caroline's abdomen.

Heat surged through her, and she silently damned Guthrie Hayes for his power over her.

He parted the moist silk that sheltered her and nibbled brazenly at the morsel he'd unveiled. With a groan of helplessness and passion, Caroline reached over her head to grip the railings in the headboard and arched her back.

Guthrie's chuckle vibrated against her flesh, but then he began to enjoy her in earnest and soon the only sounds she could hear were those of her own muffled groans and hard breathing.

Jardena brought Caroline's breakfast tray only minutes after Guthrie had gone.

Caroline didn't bother to hide her tears from the woman who had become her friend. "He won't be back," she whispered brokenly. "Flynn will kill him."

Jardena set the tray carefully on the bedside table, after moving a lamp aside. Her expression was troubled and her eyes were filled with compassion. "You can't think like that," she scolded. "Bad thoughts can make things happen, just like good ones."

Now fully dressed, although her body was still humming from the tune Guthrie had played on it, Caroline reached with a trembling hand for her teacup. She gave a bitter, humorless little laugh. "He expects me to turn right around and marry someone else if he's not back by Christmas. Just as if the last few months had never happened. Can you imagine that?"

The housekeeper sighed and laid one hand on Caroline's

shoulder. "You'd be happy here," she said. "Roy's a good man, Caroline, and you'd never lack for anything if you were his wife. Neither would your child."

Caroline stared at Jardena. "You too?" she marveled, with quiet anger. "It's as though everyone thinks—"

"Guthrie's strong," Jardena interrupted calmly. "And he can look after himself."

Disconsolately, Caroline began to eat from the food on the tray. She wasn't hungry, but she knew her baby needed sustenance to grow. "It'll be purely my fault if Guthrie dies," she said. "Before I came along, he was happy, working his mine and planning . . . planning to marry Adabelle Rogers."

Jardena shook her head. "Guthrie wouldn't have been happy married to anybody besides you. Now, you straighten yourself up and stop carryin' on like some queen locked up in a dungeon. You've got your work to do, so do it." With that, she left.

Knowing full well that there was nothing she *could* do besides wait and pray and conduct Ferris's lessons, Caroline finished her breakfast and carried the tray downstairs.

That night, when she was standing out on the porch, gripping the railing in both hands and counting the stars to keep from fretting about Guthrie, Roy Loudon joined her.

Pipe in hand, he stood beside her at the railing, and she was struck once again by his uncommonly good looks. He was a fine man, stern but fair in his dealings with his son and the men who worked for him, and Caroline knew she might even have loved him if she hadn't met Guthrie first.

"We're old friends, your husband and I," he said quietly, tamping fresh tobacco into his pipe with a practiced thumb.

Because she liked Mr. Loudon, and because she was lonesome, Caroline tried to make polite conversation. "I guess you both served in General Lee's army," she ventured.

Roy chuckled. "Hardly, Miss Caroline. I was once a personal aide to General Grant. Carried messages to Mr. Lincoln himself on occasion."

Caroline turned to look him full in the face, her mouth open in surprise. She remembered her manners shortly and closed it. "But that would make you a Union man, and Guthrie was definitely—"

"I know," Roy interrupted good-naturedly. "Hayes was a Reb. Still is, deep down."

"How could you have become friends?"

"Later in the war, the President ordered an inspection tour of some of our prison camps. Mr. Lincoln was deeply concerned with reports that Rebel soldiers were being mistreated—both sides were running short of food and medical supplies, naturally, but he'd heard stories of intentional cruelty. General Grant sent me on the mission."

Caroline's eyes were wide. "And you encountered Guthrie?"

"You might say that. I'd just gone through the second camp, somewhere in Pennsylvania, and I'd found some things I knew the President wouldn't like. I was in my tent, writing my report, when all hell broke loose outside. There was a lot of shouting and gunfire, and I grabbed my pistol and rushed out to see what was happening.

"That was how I found myself square in the middle of one of Hayes's famous raids. Before I could make heads or tails of things, I'd been struck over the head and two of the prisoners came after me with pitchforks.

"Guthrie saw what was about to happen, and he stopped them. I'll never forget what he said. 'The name's Guthrie Hayes, Billy Yank, and the way I see it, you owe me a favor. One day, I might just want to collect it.'"

Caroline smiled because the image was clear in her mind and the remark sounded so much like something her husband would say.

"Sure enough," Roy went on, "he showed up on the ranch years later and asked for a job. Of course, I gave him one, and that was when we became friends."

"Remarkable," Caroline said, thinking how strange it was that the two men should encounter each other again when so much time had passed.

Roy shrugged, but the look in his eyes as he gazed down at Caroline was a tender one. "I know all about what you did,

Caroline—about Seaton Flynn and the possibility that you'll have to stand trial for releasing him."

She swallowed, half expecting her employer to say she wasn't suitable to teach his son and ask her to leave.

Cautiously, he laid one big hand on her shoulder. "I have a degree of power, and more money than one man rightfully deserves," he confided. "If anything happens to Guthrie, I'll look after you, and I'll raise your child as if it were my own, but there would be no demands made on you."

Caroline was moved by his declaration; while Mr. Loudon had always behaved in a gentlemanly fashion toward her, she'd never guessed that he actually bore her any tender feelings. Now she suspected he did.

"It wouldn't be fair to ask you to sacrifice like that," she said softly. "There must be plenty of women willing to take your name and be a real wife to you."

His smile was gentle and sad. "I know it's Guthrie you love, Caroline. But if he doesn't come back, you'll need a man. I want to be that man."

Hearing Guthrie make her promise to seek Roy's protection if she needed it was one thing, but actually having him offer himself was something else. Roy Loudon deserved better than a wife who couldn't love him, a wife who would soon be burgeoning with another man's child.

"Guthrie will come back," she insisted. If she couldn't believe that, she couldn't go on.

Roy touched her face with a big, calloused hand. "I hope you're right," he said, "though, God help me, there's a part of me that wants you enough to wish he wouldn't."

With that, Mr. Loudon turned and went back inside his house, leaving Caroline to resume her count of the stars.

But she had to stop, because they kept blurring together.

Presently, she went inside, climbed the stairs to her room, and threw herself down onto the bed to beat at the mattress with her fists in a burst of fear and frustration.

The very next day, it was Ferris who brought her the parcel that would change everything, including her reluctant promise to Guthrie.

She was sitting by the pond, writing another of her endless letters to Lily and Emma, when Ferris scrambled through the trees on foot, a big smile on his face.

"Somebody sent you a present," he said. "The foreman brought this back from the post office in town."

Frowning, unsettled for a reason she couldn't quite define, Caroline reached for the small package. She knew instinctively that Guthrie hadn't sent it, but the handwriting was familiar, in a vague and disturbing way.

With awkward fingers, she undid the twine that bound it and unfolded the plain brown paper. Inside lay the small oval frame that had held Annie Hayes's photograph, though now that had been replaced with a picture of Caroline and Guthrie taken on their wedding day in Cheyenne.

The whole world seemed to shift and sway dangerously, and Caroline let the picture frame lie in her lap while she gripped the rough bark of the log with both hands to keep her balance.

"Is something wrong?" Ferris asked, squatting down in front of her and peering into her face.

Caroline swallowed, unable to answer, and unfolded the yellow sheet of paper tucked into the back of the frame.

I've got him, boasted the strong, distinct handwriting she now recognized as Seaton Flynn's. *If you don't want Hayes to die, you'll be on the two o'clock stage to Laramie, out of Cheyenne, on Friday afternoon. And you won't mention this to anyone. Regards, S.F.*

Bile rushed into the back of Caroline's throat and, for a few seconds, she struggled not to throw up. A moment later, she even managed a smile. "It's our wedding picture," she said, holding up the frame with a hand that only shook slightly. "See?"

Ferris was still frowning. "Miss Caroline, you don't look so good."

She stood up resolutely, praying she wouldn't swoon. "I'm just fine, thank you," she said, in her no-nonsense tone. Her mind was frantically figuring the day of the week, and the realization that it was already Friday nearly paralyzed her.

"I'd like to go riding, Ferris," she told him, in a voice she barely recognized as her own. "Would you please saddle my horse?"

"Sure, but—well—I think I'd better go with you."

Caroline shook her head too hard, too quickly. "No, Ferris. I want you to prepare that essay we were talking about yesterday."

The boy screwed up his face. "Now? But we're finished for the day . . ."

"Ferris," she blurted sharply, "just do as I say!"

"Pa won't like it, your going riding alone," he protested, but he was already turning around and starting back toward the house and barn.

Caroline followed him in a haze. She couldn't take the time to pack anything, and if she tried, Jardena might guess what she was planning to do. Still, she would need money for her stage fare.

She went into the house, took her wages from the drawer in the nightstand, and tucked them into the pocket of her green corduroy riding skirt, another garment she'd made for herself, along with the little picture frame. The thought of Guthrie being held in some hideaway of Seaton's, hurt and maybe dying, made illness threaten again.

But Caroline forced herself to be strong. Trying to pretend nothing was out of the ordinary, she set out for the barn.

Ferris had her horse ready, but he still looked worried. "If something's wrong, Miss Caroline, you could tell me," he said.

She bent and kissed his cheek, an act that obviously increased his confusion, rather than soothing his worries. But it couldn't be undone. "Work on your essay, Ferris," she said, and then she mounted the horse with only minimal help from her pupil.

There were many dangers between the ranch house and Cheyenne, especially for a woman alone, but Caroline didn't think of them as she rode at her mare's top speed. Her mind held no room for anything or anyone but Guthrie.

Reaching Cheyenne, she went immediately to the Wells

Fargo office and bought a ticket to Laramie. Uneasily, she watched as the driver and the man who would ride shotgun loaded trunks and baggage onto the top of the coach. These men were in real danger, and so were the passengers, and yet she didn't dare warn them.

Guthrie would die if she did.

Still, Caroline's conscience wouldn't permit her to simply leave everyone's safety to chance. She went to the driver, a weathered middle-aged man with a big mustache, and touched his sleeve.

"Pardon me, sir, but I'd like to ask if you're properly prepared for any highwaymen we might happen to meet."

He grinned at her and spat a stream of tobacco juice into the dirt. "Highwaymen, ma'am? You've been reading too many of them dime novels."

Caroline bridled. "Robberies happen virtually every day," she pointed out.

"Not to me," the driver answered, with insufferable arrogance.

Caroline glared at him, tempted to show the man Seaton Flynn's note and prove him wrong. But such a rash act would certainly bring on Guthrie's death. She turned on one heel and climbed aboard the stage.

An elderly lady and a young man with a very bad complexion soon joined her, and once again Caroline felt terrible guilt. Mr. Flynn had killed before, and she knew he wouldn't hesitate to kill again. Neither age nor youth would be any particular deterrent to him.

"May I read your palm?" she said, in a burst of near hysterical inspiration. Caroline knew nothing about telling fortunes, but she couldn't let that stop her.

Twittering, the elderly lady extended her hand. "I just hope you see a handsome stranger in my future," she said.

"No, you don't," Caroline argued—whatever else he was, Mr. Flynn was undeniably handsome—pretending to study the woman's outstretched palm. She frowned thoughtfully. "It certainly looks as though you shouldn't travel any time this month," she ventured. "I see potential disaster."

The woman laid one plump hand to an equally plump bosom.

"Horsefeathers," said the pimply young man with disdain.

Caroline reached out and grabbed his hand, turning it over to examine the palm. "You will be captured by hostile savages," she predicted, purely to pay him back for being so uncooperative. "They'll stake you out in the sun and . . ."

The scoffer had gone deathly pale beneath his many blemishes.

"But," Caroline finished triumphantly, "it will only happen if you travel to Laramie within the next ten days."

To her secret relief, and amusement, he got off the coach immediately and demanded that his baggage and ticket money be returned.

The lady was not so easily led. "You're not a fortune-teller," she accused good-naturedly, squinting at Caroline.

Caroline settled back against the hard seat and sighed. "You must get off the stage," she said wearily. "I cannot tell you why, but I beg you to delay your journey for at least one day."

"Oh, dear," murmured the lady. "You do seem sincere."

"I've never been more sincere in my life," Caroline retorted. "Everyone on board this stage is in danger." *Including me,* she reflected philosophically. She'd have to come up with some plan to protect herself from Seaton Flynn when the time came, but so far nothing had come to mind.

Caroline's companion was already reaching for the lever on the door. "Oh, driver," she called. "Please get my things down again." Her attention returned to Caroline. "If something is going to happen, then surely you should get off the coach, too."

Caroline only shook her head, unable to explain. No matter what happened to her, she couldn't stay away and leave Guthrie to die because of her cowardice. She was sick with relief when the woman disembarked.

Almost immediately, the driver put his head through the

window of the coach and studied Caroline indignantly. "What have you been tellin' these people?"

She smiled and smoothed her riding skirt. "Not a thing," she lied. "They decided to change their plans, that's all."

He glared at her for a moment, then retreated. A few minutes later, the stagecoach was rolling toward Laramie. They would stop at the mountain way station for the night, provided they made it that far.

Only when the journey was underway did Caroline pause to consider her own fear. She was walking right into Mr. Flynn's trap, and yet she saw no other choice. She reached into her pocket and pulled out the little frame with the crack across the glass.

Opening it, she found Annie's photograph beneath the one of herself and Guthrie. Nothing short of total incapacitation could have persuaded him to give the item up; it was the one thing Caroline had ever known him to cherish.

She touched Annie's sweet face with the tip of one finger, and felt a painful twist in her heart. Even though Guthrie had covered the first picture with their wedding likeness, his love for Annie would always be there, underlying what he felt for Caroline. Once, she would have minded that very much, but now she only wanted to see him, and hold him, and say, "I love you."

She replaced the portrait of her and Guthrie and, after kissing his image, returned the frame to her pocket.

Of course, if Guthrie was still alive, and Caroline prayed he was, he would be furious with her for obeying Mr. Flynn's summons. In fact, she'd probably be in for a loud lecture, sprinkled with didn't-I-tell-you's and those empty threats to turn her over his knee that seemed to give him so much solace.

Right now, Caroline thought with a sniffle, she wouldn't even mind that if she could just be with him.

As the afternoon dragged on and nothing happened, however, she was beginning to think that Seaton had only been bluffing. And she still didn't have an idea to save herself.

CAROLINE AND THE RAIDER

Then when it was almost twilight, and they were climbing steadily up toward the mountain trail, the riders came. Their horses galloped alongside the coach, and one man jumped into the wagon box with a defiant shout.

Caroline was leaning out the window by that time and she watched in horror as the driver was thrown to the ground and nearly run over by the wheel. When shots were fired, she closed her eyes tightly and sank back into the coach.

Only moments later, the stagecoach was brought to a noisy halt and a rider in a long canvas coat reached down to open the door on Caroline's side.

Even though the man was masked, Caroline recognized his dark, shining eyes. Seaton Flynn pulled the bandanna from his face and smiled.

"I knew you'd come, darling," he said formally, dismounting to stand on the ground, looking up at her. "You'll never know how much I've missed you."

"Stop it before I vomit," Caroline responded contemptuously, stepping out of the coach with as much dignity as she could summon.

Seaton laughed. "You have spirit—a quality I particularly appreciate in my women."

"I'm not your woman," Caroline replied, "and I never will be." She was scared to death, but she knew that the less fear she showed, the better.

He caught her chin roughly in a leather-gloved hand, while his men looked on, all mounted, all wearing masks and carrying rifles. "That's where you're wrong, Caroline, my love. Tonight you'll share my bed, and I'll see what tricks you've learned from your persistent lover."

The men laughed at that, then one of them climbed up on top of the stage to open the strongbox by shooting off the lock.

Caroline couldn't help starting at the sound, even though she'd known it was coming. "I don't care what you do to me," she said, lifting her chin, "as long as you let Guthrie go."

Seaton mounted his horse and then bent to curve an arm

around her waist. Before she knew it, she was in front of him in the saddle. "I don't have to let him go," he breathed into her ear. "I never captured him in the first place."

Twisting to look up into Seaton's face, Caroline blurted out, "But you had the picture!"

A gloved finger traced the outline of her jaw in a familiar, proprietary way that chilled Caroline's blood. "Some cowhands jumped Hayes outside a saloon a few days ago," he replied indulgently. "While he was kicking their asses from one end of the street to the other, Charlie here went through his saddle-bags and helped himself to the photograph. It's charming, by the way."

Caroline closed her eyes as pure terror swept over her. "How could I have been such a fool?" she whispered.

Seaton's lips touched hers, sending revulsion rippling through her, and his hand cupped her breast. She pushed him away, only to have him grasp her again, harder. "You'd better get used to my attentions," he warned, in a husky undertone, "because you and I are going to be together until I get tired of you. And that's likely to be a long time, judging by the way you've filled out."

Although she instituted a fresh struggle at that, Caroline couldn't break free of Seaton's hold. He reined the horse away from the stage and spurred it hard, and Caroline held on tight to the saddle horn.

The branches of trees clawed at her hair and face as they rode farther and farther from the trail, but Caroline was too proud and too frightened to complain. The other bandits did not follow, though she suspected they were simply taking a different route so that anyone who tried to track them would be confused.

Just at dark, Mr. Flynn pulled his horse to a stop in front of an isolated cabin. The place was weathered, all its boards crooked, with gaps between them in places.

Seaton swung down from the saddle and reached up to lift Caroline after him. She could hear his men arriving from various directions, and desperation fairly choked her.

Her escort gripped her by the arm and fairly flung her into the cabin. While she leaned against the cold stone face of the fireplace, the breath knocked out of her, Seaton lit a lamp. Light flared to reveal a dirt floor, a working stove, a spindly chair, and a bedstead with a stained mattress but no blankets or sheets.

She drew a deep breath and stood up straight, only to have her captor grab her by the shoulders and fairly lift her off her feet.

"Why did you do it?" Seaton rasped, baring his fine white teeth as he spat the words. "Why did you give yourself to that saddle bum?"

Caroline raised her chin another notch. "I love him," she answered starkly. "He's my husband."

"We'll see if he wants you when I'm through with you," Seaton bit out, slamming Caroline down hard onto the dirty mattress and bending over her.

She closed her eyes for a moment, so terror stricken that she could barely think. But she hadn't forgotten her baby for as much as a moment, and she made a frenzied bid to protect it. "In the name of God, Mr. Flynn," she whispered, "let me go. I'm expecting a child."

Seaton's eyes widened, then narrowed. He thrust himself away from Caroline, turning his back. "The bastard planted his seed in you," he breathed. "I'll kill him for that!"

Slowly, Caroline sat up, thinking of Pedlow, the man who'd killed Annie. "No, Mr. Flynn. He'll kill *you*. I know Guthrie Hayes, and if you harm me or this baby I'm carrying, there won't be a place on earth for you to hide. He'll find you, and he'll have his vengeance."

Seaton turned to her again, slowly, distractedly. If he'd heard her warning at all, he gave no sign of it. "There's a woman who'll know how to get rid of the brat," he said, running hot eyes over Caroline.

And then he strode over to the door, wrenched it open, and went out, leaving Caroline to stare after him, rocked to the soul by the horrible words that echoed over and over again through her mind. *There's a woman who'll know how to get rid of the brat. . . .*

Chapter
❧ 23 ❧

Caroline tried to ignore the raucous laughter and coarse talk outside the cabin. For the baby's sake, and her own, she had to pull herself together and try to think in a coherent, productive way. Somehow, she had to escape.

But Mr. Flynn's henchmen were all around the shack, standing guard.

After drawing a deep, steadying breath, Caroline squared her shoulders, lifted her chin, and smoothed her hair and her soiled, rumpled clothes. She would waste neither time nor energy wishing she hadn't been taken in by Seaton's trickery. The photograph had seemed to be incontrovertible proof that Guthrie had been captured.

Given that belief, Caroline would have done the same thing all over again, once, twice, a thousand times.

She began to pace the dirt floor as the din outside grew in intensity. Heaven knew Mr. Flynn was vile, but his men, if possible, were even worse. And he'd left her alone with them in his insane eagerness to fetch this mysterious woman who could erase all traces of Guthrie's possession from Caroline's body.

A chill moved up and down her spine. Somehow, she had to get away before she was forced to sacrifice her child.

Guthrie, she called, in desperate silence.

"I say we don't owe Flynn nothin'," one of the outlaws said to another, and Caroline went to the window to see two men arguing in the shadow-streaked light from the lamps inside the cabin. "We got a right to a share of the woman, just like the gold we took."

Caroline laid one hand to her chest and ordered herself not to panic, then looked wildly around the shack for something she could use as a weapon.

"This ain't just any woman," argued another voice. "You heard what Flynn said when he left here—any man as touches her, he'll kill. Maybe he's bluffin', but *I* sure as hell ain't gonna make him show his cards."

"I'm goin' in there," replied the first man, and Caroline's hands tightened around the handle of the rusted skillet she'd found as she waited for the door to open.

Instead, a shot made a bone-chilling *twang* sound in the deepening darkness, and a man screamed in rage and pain. "Godammit, McDurvey, *you shot me!*"

"The boss gave orders and I mean to see that they's followed," was McDurvey's answer.

Caroline was peering through the window again by then, but she couldn't make out McDurvey's face, only his rangy frame and big, misshapen hat. A motion of his hand told her he was reholstering his gun.

The injured man began to moan as his disbelief and his agony grew. "Somebody's got to help me," he whined, but as Caroline watched, the other men resumed their posts.

She tried to ignore his suffering—after all, the man had meant to rape her—but the effort ran contrary to everything Caroline had ever been taught. Finally, she wrenched open the cabin door.

Her would-be attacker was lying on the rough, filthy boards of the step, clutching a wound in his side, and she crouched to assess the damage.

"Bring him inside," Caroline ordered flatly, rising to her feet again.

McDurvey and the others just stared at her, unmoving, their faces invisible in the darkness, while the wounded man tried to stand. With Caroline's help, he managed to pull himself up by clutching the wood of the doorjamb.

He was small and wiry, no taller than Caroline herself, with dirty blond hair that trailed past his shoulders and strangely guileless eyes. Behind them, Caroline knew, lurked the mind of a fiend, but she couldn't leave him to suffer and die unattended, no matter what he'd done.

No one protested or moved to stop her as she positioned herself under the man's arm and walked him to the bed. After depositing him there, she began opening and peeling back his bloody shirt for a look at his wound.

"What's your name?" she asked, glad of something to distract her from her own impossible predicament.

"Willie Fly," he answered, and the only feature in his childlike face to betray his real character was a slight curl to one side of his lower lip.

McDurvey had blown away some flesh and part of a rib. Willie Fly was standing on the threshold of eternity without much to say in his own defense.

Caroline glanced toward the stove. She'd need hot water and a clean cloth to accomplish anything, and it seemed to her that there was virtually no chance of Fly's surviving. Still, she had to try. "Where are you from, Mr. Fly?"

"Coffeyville, Kansas," he replied, shifting uncomfortably on the bed.

Caroline went to the door, opened it, and asked for water. "Do you have any family?" she inquired, when she returned.

Fly's forehead was beaded with sweat, and his eyes were sunken. Dark smudges seeped through the skin beneath them. "Just a sister, Eudora. She won't miss me none."

He knew, then, that he was probably going to die. "What made you take up with somebody like Seaton Flynn?" she asked, finding a valise and opening it. Sure enough, Seaton had a supply of clean shirts.

"I might ask the same question of you," Fly retorted insolently and, even in his dire position, he ran his eyes boldly over Caroline's body, making no apologies for what he'd meant to do.

Caroline flushed as she tore one of the shirts into strips "Mr. Flynn had me believing he was a fine, upstanding citizen. But you don't have that excuse, Willie."

Willie let out a raspy sigh and gazed up at the ceiling. For all that he was surely damned, he seemed resigned to his fate. Then Caroline realized he probably didn't accept either God or the devil as being real. "Fine, upstandin' citizens are for spittin' on," he said. "It was *fine, upstandin' citizens* that stole my pa's farm after the war."

One of the men opened the door and set a bucket of water inside, but no words were spoken. Caroline collected the bucket and set it on top of the stove, adding a few chunks of wood to the fire before she claimed a pint bottle of whiskey from a shelf near the bed.

"You'd better have a sip of this," she told her recalcitrant patient. "And you're not the first man who's ever been cheated. It didn't give you the right to go bad."

Willie unscrewed the cap and tipped the bottle, grimacing as the liquor coursed over his tongue, coughing when it went down. That caused him pain; he gripped his wounded side and his hand came away bloody. "If it's all the same to you, ma'am, I could do just as well without the sermon," he said, rubbing his crimson palm down his pant leg.

"It wouldn't hurt you to look to the welfare of your immortal soul," Caroline replied, going to the stove to check the water. It wasn't hot, but the chill had been taken off, so she dipped a piece of Seaton's torn shirt into it and went back to the bed to begin cleaning Willie's wound.

"Why would you want to help the likes of me?" Willie asked, without a sign of remorse for his earlier intentions. "If McDurvey hadn'ta shot me, it'd be you lyin' on your back on this bed, not me."

Caroline didn't even attempt to hide her shudder of disgust. "A person has to do what's right, even when they'd rather turn away and pretend not to see."

Willie flinched as Caroline tried to clean the wound. It was deep, and more internal damage had been done than she'd thought. She turned the outlaw onto his side so that she could get a closer look, and one of his hands locked on the back of her thigh.

She slapped it away and went back to check the water again. "The bullet went right on through," she said. "I guess you're lucky that happened."

At last, Willie was beginning to get a grasp on his future, and he was panicking. "I need a doctor! You send one of those weasels out there to fetch me a doctor!"

Caroline decided the water was hot enough and carried the bucket to Willie's bedside. He'd bled so copiously that the filthy old mattress was soaked with crimson stains. "They're not going to do that, Willie. If they did, the doctor would know where the hideout is."

"I don't give a damn!" Willie cried, straining to sit up. "For all I care, they can shoot the bastard between the eyes, once he's sewed me up."

Caroline pressed him back onto the mattress. The sharp, salty smell of Willie's blood filled her nostrils, and she felt sick. "I'm the best you're going to get, Mr. Fly, and you'd better accept it," she said, moistening her lips with the end of her tongue.

She cleaned the wound the best she could and applied compresses in an effort to stop the bleeding, but it was like trying to soak up a river with her Sunday handkerchief. Willie's wounds required a surgeon, not a schoolteacher who'd nursed two gentle old maids through periodic bouts of rheumatism and the grippe.

"I'm going to die," he rasped out, and his color had gone from pure white to a sickly gray. "Damn it, McDurvey done killed me!"

Privately, Caroline agreed, but she didn't think saying so would do any good. "Please try to lie still."

Willie began to shiver. "I'm cold!" he cried, hugging himself as his teeth started to chatter. "Sweet Jesus in heaven, I'm so cold!"

Caroline found a blanket and covered him. "If I were you," she said quietly, "I'd be asking His mercy, not taking His name in vain."

Willie's shivering progressed to a sob. Then he suddenly went still, and his eyes rolled toward the ceiling in a glassy stare.

Caroline knew before she touched the pulse point at the base of his throat that Willie Fly was dead. "God have pity on his wayward soul," she whispered, and then she closed his eyes and pulled the blanket up so that it covered his face.

After washing the blood from her hands, Caroline went to the door and opened it. "Your friend is dead," she said to the shadowy figures keeping their vigil outside.

"Weren't no friend of mine," muttered a voice, and those were the only words to be offered for the misguided boy from Kansas.

Caroline closed the door and looked back at the covered figure lying on the bed. Willie Fly seemed so small now, hardly more than a boy, and she hoped he'd somehow managed to make peace with his Maker before the spirit left him.

There was a broken-backed chair at the table, and Caroline sat down and rested her head on her folded arms. Wherever Guthrie was, she just hoped he had the good sense to stay clear of Seaton Flynn's hideout.

Guthrie's frustration was supreme.

He and Tob had been following Flynn for a day and a half, waiting for the right moment to strike. When the murdering thief had stopped the stagecoach, Guthrie hadn't been surprised. But seeing Caroline step down from inside it had set him back on his heels.

He'd had to watch, not daring to let so much as a single muscle twitch, while Flynn pulled her up onto his horse. Although he'd wanted to move in, he'd known Caroline and his child could well be the first casualties of such a rash action.

Guthrie had tailed Flynn and his gang to the hidden cabin. By then, it had been dark, but he'd known Caroline was alone in the shack with the man who'd sworn to avenge his alleged betrayal.

A cold sweat stood out on Guthrie's flesh as he checked the chamber of his rifle for the hundredth time and prepared to bring down anyone who got in his way.

But then, just when he'd been about to risk everything, just when he thought he was fresh out of choices, Flynn emerged from the cabin like a bullet out of a red hot stove. Guthrie watched and listened, holding his breath, while the leader argued heatedly with his men.

When Flynn rode off, Guthrie waited as long as he could bear to, then followed. Tob remained behind, whimpering low in his throat and staring at the cabin where his mistress was being held.

It was nearly dawn, and Flynn was crouching beside a mountain stream, drinking water from his hands, when Guthrie finally closed in. Approaching soundlessly from behind, he pressed the barrel of his .45 into the back of Flynn's neck.

Flynn eased his hands out from his side, and Guthrie bent to pull the pistol from his captive's holster and toss it into the stream.

"Hayes?" Flynn asked, and he sounded resigned and even a little amused.

"If I didn't think it would be a waste of good tobacco, I'd give you a cigar," Guthrie answered, by way of congratulations. "Lay down on your belly and put your hands behind your back."

"We can work this out," Flynn offered, remaining upright. "All you really want is the woman, right? And I can give her to you."

Guthrie planted one boot between Flynn's shoulder blades and gave him a little help lying down. He landed sprawled in the chilly creek, sputtering and cursing.

Dragging him back out by his feet, Guthrie repeated his earlier request, though less politely than before. "Put your hands behind your back."

Still swearing, Flynn drew both wrists together at the base of his spine, and Guthrie bound them with a piece of rawhide from the pocket of his coat. Then he took a handful of the outlaw's wet hair and jerked him up onto his knees.

"I want the woman," Guthrie clarified, as if there had been no break in the conversation, "but there's something else I've got a fancy for, Flynn—seeing you hang."

"There are six men standing guard over Caroline, Hayes. How do you plan to get past them?"

Guthrie took a cheroot from his pocket, clasped it between his teeth, and lit the end with a wooden match. "If I thought there was a shot glass full of loyalty between the whole half dozen, I'd use you to get in. Since those bastards would probably poison their own mamas for a beer token and five minutes with a whore, I'll have to come up with another plan."

Flynn started struggling to his feet, and Guthrie waited until he'd almost made it, then kicked him back into the stream again. He came up screaming profanity.

Guthrie smiled slowly and flicked the ashes off his cheroot. "I'm pretty sure I didn't understand you right," he said indulgently. "But it sounded like you called my mama a nasty name just now."

"You heard me right," Flynn spat.

After drawing deeply on the cheroot and exhaling the smoke, Guthrie sighed. "That's a real pity," he said. And then he returned the .45 to its holster, unbuckled his gunbelt, and set it aside. After that, he took a knife from the top of his boot and bent to cut the rawhide that bound Flynn's hands.

While the outlaw was still recovering from that development, Guthrie caught him in the jaw with a hard right cross and sent him tumbling into the creek for the third time.

Flynn came up fighting; his fury gave him a maniacal strength. It also made him reckless.

The battle began in earnest when Flynn landed a hard punch in Guthrie's midsection, and it raged on one side of the creek, then the other, and, for a while, in the middle. Finally, Flynn went face down in the water, and he didn't get up.

Guthrie dragged him ashore by the back of his shirt and flung him down into the slippery pebbles, where he coughed and spit and vomited creek water. When he was through,

Guthrie bound Flynn's hands again and then hauled him upright by his hair.

Flynn glared at him. "Why don't you just kill me?" he said, and Guthrie wondered if his own face was as bruised and misshapen as Flynn's. "That's what you want to do, isn't it?"

Guthrie grinned and slapped him on the back. "You're damn right it's what I want to do," he answered, "but the law's got first claim on you, so I'll have to settle for watching you choke when the rope tightens."

"I've got money," Flynn offered, and now there was a frantic note in his voice. Thanks to all those baptisms in the creek, he was even wetter than Guthrie, and that was saying something. "I can get you the woman back and give you enough gold to last you the rest of your life."

Guthrie pretended to consider the offer. "Where is this gold?"

Flynn stumbled in the rocks as Guthrie flung him toward his horse and then helped him up into the saddle. He spat onto the stony ground. "You don't think I'm going to tell you that before we work out a deal, do you?"

Guthrie reclaimed his gunbelt and strapped it on. "You couldn't offer me enough money to let you go," he said. "I've got a front-row seat at your funeral."

"You're a bastard, Hayes."

Guthrie touched the brim of his hat, after picking it up off the stream bank and settling it on his head. "Coming from you—and you're one notch below the stuff that sticks to the bottom of my boots—that's a compliment."

When they began to draw near the cabin, Guthrie stopped, wrenched Flynn off his horse, and tied him to the trunk of a birch tree. Then he gagged him with a dirty sock taken from the depths of his saddlebag.

"You just sit right there and enjoy yourself, Flynn," Guthrie told his captive, as Tob trotted over to lick the bruises and cuts on the man's face. "I'll be back real soon."

There was smoke curling from the chimney of the shack, Guthrie observed, from his vantage point on the ridge, and he counted six horses. There were two men keeping watch in front of the house, and two men in back.

Guthrie's stomach churned. That meant two more were inside, with Caroline. His heart stopped cold in his chest when the door opened and a tall, slim man came out carrying a blanket-wrapped corpse over one shoulder.

But then Guthrie caught a glimpse of yellow hair sticking out from under the blanket, and relief swept over him. As if in answer to some silent summons, Caroline appeared in the doorway.

She was rumpled, and her clothes were stained with blood, but Guthrie knew by her bearing that she was all right. She scanned the hillside anxiously, as if expecting someone, and as her eyes moved over the rocks at the top of the ridge, they linked with Guthrie's.

He was sure she'd seen him, since she looked away so quickly. He smiled to himself. *Don't give me away, Wildcat,* he thought. *This isn't over yet.*

Guthrie had found her.

Caroline's heart leapt with the knowledge, but she was alarmed, too. The man was just enough of a brazen fool to try to take on five outlaws by himself and, if he did, he'd probably get himself killed. She approached McDurvey as he began to dig a grave for Willie Fly.

"Shouldn't one of you go and find Mr. Flynn?" she asked, surprised at how bright and happy her voice sounded when she was forcing it through her constricted throat. "He's been gone for sometime."

McDurvey, a homely man with a mournful, pitted face, eyed her as he pushed the shovel into the soft earth with his foot. "You missin' Flynn, ma'am?"

Caroline swallowed, and her heart was beating so hard that she could feel it in the bones of her face. "Well," she replied, "he and I *were* engaged to be married at one time."

"I don't think marriage is exactly what the boss has in mind," McDurvey remarked, proceeding with his digging. The body of Willie Fly lay a few feet away, still covered with the blanket.

It took all Caroline's strength of will not to turn and glance at the hillside to see if Guthrie was in plain view. "Maybe he'll be angry with you for killing poor Willie," she said, folding her arms.

McDurvey turned his head and spat into the grass. "Flynn woulda done it himself if he'd been here." He went on digging. "I can't see why you'd be mournin' Fly, anyway. He made it plain what he was meanin' to do." Sharp gray eyes studied Caroline's face. "But maybe you're one of them women as likes such as that."

Caroline retreated a step, her cheeks hot with fearful color. "What happens if Mr. Flynn doesn't come back?" she asked.

McDurvey smiled for the first time, and the sight was chilling. "Then I reckon the boys and me'll have our turns at you. It's been a while since we've took a woman."

A sour taste surged into Caroline's mouth, but before she could think of a reply, a fight broke out between the two men on the other side of the house. McDurvey dropped his shovel and started in that direction, then thought better of the action.

"You boys go on around and break that up," he told the pair in front.

They obeyed, and when McDurvey turned around to resume his work, he caught the business end of the shovel square in the face.

Caroline felt a certain chagrin when his eyes rolled back and blood spouted from his nostrils. In the next instant, his knees buckled and he toppled to the ground without making a sound.

Quickly, Caroline bent and pulled the pistol from his gunbelt, holding it in both hands. When she looked up, she saw Guthrie coming down the hillside on horseback, moving as fast as if he'd been on level ground. He was standing in his stirrups and using both arms to wield his rifle, and a Rebel yell rent the air just before the repeater started spewing bullets.

Caroline ducked behind a birch tree, still clutching the

pistol but squeezing her eyes shut, certain that if she looked, she'd see Guthrie and his gelding tumbling head over heels down the incline.

There were more shots, followed by an eerie silence.

Caroline recited every Bible verse she could remember and then opened her eyes. Guthrie's horse was standing a few yards away, reins dangling, and Tob was nuzzling at the palm of her hand. McDurvey had regained consciousness, and he was slowly rising to his feet, his gaze fixed on Caroline.

She pointed the pistol with both hands and shrieked, "Guthrie!"

To her relief, he came ambling around the side of the cabin and cocked his rifle.

"Hold it right there," he said, and McDurvey froze.

Now that the worst was over, Caroline was in a state of shock. "Are the others—?"

"They're all dead," Guthrie answered flatly, wrenching McDurvey's hands behind him and binding them together with a rawhide string that had held the outlaw's holster to his leg.

"And . . . and Mr. Flynn?" she choked out.

"He's up on the ridge, tied to a tree. With any luck, the squirrels will eat him and the territory won't have to waste a good rope on him."

Caroline wanted to fling herself into Guthrie's arms but, at the same time, she was furious at the risk he'd taken. It might have been him lying there staining the ground with his blood, instead of Flynn's men. "How could you do such a rash, foolish, *crazy* thing?" she demanded, making a wild gesture with her arm.

Guthrie carefully took the pistol from her fingers. "You did force my hand a little," he pointed out reasonably, "when you hit handsome here with the shovel."

Realizing she and Guthrie and their baby were safe, Caroline gave a sob and propelled herself at her husband. "I was so afraid—Mr. Flynn was going to make me lose the baby . . ."

Guthrie held her with one arm, but she was pressed tight against him and that felt gloriously good. "Are you all right, Wildcat?" he asked hoarsely.

"Yes," Caroline wailed, clinging to him.

He kissed her neck and simultaneously gave her bottom the kind of pat she would have found patronizing at any other time. "Take it easy," he told her. "It's over now."

Systematically, Guthrie hung each corpse over the back of a horse, then he linked the animals together with a long line of rope. McDurvey remained bound while Guthrie went back up the mountain and, presently, returned with a seething Seaton Flynn.

Soon, Guthrie was leading this strange, macabre procession behind him like a ragtag caravan. Caroline rode in front of him, glad to feel his strong arm bent around her waist to keep her from falling.

A few hours later, they came upon the way station, where the stagecoaches stopped when they traveled between Laramie and Cheyenne. The dead outlaws were stored in a shed, while Flynn and McDurvey, both still bound, were locked up in the fruit cellar. Caroline wanted a hot bath, eight hours of uninterrupted sleep, and Guthrie, in that order.

He had different ideas about the sequence of things, joining her in the tub sheltered on four sides by dirty canvas tarps. The moonlight shone down on him, emphasizing the majestic planes and hollows of his body.

His mouth covered Caroline's in a fierce kiss, and she put her arms around him, moving downward into the rapidly cooling water to kneel. Using her soap, he gently bathed every inch of her. Then, solemnly, he handed the bar to Caroline.

She washed him in the same way, and when he was clean, she fell to kissing his slippery chest and hard belly. But then he stopped her, lifting her face back on a level with his for another consuming, desperate kiss. His eyes blazed with passion when he drew back from her.

With a despairing groan, he gripped the sides of her still slender waist and hoisted her upwards. When he lowered her again, it was onto his shaft.

The slow, fiery pleasure made Caroline thrust her head back, and Guthrie bent to take one of her nipples greedily into his mouth. He suckled, all the while lifting Caroline along his length, then lowering her again. The process continued until she was moaning and trying to increase the pace.

Guthrie wouldn't allow that; he held her to the slow rhythm that threatened to ignite into flames and consume her soul. When she pleaded, he began having her with such ferocious thrusts that water splashed over the sides of the tub.

Caroline repeated Guthrie's name like a litany and then she stiffened as her body went into a series of violent buckling motions in response to the unbearable pleasure. He covered her mouth with his own, swallowing her cries.

When he came, she was brushing her nipple back and forth across his lips. He grabbed onto her with wild hunger and her flesh absorbed his moans as he surrendered without reserve.

Chapter

↣ *24* ↢

The townspeople of Laramie stared at the odd procession led by Caroline and Guthrie. Behind them rode Seaton Flynn and McDurvey, hands bound to their saddle horns, followed by the five dead men draped over their horses' backs.

Marshal Stone came out of his office to investigate the ruckus and strode forward when he saw the grim caravan.

"So you did it," he said, with a half smile, as he looked up at Guthrie. "I could use a man like you, if you can see yourself as a deputy."

Guthrie grinned easily and shook his head. "Thanks, but my plans are a little different." With that, he dismounted and helped Caroline down. While she stood watching on the steps in front of the marshal's office, Guthrie and John Stone dragged the live prisoners from their horses and took them inside.

Caroline sagged against the rough board wall of the jailhouse when she heard the *clang* of the cell door slamming shut. It was over; she would go free now, and she and Guthrie could make a real life. He could work his mine again, and she'd go about making up to her guardians for the grief she'd put them through. And when the moment was right, they'd travel to Chicago and start a new search, this time for Lily and Emma.

Guthrie came back out and took her gently by the arm. "Come on, Wildcat. You need some good food and some rest." With that, he started leading her across the street, toward one of the hotels. Caroline didn't pay attention to the name.

"We can go back to Bolton now," she said distractedly. Until a few minutes ago, she'd been able to keep her fatigue at bay. Now she felt exhausted.

"That's right," Guthrie agreed, with a nod. "Seems like we'll be able to build that house sooner than we thought, Mrs. Hayes. There were rewards posted for Flynn and McDurvey and for two of the others."

Caroline's heart gave a weary little leap, but any other response was quite beyond her. She let Guthrie take charge and he arranged for a room, then led her upstairs, unlocked the door, and put her to bed as gently as he would a tired child. The last thing she remembered before nodding off to sleep was the warmth of his lips touching her forehead.

When she awakened, hours later, Guthrie was sitting on the edge of the bed with a tray in his hands. Once she'd drawn herself up to lean against the headboard, pillows propped behind her back, he set the food in her lap and kissed her.

"Have you been with the marshal all this time?" she asked, yawning. She was dressed only in her underthings.

"Most of it," Guthrie answered, going to stand at the window. "I wired Roy Loudon to let him know you're all right, and I sent a similar message to the Maitland sisters in Bolton."

Caroline sensed something in his voice and manner and put down the fresh wheat roll she'd been slathering with butter. "Guthrie?"

He grasped the window casings on either side of him and lowered his head. His raspy sigh seemed to fill the room. "Something's happened," he said. And then he turned to face Caroline with bleak eyes. "I wasn't going to tell you until we were about to reach Bolton—Miss Phoebe died a week ago, and Miss Ethel was so grieved that she had a stroke."

The world seemed to stop turning, and a hum filled Caroline's ears, dulling all other sounds. "How—it can't be—I won't believe it!"

Guthrie came to Caroline's bedside and gently moved the tray onto the night stand. Then he pulled her into his arms. "The Western Union operator in Bolton wired the news back after I sent my message that you were coming home."

Caroline's shoulders rose and fell with the force of a tearing sob. "No—no! Oh, Guthrie, it's all my fault—it's because I worried them so much . . ."

His hand was entangled in her sleep-tousled hair while his other arm held her within a steely circle. He kept her in his embrace, his lips occasionally touching her temple, until her sobs were spent. Then he settled her back against the pillows and reached for the bowl of vegetable-barley soup on the tray.

She shook her head, but he lifted the spoon to her mouth anyway. "If you won't think about yourself," he said, "think about our baby."

Caroline took the soup, but for all her docility, she was frantic to leave for Bolton. She kept her composure only because she knew Guthrie would not permit her to make the trip until he was sure it wouldn't be too much for her.

That night, Guthrie didn't make love to Caroline. He simply lay in the bed beside her, enfolding her in his arms. She slept fitfully, waking often from frightening dreams she couldn't remember.

In the morning, Guthrie brought a doctor to the room. Caroline was examined and then left to wonder what the findings were. One thing she knew; she hadn't been comforted by the concerned look on the elderly man's face.

"What's wrong with me?" she demanded, when Guthrie came in with a stack of dime novels from the general store.

He set the thin, paperbound volumes in her lap. "Nothing, except that you're cussed as hell," her husband answered.

Momentary panic overwhelmed Caroline. She'd seen so much blood, so much tragedy and death, since setting out on her quest to bring back Seaton Flynn. She pressed both hands to her belly. "I won't lose my baby," she vowed. "I won't!"

Guthrie drew up a chair and took her hand in his, running a calloused thumb over her knuckles. "That's right, Wildcat. But the doctor thinks you need to spend a week or ten days in bed because of all you've been through, and I agree with him."

Caroline couldn't risk miscarrying her child, but she was anxious to get back to Bolton. "Surely I'd be all right if I took the stagecoach . . ."

Guthrie only shook his head. "You're not ready for two or three days of bouncing up and down on a coach seat," he said firmly, and Caroline knew that was the end of the discussion.

In the coming ten days, while the July sun gleamed at the windows, Caroline played checkers with Guthrie, read, slept, and ate. When Guthrie wasn't in the room, entertaining her or cajoling her to eat her vegetables, he was off doing business.

Finally, late in the month, the doctor came back and pronounced Caroline well enough to travel. She put on a fresh dress—Jardena had sent her clothes from the ranch days before, by stagecoach—brushed and braided her hair, and had a late breakfast in the hotel dining room with Guthrie.

At one that afternoon, the stage set out on the first leg of the trip to Bolton. Guthrie rode his gelding, but Caroline had Tob to keep her company inside the coach. Once she spotted Indians in the distance, but they offered no trouble.

For three days, Caroline rode in various coaches. Each night, she and Guthrie shared a bed in another way station, and Caroline's body ached for his attentions, but Guthrie didn't touch her, except to kiss her good-night.

By the time they reached Bolton, Caroline was convinced that Guthrie regretted marrying her. After all, she'd put him to a lot of trouble, and because of her, one innocent old woman was dead, while another barely held on to life. And because of the rewards, totalling up to a considerable sum between them, Guthrie could now go anywhere and do anything he wanted.

When the stage rolled to a stop in front of the Bolton General Store, which doubled as a depot, however, Guthrie was there to help Caroline down. Her cheeks flared as she became aware of all the people stopping to look at her, and to point.

She could well imagine the speculation that had taken place while she was away.

She held her head high, though, and when Guthrie offered his arm, she took it gratefully. Caroline gazed straight ahead as she and her husband walked along the familiar streets to the house that had been her home ever since she'd first come to Wyoming at the age of eight.

There was a black satin wreath hanging on the front door, and the shades were all drawn. The yard and the flower gardens, always Miss Ethel's pride, were overrun with weeds and brown with the need of water.

Guthrie opened the gate for Caroline, and she stepped through. When she took his arm again, her hold was tight.

She didn't pause at the front door but instead opened it and walked in. The inside of the house was neat as a pin—that would be the doing of the ladies' aid society—but the place was dark and it needed airing out.

"Shall I go upstairs with you?" Guthrie asked quietly, removing his hat and hanging it on the coat tree beside the door.

Caroline swallowed and shook her head. She was the cause of all the grief and heartache in this house, and she would face her responsibility squarely—and alone.

Just as she started up the stairs, she saw the pastor's wife, Mrs. Penn, start down.

"Caroline!" the middle-aged woman said, and her tone conveyed the fact that she wouldn't have been more surprised to see Mary Todd Lincoln. She was slender, with gray hair, and she laid splayed fingers to the bosom of her prim brown dress.

Caroline inclined her head slightly. "How is Miss Ethel?" she asked, advancing up the stairs.

For a moment, it looked as though Mrs. Penn would try to block her progress. Her narrow face was a study in disapproval. "It's good to know you're concerned," she said.

Caroline had neither the inclination nor the patience to explain her long absence. She stepped past the woman and proceeded to Miss Ethel's room, which was at the back of the house, overlooking the garden.

The old lady lay with pillows behind her back, and her eyes looked sightless and glazed. One side of her face seemed to droop well below the other, and spittle gathered at the corner of her mouth.

Caroline found one of Miss Ethel's precious handkerchiefs, kept in a drawer with a lavender sachet, and gently wiped the old woman's mouth. Then she kissed her lightly on the forehead and sat down in a delicate chair upholstered in rose velvet.

"It's me, Miss Ethel," she whispered, in a low, miserable voice, taking the fragile, weightless hand. "Caroline. I'm back, and I'm safe. And I'm so sorry that I made you worry."

Miss Ethel made no sound, but her fingers fluttered slightly against Caroline's palm.

A sob tore itself from Caroline's throat. She pressed Miss Ethel's hand to her forehead and wept for all that would never be again. Presently, she fell silent, though deep inside she was still shrieking with grief. She brushed Miss Ethel's wispy gray hair and changed her bedjacket and read to her from a volume of poetry she found on the bedside stand.

The book was well thumbed, for Miss Ethel had loved the

musical words it contained, and read them often. When Caroline closed the volume and prepared to leave the room, she saw a tear on the wrinkled cheek.

Miss Ethel's lips tried to form sound. "Car—Car—" she said.

"I'm here," Caroline said, her own eyes wet again.

"Li-leeee," Miss Ethel managed, with an agony of effort. "Li-leeee—"

Caroline dried her face with the back of one hand. It sounded as though Miss Ethel might be trying to say Lily, and just the idea made her heart catch and then stumble over a half dozen beats. "Lily?" she whispered.

But Miss Ethel was worn out by her struggle; she sank back into utter oblivion, staring blindly up at the ceiling.

Caroline tucked Miss Ethel's blankets in carefully, then hurried out of the room and down the rear stairs. Guthrie was waiting in the kitchen, drinking coffee from a china cup that looked ridiculously small and fussy in his hand.

"How is she?" he asked, setting aside the cup to lay his hands on either side of Caroline's expanding waist.

"I think she'll die soon," Caroline answered dismally, and the words were out before she even knew she'd planned to say them.

Guthrie drew her close against him. "I'm sorry," he said hoarsely.

"I've got to go and visit Miss Phoebe's grave before it gets dark," Caroline said, pulling away. Her brown eyes searched his face, looking for the recrimination she was sure he must feel. "She said Lily's name."

His eyes brightened. "Your sister?"

"I think so," Caroline muttered. "I hope so." She left Guthrie and took a shawl from the peg beside the back door to wrap around her shoulders. "I'll be back soon."

"Do you want me to go with you?"

Caroline needed to confront her grief and guilt alone, even though she loved Guthrie Hayes with her whole heart. "No," she answered softly, and then she went out.

Miss Phoebe was buried in the Presbyterian churchyard

across the street, and a small maple tree had been planted nearby, to cast pleasant shade on her resting place.

Caroline read the stone with dry, swollen eyes

Phoebe Elliott Maitland
Beloved Sister
Born April 5, 1800
Died June 30, 1878

"I'm so sorry," she said, in a hoarse and broken voice

It was then that Pastor Penn appeared. He came out of a side door, looking official in his frayed but immaculate suit. His white hair glistened in the fading sunshine.

"Hello, Caroline," he said in a gentle voice, coming to stand on the opposite side of the grave.

Caroline swallowed. "What happened to her?"

Pastor Penn sighed. "It was her heart. It just gave out one day."

"Because of me. She was upset because of me."

"Your disappearance did trouble her, of course," the minister admitted. "But Miss Phoebe had problems with her heart for years. You must have known that."

Caroline had known, but it was something she'd always preferred not to think about. "Didn't they receive my letters?"

"There was one wire, I believe, but both Miss Ethel and Miss Phoebe thought you'd been coerced into sending it, or that someone had sent it for you."

Caroline gathered the shawl around her, feeling chilly despite the heat of the summer evening. "Miss Ethel mentioned my sister, Lily. Do you know anything about that?"

The pastor was agape. "Miss Ethel spoke?"

"She tried."

Penn recovered himself. "Miss Ethel did tell me that a young woman named Mrs. Halliday had stopped in one day, looking for you. But soon after that, Miss Phoebe suffered her fatal illness, and Miss Ethel's stroke came only a short time later."

Lily had been right there in Bolton, Caroline was sure of

it. Lily, all grown up and calling herself Mrs. Halliday. She wondered what kind of man *Mr.* Halliday would turn out to be.

She lingered a while longer, then went back to the house.

Guthrie was in the kitchen, lifting the lid from a pot of chicken and dumplings on the stove. Caroline dished up a bowlful, took it upstairs, and fed Miss Ethel. When she came down again, Guthrie was gone.

She ate sparingly of the chicken dish, then went up to her old room.

It was the first time she'd entered it since her return. The room seemed like a very different place now, smaller somehow. She opened the wardrobe and the drawers, touching the clothes she'd left behind, and spent a good five minutes gazing at the framed drawing of Lily and Emma that stood on her dresser.

"Lily Halliday," she said out loud, smiling a little. "And what about you, Emma? Who did you marry? Are you looking for me, too?"

Presently, Caroline took a cotton nightgown from her bureau drawer, and a wrapper from the wardrobe. Then she went downstairs to take a long, luxurious bath in the famous Maitland tub. Miss Phoebe and Miss Ethel had been the first in Bolton to own such a modern contraption.

Caroline was in the kitchen, heating milk at the stove, when Guthrie came in the back door. He'd obviously bathed and changed clothes himself, and he'd had a shave, too, and gotten himself barbered.

Somewhat surprised to see him, Caroline stared. "What are you doing here?"

His eyes moved over her thin nightgown. "Looking for my wife," he answered. "Have you seen her?"

Caroline couldn't help smiling, and deep in her heart a little flame of joy flickered because he hadn't washed his hands of her and walked away without looking back. "She's standing right here."

Guthrie came and took her into his arms, holding her close. "I've been afraid to touch you, Caroline," he confided in gruff tones.

She straightened his collar, even though it didn't need straightening. "Why?"

"Because of the baby. You've been through so much in the last few months . . ."

"Then you still want me," she marveled. "You're not planning to go away."

He frowned. "I wasn't planning to go anywhere, Wildcat —not without you, anyway. You're my wife."

Caroline's heart fluttered into her throat. "No one could have blamed you if you hadn't wanted anything to do with me, after all that's happened."

Guthrie laid an index finger to her mouth, then took the pan of milk off the stove and set it on the floor for Tob. Having done that, he lifted Caroline easily into his arms and started up the back stairs.

"Where's your room?" he asked, when they reached the hallway.

Caroline pointed to the appropriate door, feeling like a traditional bride on her wedding night. Her throat was thick with emotion, and a little coal of passion was already burning bright deep inside her.

The small room seemed even more crowded with Guthrie inside. The sheer power of his personality seemed to push at the ceiling and the walls. He laid Caroline gently on the bed, then sat down to kick off his boots.

"We'll stay here until our house is ready," he said.

Caroline laid a hand on his muscular back, trying to assure herself that he was really there. "I wouldn't want to leave Miss Ethel now anyway," she said.

He turned to look at her, pulling his shirt from his trousers as he spoke. "I'll make sure there's a room for her at the new place," he said, but they both knew Miss Ethel wasn't going to last until the new house was built.

"You're a very special man, Guthrie Hayes," Caroline said, and tears brimmed in her eyes.

Guthrie's eyes danced as he unbuttoned his shirt, took it off, and tossed it over the bedpost. "I'm glad you think so, Wildcat," he answered. And he stood up to remove his trousers.

Caroline couldn't help admiring him; she'd missed the special dimension his lovemaking gave to her life. "Maybe in the spring we can look for Lily and Emma," she said.

The lamplight glowed on his naked body as he bent over Caroline, placing one hand on each side of her waist. "By then, the baby will be big enough to travel," he agreed, and then he dipped his head to kiss her.

His tongue teased her lips and then conquered her mouth, and Caroline gave a little whimper and arched her back, needing his weight upon her, and his uncompromising masculinity inside her. But he soon made it plain that he wouldn't be rushed.

Slowly, still kissing Caroline, he dragged her nightgown up around her waist. Then he spread her legs and poised himself between them, teasing her with his manhood and the promise of pleasure.

"Is this what you want?" he whispered against the tingling flesh of her lips.

"Yes," Caroline groaned, unabashed. "Yes, Guthrie, all of it—hard and fast and deep—"

He chuckled and slid down to nibble at her neck. "Still my Wildcat. Do you know what I want?"

In answer, Caroline pulled her nightgown the rest of the way up, so that her breasts were bared to him. With a contented moan, Guthrie found a nipple and took it into his mouth, teasing it with his tongue and his teeth before suckling in earnest.

Caroline responded with a low groan and raised her hips against him, seeking him.

He gave her an inch, just to torment her, and continued to take suckle at her breasts.

Finally, Caroline could bear it no longer. Her need was great, in spite of and because of all the things that had happened to her in recent weeks. And there was the fact that Guthrie hadn't touched her intimately since that night at the way station, when he'd made love to her in the outdoor bathtub surrounded by canvas walls.

She laid her hands to Guthrie's buttocks and they went taut under her palms.

"I won't wait any longer, Guthrie," she warned, and then she guided him into her.

He moaned helplessly as she took him deeper and deeper, her sheath closing around him, pulling at him, caressing him. His mouth covered Caroline's as his hips moved faster and faster.

Her body was moist with the effort of her response as she met every thrust, each one taking her closer to the silver fire that would exalt and purify her. When the tight coil of pleasure suddenly unwound, she wrapped her legs around him and, with little twisting motions of her hips, milked him of his seed.

With a muffled shout, Guthrie spilled himself into her and then sank to her breast to take the nipple again, between gasps for breath. Caroline drifted into a contented sleep, her body sated, her spirit calmed.

When she awakened early the next morning, Guthrie had left her bed. She washed and dressed hastily and hurried down the hallway to Miss Ethel's room. Mrs. Penn was there, spooning thin cereal into the slack mouth, and she didn't smile when she saw Caroline.

"Good morning," Caroline said, all the same.

Mrs. Penn nodded curtly and raised another spoonful of cereal to Miss Ethel's lips.

Determined not to be shunted aside, Caroline came to stand at the side of the bed. "Yesterday, Miss Ethel spoke to me," she said.

Mrs. Penn looked unconvinced. "About what?" she asked.

"I think she was trying to say my sister's name, Lily."

The pastor's wife nodded. "There was a young lady here by that name a few weeks ago," she allowed.

Caroline couldn't help the eagerness in her voice. "Did you see her? Talk to her?"

"No," Mrs. Penn answered flatly. "I know only what Ethel told me—that she was quite charming and that she asked for you." She paused and cleared her throat. "About that young man you've been traveling with—"

"He's my husband," Caroline interrupted. "He has a copper mine outside of town, and we're going to build a house right here in Bolton."

Mrs. Penn had the good grace to look uncomfortable. "Well, I suppose if you're married, it isn't wrong for him to be spending so much time here."

"I'm so glad you feel that way," Caroline said politely. Then she sent Mrs. Penn away and spent the morning taking care of Miss Ethel herself. She was reading poetry again when suddenly Miss Ethel's whole countenance brightened, and it seemed that she sat up a little straighter against her pillows.

"Sister," she said clearly, and then she sank backwards.

Caroline knew before she touched Miss Ethel's wrist that she would find no pulse, but she tried anyway. Then, vision blurred with tears, she gently closed the old woman's eyes and stumbled out of the room.

She went down the stairs and out the front door, nearly tripping over Tob, who was stretched out across the top step.

He whimpered and stood up to greet Caroline, his cold nose nuzzling her palm. She petted him and proceeded along the walk and through the gate.

People called out to her as she walked through the main part of town, but Caroline didn't pay any attention. She was intent on only one thing, and that was finding Guthrie.

He was at the mine, as she had known he would be, but there were other men there, too, setting up equipment of some kind. The mine was now being worked in earnest.

Guthrie spotted Caroline right away, left what he was doing, and came to grip her shoulders in his hands. "Miss Ethel?" he asked.

Caroline swallowed and nodded. "Gone. She's gone." She wanted and needed to cry, but she couldn't make a single sound, not even when Guthrie took her into his arms and held her close.

"It's all right," he whispered. "I'll take care of everything."

And he did. He explained briefly to his companions, put Caroline into the seat of his wagon and started back toward town. He stopped on the way to leave word with the undertaker, then proceeded to the church. After informing Pastor Penn, he led Caroline inside the house and sat her down at the kitchen table.

While the minister was upstairs, Guthrie brewed tea for his wife and set a cup before her.

"I've ordered the lumber for the house," he told her, and the words were like a lifeline flung out into the dark seas of death. "Our children will grow up there, Caroline. I'll make love to you in the master bedroom, and you'll fry chicken in the kitchen."

She knew he was telling her that life goes on, and she was grateful for the reminder. "They were good to me," she told him brokenly.

Drawing his chair close to hers, Guthrie clasped her hand and lifted it to his lips. "I know," he replied.

"It would have meant so much to them to know we were married . . ."

"Maybe they do know," Guthrie broke in gently. Then he drew Caroline onto his lap and her tears came, wetting the fabric of his shirt where she laid her head on his shoulder.

He carried her upstairs and put her to bed in a thin satin chemise after the pastor and the undertaker had gone, the latter taking Miss Ethel away in his special wagon.

"Don't leave me," Caroline whispered, rising to her knees in the bed and putting her arms around Guthrie's neck. The heat she felt at this close contact with him shamed her, given the fact that one of the dearest people in her life had just died, but it would not be denied. Somehow, this sudden and violent passion she felt was a response to death, a rebuttal of its power.

Astraddle of Guthrie's lap now, she kissed him hungrily, while her hands fumbled with the buttons of his trousers.

He seemed to understand. Very gently, he gathered her chemise in both hands and pulled it off over her head. Then he pushed his trousers down far enough to free his shaft, which Caroline had already teased to full readiness.

Guthrie entered her with caution, but she would not, could not be careful. She rode him hard, until her flesh was damp with her exertions and tendrils of hair clung to the skin around her face. Then, with a low cry, she spasmed, her head thrust back in triumphant submission.

He moaned her name and then stiffened, and she could feel his essence flowing into her.

"I love you," he rasped out.

Caroline heard the words and cherished them, but her need for Guthrie had not been appeased. Still joined with him, she put a breast to his mouth and stroked the back of his head, all the while whispering tender things too precious to be said aloud.

He suckled for a long time, and then his hands started roving over Caroline in motions that grew more and more frantic by the moment. His rod towered strong and hot inside her.

Caroline pushed him back, so that he lay prone on the bed, and slowly began to move upon him. Not until she had reduced him to delirium and drained him of his essence did she allow the pleasure to take her again. When it did, she gave herself up to it, glorying in the buckling of her body and the feel of Guthrie's hands on her full breasts.

It was a long time before they'd recovered enough to move and, this time, it was Caroline who put Guthrie to bed. After teasing his kiss-swollen mouth for a few moments with her index finger, she lay close to him and gave him a breast. He tasted the nipple with his tongue and then suckled in earnest, one hand making slow circles over Caroline's belly.

They made love again in the morning, and then Caroline got up, washed, put on a black dress, and began the business of bereavement.

That afternoon, Miss Ethel was buried in the churchyard beside Miss Phoebe, and it seemed right that the two sisters were together again, in some finer and brighter world.

Although she mourned, Caroline went away from the grave with peace in her heart. Someday, she would see her guardian angels again, and when she did, she would have a great deal to tell them.

Chapter

❧ 25 ❧

Winter snow was drifting past the windows, and Caroline was great with child, that late January day when she found the letters resting in Miss Ethel's jewelry box.

Hands trembling, Caroline stumbled to the padded chest at the foot of Miss Ethel's bed and sat down. She splayed the fingers of one hand over her distended belly as she fumbled with the flap on the first envelope.

The missive was from Kathleen Harrington, her mother, and there was a bank draft for seven hundred and fifty dollars inside.

Filled with a tangle of emotions—hope, disbelief, outrage —Caroline read the letter twice before she made sense of the woman's words. Kathleen had sought her, as well as her sisters, for years. Giving up her children was the greatest regret of her life, she said, and now she hoped for a reunion in Chicago.

Caroline's throat worked as she stared at the bank draft. She didn't need the money; Guthrie's mine was producing, the new house stood sturdy and imposing at the edge of town, and there had been small legacies from both the Maitland sisters.

341

She crumpled the check and tossed it away, and it landed in the middle of the hooked rug.

The other letter carried a return address of Fox Chapel, Pennsylvania, and it had been mailed months before, at the end of July. Caroline's throat ached with hope and the fear of disappointment as she opened it, took out several folded pages, and began to read.

July 28, 1878

My very dear Caroline,
  It is my devout hope that, by the time this letter reaches you, you will be home from whatever quest you have undertaken, safe and sound. . . .

A quick look at the closing of the letter told Caroline it was from Lily, and her eyes filled with tears of joy as she read on. Lily was happy—except for the fact that she still hadn't found her lost sisters—and she'd married a man named Caleb Halliday, formerly a major in the United States Army. She was expecting a child in the winter, and hoped to return someday to the homestead she'd founded in Washington Territory.

Caroline was reading the precious words through for the third time, tears trickling down her cheek, when the door hinges squeaked and she looked up to see Guthrie standing on the threshold.

"Lily," she said, holding out the paper.

Guthrie took it and read it quickly, his grin broadening with every word. "Married a Yank, did she?" he teased, handing back the delicate pages and bending to kiss his wife's forehead. "Oh, well. She's your sister, so chances are, I'll like her anyway."

With Guthrie's help, Caroline managed to rise to her feet. She put her arms around his waist and rested her forehead against his shoulder. "Miss Ethel was saving the letters for me," she said. "All these months, they've been right here. All I would have had to do was look."

Guthrie hooked his hand under her chin and lifted. "You

had your grief to deal with," he reminded her. "Besides, I believe things happen at their appointed times."

Caroline grimaced as the baby gave her a lusty kick. This was followed by a pain of startling intensity. "You may be right," she managed, with a gasp. "Guthrie, I think your child has just decided to make this his birthday."

His eyes widened as he looked at her and, for a moment, his flesh was white as paper under its winter tan. "What?" he choked out. "You mean . . . ?"

"I mean I'm going to have this baby. Right now. Today."

Guthrie looked at her in quiet terror and started ushering her around to the side of the bed.

She stiffened. "Not here. I want to be at home, Mr. Hayes, in our bed."

He looked horrified, as though she'd asked him to drive her to Denver or San Francisco. "What if you—what if he's born in the wagon?"

Caroline laughed, then flinched as another hard pain turned the muscles in her middle to flexible steel. "He—or she—won't be born in the wagon, Guthrie," she answered patiently, waddling toward the door. "But I do think it would be a good idea if we stopped by Doc Allen's office on the way home and left a note on his message board."

At a definite loss, Guthrie helped his wife down the stairs, wrapped her blue-and-gray plaid woolen cloak around her when they reached the entryway, and maneuvered her carefully across the porch, over the steps, and up the walk to the gate. His sense of humor had returned by the time they reached the waiting buckboard, and he grunted as though he were hefting a side of beef into the seat, instead of the wife he'd so often termed "skinny."

Only then, as they were pulling away, did Caroline realize that she was still clutching Lily's letter in her hand. Kathleen's lay upstairs in Miss Ethel's room, along with the unwanted bank draft.

Guthrie drove as fast as he dared through the snowy streets, jumping from the wagon box before the rig had come to a complete stop in front of the doctor's office.

Typically, Doc Allen wasn't around, and Caroline smiled through another contraction as her husband scrawled Hayes Baby Coming, Get There Quick! on the blackboard affixed to the wall beside the physician's front door.

By the time they arrived at their own house, a white three-story place with gables and a turret and a southern-style veranda, the snow was coming down in flakes the size of chicken eggs and Caroline's skirts were soaked. Mary O'Haley, the middle-aged Irish housekeeper Guthrie had hired as soon as the construction was complete, was waiting on the porch.

"I knew it!" the red-headed woman crowed, as Guthrie helped Caroline down from the wagon and shuffled her through the gate and up the walk. "I saw it clear as glass in a dream last night."

Upstairs, in the master bedroom, which ran the width of the house and half the length, Mary built up the fire while Guthrie stripped Caroline and put her into a fresh nightgown. She was not so far gone that she couldn't have removed her own clothes; it was just that her frantic husband never gave her the chance.

"It'll be a boy," Mary insisted, shaking her finger at Caroline as Guthrie tucked her into bed. "You mark my words, Mrs. Hayes. My dreams don't lie."

Caroline was seized with another pain, this one more ferocious than the others. She gripped Guthrie's hand hard and made a confession she knew he wouldn't find comforting. "I'm afraid."

He sat on the side of the bed and brushed her knuckles with his lips. "Me, too, Mrs. Hayes," he replied hoarsely. As always, he looked incongruous sitting there beneath the lace-trimmed canopy of the bed.

The labor progressed rapidly, and it seemed remarkable to Caroline that when the pain took her, she made almost exactly the same sounds as when her passion was greatest. The paradox was that, even though she'd never hurt so badly in her life, she wouldn't have traded a moment of the experience for anything.

Guthrie left Caroline's side only to keep the fire crackling on the bedroom hearth. The rest of the time, he gave her his hands to grip and whispered words of encouragement. Between contractions, when she lay panting for breath, he deliberately made her laugh. When she arched her back and screamed, he cradled her head against his chest and rubbed her rock hard belly with a gentle hand.

It was dark outside when the doctor arrived, but Caroline could still see the snowflakes, fat and white, through the bay window across the room from the bed. Beyond were the lights of the town, twinkling like stars fallen from the sky.

The doctor was elderly, his manner reassuringly calm. He rounded the four-poster bed to stand opposite Guthrie and addressed him quietly. "I wonder if I could prevail upon you to boil some water for us, Mr. Hayes. We'll need it in the next little while."

Guthrie, anxious to be of help, nodded, kissed Caroline on the forehead, and left the room.

Between pains, her body drenched with perspiration, Caroline gave the doctor a faltering smile. "You just wanted to get rid of him," she accused good-naturedly.

Dr. Allen chuckled and shrugged out of his jacket. After laying it aside, he undid his cufflinks and rolled up his sleeves. "Husbands aren't usually much help during examinations," he conceded. "Besides, the poor fellow looked like he was about to pass out." Once he'd scrubbed his hands and forearms at the washstand, he came back to the bed and turned back the covers.

Caroline was caught in the jaws of a fresh pain when he began examining her, and when the spasm subsided, the doctor was smiling. "It won't be long now, Caroline," he said. "This little one is in a hurry to be born."

Mary came quietly in and emptied the basin, then poured fresh water from the matching pitcher. Dr. Allen washed his hands again, but he didn't roll down his sleeves.

Yet another contraction lifted Caroline's hips off the bed and wrung an animal cry from her, and Guthrie burst in, carrying a bucketful of steaming water.

"Can't you do something about the pain?" he demanded impatiently, as though Caroline's situation were somehow the doctor's fault.

Patiently, the physician shook his head. "Nothing to do now but wait," he said, "though it might be good if Caroline walked around a bit."

Before Caroline could protest that she wasn't going anywhere, Guthrie had her on her feet. He took her out into the hallway, where they paced, together, up and down, up and down. An hour passed, and then Caroline's agony was so great that she sobbed and said she couldn't go another step.

Guthrie carried her back to the bed, which Mary had stripped of its fancy silk sheets and lacy coverlet and spread with freshly laundered, but old, blankets and flannel sheets.

The bedding was soft and worn, a comfort to Caroline, like a nest.

"I think we're in business," Dr. Allen mused, after giving Caroline another quick examination. And then he suggested that Guthrie leave the room.

Mr. Hayes refused in colorful terms and sat sideways on the bed, supporting Caroline's back as she raised her knees and pushed to deliver their child.

The process was long and it was arduous, and just when Caroline thought she'd die of the pain and the effort, she felt the child leave her body.

Laughing with delight, as pleased as if the experience were entirely new to him, Dr. Allen received the child into his hands and deftly cleared its mouth.

"Mr. and Mrs. Hayes," he said jovially, placing the squalling infant in the crook of Caroline's arm, "may I present your son."

Dazed, Caroline stared at the baby boy, then at her still-burgeoning belly.

"It appears that the young man didn't arrive alone," the doctor explained, as he cut the cord between Caroline and the first child.

Mary took the baby from Caroline's arms to bathe him

and bundle him up, and Caroline was caught up in the rigors of bearing yet another little Hayes. Again the violent spasms tore at her body, again she screamed, again she presented her husband with a son. She looked back at Guthrie as the cord was being cut and the first baby was being returned to her arms, and there were tears glistening in his eyes.

"I love you," she said.

He moved to kneel beside the bed and kissed her soundly. "And I love you," he answered hoarsely. He touched his firstborn son's fragile little head in a motion of gentleness and wonder.

Caroline was exhausted and, though the pain echoed in her body, she felt transported. Emotionally, her state was much the same as it was when Guthrie was making love to her and the pleasure became almost too keen to bear.

Mary laid the other bundle beside Caroline, then she and the doctor went out, leaving the Hayes family alone.

Reverently, Guthrie picked up a tiny hand and kissed it, his eyes still shimmering with emotion. "How can I thank you for a gift like this?" he whispered, gazing into Caroline's face as if he'd never seen anything more beautiful.

"You can give me a dozen more," Caroline replied, and now her own eyes overflowed. "Oh, Guthrie, I've never felt so close to you. It's as though our spirits have mated, just as our bodies have."

"I felt it, too," he whispered. And then he took the babies, one by one, and carefully placed them in the beautiful wooden cradle he'd built and carved himself. That done, he came to the bed and stretched out on top of Caroline's covers, taking her gently into his arms, his hand lightly fondling one of her breasts and making the obedient nipple bud against his fingers.

Caroline trembled and then sighed as her very soul seemed to join with Guthrie's, producing a release far more poignant than anything she'd ever felt physically.

Late the next day, Caroline's milk came in, and Guthrie watched, rapt, as she fed one son and then the other.

"What are we going to name them?" he asked.

Caroline smiled, stroking her second-born's head. He suckled as greedily as his father did, but her eyes were on the other baby, lying sated in the cradle. "That's Guthrie Hayes II," she announced. "And this," she paused to kiss the tiny downy head, "this is Robert—Robert Edward Lee, for the general his daddy served so bravely."

Once again, there were tears in Guthrie's eyes, and he went to stoke the fire until he'd recovered himself.

February was snowy and cold, but the babies thrived, and when March came, Caroline left them with Mary, bundled up in her warmest cloak, and drove to the mine. Finding Guthrie in the small frame office building, alone, she went to him and took his hand.

She placed her lips close to his ear and spoke softly. "I have need of my husband." Then, hardly giving him time to respond, she led him to the door and handed him his coat and hat.

He looked as nervous as a boy, but he was eager, too. After all, long weeks had passed since he and Caroline had lain together, and his body was surely as hungry as her own.

Reaching their house, they went up the stairs together, ignoring Mary, who called out cheerfully that there'd been a letter for Mrs. Hayes.

Behind the closed door of their room, Caroline stripped away Guthrie's coat and hat, tossing them aside, then pushed down his suspenders and pulled his shirt out of his trousers. When she opened the shirt and spread her fingers over his chest, she felt his nipples grow hard against her palms and reveled in his groan of need.

Some new bond had formed between them with the birth of their children, and Caroline felt a sweet agony of joy as she knelt before her husband in front of the fire and slowly undid his belt buckle, then the buttons of his trousers.

His manhood jutted out, proud and ready, and he moaned as Caroline eased his pants down around his thighs and took him boldly into her mouth. His fingers delved into her hair, and gruff incoherencies tumbled from his lips as she pleasured him.

"Let me take you," he pleaded raggedly, when she knew he would not be able to withstand the attentions of her lips and tongue much longer.

But Caroline's love for Guthrie had reached a new dimension, and she could not let him go. She squeezed his taut buttocks in her hands and held him captive until he'd given everything.

He dropped to the hearth rug, bringing Caroline with him, and she knew his vengeance would be protracted because she had appeased him so well. Their clothes seemed to fade away, and then Guthrie was caressing the full breasts that fed his babies.

"So beautiful," he rasped, but Caroline felt embarrassed because a droplet of milk came from her nipple.

Guthrie touched his tongue to her, teasing her with it, then taking suckle when the nipple grew rosy and hard. With his hand, he found Caroline's secret garden and invaded it, claiming the quivering treasure hidden there for his own.

She whimpered as he rolled her between his fingers, all the while alternately kissing her nipple, licking it, and scraping it with his teeth.

"Guthrie," she pleaded, as her bottom rose off the rug, seeking closer contact with his hand, "I need you so much—I can't bear it—"

He moved downward, kissing her belly as he went, and then placed himself between her legs. Draping her knees over his sturdy shoulders, he looked down the slope of her silky white body and smiled a cocky smile. "You're about to start needing me a whole lot more," he warned huskily. And then he burrowed through and took her brazenly into his mouth.

Caroline gave a low cry and flung her arms back over her head, and Guthrie's hands came smoothly over her hips and her rib cage to lock possessively on her breasts. She dug her heels into his back and arched as he gave her a merciless teasing with his tongue.

Her head moved from side to side on the rug and her flesh

shimmered in the firelight as the pleasure heightened to savage proportions. "The whole town—will hear—" Caroline gasped out, as her body surged to meet the tender ecstasy Guthrie was bringing her to. Her legs locked behind him as the first spasm loomed over her like an emotional tidal wave. "I'm going to—oh, God, Guthrie—I'm *coming . . .*"

He was relentless, making her give up the last quivering response, the last sweet sigh, the last husky groan, before lowering her to the rug. She had hoped to rest, but Guthrie was intent on arousing her again, and he was damnably skillful at it.

Lifting one of her legs from his shoulder, he kissed the tender skin behind her knee, then her calf, then her ankle and her instep. He repeated the whole process with her other leg, then lay beside her and idly toyed with a nipple while tasting her earlobe.

"It's going to be very good to be back inside your body, Mrs. Hayes," he told her, in a raspy whisper, and a shiver of joyful anticipation went through Caroline.

"It's going to be very good to have you there, Mr. Hayes," she responded, running her hand down his belly until she found his shaft. He was already hard as a tamarack log, and Caroline loved the feel of him flexing between her palm and curved fingers.

Presently, he moved over her, resting his weight on his elbows and forearms, and lowered his mouth to hers.

His kiss was in itself a possession so bittersweet, so powerful, that Caroline felt swept up in its force, like a leaf tossing on a swollen river. When Guthrie glided into her in a powerful thrust, she lifted her hips in welcome.

He broke the kiss with a gasp and, raising himself up on his palms, eased out of her, and then in again. His hooded green eyes cast a spell even as they held Caroline's brown ones captive. With excruciating slowness, he claimed her again.

His very control was Caroline's undoing. Her body leaped toward him, seemed to explode around him, and Caroline was dazed by the flash. She locked her legs around him and cried out, long and low, aware only of him and his complete and utter dominion.

When she lay still at last, weeping because it seemed her very soul had been taken out of her and then put back in again, she had the joy of watching him mount the pinnacle.

A ragged, soblike sound came from his chest as he delved into her, and Caroline gripped his buttocks and squeezed, as if to force him to give the last drop of his essence. His eyes glazed over and he panted for breath and still his body buckled against hers, giving and giving.

"Caroline," he pleaded. "Oh, God, *Caroline* . . ."

Finally, his powerful frame went still, and he collapsed beside her, his head on her breast. She stroked his back and his hair until he'd caught his breath, and as soon as he had, he claimed a nipple and the whole fiery rite began all over again.

The letter was resting on Caroline's plate when she came down to dinner two hours later, cheeks flushed, eyes bright, hair a scented ebony cloud around her face.

She frowned when she saw the postmark, seeing that the message had been written very recently. Although the handwriting was unfamiliar, the return address wasn't: The stiff white envelope had been mailed from Fox Chapel, Pennsylvania.

Caroline's smile faded as she awkwardly ripped open the envelope. Had something happened to Lily? Had she at last gotten a clue to her sister's whereabouts only to lose her again?

"She's gone to Chicago!" Caroline cried, when she'd read the entire letter. She waved it at Guthrie. "This is from a Mrs. Joss Halliday, and she says Lily's gone to Chicago to search for us—Emma and me!"

Guthrie grinned and reached for the biscuit platter. "Then I guess we'd better head east, Mrs. Hayes. It seems to me that if you got a letter and a bank draft from your mother, your sisters probably did, too. We'll start by paying a call on the mysterious Kathleen."

"I don't know where she lives!" Caroline wailed. "I threw away her letter—"

"And I went back to get it after you were through having my sons. It's in the top right-hand drawer of my desk."

Her supper forgotten, Caroline jumped out of her chair and bent to kiss the top of her husband's head. "You're an angel, Guthrie Hayes!" she cried.

He chuckled. "That isn't what you were saying an hour ago, when I arranged you on the side of the bed and—"

"Guthrie!" Caroline interrupted, her cheeks flaming. But already she was hoping he'd put her through her paces again, once the evening was over and they'd retired to their room. She pretended indignation when he swatted her bottom just before she walked away.

She found the letter where he said it would be and read it until she could have recited every word, from the date to the closing sentiments.

The next morning, Guthrie put his foreman in charge of the mining operation and the Hayes family boarded an eastbound train, bringing Mary along to help tend the babies. Caroline's hopes were high, and even though she tried to bridle them, in an effort to avoid disappointment, they kept flying away from her.

For five days they traveled, spending their nights in cubicles hardly bigger than a closet. Caroline could barely stand the suspense and the enforced containment of her energies.

When they reached Chicago, she would not even wait until they'd booked a hotel room. She insisted on summoning a carriage, and Guthrie watched her with a smile in his eyes as she fed their sons, first one and then the other, while the coach rattled toward the address Kathleen had given in her letter. Mary kept her face discreetly averted, and it was no secret that she didn't entirely approve of Mr. and Mrs. Hayes and the frank way they dealt with such matters.

Caroline was leaning halfway out the window when they arrived at their destination, and she saw another carriage waiting in front. Her own had barely stopped before she was out the door and hurrying along the sidewalk toward the gate.

Guthrie didn't follow, though Caroline knew he would be there to lend strength and support, whatever happened.

She was in the middle of the walk when she heard the piano and the two voices inside the house, blending in perfect harmony. Tears filled her eyes and a sob surged into her throat as she made out the dear, familiar words . . .

> *Three flowers bloomed in the meadow,*
> *Heads bent in sweet repose,*
> *The daisy, the lily, and the rose . . .*

Dashing away her tears with the back of one gloved hand, Caroline wrenched open the front door without bothering to knock and followed the continuing notes of the song through an arched doorway.

There she found Lily, lithe and blond and unbearably beautiful, her face wet. And at the piano sat Emma, with her glorious copper-penny hair and her wonderful dark blue eyes.

Just as the chorus started, Caroline added her voice to the song, and both Lily and Emma turned to stare, their faces alight with amazement and wonder.

"Caroline!" the two younger sisters chorused, looking at her as if they couldn't quite believe she was there. And then, for the first time in fourteen years, Lily and Caroline and Emma embraced, all of them sobbing for joy.

"Where have you *been?*" Lily demanded, when they'd all calmed down a little, looking from Emma to Caroline.

"Oh, it's a very long story," Caroline sniffled, beaming, kissing Emma's cheek and then Lily's, wondering how it was possible to contain the happiness she felt, the completion. Arms around her sisters' trim waists, she guided them to a long sofa nearby, where they all sat, oblivious of the rest of the world.

"I was told you'd been kidnapped by an awful man with a drunken dog!" Lily cried, brown eyes wide.

Caroline laughed. "I've married the man and reformed the dog," she said, and then she gave a brief version of what had happened to her in the years since they'd been parted. She finished by announcing the recent birth of her twins.

Lily sat between Emma and Caroline, holding one of their hands in each of her own. "And you, Emma? Where have *you* been all these years?"

Emma smiled and delicately dried her eyes with a lace-trimmed handkerchief. "I fell in love with an outlaw," she said. "We have a lovely home in New Orleans now, and a brand new baby girl, named for the two of you."

Lily gave a cry of delight; Caroline recalled that simple things had always pleased her youngest sister. She brought a locket from beneath her bodice and showed a small likeness of her infant sons.

Caroline didn't know where the next hours went. Guthrie came in from the carriage at some point, bringing the babies and the maid, but he was careful to keep himself out of the way. The other two husbands, Lily's tall, imperious Caleb Halliday and Emma's suavely handsome Steven Fairfax, arrived in good time as well.

"So," Lily sighed, standing at the hearth with her back to the room, when the three girls were alone in the sumptuous upstairs chamber that had belonged to their mother, "this is where Mama was, all that while. I imagined her living in squalor, drinking her life away."

Emma put her hands lightly on Lily's shoulders. "Let's agree to forgive her," she said softly. "We've found each other at last, and we all have husbands we love and beautiful children. The past has made us suffer enough. I'm not going to give it another moment's thought."

Caroline stood at the vanity, holding a small photograph. She couldn't remember posing for it, or even seeing it before the infamous day she and her sisters had boarded the orphan train, but there were three small, familiar faces gazing from behind the glass. Her own, Lily's, and Emma's.

"She loved us," Caroline said. "She wanted to make amends. It's enough."

With nods of their heads, Lily and Emma agreed.

The next day, the three families gathered at the house Lily and her husband had taken, and Caroline was pleased with her sister's choice—Caleb was a fine man, handsome and strong-willed enough to look after Lily properly. Emma's Steven was not so tall as Caleb, but he was equally good-looking, with his brown hair and quick, discerning eyes, and he moved with an easy grace that Caroline admired.

After dinner, the husbands—two Rebels and a Yankee, Caroline thought with a smile—stood close to the parlor fire, drinking brandy and smoking cigars. Meanwhile, Caroline and Emma and Lily sat in three chairs pulled into a tight circle, still catching each other up on the myriad things that had happened since they'd been taken from the orphan train. The babies slept nearby in assorted baskets and boxes padded with cushions, carefully watched over by their nurses.

The hour grew late and still the sisters chattered, pausing now and then to weep at some memory, or just because the joy of finding each other again was so sweet. Caleb, Steven, and Guthrie went off to their appointed rooms and the babies awakened, wanting to be fed.

Caroline, Lily, and Emma talked on as they held their children to their breasts and then put them back to bed.

Dawn was breaking when Lily said sadly, "I can't bear the thought of parting from you both. I wish we could all live in the same town, but Caleb and I have to get back to our homestead in time to plant."

Emma nodded, her fiery hair glowing in the early morning light. "And Steven and I have a life in New Orleans."

Caroline thought of Bolton, and her lovely house, and the mine, and she knew she could return there in peace because she'd found the missing parts of herself—her sisters. "We can all get together once or twice a year, perhaps in San Francisco, or Denver."

Emma and Lily nodded, looking happier.

"And we can exchange letters. The important thing is, we're not lost from each other anymore. When I stop and think of you, I can say to myself, 'Lily is here' and 'Emma is there.'" Her eyes filled again, but the tears were happy ones. "I love you so much," she finished.

Lily and Emma gave a laughing sobs, and drew close, each putting an arm around Caroline's waist, and all three sisters stood with their foreheads touching. Somewhere, far off in another part of the city where their adventure had begun so long before, a train whistle blew, offering a shrill benediction.